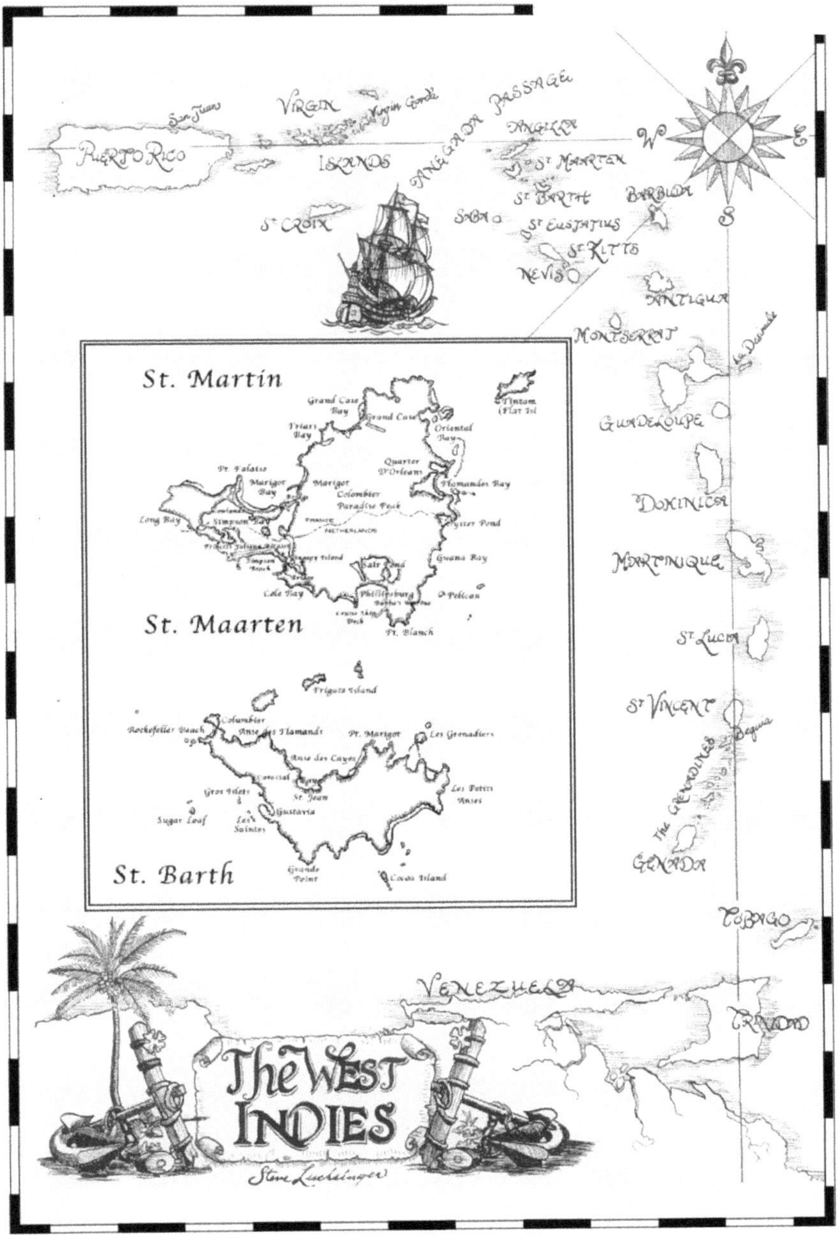
San Juan
PUERTO RICO
VIRGIN
ISLANDS
Virgin Gorda
ANEGADA PASSAGE
ANGUILLA
ST MAARTEN
ST BARTH
BARBUDA
SABA
ST EUSTATIUS
ST KITTS
NEVIS
ST CROIX
W
E
S
ANTIGUA
MONTSERRAT
La Desirade
GUADELOUPE
DOMINICA
MARTINIQUE
ST LUCIA
ST VINCENT
Bequia
THE GRENADINES
GRENADA
TOBAGO
VENEZUELA
TRINIDAD
St. Martin
Grand Case Bay
Grand Case
Oriental Bay
Tintam (Flat Isl
Friars Bay
Pt. Falatso
Marigot Bay
Marigot
Colombier
Paradise Peak
Quarter D'Orleans
Flamandes Bay
Long Bay
Simpson Bay
FRANCE
NETHERLANDS
Oyster Pond
Simpson Beach
Salt Pond
Guana Bay
Cole Bay
Phillipsburg
Pelican
Pt. Blanch
St. Maarten
Frigate Island
Columbier
Rockefeller Beach
Anse des Flamands
Pt. Marigot
Les Grenadiers
Anse des Cayes
St. Jean
Gros Islets
Les Petits Anses
Sugar Loaf
Gustavia
Les Saintes
Grande Point
Cocos Island
St. Barth
The West Indies
Steve Luchsinger

Copyright © 2024
Cheryl du Bois

All rights reserved. No part of this book may be reproduced in any manner without the express written consent of the publisher/author, except in case of brief excerpts for critical reviews or articles. All inquiries should be addressed to

A Place in Time.Press
8594 Wilshire Blvd., Suite 1020, Beverly Hills, CA 90211
310 428-1090 or info@aplaceintime.press

This is a work of fiction. Names, characters, businesses, places, events and incidents are either the products of the authors' imagination or used in a fictional manner. Any resemblance to actual persons, living or dead, or actual events is coincidental.

Author: Cheryl du Bois
Cover Design and Layout:
Christopher Staser, brandweaver.tv
Photography: Cheryl du Bois
Map Design & Illustration: Steve Luchsinger

Library of Congress Cataloging-in-Publication Data is
Available on file.
Print ISBN # 978-0-9745414-5-7
Ebook: ISBN #979-8-9893814-0-1

A Place in Time.Press
8549 Wilshire Blvd. Ste. 1020,
Beverly Hills, CA 90211
310 613-8872
e-mail: info@aplaceintime.press
Website: aplaceintime.press

HISTORICAL FICTION
Printed in the United States of America
Our books may be purchased in bulk for promotional, educational, or business use. Please contact your local bookseller or the publisher:
info@aplaceintime.press

First U.S. Edition 2024
Copyrighted Material ©2024

Island Fever
Running From Paradise

TABLE OF CONTENTS

Chapter	Title	Page
	Introduction	vii
	Author's Note	ix
	Dedication	xi
1	Discontentment	1
2	Guardian Angel	10
3	Paradise Lost	16
4	Hook, Line & Sinker	27
5	Survival	39
6	Dead to Weather	51
7	Celestial Navigation	59
8	Approval	68
9	Excess Baggage	79
10	Some Otters Don't Swim	93
11	Guilt	105
12	Innocence	113
13	Freedom	119
14	Flotsam and Jetsam	127
15	Ego or Eating Crow	135
16	Lambchop or Mutton	141
17	Bankrupt	149
18	Dirty Laundry	153
19	Wisdom	159
20	Fear	167
21	AC – DC	175
22	Black-Out	181

23 —	Dinghy Fever	189
24 —	Lost at Sea	197
25 —	Paradise Peak	205
26 —	Mistaken Identity	211
27 —	Heart and Sole	217
28 —	Tropical Depression	223
29 —	Changes in Latitude	231
30 —	Hurricane Hole	239
31 —	Weathering the Storm	250
32 —	Overboard	260
33 —	Eye of the Storm	270
34 —	Dead Reckoning	281
35 —	Life & Death	291
36 —	The Payoff	297
37 —	Paradise Found	311

VI

INTRODUCTION

In the tradition of Herman Wouk, I would like to offer up the following words of wisdom about 'life in Paradise' and dedicate this story to all of its misguided seekers. I thank Mr. Wouk for his contribution to the world of "Don't Stop the Carnival," a book read by few, but treasured in the Caribbean by all sailors and land lovers alike who have been stricken at some time or another with that dreadful disease known as 'island fever.'

•

All of the following events and many of the people have indeed been inspired by actual occurrences and real characters – either experienced or witnessed by the author while living in Paradise between 1980 and 1986. The circumstances and names have been changed however, in order to protect those survivors of Paradise.

*"Your reason and your passion
are the rudder and the sails
of your seafaring soul.
If either your sails or your
rudder are broken, you can
but toss and drift or else
be held at a standstill in mid seas."*
                              Kahlil Gibran
                              "The Prophet"

AUTHOR'S NOTE

*"He who looks outwardly dreams,
but he who looks within awakes."*

Carl Jung

I lived I thought, in 'Paradise.' Six years of my life were spent in the West Indies searching for that elusive destination in the tropics. Buddhists know it as Nirvana, Existentialists find true bliss in just 'being,' Adam and Eve knew it as Eden, Robinson Caruso called it shipwrecked, and westerners have their own vision of this state of ultimate 'being' – they call it 'Paradise.'

I ran a yacht for charter for four of those six years that I lived in 'Paradise' – believing that simply living that romantic island lifestyle would surely fulfill the quest. Even though I thought I had arrived, I was mistaken. Somehow, I had followed the wrong heading along the way – I had failed in my quest to discover true Paradise in my search for ultimate happiness. I failed because I was searching from the outside and not from within – for a place instead of a way of perceiving and accepting reality, or at least what we define as reality. I was searching for something or someone to supply it for me instead of creating it from myself.

It wasn't until I had nearly finished this book, now many years later, that I felt truly enlightened as to the whereabouts of Paradise. As I dove into the depths of this tale which mirrored my own biographical pilgrimage, it was as if all my lifetimes of inner knowledge were slowly regurgitated into consciousness by my inner being, or possibly even by my inner guide in order to make me take stock of my own good advice and see the light. They say that when the horizon seems the darkest – we can finally see the clearest. It wasn't until I had found myself in a great black void that I realized that I was looking at the world, and at my life, with binoculars in order to see what my life might be like way down the road instead of what it was now. Writing this book was a cathartic process of learning to see the horizon as it stretched out ahead, without worrying about what it would bring. It helped me to learn to live in the now, which in turn allowed me to plot my current position in order to navigate my course without the aid of an external compass.

For me, sailing represents a metaphor for freedom. Through this humble comparison of life to the Zen of sailing, I have attempted to offer my own process of discovery of nearly every human's desired destination – even if everyone's perception of 'Paradise' is different, as is their route by which to get there. It's the acceptance of the trials and errors of the journey along the road as valuable lessons for growth, that truly allows one to appreciate the achieved destination – if and when they finally do arrive.

Too often I have prematurely weighed anchor to journey farther across the seas of life in search of something to nourish my soul, instead of simply setting a secure mooring and searching the depths within. Like a lost sailor I found myself stranded on a desert island over and over again, thirsting for sustenance – in need of the food and water necessary to keep my soul alive, never realizing that I was indeed the island I had yet to discover and that life was my vessel. I have since learned that everything I would ever need, had been aboard all along.

"Life is like a magnifying glass – if you get too close to something, it's fuzzy."

Elizabeth Claire Prophet

DEDICATION

This tale of Paradise is dedicated to all of those in my life who have inspired my love of sailing – my brother, Roy, who first inspired the awe of sailing in me as we both learned to sail by bouncing off sandbars on the Piankatank River in a centerboarder; to Buddy Bond who taught me to love catamarans, encouraged me to make sailing my business, take my Captain's test, and ran me away to the Caribbean; to the U.S. Coast Guard who allowed me to become one of the first female Captains, even though they had to scratch out "he" and write "she" on my license; to Jon Westmoreland who taught me to love the ocean and all that goes with it, and the one who made a real sailor out of me; to my dear little fifty foot catamaran, Ikhaya, who made me understand the love between a sailor and their vessel; to D. Randy West, a greatly missed pirate, a comedian, and a seasoned sailor known and loved by all in the Caribbean, who advised me and supported me during the writing of this book, and who loaned me his extraordinary hurricane stories; to all those on 'The Otherside' who have inspired and assisted me with the writing of this book...

...and last but not least I would like to dedicate this book to Lorna Steele, a black, West Indian poet, who taught me how to live life in the tropics, even if it did take me several more decades to grasp living life in 'Paradise.'

THIS HOLLOW CRY

Show me your chains, my Afro'd friend,
Who chants so vibrantly for "Freedom!"
What binds you now to this or that,
Or even – God forbid, to anyone?
Show me the blindfold keeping you
Ever in darkness, away from sunshine,
Or from reaching upwards to the green hills of life!
And who draws for you the line between
The good and evil areas of strife?
Who enforces what you do (or fail to do!)
In order to attain the best or worst
Of being within you?
Where is the Cross you carry, the scar you bear?
Tell me little puppet, whose whine for 'freedom,'
Rings so falsely on my ear,
When they hanged your slave ancestor –
Were you there?

Lorna Steele

"Nothing shortens a journey so pleasantly as an account of misfortunes at which the hearer is permitted to laugh."

Quentin Crisp

CHAPTER ONE

Discontentment

"There is no sorrow like the memory of a love,
knowing it is lost forever."

Ian

It was a typical Monday morning in Rob's life as he awoke to the smell of coffee from his automatic coffee maker, which he religiously set for 5:00 AM every evening except Saturday. As he arose in his chic yet modest penthouse high above the still sleeping city, he poured himself a cup of java – black as always, shaved, dressed, and headed off to the gym for his hour workout and shower – a quick protein-shake at the snack bar, and another coffee on the run to the Chicago Stock Exchange. Opening at 7:00 AM like a race started by a shot from a starting gun, the trading floor delivered Rob into a sea of chaos and unrelenting pressure each day until its close at 4:00 PM sharp. Somehow, Rob managed to survive the day on caffeine and protein bars – never letting up his pace until he joined his fiancée, Sydney, every evening at seven for dinner at the newest, trendiest restaurant that she had uncovered from the gossip of her peers – at one of the many social events the city had to offer. A true dilettante, Sydney offered Rob entrée into a world that was about as alien to him as the Pleiades,* since Rob had grown up in a small farm town in central Iowa – as far away from Chicago as one could get and still be in the corn belt.

      Rob considered Sundays as a day of rest as far as the alarm went, and instead of the gym he partook in his and Sydney's weekly routine of sex before

---

• PLEIADES – *A small cluster of stars in the heavens, also known as 'The Seven Sisters.'*

mass, which they attended with her parents. Sydney had taken it upon herself to convert or more accurately recruit Rob into the church – a firm prerequisite of her father's to marry his only daughter. For Sydney, who was raised to be a devout Catholic and a 'good girl,' sex on Sunday was a deliberate desecration of the Sabbath which titillated her and verily pushed the envelope of her deviant behavior. Thanks to her mass-produced childhood and puritanical bourgeois upbringing, Sydney was a tad straightlaced and pedestrian when it came to her imagination – especially where sex was concerned.

Raised in a mixed household comprised of Protestant and Catholic, Rob felt somewhat familiar, if not comfortable in church – considering that over the years he had come to qualify himself as an agnostic, or at least, a skeptic at best. Becoming religious at this point in Rob's life was highly unlikely and conforming to the strict dogma of the Catholic faith was simply not in his cards. He was the first to admit his skepticism of God, and heaven, and hell. All he was sure of, was that he was one more rat in the maze of life racing to get ahead of his own shadow. But to appease her parents, Rob attended Sunday mass with Sydney, realizing of course that it wouldn't hurt to enhance his social and future business connections amongst the well-heeled parishioners of their affluent congregation.

Rob Mariner was bright, attractive, ambitious – most importantly, Rob was a success by that point in his young career as a stockbroker in Chicago. Only eight years out of college with his master's degree in business, Rob had already achieved certain respected measures of success amongst his peers. He wore the right clothes – Armani, of course – drove the right car, worked hard at the right job, lived in the right building, dated the right girl, and had managed to put away a fair amount of money for a rainy day, or a sunny one should it ever come along.

Five years at this pace was usually enough to burn out even the toughest of individuals, and Rob was fast approaching that mile marker since this was his 56th month on the floor as a trader. The business had been good to Rob who was enviously referred to by his fellow traders as, 'Houdini,' since his uncanny feel for the market and its unpredictable vacillation had always been more than just a hunch to him. Somehow, he had a sixth sense of knowing when to take a risk, when to invest, and when to get out. Rob could smell a downturn coming the way a professional gambler smelled a streak of bad luck and always managed to escape in time, totally unscathed. Too bad this extrasensory perception failed him when it came to his personal life.

Although Rob's life was apparently blessed, there was only one small problem – he hated it. His job was killing him, his boss was an asshole, his girl-friend a prima donna, and he needed a vacation – desperately! Contrary to the appearance of perfection in Rob's world, life was beginning to feel like a prison comprised of unfulfilled expectations, obligations, and shallow meaningless existence. That Sunday night dread of Monday morning coming all too fast was now starting for Rob on Friday night. Rob knew there was a time when he had truly loved Monday mornings and his job. He had looked forward to that shot of adrenaline which surged through his body when he stepped onto the trading floor. But somehow, he had drifted into a fog, almost a numbness – an absence of all feeling.

He just couldn't seem to remember how it felt to be passionate about one's work – about one's life. Rob's success had become empty – meaningless – he was living in the season of his own discontent. He had lost his joie de vivre. He felt passionate about nothing, not even his fiancée, Sydney. Maybe he was just one of the sixteen percent of the U.S. population that was clinically depressed. Or was he just, bored? He wasn't sure any longer that he could tell the difference. Maybe he should just join the other five-million people in America who were on Prozac or some other designer, mood-elevating drug, and get it over with. Or, quite possibly, it was just simply time for a change of scenery.

Even though Rob realized he was somewhat dispassionate about his current engagement to Sydney Corandini, the daughter of one of Chicago's wealthiest businessmen, he sincerely believed that he had everything he'd ever wanted in a woman. She was tall, beautiful, had a great body even if it wasn't all original equipment, long dark hair, and a business degree from Harvard, which she had no intention of ever using. Daddy had made certain that his little girl – an only child since her brother died at three, got the best of everything and would never find the need to work a single day of her life. In fact, work was included in Sydney's list of distasteful four-letter words. She felt that even Rob's job was only a temporary disgrace until they were married and Rob would of course be made a partner in Daddy's firm.

Rob sat across from Sydney that night at dinner in a posh, Chicago, Damen Avenue restaurant – exotically decorated in a multi-cultural motif, as Sydney had immediately pointed out to Rob who sat staring up at a bigger than life-size Hindu Shiva with his many arms intertwined amongst his multitudinous consorts.

"The restaurant's only been open two weeks and already it's been graced by the Maharishi himself, four movie stars, and the President," prattled Sydney to a disinterested Rob. "Don't you find it strange that there was nothing in the paper about the President's visit to Chicago?" Sydney continued, barely even pausing for a response.

Rob sat across from her all through dinner listening to the events of her uneventful day of shopping with her friends Karla, Marla, and Wendy in the morning; and more shopping with her mother in the afternoon. Sydney and her mother had a weekly routine of two sacred days for shopping – Monday and

Thursday, which to miss would have been as dire as the desecration of a holy sacrament – her other days being comprised of either bridge or charitable luncheons. Sydney, it seemed, was destined to follow in her mother's footsteps. Since her marriage to Sydney's father, Mrs. Corandini had defined her whole identity as Jack Corandini's wife and society's maven – chairwoman of all the right charities in town.

Rob sat thinking to himself that maybe he had been wrong about Sydney's joblessness. Indeed, it was Sydney's job to shop all day – everyday, luckily on daddy's open accounts which were available to her at any and all establishments she chose to frequent. Rob carefully studied her beautiful face as a botanist might scrutinize a specimen for its inherent attributes, hoping to find one feature that had not had some means of alteration perpetrated upon it by a rich, Chicago plastic surgeon – made wealthy from hundreds of rich girls like Sydney whose fathers and husbands had spent small fortunes paying off their revolving charge accounts. Rob searched Sydney's face for that cute little mole she used to have on her right cheek when they'd met, but strangely it seemed to have disappeared. Likely, he thought, into some surgeon's collection of unwanted fat, wrinkles, eyelids, and nose cartilage. Maybe it was his imagination. Maybe it had never really been there at all, but he had fairly good recall for such detail and decided to simply file it away in his cerebral database along with the memory of Sydney's laugh lines.

Rob had met Sydney about three years out of college when he was just learning the art of making money for his clients, and most importantly, as far as Sydney was concerned, for himself. Rob had never felt that he needed a lot of money; after all, he had come from a modest but comfortable home on his parent's small farm in Iowa which raised, as most farmers did in that part of the country – corn. Their roots having come from poor farmers and immigrants who had never had much more than the daily bread on their tables. Rob had known though, that he would do well at whatever he decided to pursue since he'd always done well in school and had graduated top in his class from the University of Chicago* with a degree in business and finance. Rob's mother had encouraged his green thumb, when he was young, and had made him tend her vegetable garden for her, producing his award-winning zucchini each year for the county fair. Regardless of his apparent talent for making things grow, Rob had chosen in the end to seed a more profitable garden. Since he'd come to the city he'd discovered that indeed his green thumb had not deserted him, and he was now adept at raising a different type of green crop.
"Who said money doesn't grow on trees," thought Rob.

* UNIVERSITY OF CHICAGO — The University which spawned the term 'Chicago School' – the monetarist, conservative approach to economic policy.

As far as he was concerned, business got right down to the bare essentials of things. All making money entailed was planting the right seeds under the right conditions, with other people's money whenever possible, watching the weather forecast to ensure the proper growth period and conditions, and reaping the harvest when the crops, or stocks, were right for the picking.

Since Rob had asked Sydney to marry him, or had it been the other way around – he could no longer remember, he had begun to realize the future importance of a lucrative career seeing that Sydney was quite accustomed to life in the lap of luxury. The lap of a downright filthy rich father who had his eye on Rob's business acumen. In fact, he already had Rob's name painted on the door across from his. A room with a view was an understatement since the office, which Sydney had secretly spent the last year decorating for Rob as a wedding present, had a one hundred-eighty-degree panoramic view of the city and Lake Michigan.

Of course, much of this was still unknown to Rob who actually had his eye on a small brokerage house he had dreams of buying with his best friend, Kyle, another successful trader who had already been on the floor a year when Rob had arrived to claim his own territory. Sydney couldn't fathom how Rob worked on his feet all day, without even a window to look out of not to mention a million-dollar view – in that horrid animalistic pit called the trading floor.

Maybe that was part of his recent frustration, thought Rob to himself, as the Chateaubriand was delivered by a waitress wearing a red Chinese ceremonial robe and headdress – followed by the wine sommelier who approached the table in a blue sari and silently refilled their glasses, then stole away as quietly as she'd come. Maybe Rob had just been cooped up too long. Maybe he had that syndrome he had read about in Newsweek that executives get from all the positive ions in office buildings. What had they called it? At least if he could put a name on it he could start to understand the problem and attempt to do something about it.

What more could any man ask for from life, Rob thought to himself. He owned his own penthouse, a new BMW, he was tall, good looking, well educated, and had a respectable savings account for a guy of thirty-two. All of those wonderful attributes, it seemed to Rob, should have constituted happiness, and in essence a sense of 'Paradise' in his life. But, for some reason, something important was missing.

"What am I doing with my life?" thought Rob. "Have I sold my soul for comfort, status, and success? Do we all just trade our childhood in for responsibility? Are we afraid to escape from the security of nine to five, afraid to venture out into the unknown? Or am I just too ambitious?" Rob questioned. "I don't think so. I really don't want much. I actually get up five days a week to make money in order to support Sydney in the style to which she's accustomed.

5

Is it because of women, men are destined to slave their entire lives away, unhappy, in order to make them, if not happy, at least comfortable? If Eve hadn't eaten that apple, maybe things would have been different," he pondered. "*Maybe mankind wouldn't have been evicted from Eden and doomed to live in search of Paradise for the rest of eternity. Or, am I trying to find someone else on which to place the blame? In truth, it is probably for the power that we enslave our lives to money in order to prove oneself and take control of our lives? Or, do we indeed have control – has money become my true master?"*

As much as Rob tried, he would never have remotely suspected that the root of his unhappiness might be his underlying uncertainty of his true love for this woman who sat before him, immaculately dressed in chartreuse Valentino, who was considered by all as a 'wonderful catch.' Why, any of his friends would have jumped at the opportunity to trade places with Rob's 'wonderful life.'

But Rob was unable to uncover the source of the empty, sinking feeling in the pit of his stomach at the end of every day when he lay his head on his pillow and turned out the light. There was definitely something missing – something at the very core of his being as if he had overlooked something intrinsic to his formula for the perfect life. And of course, Sydney who lay in bed next to him in the dark extolling on and on about the extravagant plans for their upcoming wedding six months hence, would never understand that somewhere deep in his soul he felt this vast emptiness. An emptiness that neither work, nor money, nor Sydney could fill. But with what or how could he find what he needed to fill it? Maybe he was just tired. After all, it had been years since he had really taken a vacation. Maybe he should suggest a trip to Mexico or some tropical island. Maybe there he and Sydney could rediscover what happiness felt like. But no, he didn't want to go away with Sydney. What he really wanted was to go without her, far, far away. But he knew she would never understand his reasons for needing to be alone.*

Somehow, Rob just wanted to slip into that void somewhere between awake and asleep where he could be with himself and his thoughts, or even more importantly, his feelings. It had been a long time since he'd felt anything other than that numbness, that total lack of feeling in any part of his body or being. He felt an overwhelming need to find something within himself, about himself that was more intimate, higher – more connected to the Universe. That 'void,' that's where he thought he'd find it. For the first time in his life, the last thing he wanted was to be social, with anyone, including Sydney. It seemed that confusion had set into every area of his life except his work. When Rob was at work, he was a machine – a money making machine that wouldn't stop. But

---

* ALONE – (adj.) With only one's own company. Apart from anything or anyone else; singly.

when he was off, he felt moody and confused. He never even seemed to have energy for sex anymore.

"Something has to be wrong with me," thought Rob. "There was a time when I always wanted sex. But somehow, I don't feel a thing, no desire, no drive. I don't even care if Sydney and I ever make love again. I don't think that's normal for a man my age. Of course, it still works whenever I want it to, but funny enough... I don't really care."

"Did I tell you Tracy's giving me a lingerie party next Friday night?" said Sydney, interrupting Rob's stream of self-dissection.

"But you know my class reunion's next Friday night. I thought... you'd be going with me."

"You are joking dear? You don't really expect me to go with you to the 'Iowa City Corn Huskers' reunion? I mean it's so, you know, small town," Sydney lamented with a hint of indignation in her voice. "And besides, you do want me to look like a sex kitten on our wedding night, don't you sweetheart?" She whimpered, attempting a purr which sounded slightly more akin to the sound that a wounded cat might utter in its final gasping breaths after being run over by a Peterbilt.

"I guess that makes me a small-town sort of guy then," said Rob as he stared at the ceiling, wishing desperately that there was something to stare at.

"Sweetums... you know I didn't mean it that way. You know you're different. You're... cultured, you don't think like a 'Corn Husker' anymore," Sydney continued in a regretful tone, attempting to dig herself out of her subconscious blunder and correct her unfortunate choice of descriptive adjectives. "I mean, you know the difference between Geoffrey and L.L. Bean. You've been away from there long enough to lose all of those unattractive smalltown traits. And besides, small town is sort of coming back into vogue," Sydney reasoned further, working hard to extricate her size ten foot from her mouth. Coquettishly, she pursued another tactic as she rubbed her hand down the length of Rob's chest and stomach to his 'Benny,' as she called it – stroking him in an attempt to move on to a different topic.

But for some reason, Benny just wasn't responding tonight – no more than Rob was responding to her advances. When it finally became apparent that her efforts seemed to be failing miserably, Sydney slid her body onto his and began to work herself on top of him, expecting that this would surely muster up an appearance from the 'Benny Monster,' as she would teasingly refer to it on a good night. But to no avail, the Benny Monster was just not going to perform for her tonight.

"Oh God," thought Rob, "Maybe I spoke too soon. Now I can't even get it up. That's what I get for not appreciating what I have. Look at this beautiful woman sitting on top of me. How could I not want to simply ravage her right this minute? I mean, this is the woman I'm going to marry. Marry! I must be out of my mind. Do I really want to marry a woman who I hardly even know? I mean really know. Of course, I know where she shops, what social events she deems important to attend, which restaurants she has to be seen in that week, and what she feels is chic to read, wear, or which cause to support that month, but do I really know her? Have we ever discussed how she feels about anything truly important? Have we ever discussed the origins of the Universe? Things like life, love, freedom, happiness... 'Paradise?'

And love... what about love?" thought Rob, "It seems to be all about practicality and compatibility... that is why most adults get married isn't it? At least that's why all my friends have gotten married. Does anyone truly marry for love anymore? The last time I really remember feeling in love was in eighth-grade, when Julie Anne Phelps sat down next to me in homeroom. It was the first time I had ever laid eyes on her and it was the last time, since I never took them off of her again," reminisced Rob. "Not until the day I drove away to college and she kissed me one long last time in the driveway. She told me then that she loved me but she couldn't leave her mother, and she knew that I was destined for the big city and great things. I think my heart's still there in that locket I hung around her neck that first Christmas we went steady. My mother says she still wears it. It still beats there I'm sure of it, since there's no sound of it anywhere in my chest. I lie here listening, but all I can hear is Sydney, the woman I'm about to marry, repeating one of her discourses on proper etiquette for a wedding shower which her maid of honor had so inappropriately neglected to follow."

"Maybe we just leave love behind with happiness," reasoned Rob, "To keep it company when we grow up... when we leave childhood behind. Can we really love as adults having lost the innocence of childhood? Maybe The Little Prince and Peter Pan had something there. Maybe it's better to never grow up. If so, we could keep love and happiness locked somewhere inside us, instead of in a silver trinket around someone else's neck. The last time I remember not having to think about whether I was happy, or not, was when I was a child. Maybe that's because you don't have to think about whether you're happy or not when you're happy. Maybe it's when you think about it and talk about it all the time that you've lost it, and you hope that if you talk about it enough, you might find someone who can help you find it again. Maybe adults just aren't meant to be happy at all," reasoned Rob, "Maybe when we grow-up we're supposed to take the burden of the world on our shoulders and never be happy again... never find Paradise."

"That's okay," Rob relented letting her off the hook, "I'll go alone," trying to hide the fact that he was actually somewhat relieved, since he hoped to spend some time catching up with Julie Anne. He wanted to see if she was indeed still wearing the locket, even though she had married only two years after he'd left and had already had two kids.

Lying there in bed that night Rob felt lost. Not lost in the sense of not knowing his way to the therapist's office across town, who was temporarily filling in for his own therapist who had jumped off the Chrysler Building while visiting New York, two weeks prior. But a feeling somewhat similar to being lost at sea. Where you sit floundering in that trough between the swells at high noon surrounded by nothing but water, with no sign of land or buoys to mark the way. You look in every direction but there's nothing on the horizon, not even a hint. Nothing to tell you that if you head north, you'll find eternal 'Happiness,' east – 'Failure,' south – 'Hell,' and west – 'Paradise.' Suddenly, you realize that the only source of navigation you have is yourself, and that inner voice one can turn to at times like this seems to have suddenly come down with laryngitis.

CHAPTER TWO

Guardian Angel

"I am here and I shall not leave you until you have fulfilled your reason for being."

Archangel Gabriel

If only Rob could tune in and listen. But like most, he hadn't even learned how to turn on the radio yet, let alone tune into the right frequency, even though I've tried my best to guide him along this long, perilous journey called life. Most humans are usually quite oblivious to it but everyone has a Spirit Guide* whom they hired before embarking on their journey in this human incarnation. On a day-to-day basis, being one's Spirit Guide is a thankless job. Even if we are the ones that keep guys like Rob from stepping off the curb in front of an oncoming truck, if it's not their time, while their mind is on other more important things than walking and staying out of the way of large moving objects. But our real purpose is to attempt to make their subconscious minds, and hopefully their conscious minds, aware that we're always here for a little objectivity on what is referred to by humans as life, even if they are far from truly living. Our job is to somehow assist them to tune in to the needed information to fulfill their reason for becoming human in the first place. This of course, doesn't mean that we don't love what we do. In fact, it's a learning process for us here on 'The Otherside' as well, not to mention good entertainment. But most of all, we benefit from the experience in some ways more than souls like Rob.

• *SPIRIT GUIDE – The equivalent of a guardian angel, or just plain intuition if you feel uncomfortable with any reference to spirits in general and wish to take full credit for any and all divine intervention.*

To back up a little, maybe this story of one man's search for Paradise would be best told if I were to introduce myself and provide my qualifications for the afore-mentioned job. I, am Rob's Spirit Guide. On 'The Otherside' as well as in my last life as a merchant sailor in the West Indies, my name was and is, Ian. Like most humans, I have incarnated many times before, but finally graduated from the rat race when I, in my last life, truly discovered Paradise. So, for his last time around, I was chosen as Rob's guide on his sail through life in search of himself, and of that elusive destination.

With Rob, however, I'm still working on the elementary arts, such as the art of tuning-in, in order to understand the bigger picture which is often quite hard to get the hang of for most participants of the human race. It can somewhat be compared to the usefulness of a sailor's most basic means of electronic navigation — the RDF.*

Of course, another seldom used means of acquiring the bigger picture is by simply climbing the mast to get a better view and broader perspective of where you are. Sometimes life is just simply too close to see it clearly. From up here it all makes perfect sense, but unfortunately most don't ever achieve that vantage point of perspective until it's all over and time to go home.

That night while Rob was lying in bed staring at the ceiling and listening to the hypnotic, whining cadence of Sydney's voice, he realized that his life had grown cliché – a caricature of what human existence had become – society's idea of the perfect life with all the trimmings of success, albeit happiness. He had been in compliance with the needs of society, but society hadn't complied with his.

Somehow that night, I managed to convince him that his only hope for happiness was to go in search of Paradise.** It would be a search not unlike Monty Python's quest for the 'Holy Grail' – an eternal quest for that elusive, amorphous treasure which Rob would hopefully devote the rest of his life to finding. In his heart he knew it was out there, somewhere. Maybe it was hiding with love and happiness – maybe it was indeed with his childhood.

What Webster neglected to qualify when defining 'Paradise' was exactly where that 'place' or 'condition' is and how to find it. Webster had somehow overlooked the true location of Paradise as had Rob, and just about every other human on the planet obsessed with everyday life and its obscured definition of

---

* *RDF – Known to the layman as a 'radio direction finder' – a rather outdated radio receiver which pinpoints the direction from which a radio beacon is being transmitted. As in life, when you're lost and you haven't the foggiest clue of which way to go, tuning into any old station within range will do in a pinch to give you some inkling of where you are and the direction to take. Unfortunately, this method of navigation can be rather hit or miss and does require a certain amount of practice, concentration, and fine tuning, until you're certain you've tuned into all the proper channels.*
** *Webster's definition of PARADISE – (n) A place or condition of great or perfect contentment, beauty, satisfaction, happiness, or delight.*

true 'achievement.' Like most of mankind, Rob mistakenly assumed that Paradise was to be found in some sort of tropical climate. So, at his high school reunion, when his old buddy and classmate, Joey Mitchell, invited him to the Caribbean for Antigua Race Week, Rob didn't hesitate for a moment to accept an invitation to Paradise.

Rob arrived at the reunion in the ballroom of the downtown Iowa City Ramada Inn, which had nostalgically been decorated in the same theme as their senior prom with the props from their production of South Pacific. It was a cornucopia of tacky, dusty crepe and construction paper palm trees, and fake tissue paper hibiscus – complete with hundreds of sheets of sandpaper taped together to create the semblance of a white glistening sand beach – the shop teacher's contribution to the prom fifteen years prior. The class nerd, Ronnie, had actually salvaged all the party decor and stored it away in the attic of his parent's store for all those years, to the dismay of the local fire chief, and had dug it out for this special occasion. Rob took it as a sign when Joey invited him to join him on his boat on a tropical island. He was so excited about the prospect of getting away, he snuck out of the party to book his ticket from his room, attempting to kill time while he awaited Julie Anne's arrival.

It was Rob's maternal Grandmother, Lilly, who had inspired his intrigue for travel, even though he hadn't yet left the country. Rob held a great fondness for Lilly, unlike any he felt for other family members, including his own mother, whom he loved dearly. It seemed that over the years, Lilly had dominated his portrait of his family mythology, since he'd spent much of his childhood in the kitchen of her little two-bedroom house next door to his own. He remembered her fresh baked bread and her laughter and how she would tell him of the great secrets she had hidden in her steamer trunk, which had come with her from her homeland. The trunk had stayed under lock and key in Lilly's bedroom, and had always served as mysterious intrigue to Rob and his cousin, Marie. Their curiosity was forever piqued and together they had begged daily – pleading with Lilly to show them its contents, since Rob imagined it to contain shrunken heads from Africa, and Marie some secret Italian recipe for a love potion. He had never learned what secrets lay hidden in that old trunk which had come five thousand miles with that young girl of seventeen, since Lilly had passed away while Rob was away at school in Chicago and her house had been emptied and torn down before it had fallen down on its own. But, the memory of that trunk had stayed with him and had always heightened his desire to travel, and now he had finally found his opportunity.

It was an hour into the reunion – they had already started giving out those ridiculous awards they give to those alumni that had managed to achieve something miraculous, like leaving Iowa City, when she finally arrived. Rob was busy searching the room for the twentieth time to no avail, since Julie Anne was simply not there, when his name was called. "Rob Mariner, for the 'Most Exciting Job Award.'"

Rob stood there confused, listening to the applause, certain that he had heard incorrectly since surly he couldn't possibly have the most exciting job. What about that strange girl who'd joined the circus and become a sword swallower? But then he had heard that, due to her allergy to cats *(actually lions in this case),* she had unfortunately sneezed while swallowing a rapier *(a double-edged sword)* and severed an artery. Prodded by some classmate next to him whom he didn't recognize, Rob hesitantly stepped up to the podium to accept his award – dinner for two at the Corn Husker's restaurant and a truck wash and wax at the local truck stop. Rob laughed as he was handed the award by Jodie Crabtree who seemed quite reluctant to give up the coveted prize. "Well," said Rob, "I don't quite know what to say other than I guess this means I should enjoy work more, shouldn't I?" prompting everyone to laugh as if it was the funniest joke they'd ever heard. Looking around the room, Rob sadly realized that his was likely the most exciting job of all his classmates since only he and three others, all women, had managed to escape the pull of the small town's magnetic field that so surely kept most people secure in their familiar habitat, if not in the cornfield itself. And in a town of farmers, exciting jobs were not exactly run of the mill. Maybe his life wasn't so bad after all – but maybe he just simply hadn't seen enough to know the difference.

Then suddenly, Rob felt her eyes on him. Looking up, he spotted her just as she walked through the door. She smiled at him.

"It's her!" shouted Rob in his head. *"God, she's still beautiful!"* he wanted to scream out loud. *"She hasn't even changed a bit since I last saw her. What a fool you were Rob, you left her. What did you expect, that she'd wait for you and never get married?"* thought Rob berating himself as he watched her from across the room looking just like he remembered her.

She was even wearing blue like she always did to match those amazing blue eyes. And there it was, hanging from that incredible neck of hers – right where he'd left it fourteen years before – his heart.

It wasn't until the crowd at the door thinned that he noticed she was about ten months pregnant, but nonetheless, he had to visit his heart to see if there was still any hope of freeing it. Or, would it just stay locked away in that little silver locket forever? Looking at Julie Anne, Rob felt a great sadness deep within him. A sadness, it seemed, that had filled that dark empty space in his chest where his heart once had been. Quickly, Rob stepped down from the podium and away from the limelight, and headed through the crowd in her direction.

There she stood, pregnant – with twins no less, she told him as she giggled like the young-girl he remembered necking with in the back of his pickup truck. His hand was drawn to it – he wanted to touch it, to see if it was alive.

Not the babies, his heart – to see if it was still beating inside that tiny silver trinket that had served as a home for his heart all those years. He was convinced that what was keeping him alive must be some cold, hard mechanical device implanted in his chest – designed to keep the blood circulating to his brain, and to the rest of his body and vital organs. An artificial heart. Surely, he would be the first man in history to survive for more than fourteen years with an artificial heart. He was reaching out to touch it just as Dirk, Julie Anne's husband, appeared out of nowhere.

"I finally found a parking spot honey, only nine blocks away," Dirk panted out of breath.

"Rob, you remember Dirk."

Rob was confused – "Don't they have valet parking here?"

"Oh yeah but it's two-fifty. Why would I want to pay when I can park for free?"

Julie Anne just laughed nervously and smiled.

"But what if Julie Anne goes into labor?" asked Rob.

Slapping Rob hard upside his shoulder, Dirk laughed, "Don't you remember Rob, I was a sprinter."

"Yeah, you sprinted right in there as soon as I was out of town," thought Rob as he smiled politely.

Julie Anne smiled back at him the way she always had when they were in class together and shared some secret from the rest of the world. Rob melted and he knew immediately that he was still hopelessly in love with her. But what concerned Rob most was that he'd always heard that love finally fades away once it has been replaced by a new one. Did that mean that maybe he had never truly been in love with Sydney?

CHAPTER THREE

Paradise – Lost

*"Make voyages! —
Attempt them! There's nothing else..."*

Tennessee Williams

Rob ran onto the American 727 in Miami after his tight connection from Chicago – boarding pass in hand. He breathed a sigh of relief – it was close but he had made it aboard. He'd nearly missed his flight due to a late take off at O'Hare, but somehow fate had intervened and kept the plane at the gate ten minutes longer than scheduled due to a passenger's cat that had escaped from its sky kennel. Rob was far from a world traveler and could still count the number of planes he had been on, on one hand. The butterflies at take-off had yet to alight on a resolute resignation that he would get there safely, unless of course it was his time to go. If it were, one eventually reaches the understanding that staying at home will not ward off the inevitable. If it is, indeed one's time, you might just as easily succumb to a broken neck suffered from falling from one's bed as dying in a plane crash.

Rob had booked a first-class seat with the airline, however as he looked around the plane, he realized that the only difference between first and economy class on this plane was having the only flight attendant that didn't need to shave a five o'clock shadow, although she did look as if she needed support hose. The only other difference being the fact that if it were to crash, the first-class passengers had insured themselves first in line when it hit the ground. What had happened to all those pretty stewardesses that he remembered from flight ads? Rob had envisioned a pretty blonde of about twenty-one placing a white linen napkin in his lap and serving him caviar and champagne. He glanced again at his boarding pass and checked the numbers overhead and was relieved when he found that 6F was, as he requested, a window seat. He dropped his copies of "Journal" and "Forbes" onto his seat and proceeded to stow his bag in his overhead compartment. Finding it full, he patiently opened all twelve bins in first class to find them all crammed full with passengers' luggage, plastic cups, blankets, and safety equipment. Finally, his first-class flight attendant, an overweight, overbearing drill-sergeant with a name tag which read Beatrice, came to his rescue. She proceeded to instruct him to shove it under the seat ahead of him. Rob smiled politely and obeyed her instructions forfeiting all of his leg room to stowage. Since Rob's experience with airplanes was far from prolific, he just assumed that this was standard treatment and also figured that the flight attendant was not someone to argue with. After all, should the plane crash into the ocean, the last thing he needed was a pissed-off flight attendant overlooking him when it came time to hand out life-jackets or assist him into a life raft.

Rob buckled in just as the cat was captured and returned to its sky-kennel and the jet started backing away from the gate. It wasn't until they were airborne and Rob tried to recline his seat and found a bulkhead preventing it, that he realized it was going to be a long, three-and-a-half-hour flight. Since there was no movie, Rob donned his Walkman headphones and popped in a Harry Belafonte CD. He closed his eyes and tried to settle into an island rhythm, smiling as he fantasized about what life would be like in Paradise. Of course, even Rob's wildest imagination fell short of what was truly awaiting him in the land of swaying palms, coconuts, and blue waters.

Ahhh, the seduction and the lure of Paradise. We've all been prey to it at one time or another. The dream of sailing off into the sunset and a life of total leisure, where there are no phones to ring, no schedules to keep, and best of all, no IRS. You know no dictionary or encyclopedia written to date designates that Paradise is located somewhere in the middle of the ocean just slightly north, or south of the equator. Then why is it that humans always think they can find it there? Like Rob. Somehow, he just knew that he would find Paradise on a tiny speck of dirt located at approximately 17° North and 61° West in the middle of a sea they call the Caribbean – in a chain of islands called the West Indies.

Columbus first discovered the West Indies, a chain of islands separating the Atlantic Ocean from the Caribbean Sea in 1492, and on his second voyage a year later made landfall in the southern West Indies discovering Antigua and naming it after a church in Seville, Spain. It wasn't until nearly a century and a half later that the British colonized it making it one of their most secure military bases. Unfortunately, however great at building fortifications the Brits were, they were far less than efficient in building an island economy. Once slavery was abolished, you weren't likely to see those plantation owners out in the hot sun cutting down sugar cane and loading it onto sugar cane trains. After three

ISLAND FEVER

hundred years of struggling to keep the island afloat, the British finally gave it its freedom for the natives to make a mess of it themselves. But then luckily came the twentieth-century, along with tourism – an industry without which the Caribbean would surely be a desolate place.

Rob had finally escaped for one glorious week of fun, sun, and relaxation, without Sydney, to her dismay. Not that she really cared about those hot humid islands with their miserable mosquitoes and horrible little flying sets of teeth known by the locals as 'no-see-ums, much-feel-ums.' Her real upset lay in why, what, and how Rob felt the need to vacation without her, what he planned to do to keep himself entertained without her, and how he planned to do it – without her. But none of this phased Rob in the least since he knew it was long, long overdue – the party as much as the vacation. And ohhhh... what a party it was. For Joey was the perfect host on his sleek, seventy-five foot black, Spronk sailing catamaran* named 'Island Fever,' with its all-female crew, except of course for Raymond, the cook – a tall, lean, long-haired flashback from the early seventies. Joey made certain that Rob never wanted for a thing, other than possibly a little rest. But who needs rest when you're having fun?

Rob arrived on the island late in the afternoon and finally made it through customs just in the nick of time to experience his first gloriously painted Caribbean sunset. When he stepped out of the cabin door of the 727, he stood at the top of the stairs surveying the surrounding countryside and glistening blue ocean. This was a foreign land – a first for Rob and it thrilled him to think that he was no longer on American soil. As he breathed in the tropical sea breeze which washed away the jet fumes and carried tendrils of island fragrance, laced with that distinctive scent of sea air, he was instantly intoxicated as if he had already consumed several tall rum punches. Seabirds, both elegant and awkward, soared over-head stealing updrafts from the thermals rising off the white concrete runway. Rob walked across the tarmac that surrounded the terminal to the single line of passengers that had just disembarked ahead of them from the 747 out of New York – the queue in which one must wait in order to clear immigration to be allowed the privilege of entering their little island. It took thirty minutes of standing in the glaring afternoon sun until he gratefully reached the door to enter the unairconditioned immigration terminal and the reprieve of some shade. After all, Rob was whiter than the Pillsbury Dough Boy since visits to the beach were not exactly on his daily agenda, nor were unair-

---

*CATAMARAN or 'CAT'– A boat, either power or sail with 'two' hulls of equal size, which are held apart by a rigid deck – a notoriously fast hull design for sailing vessels. This type of boat should not be confused with a trimaran which, as its name suggests, has 'three' hulls in total – one central hull and two outrigger-like hulls. A Spronk catamaran is named after its Dutch designer who built these classic boats in the West Indies for nearly three decades.

conditioned buildings. It took another thirty minutes until he finally stepped to the front of the line.

"NEXT," commanded the only immigration officer open for business the others seemingly too busy chitchatting to be bothered.

Rob stepped up to the island official's counter and handed him his virgin passport, which the officer scrutinized suspiciously since it didn't contain even a single stamp, albeit it was five years old.

"Where you be stayin'?" asked the immigration officer demandingly.

"On a boat... sir," answered Rob not wanting any hassles that might prevent his speedy ingress to Paradise. Rob imagined Paul at the gates of Heaven interviewing would-be inhabitants and stamping their approval, granting their permission to enter, and wondered where those were sent who did not pass the test.

"Wha' boat," asked the officer removing his glasses in order to stare Rob down.

"Well, it's my friend's boat, Joey Mitchell," added Rob smiling politely, "I believe it's called ah... Island Fever."

"Dat boat, eh" said the officer as if it were quarantined with the plague. "I know'd dat boat well."

"Ah..." said Rob, starting to sweat even more than he had been when he was standing out in the sun.

The immigration officer stared at him unblinking for a full minute trying to determine what, Rob didn't know. He then loudly slammed the stamp in his passport passing him on to customs who proceeded to search his bags as if they were looking for a microscopic virus. So much for Rob's first pleasant experience with clearing customs in a foreign country. Joey had warned him that everything moved at a slower pace and happened in its own time in the islands, but an hour later when Rob finally stepped out to find the sun already setting. He wondered if he could ever adjust to the island way.

As he walked from the arrival hall to curbside with his bag, Rob noticed an attractive, exotic girl standing next to a car who appeared to be waiting for someone. She was quite possibly no older than eighteen, but had large contrary, chestnut brown eyes which betrayed her years of experience. Having expected to find Joey there to greet him, Rob looked around feeling a little lost since he suddenly realized that he had no specific address for Joey other than English Harbor, which Rob rightly imagined to be overflowing with hundreds of boats and sailors. He gathered, upon Joey's absence, that he had given up waiting for him while he was baking in the hot sun and being grilled by customs. As he was surveying the parking lot in hopes that Joey might return, the young girl, Maya, silently appeared next to him and without saying a word, took his hand and led him to the car waiting at the curbside. "Well," thought Rob, "Maybe this is going to be something of an adventure after all."

Rob was in awe as he stepped out of the car and stood on the dock in Nelson's Dockyard,* looking at the seventy-five foot deck of elegance and power that stretched out before him. Even though Rob knew little to nothing about boats, he innately sensed that the Island Fever was one of the elite – the creme de la crème of the fleet, comparable only to those massive hundred foot plus racing yachts docked either side of her.

The deck of the boat was abuzz with beautiful women coiling lines, fluffing cushions, and tying up awnings. It was as if he'd landed in a scene from a movie. Surely, he had fallen asleep on the plane and was merely dreaming – conjuring up his image of the picture-perfect Paradise. Suddenly, someone slapped him hard on the back assuring him that he was awake and that indeed the vision that lay before him was real, at least as real as one perceived reality to be. He had finally arrived at the latitude and longitude in which Rob had chosen to escape his unhappiness. At present he was beginning to feel quite content, if not yet making the giant step to say that he was truly happy. But he would work on it. He had resigned himself to the fact that he would temper his expectations and classify happiness for now – 'a work in progress.' And I, well... I was feeling right at home being, once again, on a sailing vessel on the waters of my homeland—not to mention quite impressed with the scenery aboard.

"So, you managed to escape purgatory eh...?" said Joey, smiling wickedly as Rob turned to see who had accosted him in the name of friendship. As exhilarating as its alienness had been to Rob upon arriving, he was quite relieved to see a familiar face. After all, this was Rob's first venture out of the States and he was still more than a bit tentative about his comfort level alone in a foreign land. Even if it was slightly akin to being in Disneyland, albeit for adults only. So, at that moment when Maya placed a tall, icy rum punch into Rob's hand, his vacation commenced, sending him on his first true embarkation into adventure.

Rob and the crew sailed by day, partied by night, and drank rum and cokes, rum punch, and petite punches around the clock. A week passed and Rob was feeling no pain, aside from a little sunburn. He no longer knew or even cared what day it was, or even what year for that matter. All Rob knew at that point, was that he didn't feel quite so empty anymore. In fact, Rob was in a state of perfect contentment, beauty, satisfaction, happiness and delight—he was, he thought, in Paradise. At least he was until that morning he awoke sporting one hellacious hangover and an empty bank account, and Joey was nowhere to be

---

*NELSON'S DOCKYARD — Named after Britain's favorite hero, Admiral Nelson, it was built on Antigua in 1745, as the main naval station for Britain in the Lesser Antilles. After the restoration of the ruins, today it has become a center for yachting commerce in Antigua.

found. It was all just a dream, right? The check to Joey for a half million dollars to buy half of the boat and the message to his boss suggesting that he invest in pork bellies. Of course, it was all a dream—a bad one.

But let's back up a here a little, since Rob's inevitable demise actually started the moment he had accepted Joey's offer to join him in Paradise. However, it wasn't until that final night of race week that Joey's carefully laid plan had actually been signed, sealed, and delivered.

The evening had started, as had all other evenings on the quay in Nelson's dockyard, with happy hour aboard the Island Fever – having already polished off ten cases of Mount Gay Rum for the week. But tonight's events included far more festivities than seeing who could drink the most R&C's and still climb the mast. Joey, being the consummate host, was making certain that his guests fully experienced every possible nuance of race week from tormenting the 'maxi's' *(90 foot plus – three-million-dollar, monohull* sailboats)* by blowing past them on a beat to weather as if they were standing still, to joining in on the drunken debauchery which wreaked havoc at the dock every evening. Although the Island Fever had not been permitted to enter the Antigua Sailing Week** race officially, she was permitted however, to enter the closing night raft race which took place in the now grossly polluted harbor – thanks to the fact that with no dumping facilities, hundreds of boats had for the last week simply clear flushed their heads'*** contents directly into the harbor.

*MONOHULL — As opposed to a catamaran or trimaran which have at least one back–up hull to keep it afloat in an emergency, a monohull is a sailing vessel with only one hull, which has a very large, long fin made of lead called a keel attached to the bottom – designed to keep it upright at all times, even once it has dragged the boat to the bottom of the ocean after it has sprung a leak. This minor design flaw of course defines the difference between a monohull and a multihull as – a boat that will surely sink, and a boat that will not, even though the latter may end up upside down.
**ANTIGUA SAILING WEEK – Formerly part of the CORT circuit – Caribbean Ocean Racing Triangle – now an independently held race which, over the years, has become more of a tradition than an event. There hasn't been a catamaran class in the Antigua race week however, since a 'Hell's Angel' of yacht racing catamaran captain T-boned one of the classic maxis at the start of the race several years ago. Catamarans are also frowned upon by more traditional sailors, due to the fact that their multi-million-dollar monohulls are thoroughly embarrassed by those funny looking raft-like craft worth a fraction of their value, who breeze past them as if they're standing still.
***HEAD — This is not a reference to any part of the human anatomy, either large or small, but is in fact a term used to describe nautical toilets, the etymology of which there's no need to go into here other than to say that the head or bow of the boat was used to relieve oneself by the early sailors. In many cases, for years, it was simply a hole through the deck on a catamaran – especially in the islands, where they have yet to learn of such sanitary concepts as holding tanks and dumping stations. Why bother, since on most islands, the island's raw sewage is dumped directly into the town harbor anyway, and those who have no landfill simply dump their unwanted garbage offshore.

But by that evening, everyone was so polluted by the Mount Gay rum it didn't matter to them how much slime had accumulated in the tiny inlet. Whatever germs they might happen to ingest by jumping into the filthy water of English Harbor at Nelson's Dockyard would surely be sterilized by the alcohol content in their bloodstream before it had the opportunity to grow into anything more harmful than some sort of tropical toe jam.

This was Joey's chance to shine, since the one and only rule for the closing night raft race it seemed, was that the cost of your vessel exceed no more than $100 *EC (East Caribbean Currency)*, equivalent to about forty-eight U.S. dollars. So, to ensure that the Island Fever crew would be the center of attention regardless of whether or not they actually made it across the finish line, Joey constructed his raft by lashing together a harem of 'Annie O' blow-up dolls, topped off with a rubber ducky or two. The Island Fever's entry was definitely the hit of the evening, or for that matter, the week, even if it had sunk the minute three drunken men and nine inebriated women dove onto it with oars in hand from the dock at the sound of the starting gun.

Now to assist him in his plan, as Joey well knew, the end of race week was always polished off, as were most of the sailors, with one last drunken debauchery known as 'The Admiral's Ball' – held at the Admiral's Inn which was housed in a two-hundred-year-old warehouse from Captain Nelson's original Dockyard. The ball, requiring shoes, jacket, and tie, however made for an eclectic array of dress from a group of sailors who had brought none of the sort with them. Instead, they resorted to wearing Top Siders, sail ties, and foul weather jackets to accommodate the evening's dress code. Rob, of course, was one of the many who had brought none of the required dress with him to Paradise. After all, who needs anything more than thongs, baggies, and T-shirts in the tropics?

The week had proven to Rob to be, as Joey had hoped, an endless stream of tanned, beautiful girls in tiny little bikinis, sun, and fun, not to mention an endless flow of libations. By now Rob was convinced he had truly discovered Paradise, as best he could discern through the fog, even though it was one of the clearest nights of the year with the tropical sky displaying thousands of celestial bodies. His focus however, though definitely on bodies, was not on the celestial type in the least – Rob thought he had surely died and gone to heaven as he danced the night away to Jimmy Buffett and the undulating beat of the Calypso steel band.

It was somewhere in the wee hours of the morning, while staggering back to the boat arm in arm, that Joey cast the bait, well disguised of course as a tempting morsel thrown out for the quarry to nibble, only to be skillfully retrieved just before the hook was set. Joey knew well, that to insure successfully landing a fish, one must always offer a tease first and wait for the prey to bite the hook of its own accord, insuring that even if the fish changed its mind once it realized that there was a catch to the tasty morsel offered, it was far too late to get away. This was a lesson learned long ago by Joey who was well versed in the sport of trophy fishing, no matter whether it be the type of trophy with scales or the kind with tanned, bare breasted epidermis.

"So, Rob, buddy. What a week we've had. I mean it's hard to believe you have to head back to Chicago tomorrow and that relentless job of yours."

"Oh... yeah, it's hard to believe I have to head back to Chicago tomorrow," Rob repeated, parroting Joey as the thought suddenly dawned on him for the first time.

"Wouldn't it be great if you could live like this all the time?" Joey taunted dangling the bait. "I mean if you owned a boat like the Island Fever you could stay here year-round, kick back and really live the good life, not just vacation here once every five years. Too bad you can't stay man, the girls really seem to dig you I guess it's cause of all that culture you acquired in the big city," he said, patting Rob on the back. "I mean, they dig that almost as much as if you owned your own boat. Just imagine what it would be like if you did."

"Yeah?" Rob queried, while the remainder of his brain cells attempted to process the thought and sort through the sludge that a week's worth of drinking had deposited.

"But I guess you just have too many obligations, I mean that girlfriend of yours is pretty high maintenance. She wouldn't like it much if you just upped and decided to do what you wanted instead of what society thinks you should do. I mean, living life every day to its fullest is perceived by some as selfish, immature, and indulgent, but you know what I say, 'You only go around once, in this body at least. So, ya might as well enjoy it while everything's still working of its own accord.'"

"Sydney doesn't run my life you know," slurred Rob as they made their way across the dockyard lit only by the full moon which danced across the unconscious bodies strewn about the dock – sailors who had been unable to walk to or find their boats once the party was over. "You know, for that matter, no one tells me what to do with my life but me. I mean, I can do anything I want. Even buy a boat, quit my job, and move to the Caribbean if I want."

"Sounds like some pretty big talk to me. Owning a boat is a huge responsibility. You've gotta know how to take care of it and sail it. You can't just dive into that sort of thing without some experience behind you."

Reaching the Island Fever's slip, Rob stopped and turned seriously to face Joey. "I've got a great idea, why don't you sell me half of the Island Fever, I mean you've got all the experience I need."

Joey chuckled for a moment feigning amusement at Rob's request, pretending he thought it to be a joke.

"I'm not joking, sell me half of the Island Fever," Rob repeated, trying to sound as straight as his inebriated brain would allow him.

"But she's not for sale, and even if she were, you couldn't afford her."

"Try me," Rob challenged as he pulled his checkbook from his back shorts pocket. "What's she worth?"

"At least a mill. But I told you she's not for sale, not even half of her."

"Turn around."

"What for?"

"Just turn around," slurred Rob in a weak attempt at a command. Trying to pacify him, Joey turned around and Rob proceeded to use Joey's back as a desk to write a check for five hundred thousand dollars, even though he was unable to focus on the lines. With great effort he tore the check from the checkbook and proudly presented it to Joey as if to prove him wrong.

Joey just looked down at the piece of paper in Rob's hand, totally bewildered, then at Rob, and then at the Island Fever. "What's this?"

"A check for half the boat," Rob said flatly as if the deal were already closed.

"I... just don't know about this Rob, this is a big decision for me. I mean this is something I'm going to have think about," Joey insisted as a faint smile raised one corner of his mouth undetected by Rob. Folding the check, he tucked it away in his shirt pocket for safe keeping. "Let me sleep on it. I'll give you my answer in the morning."

So dim was Rob's state of consciousness, he was barely aware of the two girls Joey sent him as a present that evening to consummate their deal. In fact, he was far too inebriated to say no due to any sort of guilt about Sydney. Both Maya and a sexy blonde Swede named Inga, joined him in his bunk just in time to help him get comfortable. They undressed him as he swayed with the motion of the boat on the dock, and tucked him into his bunk – joining him to be certain he was well taken care of. Joey knew that it was every man's dream to make love to two women at once, and in light of their new partnership, he hadn't hesitated for a moment to share the wealth with Rob. They started by slathering Rob with lotion – each working on a different part of his now titillated body. Rob was in heaven with a gorgeous blonde and a brunette massaging him from his loins to his toes, but when Inga placed her well-endowed lips around Benny and proceeded to resuscitate him, he was in ecstasy. In fact, the Benny Monster had surely decided to make a grand appearance that night. But when Maya took over and climbed aboard – Rob was certain he'd died and gone to heaven as he lost all conscious recall of what was to follow – once Benny took the helm.

In fact, Rob would find that when he awoke the next morning, he unfortunately, or fortunately, didn't even recall his infidelitous evening with the two gorgeous, naked girls who lay contentedly – either side of him in the bunk. It was just as well, at least in his absent state of mind, he would remember nothing to feel guilty for, where Sydney was concerned at least. Up until that point, Rob had shown an amazing amount of self-restraint in the area of fidelity to his wife-to-be. But then, Rob had always been that kind of guy since 'sincerity' was his middle name. He had always been obsessively honest to his own detriment. Having been raised by a semi-Catholic mother and grandmother who had given up on converting his Protestant father, Rob had the market cornered on guilt and remorse in his family, which was the only remaining influence from his years of Sunday mass and weekly confessions with his grandmother, Lilly. His impulsive purging of guilt drilled into him by years of confession had made it difficult for Rob to cheat on Sydney or any other past relationship that he'd ever had without spilling the beans. Besides, other than Sydney and Julie Anne, his other relation-ships could, like his airplane rides, be tolled on a single die.

 His grandma Lilly, a devout Catholic, had bravely immigrated alone from Italy to the United States when she was only seventeen. A tall, beautiful, dark eyed Italian girl, she'd landed in New York with little money, her mother's ring, the clothes on her back, an old steamer trunk, a talent for baking, and her virginity. Within weeks her money had been spent, and her mother's precious heirloom, not to mention her virginity, had been liquidated. Her baking skills had finally landed her a job bringing in a few measly dollars a week, and a place to live above the bakery with three other girls. Although, it became quickly apparent that the baker was looking for more ovens than the wood burning one's downstairs in which to bake his strudel. It didn't take Lilly long to realize that her quickest way out of that dirty, unfriendly city was to meet a man that would take her far, far away and provide for her a life – if not an exciting life, at least a comfortable one. Lilly was a quick learner. She had astutely determined that the best way to meet a man from another part of the country would be, of course, at tourist attractions. So, on her days off, Lilly spent her time touring the sights of the city in hopes of meeting, if not her true love, the love of her life. Of course, this process required a lot of trial and error – meeting men from numerous cities, not to mention Ports of Call. But Lilly was holding out for her best shot at security after giving up on all the unreliable candidates she'd met.

 Six months after landing in America, she went to the top of the newly built Empire State building to look at the city, but more importantly, to look for a man. As she was struggling with a telescope, a kind man named Canton had gallantly come to her assistance. Canton was, it seemed, visiting New York from a state in the mid–west called Iowa, and most importantly, looking for a wife to take back to his home town. Within two days, Canton had proposed and the two were on a train west to the land where the corn grew tall, and unlike New York, the people were friendly. Less than eight months later, a robust, healthy, eight-pound baby girl, Helen, Rob's mother, was born a bit premature. Lilly had explained it away as her healthy genetic constitution and how she too had been born a preemie at eight pounds. And Canton, who was in love with Helen from the first moment he laid eyes on his blue-eyed, golden skinned daughter, never even bothered to do the math.

That night on the Island Fever, when Rob had finally drifted off to sleep with a smile on his face, although seemingly in a state of unconsciousness, he tossed and turned all night – more than Bobby Lewis had in his brief but memorable career. It was a long restless night, filled with one bad dream after the other, interspersed with dreams of Lilly's steamer trunk hidden in the bilge of the Island Fever. Rob's subconscious was somehow making a connection between Lilly's mysterious trunk and the Island Fever – both of which were symbolic of the unknown in Rob's world. Their deeper connection having yet to be revealed to Rob as he rehashed a recurring dream all night that he had bought a boat in the Caribbean, spent all his money, lost his job, his girl, and his sanity, and he didn't even know how to sail. He awoke late the next day, with the sun high and the boat sweltering hot, wondering how to interpret the previous night's hallucinations – until he started remembering the previous night's folly, like recalling a bad dream.

CHAPTER FOUR

Hook, Line, and Sinker

"Sharks are one of the dangers of swimming in tropical waters."

Ian

And a bad dream it was – more like a nightmare in fact. However, the check to Joey for a half million dollars to buy half of the boat and the message to his boss telling him where to stick his investments were unfortunately a reality. It only took three hours waiting in line at the island's phone company and three minutes on the phone to his bank in Chicago to find out that it definitely wasn't a dream at all – in fact, Joey had already cashed the check. It took only three seconds on the phone with his boss to realize that he had indeed left the message. God, maybe life in Chicago hadn't been so bad after all. But it was too late for regrets, since he was the proud new owner of one half of one very big Hobie Cat,* thought Rob, looking at his half million dollars floating there in the dirty, scummy water of English Harbor. Why, Joey had even had the decency to leave Rob a bill of sale, and a note telling him that he had slept on it and had decided to take him up on his offer. He had also added that he had important business elsewhere and would be gone for a while, asking Rob to please take good care of their boat while he was away. This time Joey had gone fishing for very big game and Rob had taken the bait and swallowed it hook, line, and sinker. Rob, it seemed, was Joey's newest prize and he was feeling quite like a fish that had been hooked, landed, and mounted, all in the course of a week.

HOBIE CAT – A small, fast, mass produced sailing beach catamaran – sixteen to eighteen feet in length. This popular beachable toy, which was designed by a man named Hobie Alter in the seventies, has inspired a plethora of copycats over the years.

Standing on the dock looking at his new purchase, the sailing of which was still as foreign to him as his surroundings, Rob scratched his head confused as to which of the two hulls was actually his. He was still in shock that he had made such an immense investment without even weighing his options or checking the market. Such a poor business decision was totally against his good judgment and his daily business practices. It was indeed the most, rash thing that his level head had ever devised and he was still reeling from discovering that the balance of his bank account was lower than a barometer during a gale. Suddenly, the intoxication of the island had worn off and Rob was more sober than he'd ever been in his life. The lure of the enticing fragrance of the island and the exotic fare had instantly become yesterday's news – some fast-fading fantasy that he had breezed past on the roadway of life. Oddly, the infidelitous affair, both with the island and the women, which had been his one and only departure from his faith-fulness to Sydney, had all but evaporated in light of the seriousness of his current financial indiscretion. Rob studied the boat with a surge of fear in his heart, realizing that he didn't have the slightest clue what to do with his half-million-dollar faux pas.

It wasn't that he didn't think the boat was worth the money he'd just spent. She was beautiful and well built – with no detail left unaddressed. But then, that was Joey. He had always covered all the bases. She had six foot–two headroom in her hulls and deckhouse, and she slept fourteen comfortably below deck, not to mention the amount of seating in the deckhouse that had been used on numerous occasions as a place to crash by those so inebriated that they couldn't find their way down to their bunks. Her deckhouse also housed a gourmet galley *(better known to the layman as the ship's kitchen),* a navigation station somewhat resembling the cockpit of a 747, and enough seating in the main salon to accommodate the island soccer team for dinner.

The Island Fever's decor was close to that of an Upper East Side townhouse with plush velvet cushions, Tibetan and Afghani carpets and a gold and mahogany inlaid table – a floating den of iniquity as it were. A chick magnet thought Rob cracking a small smile as he tried mulling over the vagueness of the past week's activities. But then reality hit him like a ton of bricks. In all his years as a broker he had never once felt any anxiety on the floor. But there he was for the first time in his life experiencing what he assumed had to be the syndrome that he'd sadly witnessed his fellow traders and clients suffer in the past when their investments were waning – his first anxiety attack.

"What have I done?!" thought Rob. *"I've just spent my entire life savings on a floating bachelor pad, and I'm not even single. I mean I wanted change in my life, but this is ridiculous. Sydney's going to kill me. She'll never understand why I'd spend everything I have on a giant raft with sails."*

Rob stood there hyperventilating, trying desperately to think about what he would do if he were on the trading floor, which generally boiled down to knowing when to buy and sell. Suddenly, an alarm went off in his head like it might on the trading floor.

"That's what I'll do!" Rob thought, *"I'll sell! There has to be someone who'll buy my half, it's a great boat."*

Once Rob had managed to control his panic and somewhat normal breathing had resumed, he settled into a mild nervous breakdown, and was able to start regaining some sense of reality about his current predicament.

"What was I thinking?" thought Rob. *"That's just it, I wasn't thinking, I was drinking."*

At the time everything had made perfect sense. But now his head was so fuzzy from the hangover that he was still having trouble tracking a coherent thought. Rob had always heard that a Bloody Mary was a sure cure for a previous night's binge to clear one's head, so in order to get a better handle on things Rob quickly poured himself a tall, stiff one. If a Bloody Mary was the answer, then he would have to consume gallons to wash away the previous week's fog, he thought. But, somehow one stiff cocktail had calmed his nerves and he'd actually started to regain his wits about him.

Aside from the terror of the unknown stretching out ahead of him, Rob was strangely quite titillated about this new adventure he was facing. After all, he had never ventured much past his own backyard. When he graduated from high school, Chicago had been a huge step for him since no one in his family had even visited a big city since Canton had brought Lilly back from New York, let alone gone to college. And the farthest Rob had dared to venture by this point in life, prior to his plunge into Paradise, was twice to New York City with Sydney on her yearly shopping sprees, and once to Disneyworld as a Christmas present from her dad. Aside from an oversized mouse and a big apple, Rob hadn't seen much of the world, and he was still a virgin as far as intercourse with life went. He had by that point experienced little of what life had to offer.

As a young boy, Rob had voraciously devoured books in the local library about faraway places, Grandma Lilly's stories about the old country, and television shows on travel to exotic lands. The spark was there from the beginning. But, like most humans who become domesticated by society before they are old enough to truly decide their lives for themselves, the fuel had been diverted into society's dream, and the spark had never been ignited. Rob had fallen into what had been his parents' safety net of security instead of pursuing dreams of studying abroad. Like most, he had not chosen his life, he had simply accepted what had effortlessly fallen in his path – he had only been courageous enough to venture as far as Chicago for college, which if the truth be known, had even caused concern in Rob at the thought of venturing out of the nest on his own. In fact, Julie Anne's decision to stay in Iowa City had nearly nixed the idea of Chicago for Rob. For her, he was ready to spend the rest of his life in his own hometown working in some sort of farm-related business. But Julie Anne had been far more astute than Rob about his longing to experience more about life and the world than corn fields and truck stops. She had been mature enough to realize that no matter how much he loved her, he would always have a longing in his heart for more. That night at the reunion when Rob had told Julie Anne about his plan to visit Joey in the West Indies, he had noticed a little sparkle in her eyes as she nodded and said, "It's about time."

As far as really living life and enjoying oneself went, Rob hadn't taken more than three weeks off in the past nine years, since he'd graduated and gone to work immediately in a broker's office and then on to the stock exchange. But he was finally awakening to the reality that he was letting life pass him by like most humans caught up in the race to gain success, money, and power. Suddenly, Rob was starting to realize that maybe there was more to living than conforming to society's measure of success for him.

"Why do I have this guilty sensation in the pit of my stomach?" he *wondered as he walked back on deck and purveyed his new holdings. "I feel like I'm not doing what society expects of me, especially Sydney's society. But then what do I really owe society? For nearly a decade I've put in the expected eight-hour work day in order to support my future wife, my future family, and my future grandkids and I'm not even married yet,"* he suddenly realized. *"I'm considered successful by most of society, especially for my age. But am I happy? What if I want more out of life? Or am I just being selfish and childish? Forget society, that's the least of my worries. What I've really done is to give up the security of knowing where I'm going to be ten years from now, or a year from now for that matter, and it's kinda scary. I'm stepping off the crowded ferry into a one man row boat and I don't even know how to row, let alone sail."*

Rob had never really considered himself afraid of anything. As a matter-of-fact 'fearless' was one of the adjectives used daily to describe him on the market floor. But this was very unfamiliar territory in more ways than one for Rob. His heart was racing the way it did on the floor when he had only seconds to make a multi–million-dollar decision and he was starting to realize that it was less fear and more exhilaration about what the future might hold that was surging the blood through his body at what felt like twice its normal rate. Of course, on the floor it was different – there, it was someone else's money he was gambling with. This time Rob had placed his bet and had to go double or nothing or he'd lose the hand, since it didn't take him long to find out from the local boat brokers that his option of selling his half to some other sucker was extremely slim, since practically every boat in the harbor was already for sale. Rob unfortunately had no job to return to and no money to speak of, since the check to Joey had emptied out his entire bank account, except for enough to cover maybe a month's bills at home. Of course, he had his credit cards, but how far would they go between his expenses in Chicago and his new responsibility here, and how would he pay them when the bills started to flow in

ISLAND FEVER

Like the high tide? So, Raymond, who had no explanation for Joey's disappearance, and who's loyalty lay with the Island Fever regardless of its owner, since it had been his home for the last five years, suggested the tried-and-true means of earning a buck for every professional sailor at some time or other in their career – charter.

It seemed that Rob was faced with the plain simple fact that he had no choice at this point but to fish or cut bait. He had to dive into the deep-end head first and hope he could tread water well enough to at least keep his head clear. How could it be that bad, he thought. *Why, living in Paradise and sailing this great boat around with pasty white tourists onboard every day didn't sound that tough, reasoned Rob. And, look at the going price of a charter these days, I might even come out ahead and have a hell of a lot of fun doing it.*

But no one had let Rob in on the big secret about the islands. He didn't have a clue what the West Indies was really like or what it had in store for him – but he was soon to find out. No matter how much I, or anyone else, might try to warn him, I was well aware that he'd only believe it once he experienced it for himself. Yes, of course I realize the West Indian islands seem like exotic, tropical Bali Hai's floating in the midst of a glistening turquoise sea, with swaying palms, naked girls, and tall rum and Cokes. But you see, life in the islands is kinda like marriage. It keeps you fooled through the honeymoon, and maybe even through the first few months – then reality starts to set in, along with the dreadful, inevitable disease known as 'island fever.'*

It's not the islands themselves that make life here interesting – it's their inhabitants. I should know this fact all too well since I was once one of them, even though I was of mixed European and African descent. You see, today's West Indies are inhabited by a people that Columbus named the West Indians thanks to his geographic disorientation – thinking he was on islands off the coast of east Asia. However, the indigenous Indians, the Arawaks,** were eaten by the Carib Indians,*** and the Caribs, well, they're almost extinct now. Columbus and the rest of the Europeans saw to that. The West Indies now belongs to the African ancestors of the slave trading days, and Indians, as they are known in America, they're not. The Indians only hated the white man. Today's West Indian loathes the white man. Yes, they may smile at them politely as they take their tips and watch them race around their island under de hot sun in a frivolous attempt to accomplish nothing – but the West Indian knows, that like all the others, they will at some point give up and go home. But not before they have parted with a generous amount of American dollars, which

---

*ISLAND FEVER — A disease which eventually affects most non-West Indians – some sooner than others – attempting an extended stay in the Caribbean islands. After a while, the smallness of the island takes its effect on you and you begin to go a little crazy, since you know every one you see on a first name basis, and everyone on the island knows every move you make. Plus, the fact that nothing works.

are widely accepted in the Caribbean as preferred currency. For the few expatriates who do manage to stay, chances are they have nothing more pressing in a day's work than making certain that they walk to the corner store to fetch a new bottle of Mount Gay Rum. The true West Indians were smart. They got the hang of survival in the islands a few hundred years ago – they simply learned to "Live and die in three-quarter time," as the song goes. What else would any fool want to do under de hot sun?

Aside from the inherent difficulties with island life, there was only one small problem with Rob's idea about chartering the Island Fever – Rob didn't know how to sail. So, Raymond, the cook, suggested that Rob hire Captain Alex for the job, insisting that Alex was just the person experienced enough to drive that overgrown raft called a catamaran around with sunburned, seasick, but paying tourists. But most importantly, Alex was the only available Captain on the island who knew about catamarans. There was only one small detail that Raymond neglected to mention to Rob – Alex was a woman. Boy was Rob surprised to find out that the attractive, young, one hundred fifteen-pound person of the opposite gender whom he found in his cockpit the next morning was soon to be his boss.

Still slightly hung over, Rob ascended from his bunk in the starboard hull expecting to find Raymond alone on the foredeck finishing up his morning mantras.

He stood in the cockpit rubbing his eyes and scratching himself when he suddenly realized that there was a woman busy at work disassembling his port* jib** winch.***

"Hope I didn't wake you," said the attractive, but slightly tomboyish, woman, who wore her hair tightly swept back from her face in a French braid, no makeup, cutoffs, and a tiny bikini top, which covered just an adequate amount of her firm but modestly proportioned breasts. She studied Rob from behind a mirrored pair of tortoise shell, sailor's Vuarnets, "I wanted to get an early start."

"On what," queried Rob looking at her somewhat confused by her presence.

**ARAWAK INDIANS — *The second known, inhabitants of the Eastern Caribbean from 2000 years ago – the first being the stone-age Chiboneys. The Arawaks were talented artists, peaceful farmers and fishermen comprised of numerous tribes that all spoke Arawak and originated in South America.*
***CARIB INDIANS — *A band of warring tribes from South America who invaded the Eastern Caribbean somewhere around 1200 AD – killing the men and taking the women as slaves. It is said that the Caribs were cannibals or caribals which is where the name Carib was derived. However, today there is speculation that since Columbus was given approval by the church to kill cannibals, rather than trying to redeem them since they were believed to be with-out souls, then quite possibly these natives were deemed as such by the Spanish to rid those desirable islands of its violent inhabitants. Although the Spanish did a pretty thorough job of killing off the Caribs, numerous tribes still exist today on several islands in the Lesser Antilles.*

"On putting the boat in order for charter," Alex said with a wry chuckle. "I know Joey all too well. He's never been one for high maintenance."

"So, you work for Joey?" Rob questioned.

"No actually, I work for you, or should I say you work for me now. I'm your new Captain, Alex, short for Alexandra," she said as she confidently extended her hand, which was covered in packing grease.

Dumfounded, Rob returned the gesture withdrawing his hand equally covered in grease, which he stared at as if it were some-type of disease, quite uncertain where to wipe it.

"You're... Captain Alex? I ah... but," he said, "But you're aaa..."

"Girl?" said Alex finishing his sentence for him

"Well, yeah," stammered Rob, scratching his head, really studying her for the first time.

"I've been a licensed captain for fourteen years," said Alex as if she'd been through this before.

"But you look so...."

"Young?" answered Alex unable to resist doing it again. I'm thirty-two, same as you," Alex said without looking up, eliciting a look of surprise on Rob's face.

"Well, but you're so... "

"Petite?" continued Alex, getting quite good at reading Rob's mind by this point.

"And this boat is so..."

"Big?" said Alex, starting to get the best of Rob.

"Well, yeah," Rob said uncertainly referring to the length of the boat as he attempted hopelessly to qualify his fears to her.

---

*PORT — The port or red-light side – the left side when facing the bow of the craft while standing onboard, and the starboard of course being the only side left, or remaining we should say – the right side or side which carries a green running light at night. Of course, the easiest means by which to remember which side is which is by the association between the actual drink and the color red, supposing of course you remember which color goes where.

**JIB — Being one of the smaller of the many choices of varying sized headsails which is triangular in shape and comes in three sizes, the storm jib, the heavy weather jib, and a working jib. The size of the headsail required on any given day is usually dependent on the wind velocity and direction the boat is headed in relation to the wind. In other words, the bigger the wind the shorter the sail. Other headsail options increasing in size from the jib would consist of the genoa, the drifter, and lastly the largest, the spinnaker, which is sometimes used with a strange additional sail called the blooper.

***WINCH — A geared device mounted on the deck or spar (mast or boom) of a boat which is used to haul a line in that couldn't be handled by manpower alone. The line is wrapped around the winch and the winch is then cranked in with the use of a removable handle.

"I grew up in Annapolis with my dad. I was sailing the Chesapeake before I could walk," Alex offered as she squeezed more packing grease into the ball bearings.

Rob just stood there shifting uncomfortably from one foot to the other, uncertain what to say next.

"I could sail her in my sleep," replied Alex casually as she nodded her head, gesturing to the Fever's modern staysail schooner rig* which sported the newest of every work saving device that money could buy. "Joey was never known to like work. He's got this cat rigged so she could almost sail herself. This rig's a piece of cake, even a novice could sail her with a quick lesson or two."

"So, you know this boat well?" Rob queried anxiously.

"Oh, a little I guess..."

Rob nodded, relieved.

"...I built her," finished Alex.

Uncertain whether to be impressed or embarrassed, Rob was now standing there looking and feeling like a total schmuck. He realized he'd reached the intersection in this conversation and it was time for him to make a quick detour and take an alternate route, or just pull over and park it. "So, does this mean I take orders from you?" Rob said, hoping he'd chosen the right road.

"Don't worry. I'm sure that compared to your girlfriend, it won't be too painful. I promise I won't make you walk the plank or anything, however, I do demand a clean deck," chuckled Alex in an attempt to lighten Rob up.

Rob attempted a smile, however fear or maybe even intimidation, made him feel like he wasn't exactly in the smiling mood. After all, this tiny little woman was exactly his age and knew so much more about the object he'd just blown his life savings on than he. The big question in Rob's mind right now was, could he accept a girl as his mentor in this new endeavor on which he was about to embark? He'd never worked directly with a woman as his superior before. Oh, why had Joey deserted him? This was not the way he had dreamed it would be. He loved the idea of women on board, albeit in a slightly different capacity. Now he found himself in an immense quandary. Keep this obviously qualified woman on to dig him out of the mess he'd made, or hope that he could find another available captain now that race season was over and everyone had already headed off to Europe and the States for the summer months.

*MODERN STAYSAIL SCHOONER RIG — Any boat with two masts of equal height, carrying five sails, from the headsail, to the baby staysail, to the upside–down angel (only in very light weather – or a fisherman in heavier winds), then comes the main staysail (its driving sail), and finally the main (providing primarily stability and direction instead of drive). However, complicated it may sound, it's a rig designed to be handled with ease due to the fact that the wind force is spread out over numerous smaller sails instead of two much larger ones, as with a sloop, a cutter, a yawl, or a ketch, whose sails are much more difficult to lower in the case of an emergency.

"I'm sure this cute little girl knows how to sail this big boat in theory but can she handle it when things get rough?" questioned Rob to himself. "After all, sailing's a man's job. I mean, think of all the famous Captains... Nelson, Rodney, Bligh, Blue Beard, and even Hook. But who the hell's heard of Captain Alexandra? She can't be serious... maybe if I just ask her to suggest another Captain. But then, she might be insulted enough to just walk away and then where would I be? Maybe I can give it a try for a few days and see how it goes. She'll probably screw up and then I'll have a reason to get rid of her. In the meantime, I can be looking around for someone else."

Rob may have had questions about the uncertainty of hiring Alex as Captain, but Alex had a few reservations of her own about her desire to work for Rob.

"Do I really want to put myself through the agony of working with some man who obviously believes that women only belong in their bunk or the galley?" thought Alex. "Even if he is kinda cute. But then again, I've always wanted a chance to skipper the Island Fever and here it is dropped right in my lap. Okay Alex, you've dealt with worse. Even the Coast Guard gave you a hard time when you were the first woman to get your license. You know how to handle this young, know-it-all who's obviously never gotten his hands dirty his entire life. Look at him – a little packing grease on his hands and he doesn't know what to do. I'd be surprised if those soft manicured hands have ever held a tool of any kind other than a corkscrew. He probably even calls in a handyman to change his light bulbs."

Alex just smiled at him as he attempted to remove the foul substance without being too obvious. For Alex, Rob's response was a familiar one, if not expected since she realized that she did fall into that stereotypical petite physicality which men, by nature, always felt the need to protect rather than respect as an equal in the physical world. And even though the type of response that Rob demonstrated was expected and understood, it stung no less for Alex each time she encountered it. Even if she understood that this ingrained masculine nature wasn't even a conscious judgment for men. It actually reverted back, as Alex well knew, to the early cavemen – who, by force of nature found it necessity to hunt for, feed, and protect, to their death, if necessary, the female that was significant in their life. For they were the givers of life, beings to be cherished and protected if their own lineage and very species was to continue onward. So, this seemingly inherent mistrust on the part of men towards Alex's nautical abilities was expected and understood by Alex as a fact of life, and human nature, if not always accepted.

The only man that had truly understood and respected Alex's love for the sea, or Alexandra as she had been named by her father on the day she was born – the same day her mother died, had been her father. She had been raised in

Annapolis by her dad who owned a sailing school, and by the age of ten, Alex was teaching her own class of seven-year-olds how to handle a tiny 'Pram' sailing dinghy. By the age of thirteen she had already won numerous races single–handedly and was building her first sailboat. By the age of seventeen, her dad bought her a rebuilt 30' Simpson Calypso trimaran, which she had named the 'Dandy Prancer' for the way it pranced around its mooring like a yet to be broken yearling.

The day Alex turned eighteen she passed the U.S. Coast Guard test for her hundred-ton Master Merchant Marine license. Then, when her father passed away two days after she'd graduated from high school, she listed their home and business for sale with a friend of the family and sailed south alone, making the long trek down the Intra-coastal Waterway* to the Florida Keys. There she found another lone sailor hoping to head south to the West Indies, and together, they set out for the Virgin Islands. There Alex earned her living for several years running day charters for a local hotel, and teaching sailing on the weekends to tourist children. Alex – a loner, who had always found good company in her own, and whose only other love was in books and writing, found day charters to be unchallenging at best, if not a painful existence. Playing social director every day to a group of a dozen new tourists was not exactly what she considered a fulfilling profession.

Eventually, she headed south to a somewhat unheard-of island named St. Christopher – known to the locals as St. Kitts – where Alex went to work at the island boatyard building overgrown catamarans in a tin shed alongside four West Indian men and one other expatriate from California named Michael, who was in charge of running the yard. There, she had also built herself a forty-foot catamaran named, Dancer, and had fallen in love for the first time in her life. Later finding out – three years later to be exact, to her extreme disenchantment, that Michael was in fact married to a woman in the States and in hiding for some tax-related indiscretion, not to mention back alimony and child support. Indeed, Michael was not even his real name. This discovery had come about one day when his wife had unexpectedly shown up at the dockyard dragging their three small children with her. Alex's broken heart had mended over time but with an impenetrable amount of scar tissue, tainting any immediate future prospect of romantic involvement. The experience had only sent her deeper into her self-sufficient world where she needed no one other than herself to make her whole, especially a man.

The only wonderful thing that had come out of her three years in that dirty, little boatyard in Basseterre harbor had been her own little dream boat Dancer, and of course, the Island Fever, of which she was quite proud. For three

---

*INTRA-COASTAL WATERWAY — *A system of waterways connecting bays, harbors, and rivers by man-made ditches all the way from Florida north to Canada, except at one place in New York where you must go offshore to get back to the waterway. It is often referred to as 'The Ditch.'*

years Alex had sweated and toiled over this seventy–five foot beauty, a Clinker lap–strake design made from Douglas Fir and the West Epoxy System.* Joey had demanded, "Only the best," as she lovingly worked every single inch of the Island Fever's topsides to a smooth finish from her bow stems to the tips of her elegantly tapered sterns. Alex had even been the one to christen her the Island Fever by pouring a bottle of Christal over her bows strung with island leis, as she was carried into the water by hundreds of locals who had come together on that special day to launch a grand lady and send her to sea with the island's love and blessing.

Joey had commissioned the yard to build the Island Fever six and a half years before Rob had hired Alex as her new skipper, so Alex understood Joey and his habits all too well. As far as Joey went, he was another one of those gentlemen sailors who had an undisclosed source of a very lucrative income, which no one ever questioned, but for which Alex suspected its source. However, she had chosen to keep her suspicions to herself, since she assumed that Rob, having invested so much money with Joey, must know the true means of his livelihood and all too comfortable lifestyle. Oblivious to these minor details of a lack of obvious employment, Rob hadn't even gotten around to questioning this issue in his own mind, let alone questioning Alex about it. In fact, Alex was beginning to assume that Rob was as likely as not, equally involved in some illicit activity and that the stock market was nothing other than a ruse and a new spin on the usual trust fund baby story – an appropriate cover for his early prosperity.

So, Alex just went about her business simply ignoring Rob's insecurities about her abilities. She knew full well that once he had seen her sail the Island Fever, he would feel secure in the knowledge that she was more than capable of handling and protecting his new investment, and even feel that the lives of his passengers, and for that matter his own, could be entrusted in her hands. So, she was slightly optimistic on that account. But regardless of Rob's opinion of her, Alex diligently performed her duties and then some, since she still felt a rather fond attachment to the Island Fever as if it were a child to which she had given birth. Again, another concept that Rob could never grasp.

*WEST EPOXY SYSTEM — *The top-of-the-line two-part resin which is designed for use in wooden boat building to seal, glue together, and water-proof the wood.*

CHAPTER FIVE

Survival

"Everything comes to him who hustles while he waits."

Thomas Edison

Up until now, Raymond had been extremely helpful in advising Rob on how to go about daily life in the West Indies. Unfortunately, the three most important lessons about island living that Raymond, Alex, or any other experienced inhabitant of Paradise neglected to teach Rob were, 'The Rules to Survival in the Islands 101.' Common sense things like Rule Number One – never, ever expect anything to be done when you need it, since the philosophy in the West Indies is based strictly upon the mañana *(tomorrow is another day)* principle. Which also means that the law of cause and effect does not work in the islands. In other words, just 'cause you need it, doesn't mean it's going to get done today, or tomorrow for that matter. The mañana principle isn't even taken literally by the West Indian. To them it just simply means, whenever it comes, it comes – all they are sure of is that it will be someday in the future, but definitely not today. The most important thing to remember is to never, ever fight this principle. Since, it's kinda like ketchup, the more you fight it, the slower it comes.

The Second Rule to remember when trying to accomplish the simplest task in the islands is to know beforehand that whatever it is you need, they won't have it on the island. Which means that you are totally at the mercy of what is known as the 'Island Purchasing Agent,' i.e. the person who sits in Miami getting rich ordering the things that those poor bastards can't buy in the Caribbean. They mark them up three times the original cost then add-on special delivery air freight, handling charges, and a three to four week wait. But, by the time it arrives, guys like Rob are so grateful just to have finally gotten what they need, they willingly pay any price.

Last but not least, the Third, but most important Rule to understand about the West Indies is that their system of running things is uniquely their own. There is no need to attempt to understand the system for it changes daily. What was yesterday's rule probably doesn't apply today and so on.

At this point, Rob still remained totally unaware of any of these great words of wisdom that Raymond could have easily imparted to him – but Raymond was a wise soul. He knew only too well, as I did, that the only way Rob would ever understand was to learn these rules the hard way. And Alex, well Alex was just staying out of it, since she figured that Rob was the boss and she shouldn't be the one to lecture him.

It was all very simple, thought Rob. All he needed to charter were a few easily obtainable requirements – a charter license, an inspection, an agent, and insurance. So, Rob proceeded to the harbor master's office to obtain these simple, seemingly routine things. What he didn't expect when he stepped into the little island office on the commercial dock was to run into Althea, the three-hundred-pound West Indian official in charge of dispensing licenses for charter. It seemed that the inspector, her husband – the harbor master, was down islan' on a fishin' trip and wouldn't be back until sometime nex' week, and the license and his insurance, of course, depended upon the inspector's approval of the 'seaworthiness' of Rob's vessel.

"So, is there another office on the island that might be able to help me expedite this process," asked Rob, a little irritated by his first taste of inefficient island bureaucracy. "You see it's kind of urgent that I get this business underway," pushed Rob a little harder. Unknowingly, Rob had made his first and second major island blunder – first by questioning the exclusive authority of the inspector – Althea's husband, and by suggesting that there might possibly be someone with even the slightest hint of higher authority than the official in charge – Althea's husband, not to mention the application here of the ketchup theory. Althea stood to her full height which towered several inches above Rob's generous six-foot frame, not to mention her girth which was at least three times wider, and removed her glasses to look him straight in the eye, "No one be higher atority tan Mista Brown de <u>o'ffishal</u> harba masta."

"I see," said Rob backing away a step as Althea got a little too close for comfort.

"In fac', I tink he be away two-week if me memry be righ'."

"But…" continued Rob stupidly attempting to question her word once more, "You just said one week."

The more anxious Rob got and the more he pushed Althea, the later the projected return date got for the inspector. In the meantime, she suggested, or rather commanded, that he go next door to the marine insurance office, which of course was run by her brother, Nathan. There Rob learned from Nathan that charter insurance would only cost him a nominal fee of ten-thousand-dollars per year to be paid in advance, of course, and that Althea's brother had the only charter insurance going on the island. Rob choked as he repeated the amount uncertainly to the agent who confirmed with a smile that Rob had indeed heard correctly. And then there was of course Alex and Raymond's salaries to be paid. It seemed that Rob was in deed in need of some kind of immediate cash flow.

Now, Rob had to make a decision – go back to Chicago and beg for his job back – or sell his precious BMW in order to try and salvage his questionable investment in the islands. The other issue that Rob had been avoiding was breaking the news of his drunken blunder to his fiancée, Sydney. He had simply left a message that he'd decided to extend his vacation for a few extra days, hoping that word hadn't reached her about quitting his job, but then, he knew he would have heard about it if she had. He had simply finished the message with an "I love you and I'll be in touch soon," or I should say, as soon as Rob got up the nerve to tell her the truth. So once again, Rob stood in line for the better part of an afternoon attempting to place a simple phone call to the states, since accessible, working telephones are a luxury taken for granted by all Americans who travel at some point to the Third World.

I should correct myself here in referring to the West Indies as the Third World since it does in fact have a First World infrastructure for most modern conveniences such as phones, running water, and electricity. However, that being said, it does fall slightly short of First World standards in that, in the First World those conveniences actually work. As compared to the West Indies, where much of the time they don't – much like its inhabitants. So, for accuracy and clarity's sake, these isles are generally deferred to the category of the Second World.

Rob stepped up to the little cinder block building and lined up in the queue that filed out the door and halfway around the building. It was one o'clock in the afternoon – lunch time for islanders which ran from twelve to three. Unfortunately, Rob had chosen to place his call at the hottest and the busiest time of the day, and had of course, come away from the boat without a hat or sunscreen. Up until the day he bought the boat Rob had been slathered constantly with suntan lotion by one of Joey's many female deck hands, thus Rob's lily-white skin had yet to suffer a great deal of direct sun. But alas, with Joey went his female retinue.

It seemed that since it was lunch time, there was only one operator working at the phone company which was known by the officious name of Telit. It was looking as if it would be a rather long wait to complete this simple task that Rob had never really thought twice about. It was two–thirty by the time Rob got to the bullet proof windows inside the building, where the operator took cover from irate tourists who often tried to grab the phone company's clerks by the throat after waiting to place a call for four hours and having the phones go down at that exact moment their call was put through. By then, Rob was certain that he had sustained sunstroke, not to mention the fact that his face was so hot from the sunburn that he surely could have fried an egg on his forehead. At least that was the thought in his mind at that moment as he rehearsed what he was going to say to Sydney. Surely, he would feel as if he indeed had egg on his face, but at least he reasoned, it would be a cooked one. Normally, Rob would have opted to wait outside the filthy waiting room strewn with candy wrappers, empty drink bottles, and island trash, but shelter from the heat, although unairconditioned, made it an easy choice for Rob to remain inside the standing-room only lobby.

On average, it took one to two hours to put a call through to the States from one of the eight phone booths in the adjoining room. Rob's other concern was that he would wait the two hours and his name would be called and he'd be unable to understand it due to the bad PA system and the thick West Indian accent of the operator. That day the phone company seemed especially busy for some unexplained reason and it appeared that everyone had brought at least two children with them or a child and a dog since the little room was so overwhelmed with screaming, crying, and barking it made it even harder to hear anything over the din. Finally, at about ten after four, a voice called over the public address system – "Rib, geta boot numba eit."

Was that his name or was that the operator's take out order for dinner, Rob wondered as he fought his way to the window to confirm the call. It seemed that the operator had indeed announced Rob's phone call which was awaiting him in booth number eight. So, he quickly made his way back through the crowd to the specified phone booth, stepping over crying children, and just avoiding a nip from a rather irritated island dog which some child had been tormenting. Finally, he reached the booth and stepped in, but as he attempted to pull the door shut, it came right off its hinges nearly falling on top of him. Struggling to get rid of the heavy door, he dragged it away from the booth and propped it against the wall as he heard once again, "Rib ta boot numba eit." Just as Rob turned to step back into the booth a rather large woman, obviously some relation to Althea, was attempting to squeeze between him and the phone booth in the narrow aisle between booth numbers one through four and five through eight. Somehow, she managed to wedge herself between Rob and the phone booth, and a man who was just stepping out of booth number four.

For an uncomfortable moment, Rob was trapped between this woman's overly robust posterior and the man who was carrying a large sack of tanya root* and Christophine.** Willing himself thinner, Rob twisted and struggled his way out of the bottle neck and snatched up the receiver on the phone just in time to hear the operator tell Sydney, "He musta leff misus, he no pik up."

*TANYA ROOT — A starchy, type of root that is known as the West Indian potato.
** CHRISTOPHINE — A vine grown, pear shaped vegetable with prickly spikes – a Creole staple in the West Indies – known to most of the world as Chayote squash.

"WAIT," cried Rob, "I'M HERE!," he shouted desperately trying to catch Sydney before she hung up, but instead of Sydney's voice, the only answer he heard was a loud click. Frustrated beyond sanity, Rob pushed his way through the crowd once again, cutting ahead of a long line of Antiguans to speak to the operator. "You hung up my call before I could get to it," said Rob with a rather sharp edge of irritation having pretty much lost his patience by this point – another foolish mistake to make in the islands, especially since Antiguans take Americans' impatience as an open opportunity to torment the poor bastards that much more.

"Wha be you cal suh?" asked the new woman behind the glass cage as if she didn't have a clue.

"Rib, boot numba eit," answered Rob, "I mean, Rob, booth number eight," repeated Rob on the brink of insanity.

"I call you nam' suh, bu' you naw tear," answered the clerk as if she could have cared as much about Rob getting his call through as she did about who had won the Superbowl that year.

"I was there, but I wasn't tear," said Rob getting more and more frustrated by the second.

"You have ta wet you tun suh, we be callin' you bek suh."

"What do you mean wait my turn! I've waited nearly four hours and--" before Rob could finish his sentence the woman had shut the window in his face and gone to the next man in line at the next window over, totally ignoring Rob, who was getting pretty hot and bothered by this point – as much now from his blistering face as he was from his rising blood pressure. It was impossible to see the redness from the anger rising in his face, since it was already a deep shade of crimson from the sunburn. Rob was quickly beginning to look like an over–ripened mango about to burst as beads of sweat broke out on his forehead. On top of it all he suddenly realized that he desperately had to relieve himself, but alas, there was no restroom in the Telit building. As desperate as he was to go, he didn't dare leave the building to walk next door to find a public toilet should they call his name the minute he'd stepped out the door. Another forty minutes passed as Rob crossed his legs dancing back and forth impatiently while the waiting islanders looked on as if he were some-alien from another planet. To them he was just another yachty who was likely wealthy enough to buy the phone company and who would dare to complain about such minor inconveniences as waiting a few hours to place a phone call. But they knew that none of that truly mattered since he was one of those spoiled Americans that would at some point simply give up and go home.

So much time had passed since he had started out to make that dreaded call to Sydney, that Rob had nearly forgotten what he had so carefully rehearsed to say to her. Boy had Rob underestimated Sydney's wrath when he finally got her on the phone. At that point Rob was feeling pretty grateful that there was more than a thousand miles of ocean between him and his loving, understanding 'wife to be,' or 'not to be,' as it seemed this was now the issue in question.

"YOU BOUGHT WHAT?!!!!!!!!!!!" screeched Sydney through the receiver loud enough for callers in booths one through seven to hear. And Rob had been worried that he wouldn't be able to hear her over all the noise, especially since booth eight was now sans a door.

"But Sydney, I was thinking of us," lied Rob in a feeble attempt to defuse the tongue lashing he was about to receive.

"How could you do this to us?! All that money for our house... our future! You spent on some dumb boat!"

"But Sydney, you've always talked about having a second home once we were settled, so think of it as a mobile second home. So, I bought the second before the first, what difference does it make," said Rob attempting to sound rational about the most irrational thing he'd ever done in his life.

This, of course, went over about as well as 'mozel tov' at a Roman Catholic wedding. "Just what I've always wanted... a mobile home!" sneered Sydney.

But the phone company somehow managed to come to the rescue as Rob heard, "You deposit be finish," followed by a loud click and a dial tone.

Rob was quite thankful that Sydney had a good hour to cool down while the operator, who was now appearing quite reasonable, compared to what awaited him on the other end of the line, attempted to place the call one more time. By the time he finally got Sydney back on the phone Rob managed to convince her that everything would be just fine if she would simply sell his car for him as quickly as possible in order that he might still be able to get to work before tourist season was completely over – along with any chance he had of making back any of his investment. He hung up satisfied that his future in the islands looked a little brighter, however Rob still felt terribly depressed. Oh, how he was going to miss her. Not Sydney – Marlena, his car, which he had pampered and babied since the day he bought it – too late for regrets, Rob. Paradise was waiting.

Alex was shocked when Rob returned to the boat that evening and she saw his now badly blistered and swollen face. Although resistant to her concern, Alex insisted that he lay down in the deckhouse while she ministered to his second and third-degree sunburn. She feared that Rob might actually go into shock from dehydration, since she'd seen many a badly burned greenie succumb due to over exposure to the sun without knowledgeable medical attention. She handed Rob a large glass of water and made him swallow an antihistamine and some aspirin to reduce the chance of further swelling, and then fresh garlic to counteract the potential of infection. Rob was a little nervous about Alex's layman medical practices, however by that point he was on fire and feeling quite light headed – certain, in fact, that he would faint if he took another step.

Alex ran to the far side of the dockyard to cut fresh aloe leaves from a plant she had used many times before, and she carefully scooped out the clear jelly inside the long pulpy green leaf and gently smeared it on his sunburnt and rapidly blossoming face. Once she felt assured that she had applied sufficient aloe, she covered his face with cheese cloth compresses soaked in ice water in an attempt to cool the burn and provide relief from his immediate pain. Once Rob had given up control to Alex, he had begun to grow slightly delirious – before the drugs kicked in and the cooling bath relieved some of the intense heat that swelled waves of nausea over him like heat-waves rolling in off the Sahara.

Laying there helpless in the deck house as Alex nursed his wounds. Rob was surprised at how feminine she suddenly seemed hovering over him as his mother had done when he had been a small boy – an only child that always received too much fussing over. Laying there with his eyes closed, Rob drifted back to that place where he had felt taken care of – safe in his mother's hands. Was that what was missing from his relationship with Sydney – the nurturing? She didn't have any of his mother's tenderness, but strangely, like Julie Anne, Alex – a woman who appeared totally unfeminine to him by day, had suddenly become more feminine than even femme fatale Sydney. Alex had stepped out of the role of Captain and donned the cloak of Florence Nightingale.

I watched as Rob soaked in the touch of her arms on his chest as they brushed over him to apply more cold water to his compresses. He breathed in the smell of her skin – the smell of sun warmed flesh mixed with the sweet scent of coconut oil from the suntan lotion she had applied earlier in the day. A smell he'd remembered on Julie Anne's skin the day after graduation when they lay on the beach at the lake wrapped in each other's arms. The day of his loss of virginity. It was a smell that triggered a warm sensual surge throughout his body. But now Alex possessed it, exuded it – he drank it in. I knew then that Rob had opened himself up to new possibilities. If this woman with whom he didn't even get along could trigger this kind of sensual sensation in him, maybe there was still hope for him to find some sort of feeling again.

Finally, Alex felt Rob relax under her care as she smoothed the wet compresses over his burning face. Oddly, Alex felt a tingling sensation in her forearm as she brushed her arm over Rob's chest – the hairs rising on her arm as if there were some sort of static electricity between them that had been charged the moment, they had come into close enough proximity with one another. Strange, this was a sensation she had never felt before. Till that moment, Alex had yet to feel physically charged around any man. And now, with Rob of all men, her sexual arousal had been piqued. It scared her – titillated her. But she fought it – found herself stuffing her feelings back behind that big steel door that kept her safe. She tried to ignore it rising up from her root chakra – the sensual rush of passion. She quelled it – denied it and commanded it to return to its hiding place deep in her soul. Her discipline took over. She was a slave to it. She had lived in denial all her life of her desire. She felt it selfish and weak. Once again, she had managed to take control – she had doused the flame of pleasure in lieu of being professional, and now her job was to don the disguise of nurse and also douse the fire that burned on Rob's face.

She sensed his breathing as it shifted from tense and pained, to relaxed, shallow breaths – like the breath of relief and trust which a scarred puppy or kitten might settle into once they felt they could trust the hand that cared for them. Alex had saved many a baby kitten and puppy from the West Indian versions of birth control – a burlap sack and a cinder block dropped into the harbor. She had a soft heart where small living things were concerned even though she'd never been around children, since like Rob, she never had any brothers, sisters, or children of her own. She had never even been afforded the opportunity to play nursemaid to a man before, except her dad when he was sick, since Michael had been the type to push her away when he wasn't feeling well, and likewise, he had left her to fend for herself whenever she'd been under the weather. She liked the feel of it she decided – nursing Rob. Maybe he wasn't so tough after all. Maybe she just needed to give him a chance to get his sea legs.

Alex sat by his side for hours drizzling cool water over the cloth until the heat in his skin had finally abated. As much as Rob hated to admit it, he felt immensely better thanks to Alex's ministrations, leaving him impressed by her knowledge. However, he was shocked by how gruesome he looked when he finally took a peek in the mirror. It would be weeks before his face was normal again, but he figured he wasn't out to win any beauty contests. And thank goodness Sydney would be nowhere near until he had resumed his normal boyish good looks.

Once Rob had recovered, daily island life in Paradise commenced for him. He had blown off his night of sensual awakening to Alex's more feminine qualities and ignored it as simply a delirious episode due to his second-and-third degree burns. Alex, however, had very clear memories of that evening due to the fact that she had more than possessed all of her faculties, contrary to Rob. But, thanks to her big steel door, all that remained was a pleasant memory. She went about her duties readying the boat for the inspector and buying gear on Joey's account at the local marine store, which the boat would require for charter. And, since Rob was busy with the legal aspects of his new venture, he managed to stay out of Alex's way, somewhat to her dismay, at least for the first few weeks.

Finally, the inspector arrived on the boat early one morning unannounced, with his checklist and magnifying glass and proceeded to religiously inspect every square inch of the boat, not missing a single hairline fracture in the rigging *(invisible to the naked eye)*, or a missing fluorescent tape from a life-preserver. The outcome – he was terribly sorry, but the Island Fever had failed miserably to meet his undisputed safety requirements. However, he would be happy to send his cousin, Ethan, over right away from the marine supply store to make a list of the things that Rob would need to buy in order to pass his safety inspection, in order that he could buy his charter insurance, in order that he could receive his charter license, in order that he could obtain a charter agent, and so on, until Rob could take out his first tourist on his million-dollar, 'inspected' raft. When he was finished, Mr. Brown handed Rob his bill for five hundred U.S. dollars with an outstretched hand and waited while Rob dug out the cash.

Weeks passed and repairs were made, to Mr. Brown's strict specification of course, and Rob and Alex grew more distant than if they were residing on different shores of the Caribbean. Rob's car was sold and his insurance premium was paid, Althea promised to process Rob's charter license, and Fritz, the agent, promised Rob that if he would just do him a favor and handle a week's worth of 'day charters,' he would be eternally grateful and was certain to have a real charter for him within the week. In other words, the agent wanted Rob to run the Island Fever as a picnic ferry for a week or so, or a 'cattlemaran' as it's known in the islands. Fair enough, thought Rob, a charter's a charter as far as he knew. But Alex knew better. She knew that day charters meant trying to cram forty sunburnt, seasick tourists, who were determined to drink their passage fee's worth of Heineken, onto a vessel that should legally be allowed to carry only twenty at best. It also meant preparing a lunch for forty, which was scarfed down by the first twenty before the second twenty returned from their snorkeling outing, which Alex would of course have to escort them on. But Rob was new at this and he was desperate – the two extra weeks spent in port awaiting the inspection had cost him, and the bills were pouring in faster than the tide to Alex's dismay, he accepted Fritz's offer. So, she resigned herself to the fact that if a 'head charter' *(as in head–count or ferry run),* meant she would be able to immediately commence her position as captain of the Island Fever, she was certainly willing to grin and bear it. Even if she knew that Joey would have heart failure when he found out that forty tourists were being crammed onto his boat every day.

"*What can I say?*" *thought Alex in resignation. "It is half his boat and if he wants to beat it to death as a ferry boat, that's his prerogative. I guess I can't complain too much... the Captain's the Captain no matter what type of charter I'm taking out, so, I should just be happy with the fact that I'm her new skipper..*"

But Alex was not all too happy with the state of affairs aboard the Island Fever since Rob was yet to be useful as a 'first mate,' which left only poor Raymond to look after all those green sailors while she sailed the boat.

Thankfully, at the end of each day, when Alex had finished putting away the boat from charter, she would climb into her rubber Avon and row out to her own little boat in the harbor, where she lived. As much as she loved the Island Fever she was always excited to row those last few strokes up to the inside port stern of Dancer and climb aboard, experiencing a rush of pleasure at the feel of her decks beneath her feet and the tranquility of her modest deck house which paled in comparison to the Island Fever's. But somehow, it offered her a kind of inner peace and homecoming, since Dancer was in fact the closest thing to home Alex had known since she'd left Annapolis ten years before.

Alex tied the dinghy off between Dancer's hulls and stepped into the cockpit that night before the first charter. She reached into the portlight* to her hiding spot, and found the key which hung on the cabinet wall inside the deckhouse, then unlocked the padlock on the back door and flipped on the switch for the twelve-volt lighting in the companionway. She replaced the key and stepped into the house, sliding the side companionway hatches** open in order to let the fresh sea air in.

Alex loved lying in the deckhouse on the soft corduroy settee reading the latest novel she could get her hands on, or just browsing through the World Almanac if nothing else suited her. She relished stretching out after a long day in the sun which had evaporated all of her energy, the way it drank up the ocean into fluffy gray rain clouds – clouds that blew through in ten-minute squalls at the end of the day leaving a double rainbow behind as if to offer a gift of apology for crying great tears of rain over the island's inhabitants below – disturbing the otherwise perfect weather that the long summer days brought before hurricane season. Alex loved the solitude – the subtle sound of the water lapping at the underside of the hulls and the way it echoed up through the boat – the way a gust of wind would swoop down off the hillside and catch Dancer and spin her quickly sideways on her mooring. She loved the soft undulating motion of the water passing under her hulls which lulled her to sleep every night. She hated living on the dock and would avoid it at all costs. The noise of the other sailors and the clanging of their unkempt halyards against their masts all night drove her mad, not to mention the surging and pulling as the boat fought its dock-lines like a tethered stallion straining to break free from its restraints.

Alex was a voracious reader and would gobble up paperbacks, especially stories of adventure and travel which made her mind wander and her soul hungry to sail off to explore the world. She'd made boat deliveries since

---

*PORT LIGHT — A small watertight hatch or window-like opening in the deckhouse or topsides** of a boat.
**TOPSIDES — The sides of the hulls which are above the water as opposed to the top or deck of the boat.
***COMPANIONWAY HATCHES — The lateral sliding hatches which flip down and slide across the deck outboard to allow one to stand to climb down the steps into the hulls rather than crawl. Usually there is one on each side of the deckhouse.

ISLAND FEVER

she lived in the islands. She had gone several times with racing yachts to Europe delivering them to the Mediterranean for the summer, then traveled around for a time before returning to her own little boat in Antigua in time for hurricane season. A few times she'd been asked to take boats back to the States but she preferred more adventurous deliveries – places to which she had never gone. The year before she'd delivered a sixty-foot Swan* through the Panama Canal and on up to the west coast of Mexico.

On a whim, Alex had used the money to travel to Tahiti, Bora Bora, and Tonga, and then on to Micronesia to the Caroline Islands. Upon arriving, she had regretted that she had gone there alone, for the beauty of the islands had evoked a need in her to share it with someone. Alex had grown accustomed to traveling alone, but there in the South Pacific, she had suddenly experienced a loneliness she had never felt before. Unfortunately, that feeling had followed her home and as hard as she'd tried, she had been unable to shake it when things got quiet, especially when she watched the sun setting under a double rainbow over that magnificent ocean. At times like that, she wished she had someone with whom to share it all.

SWAN — An elegant, expensive, production monohull which could be likened to the 'Mercedes' of mid-size yachts.

CHAPTER SIX

Dead to Weather

*"You can sail across the ocean of life
or you can drown in it."*

Ian

The Island Fever's first week of charter had been initiated with their first happy troop of 'greenies' – meaning a boat full of tourists, who's closest experience to sailing had probably been a trip across the Upper Bay on the Staten Island Ferry. And, of course, as luck would have it, the little bay to which they were instructed to deliver these disciples of the canvas was a two hour 'beat to weather'* – around the southern end of the island. During which, at least half of the boat succumbed to the 'domino effect – it only takes one to heave their breakfast over the side, and before you know it, you've got twenty passengers

*BEAT TO WEATHER — Beating to weather simply means, forcing your sailing vessel to go in the only direction to which the law of physics does not permit it to go – into the direction from which the wind is blowing, known as 'dead to weather,' or more appropriately, 'dead in the water.' Due to the air foil dynamics of the mysterious workings of a sailing rig, which are somewhat akin to the dynamics of an airplane wing, it is physically impossible to approach the wind from any direction closer than approximately thirty degrees from either side, if you're lucky, requiring what is known as 'tacking.' Meaning, sailing for some distance pointing forty degrees away from your intended destination then turning and doing the same thing in the opposite direction, also forty degrees away from your intended target. One must do this maneuver over and over as many times as it takes to reach your final objective, which means it is necessary that one sail nearly three times the actual distance of your intended target, in a manner which could easily be compared to riding the Giant Himalayan at the state fair in a torrential downpour in order to reach your final destination. And, of course it never seems to fail, as in life, that the direction in which you wish to go is always, 'dead to weather.'

whose complexion had changed to a rather interesting shade of chartreuse with their heads thrust into plastic ten-gallon garbage bags. The worst part was always finding yourself downwind from someone with poor aim.

Of course, their first day out had to be a tough one, thought Alex as she watched even Rob toss his cookies over the stern of the boat. It was days like this that Alex was glad Hefty had created the 'Cinch Sac,' which enabled them to trap those God forsaken contents until they could be carefully disposed of. There was something about watching a boatload of tourists chucking up their morning orange juice and bacon, not to mention the three Heinekens they had already managed to down before the queasiness took hold of them, that made Alex wish in secret that she could just pull the drawstring tight around each of their hopelessly unseaworthy, land-lover heads until they gratefully reached the shore. Alex even had thoughts about how practical it would be to just simply remove the cockpit tables and replace them with troughs, so as to save on garbage bags. Overall, she was relieved that due to the mass sedation from the Dramamine, she didn't have to answer too many stupid questions, since on the way there, they either had their heads buried in a bag or they had the fear of God instilled in them from the bouncing and heaving of the boat. Not to mention the fact that they were nearly drowning in bow spray, which due to the heavy salt content of the Atlantic, and the aeration process, left one feeling and looking quite like a Cony Island pretzel – with salt.

The one thing about sailing that Alex never quite understood was, why the moment anyone felt sick, instead of being thankful for the fresh air on deck, they immediately made a bee-line for the cabin, thinking that somehow being down–below deck would make them feel better. But, as Alex well knew from experience – even the most well-seasoned sailors can turn green in that stuffy, bouncing, confined compartment below deck. So, Alex became the cabin monitor, making certain that no one entered the deck house next to her station at the helm, even if they were pleading their case to be a head break. Alex was relent-less on this measure, resorting to dragging anyone out by their collar who had managed to sneak past her watchful eye. This was not totally a selfish act on her part, since she was sparing those poor unsuspecting bastards the added agony of retching their guts out down below. Alex also knew all too well, how Joey would react if he found their presence left on his antique carpets.

Unfortunately, Rob's seasickness and uncertainty of what was going on did not help instill confidence to a great degree in his passengers, but somehow Raymond's calm, confident demeanor and the routine way in which he went about his duties – primarily handing out beers, bags, and suntan lotion – seemed to help both Rob and the tourists settle into a kind of uncertain resignation to their fate. Rob was so nervous the morning he awoke before his first charter, he had pretty well worked himself into a frenzy by the time they had tied up

ISLAND FEVER

at the dock to load up their thirty-five passengers for the day's sail. He wasn't certain if he was feeling queasy from the motion of the ocean or from the fear of his first trip to sea with the lives of three dozen people in his hands. By the time Raymond had passed out the second round of beers and soft drinks, Rob had already been the first to be dragged by Alex from the deck house by the collar and redirected to the back of the bridge deck. Alex had seen it in his face as he had raised his head from the cooler in the cockpit with two beers in his hand for Raymond to pass to a couple of tourists on the foredeck. By now Rob's sunburn was really starting to peel and the multicolor hue of the white flaking skin and the red beneath, mixed with his present shade of green made Rob's face somewhat reminiscent of the Italian flag.

For Rob, sea sickness was the newest in a list of adjustments he'd have to make to island living, but he'd quickly come to the conclusion, as do most, that he'd much rather be dead than live with this miserable sensation on a daily basis. Indeed, I've seen many a sailor, try to jump overboard in order to bring a quick end to their torture. In fact, I've even found it necessary to lash a few on deck to save them from that fate during my lifetime as a sailor. But what truly baffled Rob was that he had in excess of thirty passengers aboard who had just paid him fifty dollars each to experience this very misery. By the time they arrived at Green Island, appropriately chosen for the day's journey, Rob was only slightly greener than the frozen margaritas Raymond, the Twelve Volt Man,* was serving.

It's important to remember the first rule of thumb on a sailing vessel – no matter what luxuries one must do without, a blender, although a tricky accessory on a boat with no generator, is always an absolute necessity. But leave it to Raymond's wizardry to be certain that there was always an ample supply of that frozen concoction on board.

Somehow, Alex had managed to make it through the morning with no major mishaps. Once on Green Island, snorkeling went smoothly, even if there were little or no fish to see – thanks to the local fishermen's lack of concern for the environment and the islanders' voracious appetite for fish. And, while Alex was off dragging overweight tourists through the water to look at sand and coral, Raymond was preparing lunch on the shore of their little anchorage. Grilled chicken and rice was the standard picnic charter fare, and Raymond had

---

*TWELVE VOLT MAN — The term being just another of those many Jimmy Buffettisms.** Actually, the power on the boat was run off of twelve volt batteries which were topped off by either the boat's solar panels, the wind charger while in port, or a portable generator, which one had to drag out and fire up at least every few days while sitting on anchor to insure that they had power aboard.
**JIMMY BUFFETTISMS — A phrase coined by the infamous Jimmy Buffett – that singer–songwriter–storyteller who is better known as the 'King of Someplace Hot,' an expert on Margaritaville, and in general, our modern–day 'prophet of the tropics,' who possesses a truly outrageous imagination. Rest in peace dear friend.

quickly gotten it honed to a science by pre-roasting the chicken the evening before and pretending to cook it over the hot coals of the bar-b-que that he'd built on the beach.

It was time for lunch, but Rob was still recovering from his morning purge and was floundering around on the boat, pretending to look busy doing something unimportant in order to avoid having to assist Alex and Raymond play nursemaid to thirty–five mainlanders. Of course, this did not sit well with Alex since she was hired to captain the ship, not babysit tourists. She would have to speak with Rob about defining their roles aboard the boat, or at the very least, hire another crew member. But, for now, she would just have to get through the day without him. Luckily, her passengers were nice enough, especially in light of how rough their two-hour, upwind sail to Green Island had been. They loved Alex, it seemed, and found the idea of a female skipper quite novel. She only wished that she could find a way to spare her future passengers such discomfort by somehow lowering the casualty count of greenies on the way there.

Alex had been sea sick only once as a young girl when she had delivered a boat to Florida with her dad, but that was enough to make her appreciate the misery those unsuspecting novices were suffering. She and her father had decided to venture outside of the safety of the Intra-coastal Waterway on their delivery south, and had run into some bad weather off the coast of the Carolinas on Frying Pan Shoals. Even though Alex was dying from seasickness, she had refused to abandon her father's side at the helm, and had braved it through the night with hardly a complaint. After that, her father had nicknamed her 'Skipper' which had stuck. From that point on he'd barely even used the name he'd given her when she was born, since he told her she was braver than most sailors would have been under the circumstances.

"So, Skipper," said one of the men, as she was loading the last of her passengers onto the dinghy from shore that afternoon, "I'm quite impressed with your sailing ability. Can't say's I've ever sailed with a woman at the helm before, but I'd be quite comfortable to sail with you again anytime. I was in the navy for twenty years and I didn't think I'd ever hear myself say such a thing but there you have it."

Alex looked at him and smiled, and when he smiled back, it fondly reminded her of her father – the way he smiled at her the morning after that horrible night at sea when the sun rose and the storm blew over. It was a smile that told her he was proud that she had helped to pull them through it – they had done it together.

"Well, thank you," answered Alex, taken a little off guard by his uncanny resemblance to her father, not to mention how moved she was by his confession. "Thank you, that means more to me than you know," she said warmly as she swallowed hard against the lump in her throat and fought back the flood of tears she'd never allowed herself to weep for her father. One day she was afraid that the dam would break and the reservoir she had been storing would surely flood the island.

As tough as the morning had been, there was one part of the day that Alex did in fact enjoy – the peaceful downwind sail back around the coast to English Harbor. She welcomed the reach home, since by that time the passengers were so spent from their morning's retch, passed out from too much beer and wine, exhausted from their snorkeling expedition, or just plain grateful that their white knuckling had subsided thanks to the calmer water, they were all like abandoned jellyfish washed upon the foredeck by the sea which had given them up as sacrifice. The trip downwind was likened to the disparity of riding the skyride at the state-fair as opposed to the roller coaster – converting all of the previously 'sworn to never sail again,' passengers back into, 'can't wait to sail again' ones.

To Alex, sailing had always been somewhat of a religious experience – her substitution for church – a place where she could commune with GOD. In my last life, I had found the sea to be that same comforting presence, and I had always relished the rare opportunity to experience it alone. Like me, Alex had never been at sea before with a mass congregation such as this, and somehow in a strange way, we found it hard to share this sacred space with so many unenlightened souls. If only someone could make them understand, make Rob understand the sanctity of sailing. The solace of being out on the open ocean alone with no one other than yourself and that Great One Destiny, with no one else knowing for certain exactly where you were on the planet. Would Rob ever reach that point with sailing? Somehow, both Alex and I had our doubts. Rob, it appeared at present, was more the congregational type – the type that fit right into the masses of the unenlightened.

As the days wore on into a week, it was becoming more and more evident to Alex that Rob, although quite adept at handling people, was not exactly an experienced or even a promising sailor. Let's be realistic, Rob still didn't know the difference between an outhaul and hauling out, and that a winch wasn't an old English word for prostitute, let alone knowing his aft from his beam or his head from a hole in the deck. I mean a 'ketch' was a game played in the back yard with a ten-year-old, wasn't it? Not to mention how many Southerners there seemed to be down in this neck of the woods who kept saying 'yawl.'

For some strange reason, all of Alex's experience in teaching sailing went out the window where Rob was concerned. Her enduring patience which she had always found for children became frustrated impatience every time Rob would perform some new calamity like forgetting to tie down the spinnaker pole before raising the spinnaker, or dropping the anchor and chain overboard with no line attached. It seemed that every other day Alex was having to dive down and retrieve some lost piece of hardware such as winch-handles, anchors, and buckets. And, unfortunately, the more impatient Alex got with Rob, the more sensitive Rob's ego got. In fact, Rob was still having trouble taking orders from an attractive member of the opposite sex and unfortunately, the more he learned, the more he realized how little he knew compared to Alex. It was beginning to take its toll on his confidence level which was, at that point, floundering below sea-level and in risk of drowning. And unfortunately, Rob was still utterly dependent on Alex for his livelihood and nearly the sum total of his worldly possessions.

"*As long as he doesn't kill anyone we'll be just fine,*" thought Alex. "*Luckily, that guy that he dropped the boom vang* on the other day didn't seem too pissed off, even though he probably won't father any more offspring. I'll just be sure to keep him busy with little jobs that are safe, like barf bag duty or coiling sheets.*"**

As far as Rob's sailing acumen went, there were many things he was not, and would likely never be – like – handy, mechanical, dexterous, or knowledgeable about anything requiring physical labor, use of tools, or things that required being tied up – seeing that Sydney had just never been the type. Luckily, Rob recognized and understood most of his shortcomings in this department and was beginning to realize that maybe the physical side of sailing may just not be something he was cut out for, regardless of how hard he was trying to prove Alex wrong.

Attempting to justify his lack of knot tying proficiency, at least to himself, Rob reasoned, "What if I don't know how to tie the perfect knot? Hell, I never even mastered the art of tying my own ties. I mean tying the perfect bowline is not exactly my life's ambition. Okay, so it's necessary to learn how to tie knots in order to sail a boat... I'll learn eventually. If she just weren't so

---

*BOOM VANG — *The derivation of 'boom,' is quite obvious due to its capacity to slam from side to side when the wind suddenly fills the sails from the opposite side of the boat. The boom is a spar*** that runs perpendicular to the mast and is used to extend the foot of the sail, usually used along the bottom of the main, main-staysail, and/or a self-tacking forward baby-staysail. Unrestrained booms have been known to kill, maim, and drown more sailors than the Titanic – thus the 'boom vang,' a moveable block and tackle used to restrain the boom from creating a hazard for all those aboard.*

**SHEETS — *The reference here to sheets is not about bed sheets of course. No, on a boat, 'sheets' or 'jib sheets,' refers to the lines with which to control the headsails (the most forward sails). The reasoning behind naming these ropes or lines sheets has never been qualified or explained to the modern sailor.*

***SPAR — *A spar could be used to refer to the masts and booms of a sailboat rigging; or it may also refer to gaffs and poles on a more traditional sailboat rig. Spars can be made of wood, aluminum, or other wondrous new synthetic products.*

ISLAND FEVER

damn petite and innocent looking maybe it would be easier for me to take her seriously at this Captain thing," agonized Rob watching her at the helm as she steered the boat by the sails' telltales.*   She's so tiny she has to stand on a crate to see over the deck house to steer. When I was growing up girls played with dolls, makeup, and horses; not boats, engines, and radio equipment. I didn't even play with that guy stuff. Maybe I should have. Then I'd be better at this than her," Rob realized with a certain amount of trepidation.

It wasn't totally Rob's fault that he was just a tiny bit chauvinistic towards women in what were generally considered men's jobs such as the trading floor and sailing. He had grown up on a farm where a woman's job definitely fell into the domain of the daily necessities such as food, clothing, a clean house, and personal hygiene. The thing he remembered most about his childhood was his mother's cooking and her hounding him to take his bath, brush his teeth, and wash behind his ears. His father had never asked him once to wash behind his ears. In fact, his father had never even looked behind his ears, since the only ears that his father was ever concerned about were the kind on the stalk. His father had tried to encourage him to spend more time helping him with the farm work, but Rob had known from a very early age that farming was not his destiny. Instead, he had spent most of his time doing research in the library about finance and commerce. Since the time he'd gone door to door selling his mother's corn muffins, he knew he was cut out to be a business man. For the next few years, he spent his time helping his mother set up a bakery which he'd sold for her by the time he was sixteen to a major food franchiser, providing his family with a comfortable retirement fund for the rest of their lives. But his father had never been able to accept the fact that he could retire and live off the profits from his wife's company. As far as he was concerned, it had been a disgrace that his wife had ever gone to work in the first place, and the fact that Rob had been able to provide more to the family's income than he had was something he'd never gotten over.

To Rob, it would have been different if his mother had chosen to sell tractors instead of corn muffins. In his mind there were just simply some things that women were not cut out to do. As supportive and protective as Rob had always been to his mother, it seemed that a taste of his father's determination of what constituted women's work had seeped into his genes, and Rob found himself struggling daily with the image of Alex driving his father's tractor.

Contrary to what was going on in Rob's mind, Alex's patience was beginning to wear thin. Her only excuse for staying on, she told herself, was her concern for the Island Fever – to which she had grown even more attached than she had been as her creator, as most sailors do with their vessels. And Raymond,

---

*TELLTALES — Pieces of ribbon or yarn approximately eight to nine inches long, which are located at or near the luff, (or forward edge of the sail), on both sides of the headsail and mainsail. Their movement when sailing tells the sailor how to adjust the sails by showing them just how the wind is hitting the sail.

well, Raymond in his own hands-off sort of way kept the peace on board. His quiet, peaceful presence and his unexpected moments of insight somehow managed to keep Rob and Alex on their best behavior. In other words, he kept them from throwing each other overboard, and I did just my best to get them to open up to their differences.

Now Raymond, a man of few words, was not by any stretch of the imagination a complex soul. He had simply lost himself somewhere in the early seventies on a beach in Jamaica, and had been found washed up on a beach in Antigua a decade later. He had actually worked for Joey for some three years now and felt quite content to simply go with the flow. Likened to most of the West Indians and thanks to copious amounts of 'Blue Mountain Kaya' *(or marijuana as we better know it),* during his extended stay in Negril, Raymond had gotten the hang of three–quarter-time pretty early on.

Unfortunately, their one week of day charters somehow turned into two, creating even more tension with the situation on Alex's part. As unpleasant as day chartering may have been, however, it did provide Rob with a tentative sense of financial security and left them with an enlightening experience – with several of their departing voyagers leaving them with such divinely unanswered questions to be pondered by the wisdom of the Universe as: "If you can see the moon during the day can you see the sun at night?" and "Are we east or 'west of the equator'?"

"West of course, isn't that why it's called the 'West' Indies?"

CHAPTER SEVEN

Celestial Navigation

*"In life, there are no ordinary moments.
Most of us never really recognize the most
significant moment of our lives when they're happening."*

Kathleen Magee

After several weeks of sailing with him as her first mate, Alex was beginning to realize that sailing lessons might be critically in order for Rob. But most importantly, she realized that it was definitely not a job for her to tackle or even attempt, since Rob would likely feel more than a little uncomfortable to be labeled – her student. Not to mention her persistent lack of patience with him.

Lucky for Alex, her good friend Randy had just arrived on the island to teach a seaman's course and Celestial Navigation* – an ancient means of navigation which today is nearly defunct due to the electronic age, but which was at one time the only means of finding your way across an ocean. Today's navigators of the seas and of life, have unfortunately become overly reliant on far too many electronic devices for guidance in determining their position and plotting their course. Back when Celestial Navigation was the accepted means of navigating, a Spirit Guide, or Guardian Angel's job was easy, since people didn't have much else to listen to prior to the age of electronics. Today the

---

*CELESTIAL NAVIGATION — Although used by ancient mariners, celestial navigation is an amazingly advanced means of sailing navigation which uses an instrument called a sextant** to align celestial bodies in order to ascertain one's position by taking sights of the sun, moon, planets, and stars. Also known as an advanced means of soul navigation which uses an instrument called the 'higher self' to access heavenly guidance in order to ascertain one's effect of Variation and Deviation** which must be factored into any given course which one attempts to plot, both literally and figuratively.

masses are so busy listening to TV, movies, digital, CD's, HD, radio, sideband, broadband, high–fi, boom boxes, surround sound, Walkman's, MP3 players, and iPods that they can't even begin to hear the more subtle messages that are struggling to be heard over the decibels that are being drilled into their brains twenty–four hours a day. Today, humans have become so submersed in megahertz and kilohertz that they've unfortunately reached a point of mass hypnosis by multimedia.

Thus, being someone's Guide through life is hard work even if they happen to be tuned in to my station and an avid listener. But it's especially hard if you've been entrusted with the lifetime guidance of a soul like Rob who had managed to spend most of this life navigating in a fog without his receiver or his running lights on – relying only on something as drastic as a foghorn to warn him whenever he needed to change course.

What Rob still didn't understand was that he had all the help and insight available he needed – all he had to do was ask the right questions and he would have received the right answers – that is of course, if he were listening. The real problem was that Rob had not yet reached that point in his upward evolution where he was willing to listen in order to hear those whispers of advice that I or anyone else had to offer him. Up until now, Rob's life had been as shallow as a keelboat stranded on a sandbar in a rapidly receding tide. He had yet to realize that unless he learned how to read the tides and search for deeper waters, he was destined to eventually find himself at some point permanently high and dry.

Now, please don't make the mistake of determining my role to be Rob's sole life teacher, since there is much I'm still to learn myself by helping Rob on his journey across the vast ocean of life. To Rob, I am simply his tour-guide through life, trying my best to help him on his search to navigate his own course to Paradise, and serve him by highlighting the points of interest along the way. Ultimately, Rob must be the one to do the work on his own. But unfortunately, Rob was still busy searching for Paradise, and until he stopped looking and started working to create it, he was destined to find himself on that eternal wheel of life going round and round until he finally got it right.

**SEXTANT – An instrument used to measure the altitude between the plane of the horizon and a heavenly body. This angular elevation of the star, sun, or planet from which a sighting is being taken, along with the exact time, gives one their latitude the lateral lines on the planet. However, you can't find the longitude, vertical lines on the planet, without an accurate clock – an impossible task prior to the invention of the sea clock in the sixteenth century.

***VARIATION – A compass error, for which the correction should be factored in when taking a course heading. It is caused by the fact that the magnetic lines of force at many points on the earth's surface are not toward the true north pole; whereas DEVIATION – Is a magnetic compass error due to magnetic influences on a boat, such as metal objects in close proximity to the compass. As with life, any given course must take variation and deviation into consideration when calculating where on the planet one might end up.

As his Guide, I take little to no credit for Rob's achieved increments of enlightenment, nor do I accept the blame for his lack thereof. In fact, I am only one of many Guides or pilots, if you will, that will be offered to Rob during this lifetime. Although having been a sailor myself, I feel more than qualified to direct him in this particular phase of his life, however frustrating it may be for me. It would however, also take earthly teachers to instruct Rob in many aspects of life, including, but not limited to, sailing. Eventually, Rob would grow to understand that life offers many teachers. But alas, until the student is ready, the teacher is simply just another one of many unknowingly met along the way.

True, Rob was about to attend class on sailing, but what he didn't realize was that he, as well as everyone else, was struggling to graduate from the classroom of life in order to get back to his higher existence on 'The Otherside.' Many never realize that the real purpose of their life is to take every event of everyday that they are given and use it to learn, grow, and turn themselves into more enlightened beings.

Most humans spend their entire life searching for something that will fulfill them, totally ignoring the many opportunities they are given to learn and ascend to that higher state of being. Instead, they spend their time searching for something more than they have today, or had yesterday, or hope to have tomorrow. They feel there is no logic in truly living today, because tomorrow has so much more to offer. Some work their lives away in order to buy their ticket for that boat which will take them to their ultimate final destination, not realizing of course, that it is one ticket that simply cannot be purchased. A few, like Rob, do at least start to grasp this concept and realize that simply climbing on the boat in the first place is, in fact, half the battle. After all, if one does not at least attempt to make the journey, it's impossible to ever reach the other shore. But, the most important thing to remember is that you never know what's on the other side, so you may as well enjoy the ride getting there before you reach the inevitable – old age, failing eyesight, and hemorrhoids.

I was lucky my last time around on this planet called Earth. You see, I was born in the islands to a woman who had never known the true meaning and security of an honest wedding ring on her finger. And even though my mother had been unhappy with her life, I somehow managed to learn the art of enjoying life while still in her womb. To me, Paradise always came easy. I guess you could call it my specialty. So, here on 'The Otherside,' I find myself assigned to one of its misguided seekers – a yet to be enlightened human named Rob who has at least managed to catch the boat even if it may have been the wrong one. But no matter, somehow it will be my job to help him back on track in order to find the right course which was, you see, predetermined before he ever arrived here.

Luckily, Alex had managed to convince Rob to study sailing since imparting technical information to one's assignee is less than practical for a

Spirit Guide, not to mention the advancement of today's technology which is far over my head. Alex had also managed to diplomatically sit Rob down and lay out the 'rules of the road' so to speak that first night that they had returned from charter.

Once the passengers had gone and the boat was cleaned and put away, Alex bravely stepped into the cockpit with her nightly glass of wine where Rob was having his first rum and Coke. As she sat down, her leg lightly brushed his. This time he noticed it, that electrical charge that sparked ever so subtly like a moment of recognition when one smells a pleasingly familiar scent or tastes something pleasing to the pallet – the subtle senses of touch and smell and taste which are so taken for granted, so rarely recognized for the sensual pleasures they can offer.

"Rob, I know that babysitting sunburnt, seasick tourists doesn't exactly sound like the solution to finding eternal happiness," proceeded Alex carefully, "But I need some support here. My job is to drive the boat, not to play hostess. You've got to take over some of that responsibility yourself or hire another crew member to help Raymond, at least, while we're doing day charters. I can't fix sunburns, guide snorkel trips, and run the boat responsibly, too," finished Alex, relieved that she had actually had the guts to get her frustrations off her chest.

Alex drew in her breath as Rob grew silent for a moment. She was afraid of how he would respond to her honesty. After all, she didn't really know him that well.

"You're right, I didn't realize how much work day chartering would be... I mean it's kind of like being a kindergarten monitor, isn't it?" answered Rob eliciting an acknowledged chuckle from Alex. "Somehow, I thought we would sail this boat around and the tourists would just sort of entertain themselves. I didn't realize they'd be so dependent on us. I guess it's kind of like my stock market clients," reasoned Rob, trying to relate it to something more familiar. "They're depending on us to hold their hand and tell them what to do."

"I suppose they realize that we have their lives in our hands," interjected Alex.

"In the stock market, their fortunes are as precious as their lives," contemplated Rob out loud as he thought about how everything in life was truly based on the same principles, even if they were disguised in vastly different playing fields. "I think I can handle it," Rob reasoned with a hint of uncertainty, nodding his head as he thought further of what the job might require of him, "As long as I can get past the queasiness."

Alex smiled, relieved that he understood what she needed from him. Maybe it was time to reevaluate her opinion of him.

"It'll pass, once you're able to relax and just go with the flow."

During the days to follow, Rob made an effort to be more attentive to his job as host on the Island Fever, and in the evenings, he attended class with Randy while Alex tended to the boat, which always seemed to need repair due to some calamity from that day's charter. It afforded her some quiet time on the boat alone, while Rob was busy learning to tie his knots, convert his knots to miles, and his what-to-do's and what-not-to-do's to his new nautical investment.

As the days went by, Alex could actually see a modicum of improvement in Rob's sailing skills, however small they may have been. At least he wasn't on the verge of bringing the masts down anymore. But most importantly, Rob was starting to relax and enjoy sailing instead of dreading each and every time they left the dock. By the time they had gotten to Celestial Navigation, Rob was hooked – even though he knew that he'd likely never have to use it. Learning to navigate by the stars had captured his interest and had at least refocused his sights heavenward. Now if he could only get his radio frequencies tuned-in to the right channels.

Late at night after class, with the boat at anchor in the harbor, Rob would sometimes lie on the Island Fever's deck with Alex, looking up at the heavenly bodies above them racing to see who could find the most constellations first – receiving bonus points for shooting stars. It was Rob's laughter – Alex heard for the first time – that she decided she liked best about him. When he actually allowed himself, Rob would laugh like a boy of ten with a smile that made her heart race like it had the night she'd ministered to his sunburn. Once again, Alex ignored it and kept the door closed and the lock locked on the safe of her emotions.

"I can't believe that I'm lying here on deck, looking at the stars and laughing with a man that I couldn't stand a few weeks ago," thought Alex. "I didn't think he knew how to laugh. In fact, I was sure he had the market cornered on angst." Her first impression of him left her with images of him on the trading floor buying and selling shares of angst to the rest of the unhappy, guilt-ridden populous. *"It's amazing,"* she thought, *"There's actually a charming side to him that I never saw before,"* as she chuckled to herself quite pleased with her discovery – leaving Rob in the dark about her unexpected turn of character. *"Maybe this job's going to turn out better than I expected,"* she reasoned... *"At least we're becoming friends."*

Even though Alex found Rob quite attractive, she saw them as total opposites, and at first blush had decided that there was no need to worry in the least about a compromising sexual attraction complicating the job. That was before something had started to awaken in her. It had been a while since Alex had been attracted to a man – any man. She had seldom dated in high school, or for that matter, since she had been in the islands. Only on her exploits abroad had she allowed herself to indulge in casual affairs, since they were geographically impossible and thus rated in the safe category as far as involvement went. Courtship, in fact, was something totally alien to Alex. After all, she had fallen in love with Michael working side-by-side with him on a daily basis. He had never courted her. They had simply moved in together. She had admired his talents as a shipwright and a sailor, and his steadfastness, even though it was that very trait that had kept them apart and had kept the door to true communication closed. Over the years she had sadly grown to accept it as the norm for a relationship since she had nothing more to compare it to.

Alex had not known her mother, so she had never witnessed the immense love and affection her mother and father had held for one another, even though her father had talked about it often when he was feeling low. In fact, losing Alex's mother had so devastated her father, that if it hadn't been for the child that her mother, Millie, had so willingly given her life to bring into this world, he would have surely joined her in the afterworld without a moment's hesitation. But he had this precious little girl to raise whom he named Alexandra following his wife's wishes, and called her Alex following his own. Patiently her dear father, Daniel, had waited until Alex had graduated from school and he knew that she could make it on her own before he decided to leave this world in order to spend eternity with his beloved wife. So, aside from the stories that her father had generously shared with her over the years of the love between them, Alex was still in search of the meaning of true love – not to mention the ways and means to find it, or even to recognize it.

In broadening his horizons on the subject of sailing, Rob was actually beginning to appreciate and respect Alex and her position as Captain of his ship, not to mention the fact that their newly budding friendship was starting to mend their prior frustrations and desire to cause bodily harm to one another. Of course, life was far from perfect on the Island Fever, and both Rob and Alex knew that the worst was not yet over. But Raymond was quite grateful for the truce and the blissful calm that had recently fallen over the Island Fever's inhabitants.

"I love listening to Alex talk about the stars and about tales of ancient mariners," thought Rob while lying under the constellation Orion, the great hunter of the Universe.

Rob had gone hunting for his Grail and although he was still unaware of it, he was on the trail and closing in on his prey now that he'd finally started to shed himself of his preconceived notions of duty. Rob listened attentively to Alex's voice – a voice which possessed humor and intelligence. Rob liked their evenings together on the boat – he liked that they had become friends instead of enemies. He liked that Alex was so easy and uncomplicated. He liked that she was such a good sailor and that she had come to work with him – even though he still had not totally overcome his ego. These were things, of course, that he would never share with her, he thought, since doing so might give her the upper hand – she would know his secret – Rob had grown to admire her. But more importantly, he loved looking into the depths of her eyes, which were as deep blue some days as the ocean's depths and as brilliant blue as the sky above on other days. Funny, he had never really noticed the color of Sydney's eyes – even though he knew they were brown. But if someone had asked him at that moment to describe their color, he would have been totally at a loss for words.

For the first time since Rob could remember, he felt happy. He couldn't quite put his finger on it, but he assumed that he was beginning to get the hang of living in the islands, and he was finally noticing what his new life had to offer – even the stars seemed to be more plentiful than he'd ever remembered them in the States. Looking at the endless sky, Rob was actually beginning to think he could hear voices up there. Finally, it seemed he was tuning in and turning up the volume.

Although a Spirit Guide can't tell their charge how to live their life, what decisions to make, and what paths to choose – we can inspire them to listen a little closer, look a little further, and to feel a little deeper. We can direct their attention to a glorious sunset or a blossoming flower. We can make them hear the call of new life from a young family of starlings, or see the magnificence of an end-less horizon. If only I could tell Rob how precious his human experience actually is and how short in the bigger scheme of things – how easy it is to only see the good in life if you really try to savor the fragrant, sensuous, delicious, tactile, and even carnal pleasures that can only be experienced in their human incarnation. One of the more positive attributes of being a Spirit Guide is that, on occasion, we are allowed to enjoy our charge's pleasures vicariously. And I know you're not going to believe me when I say this, but the one thing that I miss the most about the human experience is the cuisine of the Caribbean – the luscious fruits of the more tropical islands such as soursop, golden apple, sugar cane, and passion fruit turned into sweet, sweet nectar; and callaloo soup and ackee rice, not to mention succulent spiny lobsters and fresh conch stew. Life on Earth need not be solely about pain and suffering, although pain and suffering are also unique to living in the flesh and can provide a wealth of unwanted lessons to the Earthly inhabitant.

"Maybe I'm imagining things," thought Rob, "But everything suddenly seems so clear. My thoughts seem more defined as if there's someone inside my head talking to me. Was that my laugh? Or was that someone else? It's been so long I can't even recognize my own laughter anymore," realized Rob, saddened by the thought.

Rob was sad that the last twenty or so odd years of his life had passed with his happiness compromised by life. But at the same time, he felt ungrateful

– ungrateful that he questioned the life that had been so good to him. He had flourished in his career – in his finances, but there was a part of him that felt as if it had been stifled. Not only had that part been unimportant to his daily routine – it had withered and gone into hiding. But something had sparked its revival since he'd been on the island – something he had not yet recognized. Something that was just waiting for him to discover – something, or, indeed someone.

CHAPTER EIGHT

Approval

"What lies behind us and what lies before us are tiny matters compared to what lies within us."

Ralph Waldo Emerson

Let's not forget Sydney, Rob's fiancée, who was still sitting back in Chicago sulking since Rob had not quite yet figured out how to deal with appeasing her for his latest irrevocable transgression. He knew he could never convince her to move to the islands, but maybe he could figure out a way to live a double life once he had things running smoothly down here. Maybe he would be able to work it like other guys he knew. Like his clients who had businesses in several cities who commuted back and forth between the two and had people to run them in their absence. Maybe his blunder hadn't been so terrible after all. Maybe, he thought, there really was a way to salvage all of this yet. Who wouldn't love to have a home in the city where one could enjoy its culture and restaurants, yet in turn, have a little island getaway unto which one could also get lost whenever the pace of the city got to be too much. But then what would happen when, or if, Joey returned? Would he allow him to continue chartering the boat?

"*Maybe all this happened for a reason,*" Rob told himself, attempting to be convincing. "*Maybe I was supposed to take a break from the treadmill and learn how to enjoy life before it's too late. Most people would kill for this opportunity to live in Paradise so early in their lives. Usually, they wait until they're too old to enjoy it. Look at this place. It could be heaven once I get everything on track. Most of my friends would give up just about everything they have like I did, for a chance to get away from the madness and enjoy life,"* reasoned Rob. *"Then why am I so worried about whether Sydney will approve? After all, she loves me, right? She wants to spend the rest of her life with me for better or worse... for rich-er or for poorer? Why shouldn't she be ecstatic about the fact that I've just made an investment in our future? Maybe not exactly the one she thought it would be, but I'll get to that. She's gonna to love it once she gets down here,"* Rob tried to convince himself. *But deep-down Rob knew that Sydney would never in a million years approve of the poorer part of that equation.*

It seemed that all Rob's life, he had been searching for approval from others. Now he was looking especially hard for it at that moment from Sydney. But what Rob didn't realize was that all he had ever truly needed was simply, approval from himself. Having been close as a child to his mother, who had also lived her life in search of approval from others, he had grown to believe that maybe this was his true mission in life – making sure that everyone in his life gave him their stamp of approval.

Thanks to that and his pseudo-Catholic upbringing which had instilled an indomitable sense of guilt for one's actions that would in any way suggest selfish behavior, Rob's mind was running in overdrive trying to make himself believe that he had indeed made the right decision to buy the Island Fever. His only defense being that it truly wasn't a conscious decision on his part anyway, only a drunken blunder which had propelled him into this temporary detour, or alternate life path. Or, had it been an unconscious need to escape his life? He had actually almost deluded himself into believing that Sydney would eventually approve of his new lifestyle and welcome it with open arms. After all, wouldn't her friends be impressed to learn that they were well-off enough to afford a yacht in the Caribbean? But in truth, Sydney was buying none of it. Her agenda, if we remember correctly was quite different – marriage in six months, a big new house in the right part of town, a two BMW family, 2.5 kids, forget the dog, a partnership for Rob with daddy, oh, and don't forget a lifetime membership at the right country club. Somehow, his investment in a stupid boat didn't exactly fit into her plans.

Sydney begged, pleaded, and threatened Rob, attempting to make him come back to Chicago and get his job back. Even better, she would make certain daddy would give him one if he'd only give up this ridiculous idea of running a charter boat and just come home. Daddy was even willing to buy them a house until Rob could afford to pay him back from his new job. After all, it was a service-oriented business, and in Sydney's book – beneath him – the lowest type of work serving cocktails to drunken tourists and wiping-up their recycled breakfast. How demeaning it would be if, God forbid, her friends got wind of this. After all, what was a silly five hundred thou anyway. Why, Daddy could make that in a day. In her mind, the only smart thing for Rob to do, was to cut his losses and run – just write it all off as a bad investment.

As stubborn as he was, Rob did realize that this was one investment he hadn't been quite so intuitive about. But he refused to give in and accept 'charity' from her father, as he saw it. He'd worked too damn hard for that money to just walk away and write it off. He was convinced that this was his doing and he had to find a way out of this mess on his own. His pride was at stake, and even though he was hard pressed to admit it, so was his sanity. Although, Rob also knew, had he stayed lost in the rat race back home, he would have surely succumbed to urban overload. After all, he reasoned, his happiness was just as important as making money, although he knew this was a philosophy Sydney would never appreciate. Rob was determined to make this work and found the courage to tell Sydney that if she really loved him, she would stand by his decision to do so. Three months was all he would need to get the charter business up and running, and then he could return to Chicago with his head held high that he'd made a success of it and be back just in time for their wedding in November. So, after days of begging, two hundred roses, a dozen telegrams and nine hundred thirty-six dollars and twelve cents, to be exact, in phone calls, she finally relented and agreed to give him the three months.

So, life went on in the islands, and finally, Rob got his first real week charter, which infused ten thousand dollars into Rob's new charter account. But before Rob could earn his ten-thousand he had to once again deal with the issue of approval, since Althea had not signed his charter license. Day charters had been easy to book and carry illegally since it was unnecessary to clear his passengers out through immigration. But term charters* were another story if they were to leave the island. Five weeks had passed and Rob was still waiting for his license to be issued. Even Fritz, his crazy South African charter agent, had tried over and over again to plead, convince, and even bribe Althea into rushing it through. But alas, nothing was going to make her move any faster than she chose to, even if she had accepted the five-hundred-dollar bribe which Fritz had generously advanced out of Rob's charter money.

The thought of having to pass up an easy ten thousand dollars frustrated Rob to no end. Especially, since it was now late in the season and the last three weeks of day charters had been spotty at best – running only every other day with, at times, only half a boat load of greenies. The cost of equipping and setting up the boat for charter, aside from the cost of insurance, had run into the tens of thousands on Joey's marine supply account. One thing was for certain,

TERM CHARTER — *Meaning any charter averaging a week or more in length as opposed to the daily cattle–run. Often considered a sentence term to the captain and crew unlucky enough to find themselves aboard for a week with passengers from hell.*

the island had the system wired, or at least Althea's family did, and Rob had fallen for every last bit of it right down to the additional three-thousand-dollar policy to insure Rob from lost business due to inclement weather. But of course, Rob had missed the fine print which excluded all of hurricane season, not to mention any form of precipitation which left only high winds from November 20th until July 1st, during which time the steady Tradewinds blew through the West Indies on an average of ten to twenty knots, rarely, if ever exceeding the norm. But then Rob was new at this and had thought – "Better safe than sorry."

That morning Rob stepped into Althea's office with a large bag of genips,* which Rob had been told was her favorite fruit – another small bribe. To Rob's dismay, there were five much larger bags full of the small green fruit lying on Althea's desk awaiting her favor. Unfortunately, Rob did not yet understand the age-old tradition of good ole island payola – one measly sack of genips and five hundred dollars under the table was not the going price of a charter license these days. Althea was not there but a folder marked, 'Charter Licenses to be Processed,' lay open on her desk. Rob looked around the ten by twelve-foot room which had two windows and two doors to determine the likelihood of getting caught. Casually, he thumbed through the file of at least a dozen other applications, four of which were stamped "Denied," three "Approved" and several "Approval Pending." His was the last application in the folder, in the stack marked "PENDING INVESTIGATION." What kind of investigation could she be referring to, thought Rob, concerned now that he knew little or nothing about Joey's comings and goings. Especially goings since he had no idea where he had disappeared to, or what he was up to. Suddenly, a door slammed behind him sending Rob nearly through the window he jumped so far, broadcasting his guilt bigger than Althea herself.

"Mista Marner!" Althea scolded. "You mus learn pacense he'ar in de islan'. It be a plece wer'd notin' happin' fas'."

Rob smiled guiltily handing her his meager offering. "Please, I realize how busy you must be here processing these applications, but I really need to take this charter, I mean your brother and your family have cost me a fortune and I..."

"Mista Marner, like I sa'befo'. You will git you licez when I sa'so an' na befo. Now I be happi to pull it fromm de file so you caan tek it to anoder islan'."

"No, no, I mean no problem I'll be happy to wait I... I'll just ah eat less you know... maybe I can get an advance on my credit cards or something. I... I'll

---

*GENIPS — A strange West Indian fruit that is ninety-five percent pit and shell. It is however, the most addicting fruit/snack known to man – like the sunflower seed and the pistachio nut. One must deshell it by biting the shell/skin in half then pop the fleshy, juicy covered nut into one's mouth eliciting a sweet/tart sensation as one sucks the pit like a jawbreaker until there's nothing left in your mouth but a tasteless ping-pong ball.

work it out somehow," said Rob backing out of the little office. "Have a good day," he said as he quickly retreated with his tail between his legs, quietly closing the door behind him.

So, now Rob had a choice, turn the charter down or secretly pick up his passengers on the little island of Barbuda, which Fritz managed to arrange by having a local ferry drop the five rock stars on shore at night, only to be picked up on the beach by Alex in the Island Fever's dinghy and ferried aboard with all their luggage. Actually, the guys were quite intrigued by the entire clandestine affair and didn't hesitate to go along with the plan, especially since they'd heard tales told by a certain musician of the drug smugglers and pirates in the islands. The guys just thought that it was all part of the ambiance and excitement of the trip.

The morning that they were to pick up their five rock stars, Alex set out early from their previous night's anchorage at Green Island, which gave them the shortest route possible to the undeveloped island of Barbuda forty miles to the north, which was surprisingly quite sizable – being more than half the size of Antigua itself. Alex set a course of ten degrees north allowing her to sneak past Spanish Port to the east and then head in toward Cocoa Point with the noon sun, using her hand-bearing compass* to avoid the many reefs that surrounded Barbuda** – the ones that had claimed over two hundred boats over the centuries. Although the compass gave her some measure of safety, Alex knew that the only way to really navigate these waters was to eyeball your way between the reefs and shoals.

Due to their illicit status as an illegal charter on the island, Alex did her best to stay away from overly populated harbors and bays to avoid clearing in with immigration, since they had not cleared out of Antigua. Fritz, their charter agent, had chosen to qualify this as a special charter – a celebrity charter in fact, since the five guys were a rather ambiguously famous English rock band. In actuality, it turned out to be a week of babysitting five burned out rockers just off a nine-month tour, who were used to being pampered and waited on hand and foot – not to mention their affinity for any and all stray babes found in each and every port they pulled into, from locals to tourists. After of course, they had

*HAND-BEARING COMPASS — An object that looks like a hockey puck which is a portable compass for taking bearings of land or other objects.
**BARBUDA — An island originally settled by the Codrington family in 1685, who leased it from the British for one fat sheep a year – native Barbudans being the descendants of slaves imported to the island to run the Cordington's livestock interests. Although Barbudan's have been loath to accept the twentieth century's, roads, cars and TV's – those modern inventions have managed to find their way onto the island due to the fact that although emancipated from England, Barbuda is still under the rule of her southern neighbor, Antigua. And of course, Antigua has welcomed, with open arms, all the luxuries and lifestyle which have cultivated the tourist trade. Aside from a modicum of tourism, and their century-old tradition of sheep herding, the island subsists today on the export of sand – their most plentiful attribute, and a small charcoal industry.

given up on Alex who was not in the least impressed by their somewhat had to offer them. By the third day, there were so many scantily clad girls onboard, the Island Fever was beginning to look like a floating bordello. To be perfectly honest, Rob and Raymond had very few complaints about their predicament, nor did I, since there was a definite excess of women to go around, and the girls it seemed, were almost as impressed by Rob's status as owner of this magnificent vessel as Joey had indeed said they would be, as they were by the Rock and Roll luminaries themselves. Once again, Rob, was in Paradise. Alex had however, had just about enough of the carnage by the third day as she watched Rob who was quite enjoying the free-for-all that ensued amongst their promiscuous and indiscriminate passengers, and she decided to redirect their route to a deserted beach north of Palmetto Point on the leeward side of Barbuda, where the fellows could romp and play on shore to their heart's content while living out all of their unfulfilled fantasies. And, where it was unlikely that they would collect any additional groupie stowaways not to mention attention to the fact that they were on charter in the first place.

To Alex's relief, her new anchorage had been a great success since it was by far one of the most beautiful beaches on an island of seemingly endless beaches, or in the entire West Indies as far as I'm concerned, since the pale pink sand of this magnificent beach wrapped its arms around a crystal-clear turquoise bay – eleven miles long – barely marred by even a rock on the sandy bottom. It was clear to Alex why she had heard it called the most beautiful beach in the Caribbean, for although she had not personally seen all of them, she found it hard to imagine one that could come close to matching its beauty.

On shore, the only sign of civilization were the ruins of a small hotel which was surrounded by a stand of palms and Australian pines in the very center of the beach. Along the beach grew a plethora of vegetation – morning glory and yellow and orange creeper spread across the sand at the highwater mark and above the beach grew Spanish cedar, and sea grape, all decorated with colorful bromeliads and wild orchids. Although the beach was just a spit of land which separated the ocean from Codrington Lagoon, it was impossible to see the buildings of Codrington on the far side of the Lagoon from sea level in the bay – making it seem as though nothing else existed on the island than their very own little world. For the next three days Alex took the guys and girls exploring and snorkeling for lobster while Raymond barbecued their catch on shore. This was Alex's secret spot which was rarely frequented by the other term charter boats

FRIGATE BIRDS — *A black, two-to-three-pound bird with a wingspan greater than any other bird in proportion to their weight. Although masters of the air, they are hopeless on their own two feet and are unable to take off from the water should they be so unlucky as to land there. Due to being challenged in the fishing department, they have resorted to stealing fish from other birds who are more adept at the task – thus their name "frigate" or "man o'war."*

due to its isolation, lack of civilization, and its many reefs one had to navigate – the reason Alex had fallen in love with it. The area's largest population, aside from the lobster along the bottom, was a rookery of frigate birds* which soared overhead – their strange cries creating an unearthly sound which made it all seem a bit surreal. The Frigate bird colony, which was on the other side of the spit of land in Codrington Lagoon, was the island's largest nature preserve. These majestic birds high above, the abundant colorful fish and spotted eagle rays on the reefs, and their all-encompassing picturesque hideaway made them feel as if they'd actually arrived at heaven on earth.

Alex was content enough with their surroundings, although she refused to admit to herself that she was somewhat irritated at seeing Rob pay so much attention to the young attractive girls onboard, even if he was restricting his participation to a voyeur capacity. However, she did find it rather distasteful that some of the starry-eyed pubescents who had latched onto him looked young enough to be his daughter. But what did she care anyway. After all, it was his boat, and his life and it was his prerogative to do with it whatever he pleased. What she didn't realize was that ironically, Rob was in complete admiration of the professional self–restraint that Alex had maintained since she could have easily had her pick of any one of the five eligible, successful, sexy rock stars. All of whom had lean, wiry, almost emaciated bodies, looking as if they lived on a diet of booze and cocaine. In fact, Rob wondered how she always managed to avoid showing any interest in men in general. At least he had come to the conclusion that he shouldn't take her cold-shouldered disinterest personally. Alex had never discussed her love life or her past with Rob. She had never mentioned Michael or her three-year partnership with him. Even though they'd never married, Alex had felt as if such a bond had existed between them since they had been inseparable during those years. Actually, Alex spoke with no one about him. She had kept in touch with a few friends from home, but their lives had evolved so differently she felt she had no one in which to confide. And although both Rob and Raymond had become friends, she was unable to share openly with them the intimate details of her life since they fell into the category of boss and coworker.

In getting the hang of term charter, Rob was finally starting to fall into the groove of island life and decided to use some of their down–time constructively. So, he took advantage of Raymond's willingness to teach him the art of windsurfing – that sport which has masterfully combined the elements of wind and water to create the ultimate surfing/sailing machine. And, as with his general laidback demeanor, Raymond was a far more patient teacher than Alex when it came to the principles of sailing, which suddenly became much more rudimentary to Rob with twelve-square-feet of canvas in his hands and a stick under his feet than the complicated sailing rig which was carried by the Island Fever.

"So, Raymond, exactly what do I do now that I'm standing on this fiberglass board?" questioned Rob, more than a little nervous about his first lesson in windsurfing.

"Well, it's quite simple you know, you just have to become one with the elements. Like the wind man, and then you just go," said Raymond in his esoteric way of explaining things.

"Okay," said Rob contemplating Raymond's instructions. "What do I do in between becoming-one with the wind and going?"

"Well... you just pick the sail up out of the water with that rope there. Then you hang on to the boom. Lean it forward to go downwind and back to go upwind," explained Raymond very matter-of-factly as if Rob actually understood what he was saying.

"Easy for you to say," said Rob as he struggled to keep his balance on the two-foot-wide board, failing miserably – inevitably ending up flailing about in the water underneath the sail.

"Watch me," said Raymond as he climbed on and placed his left foot just behind the mast.* He pulled the sail out of the water using the knotted rope that was attached to the spot where the wishbone-boom** was tied to the mast. Then he gripped the boom overhanded with both hands and pulled back in on the sail spinning the board up towards the wind and effortlessly took off at a fair clip in the steady on-shore breeze. Rob was amazed at how easy it looked, which gave him the confidence he needed, since he wasn't exactly the athletic type outside of the gym. By the end of the week, Rob was actually getting pretty good at this new sport and had even begun to seem somewhat agile to Alex, even though, in reality, she knew better.

Upon their return to port, Rob was to learn that Althea had gotten wind of Rob's illegal pick up in Barbuda. It seemed that the illicit smuggler who had fetched their passengers was, in fact, her second cousin, and was on her husband's payroll as captain for his ferry boat which ran between Antigua and Barbuda, unbeknownst to Fritz. She had not only not approved his charter license – by the time Rob returned, she had banned him from picking up any further passengers from local waters until the license was issued, which now

*MAST — The upright spar that holds the sail and stands perpendicular to the board when sailing. Of course, since the mast on a windsurfer is hinged, it only remains upright as long as its driver does.
WISHBOOM — The wishbone shaped bar that wraps around either side of the mast and is attached to it at one end at the clew.* The wishboom serves a similar purpose as a boom on a normal sailboat.
***CLEW — The lower corner of a sail – aft – where the sheets tie to control the trim and position of the sail.

seemed to fall within some terminally indefinite time frame. Rob, it seemed, was screwed.

"Like I sai befo', you get it when I say so 'n not befo'," repeated Althea for the third time to Rob who stood before her in her office with offerings of both cash and an extra-large sugar sack filled with genips. Rob was beginning to understand how a Buddhist felt venerating the Buddha with offerings since Althea certainly fit the physical profile, and like the Buddha, her word laid down the law and was respected on the island as such.

"But what else exactly has to be done befo'/before you can approve it?" questioned a frustrated Rob – no longer willing to accept her standard West Indian answer which fell under the guidelines of – always be vague and never commit to anything definitive.

"Like I sai one mo tyme. I be workin' on it an' when I prove it, you get it, n not a day befo'."

Rob was worried. What would he do now sans any income? But to Rob's good fortune, Fritz came through for him the next day, with a temporary solution – a charter only one week and ninety–two miles away on another island. It seemed that he had arranged for him to pick up his new fare on a small half-French, half-Dutch island called Saint Martin/Sint Maarten* during Carnival week, and cruise the upper chain of the Leeward** Islands or Lesser Antilles. St. Maarten being no relation whatsoever to Antigua, Fritz assured him that he would have no problems with Althea or any other island officials where this charter was concerned as long as he cleared his passengers in and out on the more tolerant Dutch side of the island.

*SAINT MARTIN/SINT MAARTEN — An island originally discovered by Columbus on the eleventh of November, 1493 and claimed for the Spanish. After many owners, it was later taken over by and divided between the Dutch and the French. Their method of claiming their respective sides of the island was – the Frenchman and the Dutchman would consume copious amounts of champagne and gin – respectively; and then start at the peak of Mt. Concordia in the middle of the island, and walk as far as they could get in the hot sun before they each collapsed. This proved that the French are far better at holding their liquor since the French won 25 square miles of the little 36 square mile island – leaving the balance for the Dutch. A uniquely democratic solution, don't you think?

**LEEWARD — Pronounced (Loo.r.d), meaning the protected side either of a boat, an island, or even a portion of the chain of islands in the Lesser Antilles. It is the side exactly opposite of the windward side – the side from which the wind is blowing. The leeward side is in most cases the dry side of any island since the side to get the wind or weather first, also gets the rain the minute the clouds hit the hillsides. With a boat, the leeward and windward sides change depending on which direction the boat is headed. In other-words it goes from side to side depending whether it's on a starboard or port tack. In regard to which chain of islands are considered the Leewards in the Antilles – they start with Anguilla on the northern end, the first island in the Lesser Antilles down through Dominica. These islands are designated the Leewards since they are situated more westerly or leeward – further away from the prevailing easterly Tradewinds than the Windward Islands, which start with Martinique at the northern end and continue on down through Trinidad which is at its extremity near South America.

As far as the name 'Lesser Antilles' goes, I've always thought the terminology to be a rather derogatory description for a chain of islands as beautiful as the Leeward and the Windward Islands. But Columbus seemed to feel that they were of lesser value than Hispaniola *(Haiti and the Dominican Republic),* Cuba, Puerto Rico, Navassa Island, Jamaica, and the Cayman Islands which he deemed the 'Greater Antilles.' But you know what they say Chris ole buddy, "Sometimes less is best."

As for Columbus, of all the islands he discovered in the Lesser Antilles it seems that Saint Martin/Sint Maarten developed into, by far, the most unique since today it exists as, not one, but two countries. How is it that the French and the Dutch have lived together so peacefully sharing only thirty–six square miles of rock and sand for over two hundred years? The answer must be that the Dutch got the monopoly on the booze along with the main trading port, and the French got the beautiful, secluded, nude beaches. A profitable solution for both, don't you think? Maybe Europe should have just taken a lesson in harmony from this tiny island decades ago. Why there aren't even any borders to cross. In fact, the only way that you know that you've left the Dutch side and entered the French is when you've left the pot–holes behind. And so goes life in the islands. What's a pothole or two when you're surrounded by Paradise?

It was just about at that point in his journey that Rob was beginning to understand what Columbus must have felt when he had first headed off on his voyage into the unknown hoping to discover his new world. He was a very brave man Rob thought – or a very foolish one, since he was traversing terra unknown, or rather, aqua incognita, since to Renaissance mapmakers this was totally uncharted territory. How could Columbus have ever been certain that he wouldn't just simply fall off the end of the earth? After all, that was the prevailing belief at the time. Likened to Columbus' journey, Rob had ventured off into the great unknown, leaving the security of the civilized world behind. And, as far as Sydney was concerned, he was on the brink of falling off the map of society – if not falling off the edge of the earth itself. After all, she already suspected that he'd indeed fallen off his rocker onto his head and was hoping that he'd soon return to his sanity.

It was as fearful as it was exciting for Rob to know that the waters which lay ahead were totally uncharted, for him and he was yet to realize that the real search he had set out on was more in fact a pursuit of self-discovery rather than a search to discover Paradise. But most importantly, he was to eventually learn that it was not so much about the arrival at one's final port, as it was about the journey across the sea of life itself that truly mattered. Once again – a concept that always seemed to elude most present-day participants of the human race, and the thing that we here on 'The Otherside' seem to find hardest to impart to them.

So, Alex and Raymond busied themselves with preparations to leave on their mission to retrieve their passengers on this unusual little atoll ninety-two miles northwest of Antigua, and Rob went off to meet with Fritz one last time to get final instructions and to collect his deposit for their second big term charter. Rob sat in Fritz's right hand drive car in a deserted cul-de-sac feeling as if he were on some clandestine drug exchange, as he watched Fritz count off five-thousand dollars cash into his eager hands.

"Don't forget now, these people only eat kosher food... meat or fish and vegetables, so be sure to tell Raymond to buy the right food. Their agent books a lot of business with me," insisted Fritz.

"Exactly where do I buy kosher food down here? I mean I'm Catholic, what do I know about kosher," Rob questioned in a panic.

"Easy, stay away from shellfish and pork. The rest, just tell 'em you picked it up at this great island kosher deli in Antigua before you left."

That's easy enough, thought Rob, nodding his head as he pocketed the cash and smiled, "Don't worry Fritz. I won't let you down. If you book another charter for us, get in touch by Landsradio...* we'll just pick them up from there." "Do what I can," answered Fritz as he started the car and drove Rob back to the market where Raymond waited in his car in the parking lot for Rob so they could buy provisions.

Rob was finally beginning to believe that maybe everything was indeed going to work out just as he'd hoped as he tallied the math in his head – let's say fifty weeks a year at ten thousand or so a pop. Why that was a far cry better than the stock market could ever provide for him. Unfortunately, Rob was so busy counting his fuzzy little chicks that he still didn't realize that the eggs needed to hatch that golden goose had not yet been laid – in fact, they hadn't even been conceived.

"Wow, maybe this wasn't such a bad thing after all," thought Rob, excited by the thought of the easy cash in his pocket. "Wait till I tell Sydney how much I'm making a week. She has to be impressed by the potential we have to make enough in three or four years to just simply sail away for a while, drop out or maybe even cruise around the world. Cruise around the world. I like the sound of that," Rob repeated to himself. That was definitely something to work towards, he thought. "Maybe I should convince Sydney to come down as soon as things are running smoothly and show her. It's a pretty nice life here after all, she'll see," Rob repeated over and over in an attempt to convince even himself.

But what Rob didn't know, was that he would have his chance to show Sydney just how wonderful things were in Paradise and it would be much sooner than he expected.

LANDSRADIO — The now defunct radio station atop the tallest island in the area which could transfer radio reception to the telephone lines.

CHAPTER NINE

Excess Baggage

"Never pack more than you can carry."

Ian

By now Rob was starting to feel a little guilty about Sydney – leaving her all alone in Chicago while he was off having so much fun in Paradise. And Sydney was doing her best to add to his guilt with message after message to Fritz about how badly she needed him for such important decisions about their wedding plans as – puce and persimmon or celery and celadon. As far as Rob knew she was questioning the menu rather than the color scheme. As damaging as Sydney's frustration was over Rob's lack of availability on such vitally important matters, her inherent suspicious nature was twice as destructive. And she was getting pretty suspicious about the whole affair – after all, Rob was living with another woman, even if she was only the skipper of his boat. Her only satisfaction was in knowing that any woman who skippered a sailboat must be at best quite the opposite of feminine, petite, and attractive. Boy, was she surprised when she arrived at the dock in English Harbor unannounced, to find a cute little blonde busting out of a very tiny bikini, leaning over the back bridge deck of Rob's vessel to change his spark plugs. Not to mention the look on Rob's face when he looked up from greasing the shaft on his outboard engine, only to see Sydney standing there on the dock in her high heels next to ten grossly overstuffed suitcases. At that moment, there were a wealth of images running through Sydney's mind. Poor Rob – this time he'd really found himself in a pickle since the circumstantial evidence weighed heavily against him, even if he was innocent of any wrongdoing, at least where Alex was concerned. Then again, possession is nine tenths of the law, and it was apparent that Rob was in possession of one very attractive female captain. Rob felt little or no pangs of guilt regarding his earlier ménage 'a trois, compliments of Joey, since he had no memory of his transgression. However, his current compromising position with Alex proved quite the contrary. After all, they were sharing a small rubber raft while getting his engine lubed.

Rob quickly began a futile attempt at damage control while trying hopelessly to stow Sydney's baggage – ignoring Alex's insistence that it was far too much for the boat to carry.

Suddenly, he felt as if he were responsible for slightly more excess baggage* than he actually owned or cared to, and he was getting worried about how he was going to stow it without rocking the boat or possibly even sinking the ship as Alex feared. Rob was beginning to think that he should have invested in a larger boat since even the QE II would have felt like close quarters to this crew at the moment. Needless to say, it wasn't the most congenial atmosphere onboard, since Alex's first impression of Sydney was that she was a spoiled, little, rich bitch. Not to mention her sinking disappointment, since she was just starting to enjoy spending time with Rob. And, well you can imagine what Sydney's mind had conceived with regard to Alex.

It seemed that Sydney had decided to surprise Rob and come down for a little vacation when she learned from Fritz that there was a week open in their charter schedule. Why, she had even made plans to sail with them to St. Maarten for Carnival,** which luckily for them had been held late this year due to the island's mourning of the death of an important government official.

*EXCESS BAGGAGE — *Defined by the airlines as more baggage than one is allowed to check without paying an additional price. It is unfortunately a fact of life, that no matter how you try to pack it into smaller compartments, check it, or stow it away, everyone carries a fair amount of excess baggage – some more than others. Some, it seems, are simply sporting manageable backpacks while others are packing steamer trunks.*

CARNIVAL — *On the Dutch side Carnival is a two week-long West Indian version of Mardi Gras, which generally commences two weeks after Easter. On the French side, Carnival is celebrated forty days before Easter or two weeks before Lent, as in Brazil. Carnival Village on the Dutch side is centered on the Saltpond Landfill* on the north side of Philipsburg where an event is held every night such as beauty competitions, steel band competitions, calypso concerts, and costume competitions. Other festivities include: Bands such as the Mighty Arrow (formally the Mighty Sparrow) which play 'til midnight prior to Juvé Mornin' which winds into the Last Lap around the Saltpond finishing at 9:00 AM; and the Jump-up parade to the Village on the last Monday where all participants dress up in flamboyant costumes and dance around town like warring Indians. In St. Barth during Carnival, they still burn the evil Voodoo spirit Val Val – a stuffed mannequin which represents the burning of bad spirits. In essence it's a two-week long party during which the local inhabitants stop work, dress up like strange tropical birds, drink copious amounts of rum, and act like irresponsible adolescents.*

So, to Rob's surprise, there was Sydney standing in the Island Fever's cockpit with her hair falling out of the perfect French twist, her dress all wrinkled and sweat soaked, and her make–up smeared and dripping down her face in rivulets. She was more than a little hot and bothered by the nonair–conditioned island taxi ride from the airport, a broken nail due to the fact that there was no one at the airport to carry her luggage, and two missing bags. At that moment, she had no intention of holding back any accusations which were rapidly germinating in her mind and wasted no time in slinging the first insult at Alex. "So, you're the woman who's been cohabiting with my future husband for the last six weeks," she snarled.

"I guess if you call captain and owner working together on a charter boat cohabiting, then I stand guilty of the crime," responded Alex, pleading her confession in her best Mae West, while futility attempting to retain a straight face.

Of course, this only served to infuriate Sydney further, who now proceeded to fire the next round at Alex, pointblank, "Why do you even bother to wear that rag you call a bikini top, it's so skimpy that it hardly serves any purpose. But then, if I were as small as you, I wouldn't be too concerned about covering them up either."

Luckily, Alex immediately recognized the gauntlet which had been so neatly thrown down before her, disguising a simple hormone induced fit of raw female jealousy, and chose not to pick it up and accept the challenge. At least not on Sydney's terms. Instead, Alex simply whipped open the bowtie holding her top in place, and in the tradition of the islands, gallantly removed the offending object in question totally revealing her well-proportioned, firm, tanned breasts. "If it bothers you that much, I won't wear it. After all, we are in the Caribbean," said Alex as casually as if she were removing an overcoat after coming in out of the cold.

This brave act of Alex's left Sydney absolutely speechless, a condition that was quite new to her and most of all to Rob, who was extremely impressed with Alex's masterful one-upmanship of Sydney, not to mention how intrigued he was by seeing her topless for the first time. Rob stood there with his mouth open in disbelief waiting for the explosion that was surely imminent. Thank goodness for Raymond who had the insight and good judgment to intervene at

---

***SALTPOND LANDFILL — Literally the island garbage dump which encompasses the entire center of town – more than half of Philipsburg in fact. It was formally a working salt pond where salt was extracted from seawater through a dehydration process. A pond would be flooded by the early settlers with seawater and then allowed to evaporate, leaving of course – salt. This process worked especially well in the Caribbean due to the fact that the waters of the Atlantic are extremely salty. Since salt ponds are no longer used in the islands as a source of salt, the local government determined it the best place to put their garbage in order to create more Real Estate.

that critical moment with a tall frozen piña colada, Sydney's favorite drink – little parasol and all. Unbelievably enough, Alex's stand had actually caught Sydney so completely off guard that her temper was somewhat quelled by her confusion and embarrassment, at least for the time being. And Raymond's icy refreshment, seemed to serve as a relief from the heat in more ways than one – it seemed to quench the fire that was on the brink of igniting from sheer internal combustion.

"How could she have just turned up like this without calling first," thought Rob. *"I'd planned to break it to her slowly that Alex was young, blonde, and attractive. I would have told her... eventually. I've always known that Sydney was the jealous type but I didn't expect that she'd really be threatened by Alex. I'd better find a way to smooth this over fast or by next week her father will have bought a cruise ship and offered Alex a job if Sydney doesn't make her quit first."*

Although Sydney's jealousy was quite flattering in some ways, Rob was a bit concerned as to whether or not Sydney's distrust of his commitment to her was something that he could deal with the rest of his life.

"I just feel sorry for poor Alex, I should have warned her. She really doesn't deserve this sort of abuse. What if Sydney does make her quit? I guess I have to try to diffuse this thing before it ever gets started. Maybe I should convince her that Alex and I can barely stand each other."

Under the circumstances, Alex somewhat understood the purpose of estranging himself from her in front of Sydney. After all, any gesture of familiarity between them could have been easily misconstrued by Sydney as more than it truly was. So, when Rob began speaking to her like an employee, not to mention Sydney commanding her like a servant, Alex was ready to jump ship before they even left the harbor.

Hoping to pacify Sydney with sailing and a little island hopping, and dis-tract her enough to keep her mind on anything other than her competition to see who was going to be the real captain of Rob's ship, Rob decided to leave in the wee hours of the morning. Alex would just have to get by with their broken engine, which was unable to go over six miles per hour due to a prop bent on a piece of floating garbage on their last day of charter. Even though it was barely enough speed to maneuver that large, unwieldy boat in a tight anchorage, Rob insisted, to Alex's dismay, that it would have to wait until they got to St. Maarten for repair. He was desperate to placate Sydney, and luckily, his strategy worked as he knew it would, by tempting her with duty-free shopping up island. After all, Sydney was Sydney, and it didn't take long for her to take control of any situation she found herself in. In fact, she was already planning their voyage and insisted on stopping on the way to St. Maarten on that quaint but chic little French island of St. Barth that she had heard so much about. She was simply dying to have lunch on the beach at Chez Francine, and of course browse through a few of the shops on the quay. In fact, Sydney had it all mapped out even before she'd arrived on the island, since she'd managed to get the latest inside track on the chic and hip places to see and be seen in the Caribbean from her posh circle of friends.

Alex was more than a little pissed off about their change in plans, but then it was Rob's boat, and if he wanted to sail to St. Barth two days early then she couldn't stop him, or even have much to say about it. Alex just hoped that the engine would hold out until they got to St. Maarten, where she knew she could buy a new prop and make the needed repairs before their next charter.

Alex set sail from Falmouth Harbor, where they had filled their water and fuel tanks, around two the next morning, estimating their arrival in St. Barth after sunup, no matter how good a speed they might make with a fifteen knot breeze on a downwind broad-reach.* She calculated the seventy-eight mile trip to take them somewhere between five to six hours, since on a downwind leg, a catamaran averages more or less the speed of the wind. Alex preferred not to arrive at the entrance to Gustavia in the dark, even though it was reasonably well marked by a beacon on shore guiding sailors between Pain du Sucre *(Sugar Loaf)* and Gros Islets, and The Saintes *(offshore rocks and islands)*. She always tried to be a cautious sailor and avoided putting herself, her passengers, or the boat into any questionable circumstances whenever possible. After all, there were enough times where undesirable conditions could not be avoided so Alex didn't believe in using up all of her good luck up on unnecessary risks.

As angry and frustrated as she was, Alex did look forward to going to St. Barth and St. Maarten for their food and the beaches. One could find food worthy of European bistros at any one of the many French, Italian, and Creole restaurants that littered the two little islands, courtesy of wealthy drug dealers over the years. Antigua on the contrary offered only mediocre, bland dining, reminiscent of its British heritage. Alex had found the Englishman's food to be quite boring and unfulfilling, much like their lovemaking. Based on her geographically impossible rule, Alex had allowed herself a moderate sampling of lovers over the years in her travels, feeling secure that she would never encounter a foreign one-nighter again. However, with the jet age, the world had grown smaller and Alex had run into a French fling on the dock one day while hauling out her boat in Guadeloupe, convincing her that even her geographical requirements were not necessarily a reliable rule-of-thumb anymore.

Sydney stayed on deck for the first ten minutes, but since the only mode of travel that interested her was first class air, she opted to sleep through the tranquil night sail rather than fret herself about large fish and the big black sea

---

* BROAD-REACH — *Sailing off the wind, or with the wind on the rear quarter aft of the beam, which is the perpendicular line off the side of a boat.*

that seemed to swallow them up the minute they rounded Johnson Point and headed west northwest around the western side of the island. Rob helped Sydney crawl into the master bunk, which she nervously referred to as a coffin for two. She kissed Rob goodnight, popped a sleeping pill, then donned her night cream, ear plugs, and her eye mask. Once all of her senses were obscured, she lay down apprehensively for her first night at sea, which was technically also Rob's.

"Don't worry," Rob assured her, "I'll come down to join you as soon as I'm certain they have everything under control," knowing all the while that there wasn't a chance in hell, he'd be able to sleep knowing that they were on the open sea.

Of course, with her ear plugs in Sydney heard none of his assurances and had already pulled the sheet over her head – like a corpse in their coffin built for two. Relieved that she was settled, Rob turned out the light and climbed the steps from the hull, then crawled on his hands and knees through the closed companionway up to the deckhouse. He was quite happy to reach the fresh air on deck once again, since he still hadn't gotten the hang of staying below deck while the boat was under sail.

Now, Sydney was even less of a sailor than Rob, if that were possible, and by around three in the morning Sydney emerged from her bunk in the leeward hull, greener than the color of the phosphorus in the wake behind the boat. For everyone but Sydney, who was at this point suffering from that French disease known as 'mal de mer,' a.k.a. 'green at the gills,' and busy feeding the fish over the back of the bridge deck, it was a glorious full moon sail offering up a magical moonbow*.

Sydney was in the cockpit for the rest of the night, draped over the back of the bridge deck like a wet towel – drifting in and out of consciousness in between bouts of nausea and vomiting. The fact that there was no horizon to watch in the darkness made the queasiness worse. Having been a sailor myself, I know that finding a fixed point of land to stare at will usually help to still the confusion in one's inner ear, by convincing the mind that not everything on the planet is moving.

*MOONBOW — A rainbow seen only at night with a full moon – a phenomenon of nature almost as rare as a green flash.**
**GREEN FLASH — Now a 'green flash' probably requires some explanation for the non–sailor. For that matter, it is probably safe to say that most sailors have never witnessed a true green flash since it is visible at sunset under only the most optimum conditions. Yes, many a tourist and sailor alike have sat in bars at sunset drinking to that elusive little flash of green that you may catch a fleeting glimpse of as that last little piece of sun dips below the horizon. But then again who's to say whether they're really seeing a true green flash or just viewing the last of the sunset through an inclined margarita glass.

ISLAND FEVER

Rob sat with Sydney all night knowing first-hand how it felt to succumb to the motion of the ocean since his first day out he'd been armed with enough experience in the matter to last him a lifetime. Although he had grown accustomed to it, this was Rob's first outing in the boat after dark and to say that the prospect of a night sail had made Rob a bit anxious, was an understatement. The last thing he needed was to let Sydney sense his anxiety, so Rob did his best to play the courageous sailor for Sydney's sake even though it had put the fear of God into him. But, once they passed the Northern head of the island and found themselves in open sea where the Atlantic meets the Caribbean, his fears were quelled by a somewhat more relaxed state of terror which eventually settled down to a mild panic once they were well on their way past the small islands to the west of them – Montserrat,* Nevis,** and then St. Kitts, or St. Christopher where the Island Fever had been conceived and born.

Slowly, as his fears subsided Rob began to realize how incredibly beautiful it was to be on the water at night. It must have been the galloping motion, characteristic to catamarans, that made Rob imagine he was riding on a magnificent black horse over a magical carpet of starlight which stretched across the heavens. Except where the second, liquid, crescent moon danced off the wave-crests in shimmering snakes slithering across its surface it was impossible to tell where the sky ended and the sea began. For the first time in his life Rob felt close to GOD. Or, whoever was responsible for the creation of this seemingly eternal Universe with which Rob now felt as one – simply one more breath of light which twinkled in the ethers. For the first time in his life, he no longer felt the separation between his mortal existence and the rest of the cosmos. Somehow, everything aside from that moment seemed as if it were only a mere perception; for in that moment, Rob had been transported beyond the physical to a place that seemed, in truth, reality – a place beyond body, mind, and ego. He

*MONTSERRAT — A little known and sparsely inhabited island which was decimated by hurricane Hugo in '89 and then finished off by the volcano, Galways Soufriére, some years later. Boats from Nevis had gone to save the island's livestock but had capsized and sank on the way back fully loaded with cattle, goats, and sheep. The men were saved and managed to return with another boat to save the poor struggling beasts, however, upon arriving they found only the remains of a shark feast. This island is best known amongst the record industry for its now deceased recording studio, which was used over the years by many a well-known musician.
**NEVIS — A sleepy little volcanic island with its head, both literally and figuratively, in the clouds – today relying solely on tourism and its one major resort, which employs nearly half the islands natives. Dominated by the island of St. Kitts as a British federation for more than a century and a half, the island formally built its wealth, as did St. Kitts, on the labor of African slaves who toiled in the sugar cane fields – later being discovered by the British elite in 1778, thanks to its thermal baths and The Bath Hotel now closed for years, which was opened as a retreat for the rich and famous. The last few years there have been rumblings of dissension and succession for its independence from its neighboring St. Kitts.

felt as one with the very soul of the Universe. In that moment he had finally arrived. Although, to my great disappointment, it was to serve as only a fleeting glimpse for Rob instead of a new reality, since by the time the sun had come up the magic had worn off and he was now focused on one very green Sydney who lay unconscious in the cockpit. He was starting to get concerned since she was still slightly greener than the new foliage on the hillsides of St. Barth.*

By the time they reached the harbor in St. Barth, to Sydney's great relief, the discomfort she was feeling in her stomach had somehow taken away the discomfort she had felt from learning that Alex was an attractive woman. This, for at least a little while, had afforded Rob some semblance of peace onboard, even if it were just a temporary truce.

Sydney was relieved that the boat had finally reached a calm anchorage just outside Gustavia harbor in Baie de Public, however, a calm anchorage was still not terra firma, and Sydney by this point would have given up her Saks charge card to just get off that floating instrument of torture – swearing she would never set foot on that godforsaken craft of Rob's again as long as she lived. But when she learned that Alex had no intention of docking the Island Fever in the crowded harbor with a broken engine, and that she would have to climb into that tiny rubber raft called a dinghy and be driven ashore, Sydney was not thrilled. In fact, Rob had to carry her kicking and screaming into the Zodiac. Sydney spared no words in making it perfectly clear to Rob that she would be leaving the island via an alternate means of transportation, i.e, the first flight out to Sint Maarten, and would be already basking in the sun sipping a tall rum punch by the time they had raised their anchor and rounded Rockefeller Point – headed northwest to Philipsburg Harbor. Of course, she had yet to see the island

---

SAINT BARTH — or Saint Barthélemy, is an island which Columbus named after his brother, but which is better known as St. Barth by the jet set and wealthy escapists – the original of which were none other than the Rockefellers and the Rothchilds. This was one island that had never had to rely on fishing and agriculture for its survival. It had simply thrived over the centuries from the trade of goods and contraband through its port, starting with the French buccaneers who for centuries dealt in stolen and captured booty; and then run by frugal Swedes for a hundred years or more who finally gave up and sold it to the French for about the equivalent of $60,000 U.S. – the likely cost today of a two week stay at one of the island's many exclusive guesthouses. Not much has changed on the island over the years except the faces of the new influx of pirates, their stripes, and the contraband. Today and for much of the last century, St. Barth has been a center for the trade of spirits in this part of the Caribbean – not referencing any of my relations here on 'The Otherside,' but the quite profitable and plentiful liquor trade through their duty-free port. I have always found St. Barth to be not only a beautiful island, but a unique gem – quite unlike the rest of the Caribbean, due to the fact there had been no slavery on the island, and their restricted policy on immigration. Combined it left it void of the true native West Indian culture – which is neither good nor bad, just simply – different.

airport, not to mention the fact that she would first have to survive the dinghy ride to the town dock.

No one, not even Alex, was prepared for what was to happen next when Sydney, still somewhat pallid from the evening's sail, dipped her hand into the harbor in an attempt to revive herself with a little tepid water on her face. It was her diamond – a rock the size of an acorn, which Rob was still paying for that caught its attention on the second dip. To a hungry barracuda* looking for its morning meal, the early sun glinting off that rock it surely resembled breakfast – a shiny silver fish feeding on the surface of the water. That, or this was one barracuda with very expensive taste. For when it hit, it seemed to know exactly what it was after, which it plucked right out of its setting without leaving even a mark on Sydney's left hand.

Of course, Alex could have warned Sydney that this particular harbor was infested with all sorts of carnivorous creatures, due to the fact that the island slaughter house was located on the town dock and the blood, and entrails were simply drained straight into the water to feed any and all that cared to partake in the daily feast. But Alex was making an effort to keep her mouth shut and forego any and all comment, since she knew that she and Sydney were unequally matched in the commentary department. But it was inevitable that Alex was about to become the brunt of Sydney's wrath, once reality had sunken in that she had lost her precious four-carat, emerald-cut, blue-diamond, and nearly her hand, to a slimy scaly creature that couldn't tell the difference between a diamond and a zircon. Once the initial shock was over for Alex, she made a beeline in the dinghy for the harbor bar on the Quai de la Republique which had been a landmark in Gustavia for nearly fifty years, but not before Sydney had become hopelessly hysterical.

Indeed, even I have been known to polish off a bottle of rum or two at the little tavern, known as Le Select, during the years I sailed the waters of the Leeward Islands on an island trader. Le Select was a tradition frequented by many a sailor and local alike over the years. The little bar on the corner of Rue General De Gaulle had seen many a drama on the island and would have had some outrageous stories to tell, if only its walls could talk. Conversely, although its walls may not have been able to, its patrons surely would partake of a rum punch and a story or two.

---

*BARRACUDA — Chances are it was the former of these two likelihoods since 'cuda,' as we call them in the islands, are known to be vision-impaired at any distance between two and twenty feet. So, given that these prehistoric looking creatures, blessed with ample rows of needle-like teeth, are not in the habit of wearing bifocals, they tend to mistake things like divers' watches and sparkling objects on the surface for an easy meal. There is nothing quite like the rush one experiences while diving when you find yourself suddenly eye to eye with a barracuda who has mistaken your silver regulator for Charley Tuna.

As in centuries past, and much like the days of prohibition, St. Barth was a safe haven to the modern-day smugglers of the eighties – those wealthy gentlemen sailors who lived aboard their expensive yachts and dealt in the illicit trade of transporting marijuana from the coasts of Columbia to the inlets of the U.S. Not aboard their own yachts of course, but aboard some other sailor's boat who was desperate to support their island lifestyle, since aside from smuggling and chartering, unless of course one chose to live in the grossly overpopulated American Virgin Islands, Americans could not easily work ashore. No one considered these merchants criminals since they were pre-gun toting cocaine smugglers. They were simply thought of as semi-retired gentlemen who made their livelihood in the business of – let's call it agricultural import/export – with an emphasis on the import aspect. In fact, these individuals had offered the closest thing to culture that the islands had known since their taste for fine wines and food had inspired the opening of a plethora of gourmet restaurants on St. Barth and St. Maarten/St. Martin over the years – often financed in fact by those very proceeds from their questionable trade. St. Barth had also been considered home-away-from-home for numerous American musicians, stars, and the wealthy bourgeoisie for the latter half of the twentieth century. Over the years, St. Barth had hosted numerous annual sailboat regattas *(races)* and rock concerts, and to this day remains the place to welcome in the New Year on a hundred-and-fifty-foot yacht on the quay, or at one of the exclusive thousand-dollar-a-night hotels.

There at that very same bar, Rob and Alex plied Sydney with so many petite rum punches to wash down the Valium, she was at last feeling no pain. Rob could tell she was starting to recover from the shock when she asked him for his credit card and stumbled across the rue to one of the many boutiques which lined the streets of town. Rob was impressed by the quaint berg of Gustavia with its red roofs surrounding the pristine port filled with fishing boats and sailing yachts. The streets, it seemed, were abuzz with activity as locals went about their business hurrying to get out of town before the day charter boats arrived from St. Maarten and deluged the little village with American tourists. They were the local merchants' mainstay, as they converged on the island for a three-hour lunch and then left for their spinnaker run back to what locals referred to as the mainland – St. Maarten.

While Rob was busy holding Sydney's shopping bags and signing charge receipts, Alex managed to slip away to the port captain's office on the dock to officially clear them in through the island's immigration. She had cleared in on the island many times before but never on the Island Fever. Confidently, she stepped through the door and placed the ship's papers and four American passports on the captain's desk.

The handsome French captain who was dressed in his official French officer's uniform got up from his seat where he was enjoying his morning espresso, smiled and started to look over her papers. His name tag read – Captain Reneau.

"Bonjour Capitaine," Alex said, greeting him in her broken French. "Sil' vous plai. We've just arrived from Antigua and I'd like to clear my boat, crew, and my one passenger into the island."

"Ah oui mademoiselle Capitaine, no probléme... welcome to St. Barth..." replied the overly friendly captain, who suddenly stopped short upon reading something on the ship's documents. "It says here the boat is called Island Fever. Is this the Island Fever?" questioned the captain officially raising his eyebrows.

"Well, yes, I guess," Alex said hesitantly, not certain where he was going with his line of questioning. God, what kind of trouble has Joey gotten into on the island, thought Alex, fully expecting the worst at that point.

"Where's my good friend Joey?" asked the captain with a very heavy French accent. "It is still his boat, is it not?"

Alex breathed a sigh of relief and pointed to the Antiguan boat registration which had been updated with Rob and Joey as co–owners of the vessel. "Actually, Joey has a new partner... Rob Mariner... from Chicago. Joey's off on business and I'm running the boat for Rob. He's doing a little cruising with his fiancée. His first trip to St. Barth," Alex smiled.

"Wellll.... in that case, we must meet for a petite punch, any friend of Joey's is a friend of mine. I must give him a little taste of our island's customs before he leaves. And you, may I please call you, Alexandria? Would you consider joining me for a drink at five when I finish. I must say, you are the most attractive yacht captain that's walked through these doors since I've been assigned here."

Although caught off guard, Alex was quite flattered by his obvious flirtation, not to mention a little embarrassed, since, other than wolf whistles from the native boys, she always presented a facade of unapproachability. "Well... Captain Reneau," said Alex uncertainly, "It's Alex."

"Please... call me Jacques *(pronounced Zock),*" he said smiling broadly.

"I'll be sure to pass along the invitation to Rob. What if I meet you at Le Select, five–thirty?"

"Excellent!" replied Jacques, quite happy that she had accepted his invitation. "How long do you stay on our little island?"

"Unfortunately, only tonight. We'll be anchoring in Columbier tomorrow, and we plan to head to St. Maarten tomorrow evening for Carnival," answered Alex, sincerely disappointed that she wouldn't be spending more time on the island.

"Too bad," said Jacques equally disappointed. "But I insist on you docking here tonight, free of charge," he said gesturing to the space right in front of his office. "Under one condition though."

Alex looked at him almost afraid to ask.

" Only if you agree to have dinner with me also?"

89

Alex froze. It was her first invitation for a real date in years and she was uncertain how to answer. Finally, she took a deep breath and smiled, "I'll see you at five-thirty," she heard herself say as she collected her documents and headed for the door.

Leaving the Port Captain's office, she felt quite excited by the fact that this would be the first date she'd allowed herself in the islands since she'd broken up with Michael – feeling distrustful of the type of expatriates that the islands tended to attract. Especially, after her experience with him – learning of his alias identity. But then Jacques was a government official, how bad could he be if he wore a French uniform? But then again, as suspicious as she was of Joey's true profession, Alex was a little dubious of the captain's obvious friendship with Joey, being that he was on the opposing team. But then in the islands, a little payola went a long way in building friendships and working relationships. And then again, Alex felt she needed a distraction for Sydney's sake. Maybe a shill* would make Sydney realize that Alex's interest truly lay elsewhere.

Knowing that by now Rob would likely need help to pry Sydney away from the shops, she went looking for them to let Rob know that she had arranged a taxi to show them around the island. Alex had guessed right, since Sydney had already done nearly several thousand dollars-worth of damage in the French clothing and jewelry stores, and Rob was beginning to sweat about the state of his finances, since Sydney seemed to take the name on his Carte Blanche card quite literally. Even before Alex found them in the Cartier shop, Rob had decided that it was time to find a way to distract her from spending any more of his money and was quite relieved when Alex turned up. At least if she were in a taxi, instead of on foot, she may not be able to do quite as much damage to Rob's plastic. Alex was quite relieved when she finally loaded them into the little VW minivan for the afternoon trip over the hill, telling Rob that she would have the boat on the dock at three-thirty when the charter boats left for the day. She even slipped the driver, Old Yugo, a twenty-dollar tip, fully aware of what he was in for. By the time Rob had torn her away from the stores and gotten her settled in the bus with her duty-free purchases, Sydney was as happy as if she were the only shopper at a 50% off sale at Sacks Fifth Avenue. Somehow, the morning's fish calamity had been forgotten and Sydney was already planning the design of her new engagement ring and Rob could hear the sound of the cash register tolling the sale.

Alex promised Rob that she would go to the Gendarmerie to report the incident with the barracuda and Sydney's missing diamond, in hopes that his insurance might actually cover it as a passenger's loss. She had Yugo drop her at the police station on his way to his first sightseeing stop in Corossol just around the bend from town. Yugo explained to Rob and Sydney about the unique little

---

* SHILL – *One acting as a decoy, especially for a cheater.*

ISLAND FEVER

fishing village just two minutes to the north-west of Gustavia Harbor – unique in that the women of the village still dress in starched black Puritan-like garb, complete with little white bonnets – many never having even traveled the two kilometers into the main town of Gustavia. They passed their days, when not in church, weaving hats, baskets, and placemats from latania palm fronds to sell to the tourists who pass through their streets as predictably as the sun rises and sets. Of course, their wares, which were hung from the walls of their homes, were an open invitation for Sydney who spent nearly an hour going from house to house buying everything she could find – even convincing one of the poor little ladies to sell her the cap off her head so that she might have her picture taken with one of them wearing the little white bonnet. Luckily for Rob, it was tough to do too much financial damage since the straw goods were quite inexpensive compared to the chic French boutiques in town. Sydney had been a windfall for those little Puritan women since before she had finished, she had bought more of the local straw handicrafts in one outing than they had likely sold in a year. It seemed that she was finally regaining her strength and feeling her old self again since shopping was the one therapy that never failed to boost her spirits and leave her in a good mood – aside from a night with the Benny Monster.

  Once Sydney had bought three of everything the Corossolinian women had to offer for her friends and family, she was starting to grow quite bored with the quaint local culture and was once again looking for something a bit more, chic. Her friend, she said, had recently returned from a trip with her boyfriend to St. Barth where they had spent a week at an upscale boutique hotel – Manapany, in Anse de Cayes, where she had managed to rub elbows with a French movie star and dine next to a geriatric rock star. This modest little hotel, and one or two others, not to mention a restaurant or two, were the most likely locales to go star gazing during the day or night.

  Sydney and Rob stepped from the van in front of the understated lobby, which didn't appear to be filled at that moment with celestial elite. Disappointed, Sydney led Rob down the walkway to the pool deck and restaurant, hoping to spot a familiar face or two in order that she might be able to return home with stories of lunching with the rich and famous. But to her great disappointment, the dining room was quite void of anyone resembling important personages and the pool deck was equally lacking in celebrity status. In fact, to Sydney's dismay, the minute boutique was not even open in which she could purchase a few baubles to prove that she had actually been there. As far as Sydney was concerned, she was quite ready to do lunch at Chez Francine, once she had gotten a glimpse from the hillside of Columbier Bay, where the Rockefellers had built their reclusive encampment which even today, as Sydney pointed out, was inaccessible by road. Obediently, Yugo headed the little van back up the hill to finish the tour around Columbier.

Meanwhile, Alex stood at the desk in the Gendarmerie filling out an official report, as best she could translate the French questionnaire about the fish that had absconded with Sydney's twenty-thousand-dollar diamond. When she had finished, she handed the report to the Gendarme in charge who reviewed it routinely then removed his glasses and looked at Alex.

"I know this is out of the ordinary," explained Alex in an attempt to look a little less foolish. "You see, I need a report for our insurance company. "

"Oui, oui Madamoiselle, but how do you know zat zis was a Franch fish zat ate ze dimonnnd?"

Suddenly, Alex didn't feel quite as foolish anymore as she fought back a snicker, "Well, it was in your harbor sir."

"Oui, oui, I unzersand, but we cannot control ze comings and goings of ze fish in our waturs, and onless you can prove zat ze crime was perpeetrated by a Franch fish, zen I am terribly afraid zat I will be onaable to process ze repor," said the Gendarme with all finality as he handed Alex the report and placed an out to lunch sign on the desk.

CHAPTER TEN

Some Otters Don't Swim

*"From a certain point onward, there is no longer any turning back.
That is the point that must be reached."*

Frank Kafka

Even though he appreciated the quaint rural countryside they were touring on St. Barth, Rob's mind was busy touring a slightly less tranquil expedition regarding his and Sydney's future.

"What was I thinking?" thought Rob to himself as Sydney chirped away in poor Yugo's ear about the beautiful scenery and the island's charm. "I should have known that Sydney wasn't cut out for this sort of life. Now I'm really going to have to pay the price. Not only am I going to have to pay off the diamond that fish just ate for breakfast, but I'm going to have to buy her a new one," mourned Rob silently. "Maybe she won't know the difference between the real thing and a zirconia. No, no, that'll never work. Sydney can smell a diamond a mile away. That's not even taking into consideration what it's going to cost to appease her and make up for the last twenty-four hours, and the fact that I even bought the boat in the first place. What am I going to do now? She's never going to give me the remaining ten weeks we agreed to get this venture up and running."

Rob immediately realized the futility of their little sightseeing expedition, since he knew that between the Valium and the rum, Sydney would likely not even have any recall of the trip. But he also knew that it was keeping her away from any more island shops until, luckily for him, they closed for their three-hour lunch break at noon. As far as Rob was concerned, he was quite happy to extend the tour as long as possible, even to the point of paying Yugo off to take her around the island a second time since Sydney was so far gone that she wouldn't even notice that they were passing the exact same terrain they had traversed earlier. Rob figured that if he could stall until lunch, and keep her out of any retail establishments through the island's siesta time, he might be able to prevent another uncontrolled shopping spree. What he didn't know was that the restaurant had their own little boutique which conveniently stayed open during déjeuner *(lunch)* so that its patrons might leisurely shop while dining in their little beach-side bistro. To top it off, Rob's plan was flawed by the fact that Sydney was getting quite ravenous since there was little left in her stomach from the day before other than the morning's rum and the Valium and her hangry was beginning to show. So, Yugo was instructed to find the most direct route to their rendezvous with the langouste du jour that awaited them at that infamous little beach café. Even the thought of eating was a bit much for Rob to stomach with the morning's excitement, but then again that bottle of chardonnay sounded pretty good to him right about then, since he was in dire need of something to dull his nerves.

"Your wish be my command, lady," said Yugo obligingly as he turned the van around and headed back over the road towards the airport and Bai de St. Jean. Now, the locals on St. Barth were fully aware that driving over the road along the hilltop overlooking the airport without watching for approaching aircraft was about as dangerous as crossing a railroad track with no warning signals, wearing blinders. Yugo, one of the few black men living on the island, had been driving a taxi there for most of his life and knew all too well to look before crossing the approach to the runway, which was at the base of the fifty-foot slope below the road. However, since Sydney was making such a racket in the seat behind him pointing out amazing points of interest along the way, Yugo was somewhat distracted from his driving and never even saw the fast-approaching Air Guadeloupe, Twin Otter until it had bounced off the top of the van, leaving two rather large tire tracks embedded in the roof of his VW bus.

Due to the fact that the runway was not much longer than a football field, it was necessary that the plane make a touchdown directly at the base of the hill, or they would find the length of the runway insufficient to safely land the aircraft on dry land. Thanks to the impediment of their approach by Yugo's van, the Otter's landing gear made contact with the runway just a split second too late, meaning that its available concrete was about to run out just short of its ability to bring this agile little craft to a halt before landing in the drink. Had they been shooting for a different kind of touchdown however the Otter would have surely scored six points with an open field all the way to the end zone. So, Rob, Sydney, and Yugo watched helplessly from the hilltop above the airport as the Air Guadeloupe shuttle skidded to a stop in about four feet of seawater in the aquamarine bay of St. Jean *(Baie de St. Jean),* looking much like a toy airplane floating in a child's swimming pool. Unfortunately, this was not the type of Otter which was equipped for swimming and it shortly ended up resting on the sandy bottom in waist deep water. Luckily no one was hurt aside from a booby bird that was lazily floating in the shallow water at the end of the runway. Strangely enough, the prospect of sailing that last fifteen miles to St. Maarten aboard the Island Fever was not looking so bad after all to a suddenly sobered Sydney.

By this point Rob knew that if he didn't get Sydney to lunch, he would surely begin to regret it, so he slipped Yugo another twenty to get them to the restaurant as quickly as possible in hopes of distracting her from the day's overwhelming events. The traditional spiny lobster dinner avec pomme frites and a nice French chardonnay at the little beach bistro, which was nothing more than a wooden deck right on the sand in the middle of a spectacular beach, seemed to do the trick. Since they were only a few yards away from the end of the runway, they had afternoon ringside seats to view the removal of the plane's passengers and their luggage from the bay. This spectacle was by now a pretty common occurrence on St. Barth, since at least one or two times a year some private pilot over-shot the touchdown spot on the runway. As far as commercial aircraft went, this was a slightly unusual occurrence since the Twin Otter pilots were well seasoned bush pilots, quite used to challenging landing sites. Rob wondered if this fumbled touchdown would be written off to pilot err, or Sydney interference.

Rob and Sydney sat and watched as the island emergency crew, evacuated the plane's slightly shaken passengers into rubber dinghies and shuttled them and their luggage ashore as if it were the normal way in which to disembark the aircraft. Of course, Rob was trying hard to be sure that Sydney didn't notice him catching a glimpse every now and then, of the topless women on the beach – a long-standing French tradition – so he tried hard to focus his attention on the rescue.

Back in Gustavia, Alex and Raymond were enjoying a 'Cheeseburger in Paradise' at Le Select's hamburger shack and, although neither of them were big drinkers, they had both already polished off their third Red Stripe *(Jamaican beer)*. Raymond had spent the morning compiling his grocery list for St. Maarten and his upcoming charter menu, and Alex had spent the entire morning dealing with island bureaucracy. Having failed miserably at filing her police report for Sydney's accident with the St. Barth police, she had gone back to Jacques' office to plead her case. He had found her recap of her conversation with the gendarmes quite hilarious and had quickly filled out an official report for her, hoping of course, to impress her with his ability to supersede their decision to close the case of the diamond-eating, <u>French</u> barracuda.

While they were sitting there finishing off their last cold one, Yugo drove up in his dented mini bus looking about ten shades paler than he had when they had last seen him. He walked past them in a daze and headed straight for the bar, downing two double shots of rum before joining them at the table with a beer. Of course, news travels fast on a small island, via the Coconut Telegraph,* and Alex and Raymond had already heard about the Twin Otter's attempted swim across Baie de St. Jean. The minute Alex saw Yugo drive up with a huge tire mark across the roof of his van she knew immediately what had caused the crash. Yugo was still shaking from the experience – more from the time spent with Sydney in the car than the actual accident itself.

"Remin' me not to take any fares from you in de future," Yugo said to Alex in his French Creole accent. "Word's out, I don't tink you be findin' anyone to pick up your friends at de restaurant. You best be gettin' a rental car and fetch dem yourself," said Yugo. "Dat woman be dangerous. She talk more dan a gaggle of women on a church picnic," lamented Yugo, looking at his shiny new van with the roof caved in, and filled to the brim with packages and straw goods. "All mash up," said Yugo shaking his head at the sight, "All mash up. It pains me to even tink abou' pickin' she back up."

A waiter walked over and sat Yugo's burger and fries in front of him as Alex sympathetically patted him on the back. She peeled off a hundred-dollar bill and handed it to him. "Here's your fee, Yugo.

"But I not finish the trip for you."

"That's okay, you earned it," answered Alex, "Raymond'll help you unload the van and take the packages out to the boat. Sorry," she said looking at him as if she wished she could somehow make it up to him. "I guess we'd better get a car," sighed Alex to Raymond. "I'll take care of it while you get the stuff onto the boat."

"No problem," answered Raymond. "Just tell me where you'd like me to put everything.

That was one question Alex couldn't answer – she just buried her face in her hands as if she'd possibly bitten off more than she was prepared for. "Would you mind dropping me at the airport when you've finished your lunch so I can pick up a car," Alex asked Yugo cautiously, expecting to be turned down.

*COCONUT TELEGRAPH — Now the 'coconut telegraph,' – a form of communication which is somewhat akin to the jungle drum, is the only reliable means of communication in the islands and is far more efficient than any inter-island telephone system. In the islands, should you need to send an urgent message, just tell any two locals in the morning and by the next afternoon it will have spread for at least a two-hundred-mile radius; within the 'Yachty'** community, wait a week and it will have crossed an ocean. One should be certain however, never to depend on the carrier pigeon in the West Indies, since in the islands, pigeon is considered a delicacy.
**YACHTY— Is the word used in the islands to describe that strange breed of transient sailor whose worldly possessions are circumscribed by their vessel and whose definition of home is wherever they choose to drop their anchor for more than a twenty-four-hour period.

"You, my dear lady, I take anywhere. She be anoder story," replied Yugo, shaking his head.

Once she'd picked-up the rental car, Alex realized if she didn't take a nap she would surely collapse before her date at five-thirty, so she climbed in the dinghy with Raymond and motored out to the boat for an hour of shut-eye. This would allow the charter boats time to leave the island at three before moving the Island Fever onto the dock. It would be tricky with the state of her engine, but Alex was skilled at wrangling those cats into doing what she wanted. Besides, being on the dock would make her life so much easier. Not only would it mean that she didn't have to be Rob and Sydney's caretaker, she would be able to avoid, at all costs, another traumatic dinghy ride with Sydney.

By the time Rob and Sydney had finished their two-hour lunch, Sydney had emptied the restaurant's little bikini shack, care of Rob's charge card. So, with a full day of shopping under her belt, Sydney was in rare form and ready to brave returning to the Island Fever, especially since Alex had promised that the boat would be on the dock when they arrived.

As much as Rob cringed when he signed the last credit card receipt, he was quite relieved to have gotten her smiling once again. "Thank God for clothing," thought Rob. "It's the only thing that seems to keep her happy. Even more than me," he said under his breath. "This may be a great way to appease her but it's getting a bit expensive. When we shopped in the States it was on daddy's plastic... now it's on mine and I'm in no position to pay for new sail ties let alone a new wardrobe," reasoned Rob." "Why is it that money's not an issue until there's no more coming in? Now I know what my friends meant when they talked about the cost of marriage. And I thought dating was expensive. How am I ever going to keep this woman happy?" Rob asked himself. "It's never crossed my mind before that I might not be able to afford a woman. Now I understand what Joey meant when he said he'd take a boat over a woman any day when it came to high maintenance. And I thought the Island Fever was expensive," he grumbled to himself, as he made the third trip with packages from the boutique to the rental car – driven by Alex, which left Rob wondering what had happened to Yugo.

Alex's heart sank when she saw Sydney climb into the car with even more packages – quite content and ready to continue on with their adventure aboard the Island Fever. She had expected Rob to load her onto the first flight to St. Maarten, however considering the earlier fiasco at the airport, she could see why Sydney had opted for the safer bet of sail over air travel. Alex steeled herself for the onslaught as she drove Rob and Sydney back to town in silence – she and Rob were silent that is, since no one could get a word past Sydney who was still on her high – an uncontrolled shopping spree topped off by the bottle of chardonnay, the Valium, and the three petite punches. Alex deposited them at a little patisserie for café overlooking the harbor as she and Raymond weighed anchor and moved the Island Fever onto the dock. Luckily, there was enough space now that the charter boats were gone for her to come alongside since the Island Fever's sterns were so low and narrow as to make it a challenge to board when she was tied stern to the dock. Alex felt comfortable that she was not taking advantage of Jacque's generosity to use the dock for the evening, since they would be gone early the next morning and would not interfere with the charter boats' return at noon.

Once they had secured their dock lines, Alex took out the awning and tied it over the cockpit for a little afternoon shade and protection from the occasional rain cloud that might decide to blow over. She had done her duty for the day as Captain, as far as she was concerned, and she was determined to squeeze in another brief nap before she met Captain Jacques for a drink, so she left Rob and Sydney to fend for themselves. She was not their tour guide, nor Sydney's valet, so she felt no further responsibility for them that evening.

Just as she had finally drifted off to sleep in her port aft bunk the screaming started outside her bridge-deck* portlight. At the sound of Sydney's screams, Alex bolted upright in her bunk throwing open the deck hatch rather than wasting time climbing out of her bunk and up the through the companionway. In a second she was on deck trying to focus her eyes in the glare of the setting sun. Sydney was screeching at the top of her lungs as Rob dangled from the end of a sail cover on the main boom between the hulls – his legs trailing in the water. He had apparently been attempting to impress Sydney by putting on the sail covers and had forgotten to cleat in the main sheet to secure that the boom remained hard to starboard where he could reach it in order to lace up the cover. When it swung amidships from his body weight leaning against it, Rob went with it. It was actually quite a comical sight until she saw the cause for Sydney's seemingly unwarranted alarm. Cutting through the water a few yards behind the boat was a dorsal fin headed straight for Rob. It seemed that the feeding frenzy was well underway on the discarded remains of the afternoon slaughter of cattle on the dock, and Rob was about to be dessert. Without saying a word, Alex jumped into the cockpit and started pulling on the starboard main sheet as hard as she could, winching Rob in like wet laundry on an urban clothesline. By the time she had gotten him back to the hull, Raymond had emerged from his bunk in time to pull Rob back on board just as the five-foot bull shark swam past between the hulls. Alex turned to assure Sydney that Rob was okay, only to find her passed out cold on the deck. Finally, for the first time that day, Sydney was quiet.

"Nothing like an afternoon swim to get the ole juices flowing," Alex

*BRIDGE-DECK – Bridge-deck meaning the deck which is suspended over water that spans the gap separating the two hulls of a catamaran.

said, smiling sarcastically. "Does trouble follow you everywhere she goes or is this just a coincidence?" Alex asked Rob.

"I don't know, but maybe we should get off this island before one of us gets eaten," said Rob, about to soil his pants.

Without a thought, Raymond picked up a bucket of water from the deck and poured it over Sydney's head as Alex watched, wishing like hell that she'd had the pleasure. Sydney sat up gasping for air – sputtering like an engine with a broken shear pin.

Alex dressed and left Rob to wait for Sydney to shower and change into her grossly over-dressed evening attire. Although a bit late, Alex made it to the bar in time to still catch Jacques for a round of petite punch with the owner of the establishment and his son, not to mention numerous other regulars. Alex was quite enjoying the attention she was being paid by Jacques and was feeling, quite rightly, as attractive as she looked that evening, since she'd actually worn a dress and makeup, and had even worn her hair down. When Rob and Sydney finally arrived, he didn't even recognize her until she called his name and motioned for them to sit down.

"So, you're the young lady that caused all the excitement today," said Jacques, laughing good heartedly as he poured Sydney a shot of rum.

Sydney hesitated taking it since she was quite hung over from her morning's medication, but she shrugged and downed it figuring it might actually help the pain between her eyes. Rob was relieved that she had not taken his comment as an insult and that she seemed to be so overwhelmed from the day's events, she had mellowed into an unusual, manageable state. By the time they had gotten to the little restaurant called Maya's on Public Beach behind the commercial dock – she had graduated to champagne and was actually becoming quite tolerable, Alex thought.

"So, tell me Rob, where's my friend Joey. And how on earth did you convince him to sell you half of his boat. I would have thought you'd have to kill him to get him to let go of a single share of his baby," joked Jacques.

"Actually," laughed Rob, "He does seem to have disappeared... I have no idea where he is. He left the night I wrote him the check and I haven't heard from him since."

"See," chortled Jacques, "Maybe you killed him and disposed of the body."

"Well then," lamented Rob sarcastically. "I guess that means his ghost cashed the check," sending Jacques into roaring laughter.

By the main course, Jacques was holding Alex's hand and the group had already polished off a bottle of champagne and a bottle of wine. And Rob, who was starting to feel a little tipsy himself, was feeling an unexplained surge of jealousy rise in him every time he saw Jacques smile at Alex and she returned the gesture – even if Sydney was hanging all over him in an exuberant embrace. It really bothered Rob that Alex was quite obviously enjoying the attention she was receiving.

"*I can't believe how incredible she looks tonight,*" *thought Rob, totally ignoring Sydney who kept whispering in his ear and rubbing his leg trying to get his undivided attention.*

Alex had become an undeniable distraction for him that evening. Rob had never seen Alex dressed in anything other than a bikini, shorts or sweats, and there she was in a dress, heels, and makeup. For the first time, Rob realized – Alex was really quite beautiful. And, although Alex found Jacques quite attractive, she was having trouble taking her eyes off of Rob.

Rob had asked Alex if it would be possible to move the boat to a deserted anchorage before dawn, to avoid an early morning shopping spree in Gustavia before they could get the boat off the dock. So, late that night after dinner, Jacques escorted the Island Fever, around the point to Columbier Bay with more selfish reasons in mind than making certain Alex was safe. Once Alex had set the anchor, Jacques convinced her to go for a midnight stroll along the beach in Rockefeller Bay. Taking full advantage of his official standing on the island, Jacques docked the patrol boat alongside the private Rockefeller dock in hopes of impressing her. He took her hand as they strolled along the surf talking about the island and the Island Fever, which Jacques was impressed to learn Alex had helped build. Alex talked easily and laughed comfortably with Jacques until he asked about her family. That was where Alex turned cold – her personal life was just that – personal, and she was not willing to discuss it with a man she'd only known less than twenty-four hours.

Back on the boat, Rob couldn't sleep and had left Sydney snoring away in the bunk, and had gone up on deck to stare at the stars – wishing Alex were there to stare with him. But, what in fact Rob was staring at was the shore where he knew Alex and Jacques had gone – alone. It had been a long time since he'd felt jealousy towards anyone other than Dirk at his reunion with Julie Anne. But tonight, it welled up in him – gnawed at him – and made him wonder what he was doing engaged to Sydney. Rob was confused – torn by the sensation brewing in the pit of his stomach.

"*Of course, I'm doing the right thing marrying Sydney,*" *Rob reasoned.* "*But then why do I have this overwhelming desire to race ashore and make Alex come back to the boat?*" *he questioned.*

The moon wasn't full enough for him to see them on shore, but Rob sensed Jacques' arms around Alex and his lips on hers as they kissed on the beach. Indeed, Alex sat next to Jacques with his arm around her just above the hightide mark, and she did let him kiss her. And although his French accent and his uniform enticed her, something was missing – something important. That spark of raw physical and spiritual attraction that unfortunately just wasn't there – only an intellectual inquisitiveness that prompted her to pursue it a little further.

Actually, her thoughts were elsewhere. In fact, they were still back on the Island Fever in the master birth. Alex wondered how Rob could actually bring himself to marry Sydney. She knew somehow, she had to save him from his fate – somehow, she had to find a way. But unbeknownst to her, fate would intervene and assist Rob with his newest dilemma. Did he really want to marry the woman who was already known in the Caribbean as a one-woman demolition team?

Around four in the morning Alex had still not returned to the boat. But Rob was so tired he'd fallen asleep in the deck-house on the settee and never heard Alex, who'd come in just before dawn. Of course, Alex had yet to get any real sleep for the last forty-eight hours but she felt refreshingly revived by her brief affair d'amour.

Morning came way too early for Rob. When the island roosters and peacocks started crowing at the first hint of daylight, he sat up wondering if Alex had ever made it back to her bunk. He was actually quite surprised when she appeared in the deck-house around eight all bright and chipper, and quite unlike herself – refused Raymond's fresh brewed coffee. Jacques arrived in his patrol boat by nine to take Alex for café and croissants before he cleared them out to take their leave to St. Maarten. By the time she had returned to the boat at eleven, Raymond had finished his morning meditations and the breakfast dishes, and was removing the awning and sail covers. Alex had brought back fresh pastries for Rob and Sydney, courtesy of Jacques, as a small token of their new friendship.

As she was kissing Jacques goodbye, Rob stumbled out of the head, showered and dressed in his baggies and T-shirt. Of course, the sight of Alex kissing Jacques did not leave him in the best mood nor did his aching head from the previous night's libations. By now, I was wondering what it would really take for Rob and Alex to acknowledge the rapidly increasing gravity between them – a little magic that we here on 'The Otherside' are allowed to perform when the occasion arises.

A hungover Rob gulped down a handful of aspirin with a third black espresso and deposited himself on the starboard jib winch seat. Unable to speak for a good thirty minutes, he watched while Alex readied the boat motor to pull the boat in closer to shore so they could have a quick swim to wash away their morning hangovers. Alex dropped a stern anchor and motored up close to shore dropping her bow anchor just off the beach – allowing the boat to drift back slightly on her bow anchor rode* while taking in the scope** on the stern anchor. The bay dropped off quickly from shore allowing a cat to anchor, on a calm day, just yards off the sand. That way she figured Rob and Sydney would be able to wade ashore and avoid the dinghy altogether. The Rockefeller estate was private property and since they had never built a road to it, the access to the beach had remained unapproachable by land to the public, unless one wanted to make the forty-minute hike in the hot sun from Anse des Flamandes. But, since all beach-front in the French West Indies was considered public domain, the beach at Rockefeller Bay was technically deemed for public use even if the current owners of Rockefeller Bay, one of several owners since it was sold by the Rockefellers in the seventies, owned the entire point.

Rob was quite relieved to have retreated to their deserted anchorage for the day to avoid any further unnecessary expenditures or additional excess baggage – after all the deserted bay technique had worked where their rock-n-rollers were concerned, why shouldn't the same principle of simple availability apply here? By twelve, Sydney had finally regained consciousness. She arose from the bunk looking like hell – her makeup all smeared and her hair looking as if several bats had nested there. It took her an hour to put herself together and make her appearance for the day, in one of her many new designer bikinis and pareos,*** hoping to catch a glimpse of some elite inhabitants of their morning's anchorage.

Alex suggested that they go ashore and do a little exploring since the water here was relatively safe and the property was filled with exotic birds such as peacocks and some type of rare Chinese geese. Uncertainly, Sydney unwound her pareo and climbed down the ladder to swim the few yards to shore with Rob. Raymond went below to bake some quiches for lunch, and Alex stretched out on a deck cushion to read a little poetry and get a little sun – first making sure that Rob and Sydney had reached the shore safely before she lost herself in her book.

On shore Rob and Sydney walked along the beach towards the estate house and dock on the western-most point, picking up broken shells and beach glass. Alex watched from the boat as the peacocks wandered the hillside fanning their tails and strutting for the females – their screeching call piercing the silence of the peaceful scenery. Not that different, thought Alex, than guys like Joey who used their physical possessions to attract members of the opposite sex.

Sydney's curiosity was getting the best of her about the 1940's house that she'd heard so much about and she insisted on getting a closer look as she

*RODE — The anchor line consisting of either rope, chain, or cable.
**SCOPE — The length or ratio of anchor rode in relation to the depth of the water. In good conditions, four times the depth of the water is the rule-of-thumb, however in bad conditions the scope should be increased to as much as ten to one.
***PAREO — A traditional Polynesian wrap which is also known in some cultures as a sarong, and has been adopted by our culture as a designer bathing suit cover. It's a simple piece of fabric which is tied around one's body in an unlimited number of ways.

dragged Rob along up the hill toward the house. Suddenly, from out of nowhere, a pack of huge white birds appeared from behind the house marching down the hillside at an alarming rate, shouting loud cries which sounded like fussy old ladies chasing a purse thief.

Before Rob realized what was happening, the huge, three-foot-tall geese were upon them screeching and pecking as they chased them like watch dogs off the property. Alex heard the screeching of the birds but paid little attention since she was quite used to the sound, having anchored here more than once before. That is, she paid no attention until she heard Rob and Sydney's screams coming from the beach as they ran just ahead of the attacking, angry birds. She couldn't help but snicker a little at the sight of Sydney running in an undignified manner from six angry geese. However, she did feel an obligation to Rob to jump in the dinghy and go to their rescue just as Rob and Sydney dove in the water to escape the birds who stopped just short of the water's edge – having done their job to keep trespassers off the property. Alex killed the engine as the two swam desperately towards the dinghy. Rob reached it first and climbed over the rubber side as gracefully as a seal might waddle into an automobile. He turned and pulled Sydney aboard the very same vessel that she had sworn to never set foot in again, but was at that moment quite grateful to climb aboard.

"Get me out of this place," screamed Sydney, as she rubbed the beak marks on her posterior where the geese had nipped at her as she ran. It seemed it was time to leave St. Barth behind and head on their journey to the 'friendly island,' of St. Maarten.

CHAPTER ELEVEN

Guilt

"Difficulties are the very road to immortality."

Lao Tzu

Rob was feeling quite guilty at that point. After all, Sydney had experienced so much trauma in the first forty-eight hours of her visit to Paradise, not to mention how worried he was about appeasing her. He was hoping that wining and dining her and dancing 'til dawn in St. Maarten, not to mention a little gambling in one of the island's casinos, might help him make it up to her. He was a bit concerned however, about the wonderland of duty-free shopping in Philipsburg, but luckily, Raymond had told him that the stores were all closed due to Carnival – at least on the Dutch side. If he could keep her away from the French side, which didn't observe Carnival on the same date, Sydney's shopping might actually be limited to a few airport trinkets on her way out, three days hence – a moment that would come none too soon for Rob.

To Rob's relief, the downwind sail to St. Maarten was as uneventful and boring as a White Sox game with no runs, and Sydney was sleeping like a baby on the foredeck thanks to her trusty prescription of Valium, which she'd topped off with one of Raymond's famous margaritas. Although the Island Fever was riding an inch or so lower on her waterline due to their added cargo, life was tolerable for the moment, and Rob was quite optimistic about the prospects of a pleasant few days in St. Maarten. He was convinced that they were over the worst of the storm, but Rob had never been through a hurricane. Little did he know that he was merely in the deceivingly calm eye of the storm, and that brutal punch was yet to come. Hurricane Sydney had arrived early in the season, and Rob was soon to learn why, for years, meteorologists had only named tropical storms and hurricanes after women. With today's advances in social etiquette and twentieth century equality of the sexes, women had demanded that men share in the blame for one of mother nature's most destructive forces and the custom of alternating every other storm between men's and women's names had become the accepted standard.

Alex allowed Rob to take the helm once she had set the spinnaker,* but she stood close to him as she helped him to get the of steering on a spinnaker run. With a following sea and the four thousand square feet of canvas, or mylar, which billowed out ahead of the boat pulling it at wind speed over the wave tops and down through the trough of the following wave, steering was a tricky proposition. Flying a kite was a little unruly, but eventually Rob started to get the hang of it. A catamaran was light enough to ride more or less on top of the waves and due to the length of the Island Fever, which spanned several wave crests at any given moment since the waves in the Atlantic ran quite close together, this downwind sail offered a smoother ride than a Cadillac Seville. Whenever a large wave caressed the sterns of the boat, it would raise it with its forward momentum and carry it quite some distance, not unlike a surfer at Waikiki – until it decided to leave off its playmate and carry on its way northwest to the Virgin Islands. There it would wash up on some pristine beach for some surfer hoping to catch something that could qualify as a real wave in the Caribbean. Although not known for its surfing as the Hawaiian Islands are, the Caribbean makes up in its reliable sailing what it fails to offer the consummate surfer.

It took some real effort, steering downwind for one to master the feel for the subtle course corrections needed to keep a large cat traveling in a straight line. A new helmsman's first response was to overcorrect the yaw, diverting one from their desired course, as many inexperienced navigators of life might do. This was already becoming a habit with Rob – drastically overcorrecting his course when he felt as if he needed to make a change. What he hadn't yet learned was that sometimes one must adapt to the nature of things and give one's vessel a chance to correct itself.

I witnessed it as a captain of my own ship in my last life, as many a sailor overcompensated for a course correction at sea, as well as in life. This is life. This is not to say that I was an expert at this myself, since there was many a

---

*SPINNAKER — (Also called chute or kite) Generally a large symmetrical headsail designed for sailing downwind, although more and more boats today carry asymmetrical spinnakers which do not require a spinnaker pole. Unlike a jib or genoa, the spinnaker is attached to the boat at only three points instead of all the way down the forestay.** The head is attached at the top of the mast by a halyard*** just like other headsails, and the two clews, which run via sheets through turning blocks**** to the aft deck, are attached to a winch in the cockpit. A spinnaker pole is attached to the mast on one end and the windward tack of the spinnaker to keep the chute full and under control.*

time that I mistakenly steered the wrong course, like leaving the love of my life and the mother of my child behind, and making the decision much too late to return for them.

Alex's arm would brush against Rob's as she would offer a small correction of the helm to Rob – keeping him from collapsing the spinnaker as he passed nervously between Grouper rocks and left Ile de Fourche***** on his starboard quarter. Rob found himself intentionally under-correcting his steering every now and then in order to elicit Alex's assistance, welcoming the feel of her warm soft skin against his forearm, or his chest if he managed to turn just right as she leaned over to take the wheel in order to fill the spinnaker.

Alex felt it too, that electric charge that she had noticed between them before – something more than static electricity since there were far too many negative ions in the air to create static in this humid climate. Every now and then, strands of Alex's long blond hair escaped her French braid and brushed across Rob's face, teasing him with a taste of what it would be like to feel her on top of him with her hair brushing across his cheek and her firm tanned stomach pressed against his.

Suddenly, Sydney's voice broke the spell as she awoke demanding a Perrier with lime and bitters. Raymond threw in a few Saltines as a precaution to ward off any threat of queasiness that might hamper her pleasant afternoon respite, but by now, Sydney was becoming quite the connoisseur of downwind sailing. As with everything that Sydney found pleasant – it required little or no effort on her part. Caught off guard by his straying fantasies of Alex, Rob quickly deferred the helm to her, once again shifting immediately back into employer/employee mode as he joined Sydney on the foredeck and barked out an order to Raymond to bring them boat drinks.******

Rob saw why the rock wall which stood as a fortress at the entrance to Philipsburg Harbor had been named Point Blanche *(White Point)* since the afternoon sun glowed off the white rock face creating a foreboding, huge white wall. They cleared the point picking up the sight of the Fort atop the Little Bay hill, Alex released the spinnaker halyard as Raymond gathered the beautiful

---

**FORESTAY — Not to be mistaken with foreplay – the wire which runs from the top of the mast to the bow of the boat, or in the case of a catamaran, onto the front crossbar in the center of the boat between the hulls.
***HALYARD — The lines which are used to hoist sails up the mast – assisted by a halyard winch on the mast.
****TURNING BLOCKS — Pulleys or sheaves mounted on deck for rope to run through.
***** ILE DE FOURCHE OR FOURCHE — A privately owned horseshoe shaped isle comprised of steep hills and craggy peaks. The atoll is uninhabited by anything but green goats who rub against the cuprous-oxide from the copper in the rocks. They have devoured everything but the rocks and prickly pear cactus.
*****BOAT DRINKS — Buffett's version of a tall, rum-infused, colorful cocktail.

multicolored sail onto the bow of the boat and forward net,* being careful not to allow the sail of delicate, light–weight fabric to fall into the water, since it could easily be sucked under the hull of the boat. Raymond adeptly bagged the enormous pile of cloth into a sail bag, on island time of course, since Raymond moved no faster than was ever necessary due to his long-term stay in the West Indies. Once he had it in the bag, he unclipped the sheet lines from the clews and clipped them onto the lifelines – then removed the halyard which he also clipped onto the lifeline** – tightening it to avoid its clanging against the mast.

As they rounded the commercial docks in Philipsburg Harbor, they were welcomed to the 'Friendly Island' of St. Maarten by the joyous sounds of Carnival which drifted across the water to greet them, followed by that wonderful breeze – ode de Saltpond Landfill. Whatever its shortcomings were, it seemed that Paradise was a wonderful place where people could dance through the streets laughing and singing and just simply forget about life for a while. Even the immigration officials who finally arrived at the boat around midnight to clear them in had obviously taken the time to enjoy a libation or two, not to mention that infamous Carnival rum punch. They had by that point, however, exceeded the 'singing and dancing in the street stage' and slipped into the 'looking for trouble stage,' and Rob it seemed, just happened to be tonight's sacrificial lamb. This of course was due to the unfortunate fact that the Island Fever's reputation as a party boat had far preceded itself via the aforementioned Coconut Telegraph.

Once on board the Island Fever, those liberally intoxicated immigration officials were unfortunately determined to find anything that seemed to be a questionable controlled substance when one of the officers spied a jar in the galley of what, he pointed out to the other officials, looked suspiciously like ganja. Why it even smelled like weed when they smoked it, but they were so high by that point from the rum it was difficult to say for sure if the herbaceous substance had indeed had any effect on them. But no matter. What was important was that it seemed they had hit the jackpot, or 'jar of pot' as it were. What was really unfortunate was that their confiscated contraband was in fact, innocently enough, one of Raymond's special new blends of sage tea, which is infamously known to look and smell like marijuana. But the duteous officials were unconvinced by Rob and Raymond's pleas for reason and proceeded with an official 'Friendly Island' welcome for the happy troop to the island slammer.

All the way to the town jail Sydney managed to voice her opinion, even over the double 90 hp Mercs on the immigration boat.

*NET — A netting made of lines or straps which are laced between the hulls on a catamaran forward of the bridge-deck in order to cut down the windage under the boat and the possibility of the boat being buried in a wave and capsizing.
**LIFELINE — The wire lines along the sides of a boat that keep passengers and crew from falling overboard – held in place by upright posts called stanchions.

ISLAND FEVER

"ROB! DO SOMETHING! I can't believe this is happening! What's the matter with you! Don't just sit there and let these animals carry us off to jail like some kind of criminals! My God, what if they get wind of this in Chicago, I'll be humiliated! I'll be thrown out of the Ladies Garden Society! Tell them! Tell them who I am and that my father will have their jobs, their heads, and their first born for this! I'm warning you! You just wait and see! You'll be sorry! Rob! Rob, say something! DOOOOOOOO SOOMMMETHING!"

"Sydney," Rob said as calmly as he possibly could but still be heard over the high-pitched whining of Sydney's voice and the engines. "What exactly would you like me to do wearing these dear," Rob asked, displaying his manacled hands as evidence of his lack of control over the situation. Although Rob was nothing short of pissed off by their dubious reception to the island, he managed to keep an outward appearance of cool, calm, and only slightly flustered, if not collected, in an attempt to quell the worries of his crew and passenger, Sydney – realizing of course the absurdity of the situation and its certain resolution come morning. They would just have to suffer through one very uncomfortable night in this austere, disgusting island Bastille. But what Alex knew far better than Rob was that no mistake was ever rectified that simply and easily in the islands, since no West Indian was readily willing to admit to their err. So, when word came the next morning that the jar of contraband had been sent off to be tested on the island of Curacao, the island's governmental seat some thousand miles away, and that due to Carnival all of the island's judges were on vacation and would be unable to hear their case for at least ten days, Alex was not surprised. Rob was to say the least, left in a state of shock, and Sydney, well Sydney nearly ruptured a lung, not to mention their eardrums, screaming at the unfortunate police officer who had been elected to present them with the bad news – then at Rob for getting them into this mess in the first place. Hurricane Sydney it seemed, had just reached a category-five-force winds and there was no stopping her.

Just another small setback, Rob. What's a week or so in the island jail? After all, it was a jail in Paradise. Rob just sat there in disbelief pondering his current predicament – trying to figure out how best to weather the storm until he could find a way to expel his supposed guilt to the uncooperative island officials.

"What the hell am I doing here? I'm not a criminal," thought Rob. "I'm not guilty of anything. We've done nothing wrong. Then why the hell do I feel so guilty? Between Sydney and the police, I've turned from a law abiding, faithful schmuck into a cheating criminal. I've been found guilty by a jury of my peers without even having the justice of a trial. I'm in Kafka hell. Now I know how K felt in 'The Trial.' At least, unlike K, I know why I was arrested," Rob

reasoned. "A bunch of bumbling idiots put me in jail for possession of a condiment, and I don't even cook."

Even though Rob knew he had not committed any *crime (at least none that he remembered),* he was feeling guilty nonetheless – at least about Sydney's suffering. After all, he was the transgressor of Sydney's expectations and Sydney had already tried and sentenced him with no appeals, and no time off for good behavior.

Besides the guilt that Sydney was so generously imposing on Rob, Rob was sufficiently supplementing his own dose of guilt. In fact, on that count, he had the market cornered. Since the time he had been a small child, Rob had invested heavily in this commodity whenever his parents fought on some subject concerning their differences of opinion in raising their only son, being that they never saw eye-to-eye on much of anything. Especially regarding his mother Helen's encouragement in his interest in the more refined things in life, and Rob's aversion to 'man's' work, like driving heavy equipment and animal husbandry. Afterall, Rob had no intention of spending his life married to either the cows or the chickens in his father's barnyard. It was his mother who had taken him to the local cinema every weekend and to any other cultural event which proffered creativity, worldliness, or anything unrelated to farming.

As a child, Rob had always thought there would be no reason for them to fight, or for that matter work so hard if it weren't for him being part of the equation. What Rob didn't understand was that he was simply just the tool they used to annoy and torment one another in their incredibly bored and meaningless lives. In fact, it was only Rob that gave meaning to their existence at all and gave them reason to love, or to be together for that matter. What Rob never realized was that he was the sum total of all that they were, together. Love was something his father had never known how to express – not just to Rob but especially to his wife. She had always longed for and craved physical and emotional contact. In secret she had a dream of a clandestine lover who might one day sweep her away from her trivial existence. Rob knew that she had spent her days writing in her diaries which she locked away each night in a chest that had been her hope chest when she had left home, moved next door, and married Rob's father. Unlike her brave mother Lilly, she had not traversed an ocean with her chest to settle on some foreign shore in search of love. It was instead a place where her hopes and dreams were destined to live under lock and key. She had known from the start that she would never be brave enough to free her dreams from their prison in that chest at the foot of her bed and truly live her life the way she had hoped it could be.

Secretly, Helen thought she might somehow vicariously experience the thrill of adventure through her son's weekly reports of his travels in Paradise. Even though her husband, Thomas, stubbornly disapproved of Rob's stupid and impulsive move. When Rob had called to break the news of his questionable decision to stay in the islands long enough to make his investment pay off, Helen had been thrilled.

"That damned fool," Thomas had said to his wife, returning from a long day of planting, when she dropped the bomb of their son's newest news from the Banana Republic. "What was he thinking, giving up a good paying job and blowing everything he's saved on some stupid boat... on what godforsaken island?!"

Thomas ranted disapproving, as he usually did, of his son's choices. When Rob had gone to work at the Stock Exchange nearly five years before, his father had thought it was the dumbest thing that Rob had ever done, aside from going to college. But this new decision was downright incomprehensible for him – he didn't even know where Antigua was, let alone what the hell a god-found-it catamaran was. On the contrary, Helen was elated that her son – her own flesh and blood, had found the opportunity to escape the domesticity of this human existence and pursue his dreams, something that Helen would never achieve in this lifetime. She could never be as brave as her mother had been when she stepped on that ship alone to come to the new world. Helen had never understood giving up that rich old-world culture to come and live in some barren cornfield. Little did she know what Lilly knew deep in her heart – that to some, a simple cornfield could indeed be Paradise.

CHAPTER TWELVE

Innocence

"Know thyself"

Gateway of the Temple at Delphi

There are only two small differences between being incarcerated in the United States and being imprisoned in the West Indies – the fact that one is definitely 'guilty until proven innocent,' and 'one phone call' – their logic being that the phones probably won't work anyway.

So, needless to say, no one even knew that they were there under lock and key, outside of the hungover immigration officials and the policemen in charge of the prisoners. Rob was never even allowed to notify Fritz, who expected him to pick up passengers four days hence. The worst of it was the fact that poor Alex had to share a cell with Sydney, who bitched continuously over the state of her nails, the nauseating bill of fare, and her disgust over the facilities or lack thereof. The toilet, it seemed, was nothing more than a latrine and the closest thing to running water was a child seen running down the street carrying a bottle of water under his arm. Not to mention a total lack of privacy from the rest of the prisoners which included four locals sleeping off several days of rum punches. Indeed, enough rum punch had already been consumed over the last few days by St. Maartians to float a navy.

Sydney was, to say the least, a novice and an unlikely candidate when it came to tolerating inconveniences – let alone hummiliation. She was having a difficult time coping with the sentence that fate had dealt her, and unlike Alex's gracious acceptance of their temporary state of affairs, Sydney was ready to crack given the conditions and terms of their seemingly irreversible sentence. Especially, since her pharmaceutical arsenal of mood elevating drugs were onboard the Island Fever, and a palmetto bug *(a two inch island cockroach known in the islands as a Bombay Runner)* had just run across her foot.

"I can't believe I listened to you and your harebrained ideas!" Sydney scowled at Rob, "I should have insisted you come home the minute you told me of your stupid decision to buy that... damned penis extension sitting out there in the bay! What was I thinking when I came down here to give you support and a chance to show me how wonderful it was going to be to sail around this pest-ridden part of the God-damned Third World, where restless natives still hunt tourists for sport!" Sydney screamed over the din of the Carnival steel drum band, which just happened to be passing by their open window.

"Hell, we're probably on the dinner menu for all we know! Look at my hair! Look at my face," Sydney sobbed as she grabbed Alex's sunglasses which still hung around her neck, nearly giving her whiplash in order to look at her distorted reflection.

"I need to use the toilet!" cried Sydney, screaming at the officer who was asleep in his chair as she gripped the bars with her fists as if to shake them lose. "For Christ's sake, my bladder's going to burst!" Sydney sobbed.

Taking pity on her, Alex stood and removed the tatty mattress she'd been sitting on from her bunk and held it in front of the hole in the floor designed to serve as a toilet for incarcerated criminals.

"Here, I'll hold this while you go," offered Alex sympathetically, realizing that this woman was just not cut out for this type of 'roughing it.' Of course, Alex had spent most of her life on boats where modesty was not sacred and was used to using anything from a hole in the deck to a bucket as a venue for relieving oneself.

Sydney just looked at her as if she must be mad, "You don't really expect me to go <u>there</u>?!" Howled Sydney on the brink of hysteria.

"It's that or burst," reasoned Alex matter-of-factly.

"Sydney, go ahead and do what Alex says, I'm certain these gentlemen," Rob said referring to the other now curious voyeurs, "Will turn their heads to give you some privacy." Of course, this only served to pique their interest even more as they all turned to stare in Sydney's direction.

Another hour went by until Sydney couldn't hold it another moment and she relented, squatting behind the mattress in utter humiliation as she relieved herself as quickly as possible. "I'll never forgive you for this," cried Sydney rambling on to Rob through the bars as he lay on his bunk, finding himself once again staring at the ceiling wishing there was something to stare at. However, this time, rather than thinking of finding Paradise, he was running through his mind all the possible ways in which to lose Paradise. In fact, he was wondering if this wouldn't be the end of his search for that elusive thing called happiness that he had set out to find oh so many weeks ago. He was beginning to wonder if he wasn't simply doomed to a life of social service to Sydney, instead of a life filled with excitement, fulfilment, happiness, and the freedom to live his life as he chose. He lay there trying to convince himself of his innocence – trying not to hear what Sydney was ranting about. He wasn't certain which he wanted to escape more, that five by eight-foot cell he was lying in, or his impending prison married to Sydney.

The next day came and went, and Rob and his crew remained incarcerated without anyone on the outside aware of their predicament, which was still status-quo and awaiting word from Curacao. However, Sydney's father, Mr. Corandini, concerned that his daughter had not placed her daily check-in call for two days, began to call out the militia – starting with the U.S. Coast Guard, the British and French Navy, as well as every private rescue service he could find for a five-hundred-mile radius around Antigua. When that proved fruitless, he turned to telephoning every immigration official, hospital, and harbor master of every island between Antigua and St. Maarten. It wasn't until the fourth morning of their stay in jail, that the St. Maarten harbor master tore himself away from Carnival long enough to return Mr. Corandini's call, informing him that his daughter had indeed arrived in the port of Philipsburg and was presently incarcerated along with the rest of the Island Fever crew for possession of drugs.

Of course, by now Sydney was in a state of near delirium and was babbling on and on as if she were talking to her hairdresser or her manicurist about her torn cuticles and split ends. Rob was more than a little concerned at this point, as was Alex, and they begged the guard in charge for a doctor to be sent to tend to her. Of course, not only did they not see it as an emergency but the official prison doctor was also off duty for Carnival and wouldn't be back until, as with the judges, next week.

Thanks to his financial where-with-all, and the fact that graft and payola had thrived on the island for centuries, in only a matter of hours of discovering the whereabouts of his precious daughter, Sydney's father had landed at the St. Maarten airport in his private jet, bought his daughter's way out of jail, and swept her off the island – leaving behind the rest of the ship's crew to fend for themselves. Sydney's lack of concern for leaving her fiancé behind bars, was to say the least, the act of a cold-hearted bitch, the fact of which Alex was quick to point out to Rob. Alas, fate had intervened and saved Alex the ugly job of convincing Rob to cut his losses and run. However, Sydney did promise to place a call to Fritz in Antigua and inform him of Rob's predicament. It wasn't until then that Rob started to panic since he was concerned that Sydney would either not remember to call, or conveniently forget in order to spite him for getting her into this situation in the first place – aside from the fact that Mr.

Corandini swore he would see Rob rot in jail for what he'd done to his daughter. Until then he had tried to be strong in order to make Sydney feel secure that he had the situation under control. But in light of Sydney's desertion, Rob was also starting to crack.

"And this is the woman I wanted to marry?" said Rob to no one in particular, astounded that his dear Sydney would do such a thing. "What was I thinking? I must have been so caught up in the image of the perfect couple, that I couldn't see it right in front of my face. How could I miss the fact that this woman has a heart the relative temperature of a reptile. How could a woman that I've been engaged to for six years just desert me at a time like this. Like some criminal?! How could she do this, how could she just leave me here like this?!" Lamented Rob over and over – amazed that the woman whom he'd plan to spend the rest of his life with would simply desert him in his hour of need with no regard whatsoever for his freedom. "But that's a woman for you, running off the minute things don't go exactly the way they want them to. She's left me to rot here in jail for Christ's sake. The least she could have done was to try and convince them we're innocent. I mean, her father's rich enough to buy the goddamn island, let alone our way out of jail. What if she doesn't call Fritz? What if she just forgets... no one will ever even know we're here. We'll just rot away in this hell hole!"

For the next twelve hours a disconsolate Rob poured out his heart to Raymond who listened attentively but seldom responded with anything more than a yeah or a nod, except for an occasional rhetorical observation of what was obvious from the start – to everyone but Rob. "After all, sometimes it takes some bad shit to get to know someone." As usual, Raymond spoke infrequently, but when he did, it generally contained a profuse amount of wisdom. Even Raymond, who never had a bad word to say about anyone, admitted that Sydney was a royal pain in the ass and hardly worth getting torn up over.

Alex, who was immensely relieved that Sydney was no longer sharing that five by eight-foot cell with her, actually began to feel sorry for Rob and finally decided to give it her best effort to offer up a sympathetic ear, and she hoped, some constructive advice.

"Well, what can you really expect from a woman who is more concerned about the condition of her nails than world peace?" offered Alex in a valiant attempt to cheer Rob up, knowing all too well that there was nothing more humiliating than finding out that the object of your love was an unworthy recipient.

"You know," continued Alex, "I've never understood the attraction men have for women who've had ninety percent of their bodies repaired, lifted, modified, or customized. I mean, would you knowingly buy a car that had been rebuilt with parts that weren't supplied by the original manufacturer? Who knows how long they're going to last. And the upkeep must be outrageous. It's kind of like buying retreads instead of Goodyear. I mean, what happens when you have a blow out? You can't exactly change it on the side of the road."

This somehow actually succeeded in raising a faint glimmer of a smile at the corners of Rob's mouth. "Actually, I had taken out an extended warranty on her," attempted Rob with a straight face.

It took some of Alex's best jokes to actually get that full-fledged boyish laugh out of him some time in the wee hours of the morning. For the next three days and nights Rob and Alex talked through the bars, quickly renewing their friendship and realizing, with a measure of consternation, that there was an undeniable attraction between them. And I – well I just sat back and enjoyed watching the magic build between them.

Rob stared at Alex, surprised at the immense frustration he felt at not being able to even touch her. "Look at her sitting there," he thought. "Just look at her... totally natural and wholesome wearing an old T-shirt and shorts and she's still prettier than Sydney with all of her makeup and clothes. Strange, sitting here looking at her, she reminds me a little of Julie Anne. I guess I didn't really notice before," Rob mused. "I've never noticed how sexy she is underneath that strong front she puts up, but then I guess she has to. After all, she is doing a man's job. Who would take her seriously if she behaved feminine and helpless like Sydney. If I could only touch her. Just a brush of her arm against mine would be enough... feel her hair on my face."

He wondered what her lips would taste like – sweet like nectar – salty like the sea she sailed on? His desire at that moment to kiss her was dire – more so than even his desire for freedom. Locked away in a prison in Alex's arms would be far from the worst punishment a man could endure. But, locked up only three feet away from her was torture of the worst kind.

"Making love to her would be better," Rob thought, "But a simple kiss would do for now... if only. But she's not interested in me that way," reasoned Rob. "She's only being nice to me now to try and cheer me up and pass the time without going stir crazy."

Rob was beginning to wonder if he really knew himself – knew what he wanted. How could he have been so wrong about Sydney – spent so many years with her catering to her every need? Rob wondered if he'd really ever made love to Sydney. Had he simply made love to her as a function of the relationship – his daily accountability to her? The more he thought about it, sex with her was never like it had been with Julie Anne. Granted, he and Julie Anne only had one short summer to grow bored with each other since they had remained virgins until they'd graduated. Rob had finally had the nerve to lose his virginity to her on the beach graduation weekend. It had been perfect – she had been perfect – as perfect as anyone's first time could be. Rob wasn't certain which of them had been more scared as they fumbled with each other's clothing on the blanket that night under the stars. The rest of that summer they had worked to hone their lovemaking to a fine skill. Then September came and it was time for Rob to leave for school – leaving Julie Anne to Dirk's offensive tactics as he swooped right in there to claim the ball the moment that Rob had left the field. Thinking it over now, Rob pondered that maybe Julie Anne hadn't ever really loved him the way he had loved her. Otherwise, could she have pledged her loyalty so easily to Dirk's team?

Alex stared at Rob, who appeared deep in thought, and wondered, "How is it I'm sitting here talking to the guy who only weeks ago was the bane of my life and now all I really want to do is take him in my arms and hold him? Maybe Sydney hasn't ruined him yet," she wished hopefully. "Is it possible that there's still some passion left in him after being with her all this time? I bet he could be a lot of fun once I really got him to loosen up. In fact, I imagine that he might even be a decent lover with a little practice," Alex mused optimistically. "But he's still in love with her," she warned herself. "I can see right through him. Even though he's trying to pretend he's finished with her. Watch... the minute he's out he'll probably run right to the phone to beg her forgiveness and he won't even remember I exist."

CHAPTER THIRTEEN

Freedom

*"Freedom is just another word for,
nothing left to lose."*

Janis Joplin
K. Kristofferson/F. Foster

Finally, on the morning of their eighth day inside, Fritz arrived and within hours had managed to obtain the lab test results from Curacao regarding the contraband in question. It seemed the immigration officials had indeed made a grave error in judgment regarding their dubious confiscation of Rob's supposed stash. It was in fact only sage tea, as Raymond had maintained, for which they had just spent the last week in jail. Hence, hoping to avoid an utterly embarrassing situation, the police and immigration officials wasted no time in releasing Rob and his crew before the island judges returned to laugh them right out of the courtroom.

Now Fritz, to say the least, was agitated that Rob had missed his charter, however considering the circumstances, which were out of Rob's control, Fritz agreed that if Rob could have the Island Fever back in Antigua, charter license or not, and provisioned and ready for charter in two days, he would have another booking for him. He even allowed Rob to keep the first deposit and told him to apply it to the new charter. Antigua is only ninety-two miles from St. Maarten – only ninety-two miles 'dead to weather.' Once again, the only direction towards which a sailboat cannot achieve direct forward propulsion. Due to their self-generated apparent-wind,* catamarans are known to have trouble pointing close to the wind. However, they are also known to more than make up in speed, the distance that they lose in beating to weather. By Fritz's calculations, Rob should have no trouble getting there on time, or so he thought. So, Rob gave his word that they would be there no matter what – come rain or shine. "Only a hurricane could keep me from picking up that charter two days from now," promised Rob defiantly.

Fritz looked at him a moment then shook his head, "Even though it's only mid-June and it's too soon for hurricanes, with the way your luck's going, that's exactly what I'm afraid of."

Alex had gone ahead to get the boat released, while Rob filled out all the paperwork for their release. Luckily, the police officials involved were so embarrassed about their faux pas that they had even agreed to destroy all record of their ever having been in jail in the first place. And, while Rob was finishing up, Raymond had gone off to find a taxi to take them to buy provisions, since with the passing week their provisions from Antigua would no longer fall into the category of 'fresh.'

Leaving that dark, dank jail cell and entering the world of the living again as he walked out into the hot balmy breeze and the blinding sunshine, Rob felt as if he'd just received a new lease on life. He had managed to rid himself of a huge amount of excess baggage, and felt lighter than he'd ever felt in his life. Oddly, it felt like someone else's life, not the old one that he'd left behind when he'd entered that jail cell eight days ago. He suddenly had a whole new appreciation for his meager existence – especially for his freedom. To different people the word 'freedom' meant different things, but Rob was just beginning to understand all of the implications of the term 'to be free.' Since of course, Rob was now a free man in more ways than one. He was a single, free man to be exact – a state of being quite new to Rob. After all it had been years since he had been without a girlfriend, or without Sydney, to be specific. 'Life Without Sydney,' now that was a somewhat intriguing new chapter in Rob's life. And Rob was feeling quite inspired by the concept at that point, and by the last few days he had just spent getting to know Alex in jail, not to mention the start of his new journey to find true love once again. That was, if he could keep his heart beating at home in his chest – he'd actually felt the slight pitter-patter of it in jail with Alex. Maybe, just maybe, it had decided to come home for a visit. Suddenly, the essence of true lovestruck Rob like a lightning-bolt. Freedom –

APPARENT WIND — Apparent Wind is the wind perceived aboard a boat while underway – not necessarily the True Wind which is the measurement of the wind's real direction and velocity. The Apparent Wind is in fact the boat's speed combined with the True Wind and is the more important wind to consider when trying to determine one's tack, heading, and arrival time. Since the faster a boat sails the further off the True Wind the Apparent Wind clocks.

that's what it meant. True love didn't have to rob you of freedom. On the contrary, it freed you to open your heart and dive in to explore its depths, and be free in knowing that there was another being inhabiting this physical existence to share one's freedom with.

Carnival was still underway as Rob stood there on Front Street breathing in the fresh air and watching as the frenzied islanders paraded through the streets in their brightly plumed costumes and body paint, now in their eighth day of drunken debauchery. Of course, the island had run out of rum two days prior, but there was still a plentiful supply of every other type of libation imaginable since the island's largest import was liquor. After all, it was a duty-free port and every American who stepped foot on its soil couldn't resist dragging back as many bottles as they were permitted to carry in order to save a few cents on a bottle of the same thing they could buy at their local grocery store back home.

Rob made his way to the town dock and looked at the harbor for the first time in the daylight. He surveyed the long stretch of curving beach dotted in both directions by little West Indian buildings and taller modern buildings to the north, that's where the beach ran into a shelf of rock extending out to the point where the old fort sat atop the small cliff – to the south were the marinas, where the Island Fever had enjoyed her last eight days of vacation.

Rob and Alex had decided that in order to expedite their departure from the island that had so kindly extended its hospitality over the last eight days, free-of-charge, or so they thought, Alex would go off and ready the boat to sail. Meanwhile while Rob set off in a taxi with Raymond to provision the boat at the Supermarche' on the French side, since the Dutch 'Food Center' was temporarily closed due to the island's ten-day celebration.

Alex had gone off to retrieve the Island Fever, which had been impounded at Bubba's Marina, and for which she was charged an unexpected eight-hundred-dollar dockage fee, *(one hundred dollars a day for the eight days that she had taken up two slips at the dock)* which had to be paid before she could reclaim her. Alex was appalled that they would have the balls to charge an impound fee, especially in light of their grossly mistaken arrest. But she finally realized that she had no choice but to come up with the cash since the marina owner could have cared less about the unfortunate blunder made by the immigration officials. He was after all, running a business and if they wanted their boat back, they were just going to have to pay the price. Even Fritz, who had been there earlier, had been unable to convince the owner to do the right thing and let them have their boat back, free-of-charge.

Rob heard the beeping of a car horn, which shook him out of his reverie. Looking around the wharf he found Raymond waiting for him in a little red car in the town dock parking lot. Getting a taxi had been impossible since no one worked during Carnival, but luckily, Raymond had found a friend from another boat and had managed to borrow his car for a few hours. Now, simply getting out of town was going to be a feat in itself, since the roads were jammed with a sea of colorful undulating bodies which gyrated and swayed to the beat of whatever drummer happened to be within rhythmic proximity. It took the little car an average of ten minutes per block to make it down Front Street to Pondfill Road, where Raymond astutely took the back road around the Saltpond. Normally a five-minute drive, it took a total of an hour to make it through the smaller parades to the road out of town. Raymond found it necessary to take the long road through the French Quarter to Marigot in order to avoid the dancers who had formed a human Macarena train over the hill to the airport, where it was rumored – a new shipment of rum was about to land.

Once out of town, Rob was actually beginning to believe that there were still some last vestiges of hope for Paradise as they passed through the lush green back roads of the French countryside – the tiny villages seeming quite the tranquil antithesis to the pandemonium of the Dutch side. The beautiful white Tropic birds that soared overhead and the goats and cows that roamed the pastures untethered, painted the countryside serenely picturesque; and the native children who laughed and played along the sparkling beaches as they passed through the little town of Grand Case while the sailboats cruised across the channel to the neighboring island of Anguilla,* blended with the rest of the amazing scenery to complete the picture-perfect postcard. But Rob's mind was somewhat distracted from his scenic excursion since he was deep in thought about the last four days he'd spent with Alex, albeit separated by a set of steel bars, but spent with Alex nonetheless. His thoughts wandered as the little car wove in and out of road blocks made by sightseeing tourists in rental cars, goats, playing children, other taxis touring their occupants around the sights of the island, and locals stopping to chit-chat to passing vehicles.

"Did I sense a change in her once we were free to go or was it my imagination?" thought Rob. "I'm sure she isn't interested in me, she probably just felt sorry for me. I mean I was a pretty pitiful sight there in that cell feeling

---

*ANGUILLA — A small island four miles across the channel to the north of St. Martin on the French side. Anguilla is a lightly populated island whose only attributes are its beautiful, powdery white sand beaches and turquoise water, since its interior is scrubby, arid, and covered in land-locked, unused salt-ponds. Aside from the early inhabitants, Arawak and Carib Indians, who called the island Malliouhana, the Spanish explorers settled the island later, re-naming it Anguilla – meaning 'eel' for its elongated shape. In 1650 the island became a British Crown Colony, which fought off the French more than once over the centuries. In 1967 Britain decided to lump it together with St. Kitts and Nevis to create the Associated State of St. Kitts-Nevis-Anguilla, which thoroughly pissed off Anguillians who wanted no part of island rule and they bodily threw the Kittitian forces off the island. After years of failed attempts to negotiate a solution, Britain finally invaded the shores of Anguilla, only to be welcomed with an open-arm celebration, not unlike Independence Day, resulting in the continuance of direct British rule. Today the island has become the home to numerous trendy luxury hotels, villas, and spas – a new hot reclusive escape for the 'rich and famous.'

miserable for myself because I was stupid enough to believe Sydney was with me purely out of love, and not because she saw me as a likely successor to daddy's company. What happened to being with someone simply because you love them?" contemplated Rob. *"Is love something we rationalize away once we get old enough to think before we engage our hearts? The good news is that Sydney wasn't capable of breaking my heart. She never had possession of it, someone else did, and it certainly wasn't me."* Rob was now wondering if Alex, like Julie Anne, owned a little silver locket for the safe keeping of his heart.

Rob and Raymond finally arrived at the Supermarche in Marigot to find that the line for a shopping-carts wrapped nearly around the building. Luckily, Raymond had often shopped at French markets in the past due to Joey's affinity for French cheese, French wines, and French women *(not necessarily in that order)*, and Raymond was able to make sense of the products which were marked with French labels, since Rob couldn't differentiate between a can of green peas and sliced peaches if it didn't have a picture on it. Grocery shopping even in the states wasn't something Rob had made a habit of since he ate out three meals a day. Aside from his corner coffee shop and the local health food store where he bought his protein bars, Rob hadn't stepped into anything much bigger than a convenience store since he was a kid. So, when they finally managed to bribe some native kid with a big smile for a cart, Rob followed Raymond up and down the aisles of alien foodstuffs, while Raymond loaded the cart so full, that by the time they reached the register, Rob's arms were so overloaded with croissants and French baguettes that he could barely see where he was walking.

It took the cashier a good twenty minutes to ring up their purchases which came to 5000 French francs. Rob looked at Raymond in a panic, but Raymond assured him that they would indeed accept the U.S. dollar as would just about any island in the West Indies. Raymond quickly calculated the true conversion to good ole greenbacks, an amount that wasn't quite as shocking. However, at a five to one exchange rate, Rob realized that chartering was likely to be a costly endeavor since this was only enough food for the first few days, and they still needed to make a stop at the liquor store for hard stuff and soft drinks which would up the ante at least another fiver. Luckily, the cost of chartering a seventy-five-foot yacht these days was quite generous and Rob calculated that there might still be a four-thousand- dollar profit after commissions, expenses, and wages, but of course he still had to amortize his insurance, fees, taxes, and maintenance, not to mention the cost of the boat itself. Rob's mind was in overdrive doing extended projections in his head and the golden goose, that he had so lucratively projected was now looking a little more akin to a tarnished hen.

Four hours later when Rob and Raymond finally returned to Bubba's Marina in Philipsburg with the Island Fever's provisions, Rob had one important thing on his agenda before they set sail for Antigua. He'd suddenly realized that he hadn't called his parents in weeks and figured that by now they'd probably come to the conclusion that he'd disappeared somewhere in the Bermuda Triangle. So, when Rob told Alex that he needed to make an important call to the States before they left the dock, Alex immediately assumed that Rob's intent was to try and win Sydney back.

Alex sat on deck waiting for an hour while Rob tried to place his call from Bubba's office, since Bubba felt that it was the least, he could do for them considering their past week's inconvenience. Alex started running the entire phone call through her mind, and her mounting frustration only served to feed her already ambiguous opinion of men's acumen and discernment.

"*I knew it,*" *thought Alex. "I knew he'd call her and beg her forgiveness the minute he got out. What is it with men? Do you have to treat them like shit to make them fall in love with you? Are they all masochists, chasing after women that couldn't give a damn about anything other than their bank account and their credit rating? Don't men care whether a woman is really in love with them or not, she pondered. Isn't there something to be said about knowing that someone's with you because they're madly in love with you and not because you look like the most dependable and reliable ATM machine to them? I'm not doing it again I'm not going to let myself be hurt by another man. I'm just going to forget about what happened in there. Nothing happened. He was hurt and lonely and you were simply there to help him through a rough time,*" *Alex tried to convince herself.* "*What makes you think that you're the kind of girl he would ever be interested in anyway? Look at yourself. You've seen the kind of women he likes.*"

So, Alex decided it was best to tend to her own duties aboard the boat – playing it as cool with regard to their new budding friendship as a spring frost on an early crocus – freezing any chance it had of ever blossoming.

When Rob returned to the boat happy to have spoken with his mother, who was thrilled and relieved to know that he was okay. Upon his arrival, Alex offered nothing more than a cold shoulder and a professional continence towards Rob as she busied herself with duties in order to make final preparations for the boat to set sail for the long night ahead. Raymond was busy battening down the hatches and stowing groceries as Alex lowered the engine sled into the water and started up the seventy-five horsepower Evinrude. Luckily, she had four hours that afternoon to make repairs to their engine and to be certain the officials hadn't done any irreparable damage to the boat, even if it was quite apparent that more than one party had been held aboard during their detention. Rob attempted familiar con-versation with Alex and was quite confused to find that Alex's response was as unfamiliar as a taxi driver in New York City. He stepped down into the cockpit and laid his hand on her shoulder hoping to be more successful at getting her attention, but to his dismay, she simply pulled away as if he were Patrick Swayze in "Ghost" – pretending to be totally unaware that he was even there as she busily went about her business.

Poor Rob, although attentive to the duties at hand, was terribly disturbed by his awakening to the fact that Alex was an attractive, available female. He was also, at best, confused by her sudden change of demeanor. After all, she was the captain and all the responsibility did fall on her shoulders, thought Rob, trying to rationalize her sudden lack of interest in continuing their courtship dance. Understandable as it was, her renewed, cold, professional attitude only proved to be a frustrating and ego deflating quandary to Rob; and even though his attention was on the motion of the ocean, the vessel in question was definitely not the Island Fever.

"I called Immigration," Alex said woodenly, breaking the awkward silence that had covered the Island Fever like a shroud. "They said as far as they were concerned, they had never heard of the Island Fever. I think that means that they can't get us out of here quick enough," continued Alex with little emotion. "We had better get moving on getting this boat ready to sail if we want to make it there by morning. I need at least a day on the other end to get ready for another week out and get this engine tuned... it's still not running at full power even though Bubba found me a used prop."

"Aye Aye," said Rob a little confused by her brusque brush off. "I'm all yours Captain. Just tell me what you'd like me to do... swab the decks, pump the bilge, scrape the barnacles off the hull?" continued Rob with more than a bit of sarcasm in his voice.

"Well, you can start by taking the sail covers off and hank the number one jib on," commanded Alex coldly as she went about setting up her charts* and plotting in her projected coordinates. Alex then proceeded to check the weather, which predicted smooth sailing all the way. Regardless, she plotted their course and turned on the Sat-Nav** even though Alex knew the area like the back of her hand. It was a smart sailor that took advantage of every available aid to navigation that modern technology had to offer, since one never knew when those electronic gizmos might come in handy. After all, what if something happened to her, impairing her ability to sail the boat. The last thing she wanted to do was to leave it up to Rob and his elementary navigational skills to determine their fate at sea.

Once they had put all their purchases away, taken on water and fuel,

---

*CHARTS — Official seagoing maps which aid one with navigation. Back in the '80s pre-electronic wonders, sailors actually still used paper charts and a compass.
**SAT-NAV or Satellite Navigational System — a device used for navigation which displays one's position via the nearest satellite. Supposing of course, that satellite wants to be found. Today the GPS or Global Positioning System is the most technologically advanced version of this type of equipment, although all electronic equipment is subject to failure and should not be a sailor's only source of navigation.

and finished their routine pre-flight check it was nightfall – a perfect time to set sail southeast, projecting their arrival in Antigua during daylight the following day. By now, Alex was looking forward to hitting the open ocean again after being cooped up in that concrete hamster cage for the last week. Anxiously, she cast off their hopelessly tangled dock lines, and pulled out of the slip without even giving Raymond time to untangle the mess that the immigration officials had somehow managed to leave behind. Once clear of the marina dock in Philipsburg harbor, Alex gave it full power as she headed the Island Fever out to sea as fast as her outboard would carry her, barely stopping long enough to turn her into the wind in order to raise their mainsails.

    The sky was a little overcast that night and the nearly full moon had yet to make its appearance. So, losing the town lights, which their eyes were now comfortably adjusted to, as they rounded the point under power and headed off into the blackness of the unlit ocean, was somewhat akin to Ray Charles driving a black Cadillac down a dark country road, on a moonless night, with no lights at midnight.

CHAPTER FOURTEEN

Flotsam and Jetsam

"Accept whatever comes to you woven into the pattern of your destiny, for what could more aptly fit your needs."

Marcus Aurelius

One thing that I should mention here is, although it can be a beautiful spiritual experience unlike any other, and was my favorite time on the ocean, night sailing in the Caribbean can be a tricky proposition at best. The problem being that any water shallower than the deep blue sea is fish pot territory, a literal minefield of floating polypropylene lines tied to empty Clorox bottles on the surface, marking fish traps on the bottom. Which of course play havoc with propellers, dagger boards, and rudders, hampering your only means of controlling the direction of your vessel should you be so lucky as to snag one on your rudder or wind it around your propeller at four thousand revolutions per minute. The result of which being a knot that not even Houdini could untangle. So, when sailing at night it is requisite that the captain, post a fish-pot watch on the foredeck to forewarn the helmsman whenever one might fall in your vessel's path. Alex, whose eye was far better trained to spot those elusive little bleach bottles in the dark, quickly took to the foredeck, posting Rob at the helm to follow her instructions, while Raymond continued to secure the boat below for their long beat to weather.

As the Island Fever motored out to sea, the last thing Alex expected was to find the four-foot-high black, steel buoy for the cruise-ship mooring sitting a quarter of a mile offshore. So, when Alex spied this oversized fish pot dead in their path, only meters away from the bow, she shouted for Rob to turn, 'Hard to Port!' But instead, Rob, who was not yet completely proficient in the sailor's vernacular, and still thought of port as an after-dinner drink, turned 'Hard to Starboard' – taking the steel buoy, which was a foot higher than the underside clearance of the Island Fever's bridge deck, between the hulls. Needless to say, with eight knots of power underway there was no stopping the boat until the buoy, its shackle, and chain had ground their way down the length of the underside of the bridge deck and port hull. Alex's screams were quickly drowned out by thirty seemingly endless seconds of the painful sound of ripping, splintering wood. Rob was so stunned it took him a moment to think to reach down and kill the throttle on the engine. To Rob, unaware of what he'd hit, it seemed like a lifetime, during which he was certain the world had come to an end – at least his that is, as his heart stopped beating until the unknown obstacle emerged out the back end of the bridge-deck. As it exited out from under the boat between the hulls, it neatly took with it the Island Fever's Evinrude and engine sled along with a good chunk of the bridge-deck and several sections of planking from the hull – leaving the boat a floating wreck.

Suddenly, all was quiet as Rob, Raymond, and Alex leaned over the back of the bridge deck watching as the engine, sputtering its last breath, sunk to the bottom of the ocean. "Oh my God!" repeated Rob over and over again to himself as he stood there – frozen, as Alex quickly released the main-staysail halyard and dropped the sail to the deckhouse halting any further forward momentum.

At that moment, all of the hours spent in seeding their newly digested friendship were totally flushed down the toilet as Rob made the mistake of opening his mouth in a lame attempt to shed the blame of his blunder onto Alex – "How could you have not seen that... thing?!" said Rob accusingly to Alex.

Not believing what she had just heard, Alex, who was showing an amazing amount of self-restraint and composure given the circumstances, turned to Rob whom she was just about to choke on his own topsiders – "I did see it. You turned the wrong way. Starboard right, port left," said Alex, gesturing to the port side – the left side of the boat.

Realization started to dawn on Rob as he suddenly turned one shade paler than he already was, as he replayed Alex's commands just prior to the incident through his mind. Although he had every opportunity to fess up at that moment to the fact that he still didn't know his port from his starboard, Rob, dying from embarrassment that he'd totally screwed up in front of Alex once again, took the opposite tack and headed off into treacherously deep water.

"Did you have to wait until we were on top of it before you said something?" continued Rob, not knowing when to shut up.

"Did you see a beacon on it? Next time I'll be sure they put a flashing light on it," growled Alex.

"Now, now," intervened Raymond as he boldly stepped in between the two who were quite on the verge of going to blows. "It was nobody's fault... it was just there," said Raymond in his own way of over-simplifying everything and never laying the blame on anyone or anything.

But alas, Raymond's were the last civil words spoken that evening aboard the Island Fever with both Rob and Alex refusing to budge from their positions of who was at fault. In his gut Rob knew that he was wrong, but his utter humiliation, not to mention his ego, prevented him from apologizing to Alex and accepting the burden of responsibility for the unfortunate accident.

What a disappointing turn of events in Paradise, since I thought I had actually come close to getting them together. But alas, even we Spirit Guides aren't always 'all-knowing' and 'all-seeing, and are sometimes working just as hard to get it right as you humans. One thing's for certain, matchmaking has never been my forte, and maybe I would find the need to enlist an Earthly assistant on that count.

Although it thoroughly pissed her off, Alex realized that Rob's intentions and desire to get it right and to impress her with everything he'd learned about sailing over the last few weeks, had been sincere and that due to his embarrassment, he was having trouble admitting his err. However, she knew only too well, that the road to Hell was paved with half-baked good intentions and was finding it harder and harder to forgive his interminable blunders, especially when he refused to own up to them. Up until now she had been pretty patient, realizing that this was a man who had probably never been the athletic or sportsman type in his life. In fact, she guessed accurately that the extent of Rob's sporting activities comprised a membership at his local athletic club back in Chicago, which was used as much to build his social and business muscle as it was meant to build his body. After all, it was an honest mistake to confuse his port from his starboard, since some people at age thirty still didn't know their right from their left, let alone which side of the boat was which after only a matter of weeks on the water. Had Rob only faced up to his shortcomings in sailing proficiency at that point she could have easily forgiven him. But Alex, who was always the first to face the music whenever she was at err, couldn't accept the fact that Rob was unwilling to admit to his latest screwup. Not only that, he was doing his best to shift the burden of blame to her shoulders.

There is something strange about a sailboat that can turn the nicest of guys into Captain Bligh even if they are only the First Mate, providing some validity to the age-old axiom that all men are inherently pirates at heart. The part about a man being master of his own ship seems to somehow induce this metamorphosis. After all, it is an island unto itself where the owner is King and his crew are his subjects. There were rare exceptions to this condition, however Alex had been hard-pressed to find more than a handful during her years in this profession. Then there was the fact that the 'master/owner' part, was in direct conflict with the fact that the captain of the Island Fever was not the owner, which was somewhat akin to two rulers of one domain vying for the throne. Not to mention the ongoing internal conflict with Rob's ego of having a woman in charge, and the fact that as a child, Rob had secretly always dreamed of growing up to be a pirate. In fact, he had always wanted to play the pirate and the mermaid, instead of cowboys and Indians – alas, he was surrounded by a sea of corn rather than the great blue ocean, and unfortunately his cousin Marie's imagination had not been as fertile as Rob's. So, Rob spent his nights fantasizing about that other watery, magical world that he was not to see until his first trip to New York with Sydney – were he stood atop of the Statue of Liberty and looked out to sea for the first time in his life, with respectful wonder.

Rob realized that once again this recent catastrophe didn't seem to fit at all into his dream world. He was in fact beginning to wonder if there was truly any real difference between Hell and Paradise. In fact, suddenly the meaning of 'Paradise' was quickly being redefined in Rob's mind as, "A place of great discontentment." Surely Webster had never run a charter boat in Paradise. All Rob knew was that he was not 'satisfied, happy, or delighted' by the turn of events in Paradise.

Of course, disputing who was correct here was not going to change the fact that the Island Fever presently resembled the Titanic just before it sunk, and Alex was far from committed to going down with her ship as had Captain Smith. In fact, she was close to commandeering the last available life boat for herself, even if the Island Fever was in no imminent danger of sinking. And, if it had not been for her responsibility to the Island Fever itself, she would have surely abandoned ship.

Aware that the soundness of the port hull had been compromised by the buoy in some way, Alex decided that there was more imminent damage to tend to than Rob's floundering ego, which was also about to resemble the sinking of the Titanic. She decided to ignore Rob for the moment and crawled through the closed companionway – down the steps into the hull to survey the situation. When she stepped onto the floorboards in the hull, she found water flowing in through the ripped waterline plank. There was already six inches of water above the floorboards not to mention the additional six inches in the bilge. Although she was shocked to find so much water in the hull, she realized that the Island Fever couldn't sink due to the fact that she was a wooden vessel with a greater displacement capacity than its overall weight. She also knew that, unlike the Titanic, the bulkheads which were forward and aft, were luckily undamaged and fully water-tight, keeping the fore and aft compartments unaffected by the water that poured into the gaping hole amidships.

Name-calling and lambasting aside, a tow was in order to bring the crippled Island Fever back into port. Antigua bound she was not – once again leaving Rob no option but to lose an opportunity to make some much needed dinero. So, Alex got on channel sixteen to radio for help – help from the man who had just extorted eight hundred dollars from them in their unfortunate predicament. And here they had found themselves in yet another quandary – once again at Bubba's mercy.

"Bubba's Marina, Bubba's Marina, Bubba's Marina... this is the Island Fever, over." Alex waited listening for an answer over the silent radio, but received no response. "Bubba's Marina, Bubba's Marina, Bubba's Marina... this is the Titanic over... we have hit an iceberg and we are in need of emergency assistance... over," called Alex attempting to bring some levity to the rapidly sinking atmosphere aboard. Although she succeeded in eliciting a chuckle from Raymond, Rob was far from amused.

Alex waited patiently wondering if she might have to attempt actually towing the Island Fever back in with her own dinghy, but thought better of it, realizing that with the hull taking on water, the boat would also be rapidly gaining in weight. Of course, she could sail her in, but since it would require a starboard tack, which would only serve to drive more water into the hull, she thought better of it and decided to wait for Bubba, or anyone else monitoring sixteen, to get back to her. Alex had never known Bubba to miss an opportunity to make some quick cash on a salvage job so she stood by patiently, voyeur to Rob's growing panic as he tried to start-up the bilge pump as Raymond bailed water through the lower head with a bucket. Once more she repeated the call on the VHF.

"Bubba's Marina, Bubba's Marina, Bubba's Marina... this is the Island Fever... we are taking on water over."

"Islan Feva... dis Bubpa's Marina... go ta channel tree ova," answered Max, Bubba's night manager who had likely been in the back room with his girlfriend all along.

Relieved, Alex dialed the radio down to channel three as instructed since channel sixteen was reserved for contact only – the proper rule of thumb was to choose another channel on which to chit chat or discuss business unless of course it was a life-or-death emergency.

"Bubba's Marina, Island Fever over," Alex called back once again on channel three.

"Roger Islan Feva... I rea' you louw an klea.... what seem to be de problim?" asked Max in his thick West Indian accent. "You'd forget someting?"

"No but some barge hand sure did," answered Alex. "You know that rather large steel buoy the cruise ships use in Great Bay?"

"Yea shur. It been out dere's lon as I been heerd," responded Max, quite sure of its whereabouts.

"Actually, it's now about two hundred yards southwest of Point Blanche where some fool deckhand forgot to untie it before the ship drug it offshore. Seems we've just managed to take it between the hulls. It's ripped off a few planks on the waterline and we're taking on water in our port hull."

"Damn maun... you guys hav all de luk," said Max wincing at the thought as he fished around in the desk drawer for his boat keys. "All de baad luk dat is. How baad it be?"

"Well, we're not likely to sink," responded Alex, "But let's just say that we won't be making it to Antigua by tomorrow, or even back to the dock for that matter since our engine's now in fifty feet of water. Think you could manage a tow?"

"Sur ting Ms. Alex, be ride wid yu... ova an out."

Of course, the moment the harbor master heard Alex's call for help, he had switched down to three to monitor the situation. After all, they were more than anxious to get the Island Fever off the island and out of their jurisdiction, than even Alex and Rob were. To the harbor master, word of their unplanned extended stay on his island was bad news, since the crew was witness to their recent screw up and were now destined to be unwanted guests of the island for the next few months. Surely, it would not take long for word of their officious blunder to get around the island, let alone the Caribbean via the 'Coconut Telegraph.'

As the crew of the Island Fever sat quietly in the cockpit with the main cocked to windward and the rudders set to leeward to slow her drift, Rob sat wondering where he'd first gone wrong, or at least at what juncture he'd drifted so far off course.

"What have I done to deserve all of this?" thought Rob. "I'm not such a bad guy, do I deserve this? It's Sydney, I know it. She's put some sort of curse on me as payback. Ever since I stepped foot on this boat my life's turned to shit. Maybe Sydney was right all along. Maybe I should have just written the whole thing off to experience and gone home. Not only did I lose Sydney, my savings, my job, and my car, but now Alex hates me and thinks I'm a total moron." Rob, it seemed, had found himself somewhere 'West of the Equator' and was clueless on how to find his way back.

Ironically, the full moon was now peeking over the edge of the eastern horizon like a golden orb rising out of the sea between Fourche and the point, lighting up the ocean ahead of them – illuminating fish pots and their iceberg as if it were daylight. Alas, that divine will was at work once again, if only they had left thirty minutes later Rob's life would have been on course to Antigua right at that moment to pick up the other half of his charter fee. But instead, Rob had found himself dodging the floating debris that life manages to somehow place right in your path, which thankfully often serves to save some people from themselves. Sometimes it's placed there simply to teach you a lesson and other times it's a sign to tell you that you're just not on the right course – the course of events attributed to universal will and destiny.* Some actually learn to recognize the fact that obstacles are put there for a reason and take it as a warning to give

ISLAND FEVER

up and go home – others manage to find a way to navigate around them and grow to be stronger human beings. If there's one thing I've learned from this job as Rob's tour guide, it's that humans seem to need to learn about life the hard way. Rob was just taking a small alternate route from his destined course, but proof of it as an enlightened experience was yet to be seen. What humans don't remember is that this is part of the deal that one expects to run into when they agree, on this side, to take on the human experience in the first place. After all, they do design their life's curriculum that they are to live by before they get to Earth, in order to learn their designated lessons and pay off karma.

Rob had unfortunately never been an exponent of Eastern philosophy, and he was still attempting to push rivers upstream. Whether he liked it or not, he was being taught that those devices employed by the Universe to correct one's course can sometimes include large objects such as water buoys placed directly in your path. The other lesson he was still learning was that, ultimately, no great power outside himself was in control and the reality of the dues to be paid were exacted only by himself.

"Why did this have to happen now?" lamented Rob as he waited in the cockpit with his head in his hands for the rescue boat.

"Everything happens for a reason," Raymond readily pointed out to Rob. "I guess this was just your destiny. Otherwise, it wouldn't have happened. It's a lesson you had to learn."

With this new awareness suddenly dawning at the forefront of Rob's consciousness, he was beginning to understand that maybe he had indeed just been enrolled in life's crash course of enlightenment. He was just uncertain of the Universe's grand reasoning and purpose behind this latest flotsam and jetsam*** which had been strewn in his path. Rob was indeed making one

---

*DESTINY — A predetermined or inevitable course of events – the events or option-lines you choose to experience during the course of your human incarnation, before you come here to spend a lifetime. Once you are here, destiny is simply, destiny. There's not much point in fighting it because it's going to eventually run the show whether you want it to or not. So, you may as well just set your oars and raise your sails and go with the flow. After all, what have you got to lose? The Universe only acts in perfect ways. It's when you try to fight it that life gets bumpy because you're not headed in the direction in which you're supposed to be, or at least along the easiest route – kind of like beating to weather, or attempting to steer the boat north when its autopilot** is on south. Of course, everyone has the option of free will and choice over destiny, that is if we want to be so hard–headed as to choose an alternate backroad. But in time, most learn that the ride is far easier when driving on a well paved highway, than bouncing over boulders in a dried-up riverbed.
**AUTOPILOT — A device used to steer a boat on a predetermined course or heading. Confucius say, "Find smooth sailing if let big autopilot name destiny lead way."
***FLOTSAM & JETSAM — Flotsam would be those items washed overboard by the sea. As opposed to Jetsam, which are those articles discarded deliberately during an emergency, or just simply those things which are unwanted. Those outcasts who are discarded from society — Rob's current ranking amongst Sydney's peers.

mistake after the other. But, if mistakes were a learning curve, then surely Rob was in an accelerated training program and enlightenment couldn't be far off. What Rob didn't realize was that there were really no mistakes in life, only lessons, since nothing is truly negative unless you perceive it to be so. And, as they say, one must first go through Hell in order to reach Paradise.

Of course, the 'cosmic experiment' theory could easily apply here too as an alternate explanation for one's predetermined path through life, thought Rob. The theory that there is some superior race of beings out there simply using him as a pawn in their Universal game of cosmic chess. If this theory indeed were to have any validity to it whatsoever, then Rob's invisible opponent in his game of life had just called check.

Rob had always been one of those naive beings who believed that he was the sole choreographer in his little dance through life, even if he was still doing the 'Swim' to keep his head above water while the rest of the Universe seemed to think he should be already on to the 'Macarena.' So, Rob was a few steps out of time. He'd catch up, or catch on, eventually.

Prior to this, the biggest emergency that Rob had ever dealt with was a flat tire on the road, or locking his keys in the car. Up until now he had always known he could simply call AAA, but this time his ten-year membership wasn't going to save him. And, being born in September under not only a Virgo sun, but also a Virgo moon, the efficient yet unfortunate thing about Rob's personality was that he had never known or allowed disorder in his life. He had always made certain that everything fit into neat little compartments, including his emotions. Now that things were starting to go awry, Rob was finding that he had no management skills to access for handling chaos, catastrophe, and mayhem, and he was beginning to realize that he was starting to fall apart along with his life. Rather than simply heeding all the warning signs that he was definitely not on the easiest heading for smooth sailing, Rob had persisted in plowing ahead without stopping to consult his compass – that internal compass known as the 'Higher Self' – what some can only acknowledge by a standard nomenclature known as intuition.

Fritz was not pleased, to say the least, about the latest turn of events in Rob's world, however, he was not exactly surprised by Rob's latest, due to his persisting string of bad luck. So, although Fritz felt sympathetic for Rob's unfortunate predicament, he asked him to send his deposit back, wished him well, and told him to call him when, and if, the scourge lifted. Once again, Rob was on his own in Paradise.

CHAPTER FIFTEEN

Ego or Eating Crow

*"The ego is nothing more
than a part of your belief that you are here."*

"A Course in Miracles"

Since the widest boat that Bubba's sling lift could accommodate was twenty-four feet wide, and the Island Fever was just slightly more than twenty-six, Bubba suggested that he tow them just off the beach in Simpson Bay, a few bays north of Philipsburg, since it was impossible to get her out of the water and onto dry land in town. When he and Max arrived at around nine with their thirty-foot work boat, Alex already had her bow bridle set up for Max to tie onto his boat in order to tow them. Bubba, a forty-year-old Dutch West Indian, originally from Aruba, was a rough, tough, Antillian cowboy and possessed little compassion for a fellow human being in need when commerce lay in the way. Knowing the man who had just made a week's wages off of their earlier misfortune, Alex wisely climbed aboard his boat, 'The Treasure Hunter,' in order to negotiate and confirm his price for the tow. Alex knew that by International Law, *(once he had a line on the Island Fever)* he could justly claim salvage rights if he chose to be a jerk and exploit an unfortunate sailor who was at the mercy of his assistance. Luckily, Alex knew that their situation was far from life threatening, which gave her some leeway to negotiate 'the deal.' She also knew that, if worst came to worst, she could limp into Great Bay under sail and anchor until morning when she could call her old buddy Jeff from the marina in Simpson Bay Lagoon.

It was a calm night offshore and Bubba found it easy to get close enough for Alex to climb aboard even though she refused a line from Max until they had settled on a price for the tow. The situation was somewhat under control since Raymond had the generator on deck and the electric bilge pump running, which was doing a pretty good job of emptying the port hull of H_2O. Alex felt good knowing that she wasn't at his mercy, or mercenary nature.

"So," said Alex as she jumped from her port stern deck onto his starboard gunwale to the aft deck of Bubba's boat, "What's it going to cost me this time?" she asked expecting the worst.

"Well," said Bubba scratching the back of his head. "Way I figure it... seems it be costin' you a lotta bad luck if you stay on dis boat miss Alex. Maybe you should be leavin' de repairs to Joey on dis one," eliciting a smile out of Alex.

"Yeah," Alex considered seriously looking back at Rob who looked pretty pathetic sitting on the back deck of the Island Fever, "Maybe you're right on that count. But I owe it to Joey to sort it out... he's certainly not going to know what to do with it," Alex said referring to Rob who sat with his face buried in his hands.

"I tell you whot," offered Bubba thoughtfully, "Howabout dis time I give you a briek. What if I jus' charge you de cost of d fuel and a few rum-n-cokes at Chesterfields in exchange for a tow?"

Taken aback at Bubba's kindness, or was it merely his desire to have drinks with Alex – either way, she smiled gratefully knowing that this was a generous offer coming from Bubba. "Thank you, that's very good of you Bubba," said Alex as they shook on it. It took only minutes for Alex to climb back on board and throw Max their tow line.

Once they had reached Simpson Bay and picked up Bubba's mooring, their intake of water had slowed to only a quart or so a minute thanks to the fact that the missing plank was just at the waterline, not below. Because the weight of the boat had decreased by pumping the standing water out of the hull, it had allowed the boat to ride a little higher in the water. Alex shook Bubba's hand and thanked him, handed him a hundred-dollar bill, and promised to meet him for 'happy hour' the next afternoon – knowing that she could easily handle a Cowboy like Bubba.

The next morning dawned painfully for Rob, partly due to the fact that he had slept only a few hours in the cockpit to the sound of the generator and the suck and gushing noise that the bilge pump made. He also lay there feeling guilty with the knowledge that the burden lay on his shoulders to patch things up – not excluding the hole in the hull. Rob had found himself in a terrible quandary – torn between utter humiliation and the guilt of having cast his embarrassment upon Alex in an attempt to alleviate the blame from himself, and, his newly discovered romantic attraction to Alex, which magnified his utter confusion.

Rob kept telling himself that it was okay that this attractive, feminine creature was his boss and had much to teach him, however, his ego kept playing havoc with his logic. Rob had never before considered himself chauvinistic in any way, shape, or form. He was used to women who were educated, independent, and capable, however until now, none of them had been his direct superior. But he was beginning to realize now, that he was faced with the choice of groveling and admitting he was wrong and giving up the throne to Alex, or finding himself high and dry on some tropical beach. He knew he needed to overcome his pride and bite the bullet, or at least attempt to make a good show of it. Otherwise, Alex would surely jump ship and abandon him to fend for himself. Alex had made it clear that she'd had just about enough of Rob's ego, which was growing proportionally greater than his luck, as she saw it, and was indeed planning a one-woman mutiny. And as Rob's luck would have it – the calamities that still awaited him were lining up like thunderheads in a squall-line.* Alex didn't like the look of what was forecast on the horizon as far as she could see. But there was much to be said about not being able to see beyond that horizon, since what awaited them was bigger than anything Alex could imagine in her wildest dreams. What it really boiled down to, Rob's ego and bad luck aside, was that Alex didn't relish the thought of spending the next month or two covered in dust and paint in a hot dirty, buggy boatyard if her services weren't even appreciated.

It was true that Rob's ego was in tatters, but unfortunately, he was not evolved enough to intrinsically know that the ego was truly of no real importance in the grand scheme of things, and that if he let it, his ailing ego would get the best of him. In fact, egos had sunken far more ships than icebergs according to history.

Rob's ego it seemed, was currently heavily invested in pain and suffering and he was starting to identify his own self-worth with his current situation, which was at best a disaster. His self-image was threatened and it was currently in survival mode – even if Rob was managing to put on a good show of 'arrogant asshole.' But in fact, his ego was exposed – vulnerable – insecure and afraid of losing control, but what he didn't realize was that it was far better to simply cut it loose like one might cut away a diseased or malignant growth or appendage.

Even though I'd like to take credit for enlightening Rob to this important life lesson, I must admit that I accept no responsibility in his decision to beg her forgiveness. In fact, I accredit it entirely to desperation on his part. If it meant admitting he was wrong to get her to stay and help him with his most recent blunder it was worth it. Besides, Rob's feelings for Alex were still piqued and he was eagerly craving her forgiveness. It seemed however, that the plat du

---

SQUALLS LINE — A series of storms appearing as a long, dark, low line of clouds, which include sudden violent wind.

jour on today's menu was crow with a generous slice of humble pie for dessert. Oh, and don't forget, Alex's complimentary shot of her arsenic aperitif to wash it all down. So, Rob was about to learn a valuable lesson in eating humble pie.* Rob was finding himself stripped of all his worldly possessions and all the things he thought he cared about, and he was beginning to realize that he couldn't afford to lose Alex due to something stupid like pride and vanity. Obviously, this was just another lesson he had to learn, and for the first time in his life, he found himself asking for a little guidance in overcoming the jetsam that life had thrown in his path. Not to mention a little assistance in helping him to learn to digest a little crow. Rob was in need of more than a sailing instructor about now, indeed he needed the help of one of those life teachers I spoke of earlier. Little did he know that one was on the way, although not exactly in the type of package one would expect. At this point, a little celestial guidance was in order to aid Rob in his present state of confusion and I was working overtime to attempt to help, but Rob was still having trouble with that radio dial. Unfortunately, it seemed, that by the time he would get around to perfecting his celestial navigation skills, Rob would have found it necessary to acquire extreme proficiency at dodging the flotsam and jetsam rather than finding the course of least resistance.

Most importantly, Rob was currently learning a lesson in forgiveness and in taking responsibility for his own screw-ups. It wasn't Alex who he needed to forgive, for he knew that she had done nothing wrong. It seemed instead that Rob was in the process of learning how to forgive himself, and ask her to forgive him. What Rob didn't yet realize was that self-love and love of self were two entirely different things and that it was time that he learned the difference.

So, with great trepidation, Rob approached Alex once he had worked up the courage to eat that slice of pie that Alex would surely serve up.

"Ahh... Alex, ah, I just wanted to ah, apologize for, ahh... you know..."

"Yes?" Alex questioned, looking him square in the eye, just dying to hear him say it.

"Well, ah, I guess it ah, was my fault," Rob said choking on his words with a pitiful look in his eyes – garnering a look of mild satisfaction from Alex. "What can I say, you were right. I don't know my port from my starboard. I'm a total fuck-up. Please, will you forgive me? I need you to stay and help me put her back together."

Oh, how Alex enjoyed watching Rob grovel and beg as he pleaded with her, promising her total charge over the Island Fever. How could she refuse now that she had finally been passed the scepter?

*TO EAT HUMBLE PIE – (v.) Swallow one's pride, hang one's head, come down off one's high horse, look foolish, and feel small.

Alex gloated, "Finally," she thought. "Maybe there's hope for him after all. Maybe I was right about him the first time. Maybe Sydney hasn't ruined him and there is a caring compassionate man under that superficial exterior," Alex tried to convince herself.

"Well, I'll have to think about it," replied Alex hoping to make him suffer for at least a few more hours. For Alex knew that a lesson well learned was likely to make a far more lasting impression. So, she decided it best if she just let him stew in his own chowder for a while – at least until after lunch.

" A little putty and paint make the devil look like a saint."

Louis St. Bernard

CHAPTER SIXTEEN

Lambchop or Mutton

"Do what you can with what you have where you are."

Theodore Roosevelt

Once Rob and Alex had come to terms and had their treaty drafted, there were only two small problems remaining with regard to hauling out the Island Fever to make repairs – how to pay for it and how to lift a boat out of the water that was wider than the length of most of the boats on the little island of St. Maarten. Needless to say, the island was not prepared for such an emergency.

However, the great thing about a catamaran is the fact that without its rudders you have in essence a beachable raft. A fact which the Polynesians have understood for centuries and Hobie Alter got rich on several decades ago. Thinking on her feet, Alex devised a way to bring the Island Fever to a safe, dry haven on the beach under the swaying palms via the island's only back hoe. Once she and Raymond had pulled the pins and dropped the boat's rudders and removed her dagger-boards,* Alex proceeded to tie ropes around the Island Fever's bridge deck and drag her onto Simpson Bay Beach with the help of a few steel pipes to serve as rollers. Why a little creative ingenuity can go a long way – especially in the West Indies where resourcefulness is a prerequisite to survival. For the first time in his life, Rob was stranded on nothing more than a

---

*DAGGER BOARDS – The vertical waterproof blades or boards that can be lowered into the water through a catamaran's hull to serve some of the same functions as a monohull's keel, albeit a fraction of the weight. They provide lateral resistance – i.e. keeping the boat from drifting sideways when you want to go forward.

sandbar and the only inhabitants of that little stretch of beach, where the Island Fever now rested, was a watersports shack, numerous land crabs, a stray island goat or two, and an elderly couple known by the names of Grandma and Grandpa who had lived in a little cottage under the swaying palms for the better part of the century.

Rob stood on the beach that afternoon looking in disbelief, at the Island Fever which now rested high and dry on the sand. He shook his head as he surveyed the damage that jetsam had done to the underside of the bridge-deck and hull.

"She be all mash-up for sure," said a slightly horse, yet refined West Indian voice behind him.

Rob turned to find a rather small, frail looking golden skinned man of later years leaning over to look under the bridge-deck of the Island Fever.

"I'm afraid so," answered Rob shaking his head. "Seems there was a small fish pot in our path."

Not unlike my own last incarnation, Grandma and Grandpa were from that lineage of West Indian who had grasped the concept of living in the islands many decades ago. Especially Grandpa, who had done a little traveling in his time and possessed a unique understanding of life in the islands for both native and foreigner alike. They were what is known in the islands as Mulatto – an attractive, golden skinned, mixed bloodline of West Indian and European descent.

Grandpa took an immediate liking to Rob, whom he saw as a confused, misled seeker of Paradise, and immediately accepted Rob as his new drinking and domino buddy. Why it was only polite for Rob to break for a rum and Coke at eleven and four every day with Grandpa, a ritual which is widely accepted in the islands as a long-standing local custom. The morning cocktail hour known as 'elevenses' which runs into the customary three-hour lunch break from twelve to three and the four o'clock cocktail hour, which kicks off the American 'happy hour' were somehow adopted as customary in the islands due to the melding of so many cultures. It was the Spanish that contributed the three-hour lunch/siesta and the British tea time for morning and afternoon were somehow merged with the Dutchman's affinity for alcohol, not to mention the French aversion to work of any kind, which all tolled makes for a three-hour work day, since the day doesn't begin until 9:00 AM and 'happy-hour'* seems to somehow fade right into dinner. The merger of cultures also works well in the islands regarding

*HAPPY HOUR – Also known as the complaining hour – America's discounted version of the psycho-therapy session at the end of any given work day between four and seven, where, for the price of a discounted cocktail and the willingness to listen to a perfect stranger's problems, one can unload their own baggage onto some schmuck equally dumb enough to listen.

holidays, since no one could decide which nationality's sacred days to honor. Instead, as in the Dutch tradition, a diplomatic policy was adopted which widely accepted all holidays of any nation which had ever stepped foot on Caribbean soil. In turn leaving more holidays on the West Indian calendar than work days. Not to mention of course, their own string of holidays and Carnival which also attributed to the calendar's days of rest. With the recent influx of New York tourists, the latest I've overheard, is that they are considering adding Hanukkah to the holiday calendar since they learned that it constitutes eight days of present giving. After all who needs just Christmas when you can have an extra eight days of gifts?

So, although it was far better than a dirty old boatyard, Grandma and Grandpa's beach caused a bit of contention between Rob and Alex over the next months while they sawed, and sanded, and painted – trying desperately to put Humpty Dumpty back together again. Irritability was about as high as the temperature and hurricane season was approaching fast – taking with it all chances of charter until those Tradewinds started to blow once again come mid-November.

Alex would get furious with Rob, on a daily basis, when he would leave her to watch over the local workers, while he broke for a cocktail and a quick game of Dominos under the swaying palms with Grandpa. She was frustrated at first by the fact that Rob was not a lot of help to her in effecting the repairs. Eventually, she just resigned herself to the fact that Rob was simply not cut out for physical labor and assigned him the task of running to the local marine store or the airport to pick-up or order the parts and materials she needed to finish the job, which were usually not available on the island, as previously discussed.

Meanwhile, aside from his leisurely island work schedule, Rob was growing rapidly familiar with life in the islands by the day. In fact, Rob was trying hard to adjust to the principle of rule number two – "Whatever you need will not be anywhere to be found on the island," and was becoming very familiar with the function of the island purchasing agent, who created one unplanned delay after the other – from a shortage of wood to a lost engine, which somehow got misrouted to a Saint-Martin somewhere in Africa. When it did finally arrive in the right St. Maarten/St. Martin in the West Indies, it already had more miles on it, while still in the crate, than the total life expectancy suggested by the manufacturer. Oh, how Rob had taken life in the States for granted – a concept which Grandpa was all too quick to point out to him over a friendly game of dominos.

"You know, the problem with you Americans is you expect everything to be done like it is in America."

"Why is that a problem?" queried Rob.

"Well, cause, this just not be America."

"Well," answered Rob, "I do see your point, but it is the twentieth century and you would think that simple things like boat parts would be easy to find on an island."

"You make yourself crazy if you just plain expect it to be perfect," reasoned Grandpa. "You Americans want instant gratification in everything you do and you think you can be buyin' anything and everything you need whenever and wherever you want it. You want your food fast, your answers quick, and your enlightenment overnight. You keep livin' life as if it be an emergency and you end up missin' out on most of what truly matters. If you be racin' through life like a cat with its tail on fire you be droppin' dead of a stroke before you ever stop to enjoy it. It be time you just slowed down and smelled the hibiscus or listened to the sun settin' for a change," proposed Grandpa.

Grandpa was one man who had never let life rush him. A traveling salesman for most of his life – Grandpa had canvassed the islands selling the local island rum – the distillery's number one salesman. His greatest sales secret was always in his charm and the way in which he presented his product – sampling his wares with his regular clientele over a game of dominos. Poor Grandma had rarely seen him during his forty-year career, except those trips home which were long enough to drop off a little money and get her pregnant, which he had successfully done more than a dozen times. He had figured that she would be kept so busy with cooking, washing, or birthing children she wouldn't really notice he was gone so much of the time. The arrangement had suited Grandpa quite well, but then again, he had never asked Grandma if it worked for her.

In fact, it wasn't until he had retired at sixty that he finally memorized all of his children's names – even if he never did get their ages right or even the exact order in which they had been born. Grandma had survived those years on the theory that once the first wave of six was out of diapers, they were old enough to watch and help care for the second, not to mention the household chores and the marketing.

Grandpa's salary over the years had been a modest one since he'd drunken or given away most of his commissions, but fortunately, the company had offered a fair retirement plan which consisted of a comfortable pension for them to live on once the kids were grown – not to mention a lifetime supply of rum. They had even thrown in a case of Coke a week since Grandpa had been by far their most ardent promoter of their spirits. In fact, from time to time they had even used him in local commercials to continue promoting the familiar 'Grandpa' image, and his visits to their establishments. In time, Grandpa had actually become somewhat of a celebrity in the islands.

Overall, Grandpa's life had been a good one. Not much had changed for him after retirement, since old customers still came to visit him to share a familiar game of dominos and a petite rum punch. But for Grandma, the house had grown silent once all the kids were gone, and seeing Grandpa everyday had taken some getting used to, as it also had for him. But after a few years of getting on each other's nerves, they had simply learned to retreat to their corners and seek their own separate Paradise – which for Grandma was reading her mysteries and writing poetry, and for Grandpa, well Grandpa was quite content to have Rob as his new resident domino partner on the premises.

Maybe Grandpa's life hadn't changed over the years, however Rob's life was currently providing as much change as a dollar bill changer at the local Laundromat. In fact, aside from laundry – Rob didn't quite know what to do with all of the quarters that life was providing him. Somehow, he felt as if he'd received enough change over the last few weeks to handle a lifetime worth of dirty clothes.

That morning while Rob sat under the coconut palms with Grandpa drinking their first rum & Coke of the day, he couldn't help realizing as he stared at the Island Fever, how his life hadn't turned out exactly the way he'd planned. In fact, instead of being well on his way to an early retirement, Rob was rapidly finding himself on his way to being a penniless pauper.

"Some things just take time," said Grandpa reading Rob's mind. "You expect everything to be exactly the way you plan it to be," responding less than sympathetically. "If you always try to make things be a certain way... you be setting yourself up for disappointment. Dreams just don't come true exactly the way we dream them. But, then again if you be learnin' to accept things the way they come, you find you be really happy. Even if you won't always know what the future will bring."

"Not knowing the future never presented itself as a problem before I came to live in the islands," responded Rob. "The only thing that I seem to be able to count on here, other than change, is disaster and mayhem."

Rob was not only about to find that change was coming in his life like the rapid change of weather from a fast-approaching thunder storm, but he was actually about to embark on an entirely new life. As a voyeur to Rob's life, Grandpa, like myself, could plainly see the clouds brewing on the horizon, but he knew that forecasting its advance would be useless at this juncture and settled for a metaphorical approach rather than a prophetic one.

"You see," said Grandpa. "Life be like the weather during hurricane season in the West Indies, it changes from minute to minute. You just simply have to wait a while and it will be improvin'. The trick is, that you be open to change since it's the only thing you can truly count on. Even a little rain or a storm serves its purpose."

Rob thought about this for a minute as he watched Alex show a local guy how to cut a new plank for the hull of the Island Fever. "The worst part of change is watching people change."

"You just can't be bother by it," replied Grandpa, taking note of the subject of Rob's attention, "People always change... some for better, some for worse like the minister say. Especially women... they be changing their attitude 'bout as often as they change their clothes. You just got to remember that underneath it be the same woman even though she be wearing a blue dress instead of a red one." It took a while for it to sink in, but Rob did finally get on track with where Grandpa was heading with his observation. Even if the train had already left the station without him.

What Rob didn't understand was that although Alex found Rob quite attractive, she was technically still peeved at him and being too stubborn for her own good, and was far from ready to give him the pleasure of knowing she was indeed interested. If there was one lesson her father had taught her well aside from sailing, it was to play hard to get. "After all, men don't run after a train if they're already on it," he used to say. So, even though Alex was at work on the boat, she made certain that the train was on the track and that she was still the engineer. Every time it seemed that Rob was about to catch the caboose, she'd leave him standing at the station wondering what he'd done wrong,

"She's just acting so strange," Rob confessed to Grandpa with obvious concern as he watched Alex work.

"With women strange not always be so bad. Strange just be, strange. If you try to figure 'em, it'll just run your own engine right out of steam. You just have to be acceptin' how they are, an go bout your business," said Grandpa with confidence, as he chuckled. "Grandma gets so many moods, she'd plum wear out one of those mood rings."

"Yeah, but I am used to a moody woman," said Rob. "On that account no one had Sydney, my ex-fiancée beat. But Alex," said Rob shaking his head, "I think she's just not interested."

"Well, you know Rob, it kind of be like tryin' to sell a goat through a want–ad. No one be buyin' your goat, if you don't be runnin' de ad."

Now Grandpa had a point there. Rob hadn't exactly made another move to romance Alex since they were un-incarcerated. Especially since their little fiasco with the Island Fever. But then it seemed to him that she had made it pretty clear that she was not even in the market to buy a goat nor anything else Rob might be in the market to sell.

Of course, selling a goat was just about the farthest thing from Rob's mind, except owning one. But, like Grandpa said, life brings the unexpected – even if we thought we had it all well planned, it's just not meant for us to predict in advance, nor even to fully understand once it has come to pass. So, that afternoon when Rob was walking back up the beach from the local marine store, an orphaned baby goat determined that Rob looked like a good substitute for mom, and followed him back to their makeshift boatyard.

ISLAND FEVER

The last thing that Rob needed right now was a pet – a horned and hoofed one at that. For that matter, it had been years since Rob had owned an animal of any kind, and didn't have the slightest clue as to what to do with him. His last pet, a Collie named Magellan – his best friend since third grade, had died when he was in high school. He had named him after Ferdinand the explorer who was responsible for the first ship to successfully sail around the world. Rob had also raised pet show rabbits for years as a hobby, and for it his father called him a pussy especially since he refused to eat them once they were too old to show. But then again, Rob's father, Thomas, had called him that and every other name, from mama's boy to milksop often over the years. This had given Rob a bit of a complex about his manhood, especially where women were concerned – resulting in his current shyness in approaching Alex. Contrary to Sydney's modus operandi, Rob was not accustomed to making the first move in a relationship, and Alex was certainly not programmed to be the one to give up her hand and make the opening play.

Luckily, when Rob arrived back at the cottage with that little lamb in tow, Grandma and Alex immediately took pity on the creature and made a bottle from a milk jug and a rubber glove in order to feed the hungry little guy. The two women cuddled and suckled that little goat as if it were their child, then named him Lambchop, even though he definitely wasn't a sheep.

I've always found it interesting that here in the islands, the difference between goat and sheep are not defined exactly the way they are in the rest of the world. In fact, there is barely any way to distinguish a goat from a sheep in the West Indies aside from the accepted rule of thumb that if its tail points up, it's most definitely a goat, if it points down, then it is by all means a sheep. Since most can never quite get the hang of identification for the local hoofed creatures, it's usually far easier to simply refer to them all as 'Gheep.' The locals figure that there is truly no need to differentiate since they both taste the same when it comes to roti,* stew, and burgers.

This was one goat however, like Rob's rabbits, that was not destined to grow up as Christmas dinner. Instead, this odd little speckled creature was adopted by Rob, Alex, and Raymond as the Island Fever's official mascot – Little Lambchop was never really aware of the fact that he was actually a goat – for that matter he was treated more like the family dog and had quickly become so bonded with Rob, who somehow seemed to fill all of his maternal needs, that he never let Rob out of his sight. Not only did Lambchop claim the front seat of

---

*ROTI – The West Indian version of the burrito – usually made with conch or mutton and potatoes – in a curry sauce instead of salsa. Once again, a diplomatic mixture of the Mexican burrito and East Indian curry, in the West Indian tradition, which is to use anything that walks or swims that doesn't take an inordinate amount of effort to catch.

the rental car whenever Rob drove to town but he never missed a spin around the harbor with him on the windsurfer.

Between all the island chickens and their newly acquired goat, Rob was never quite sure as to whether he was living in a boatyard or a barnyard, and was feeling quite like he was back on the farm in Iowa. In fact, Grandma's rooster, Henry, had taken up standing on the Island Fever's boom at sunrise to perform his morning duty, not to mention his cocka-doodle-doos. Who needs an alarm clock when you've got a feathered wake-up service as reliable as old Henry. As much as it annoyed Rob, Henry was truly doing him a favor since there's nothing more miserable than trying to sleep in a hot stuffy boat bunk once the sun was up. Even Ole' Henry it seemed, was another life metaphor for Rob – offering a wake-up call, just when Rob was hoping to sleep in.

CHAPTER SEVENTEEN

Bankrupt

"Success is not measured by the position one has reached in life, rather by the obstacles overcome while trying to succeed."

Booker T. Washington

Once the problem of hauling-out had been solved, Rob needed to figure out where he was going to get the money to pay for everything, including a new engine – since he'd discovered that the deductible on his ten-thousand-dollar insurance policy was higher than the cost of repairs. The only thing he had left to his name once he'd returned Fritz's deposit, aside from one hull of the Island Fever which now had a rather large hole in it, was his condo back in Chicago. Rob knew that Sydney had always loved his modest little penthouse and that daddy had always wanted to buy her a home. So, he reluctantly telephoned Sydney to see if daddy would consider buying Rob's last stateside possession for his little girl. In fact, to Rob's surprise, Mr. Corandini was more than thrilled to have the opportunity to steal it from him for half its worth, taking advantage of Rob's desperate situation. It gave Mr. Corandini and Sydney great pleasure in knowing that once the mortgage was paid-off they had left Rob with only enough for one good shopping spree – Sydney style, if of course it was the yearly half off sale.

Rob hung up the phone feeling empty inside, as if he were bankrupt in more ways than just financially. It was becoming all too apparent to him that he had never really had a life outside of his career, his bank account, his condo, his car, and his high society girlfriend. Now, finding himself devoid of any of these material accoutrements, he was beginning to feel an overwhelming sense of emptiness. He felt about as lost as he would have been if he were alone at sea and at the mercy of his own inept seamanship skills. It was as obvious to me as it was becoming apparent to him, that he was in desperate need of being rescued from this floundering void in which he'd suddenly found himself. The only question being – was there a rescue in sight by some soul willing to take pity on him, or would he have to simply navigate these uncharted waters all by himself?

It was really too bad that Rob had never developed any strong sense of direction outside of the financial world. Had it been a question of whether to invest in futures or options, Rob would have been right in his element. But, when it came to investment in his own future, Rob was running out of options fast and had suddenly found himself sailing on more than one sinking ship – floundering like a boat without a rudder.

"It's hard to believe that only a few short weeks ago I had a totally different life," thought Rob. "I don't even know who I am anymore. How could this have happened to me? Just sixty days ago I was in my prime... knocking 'em dead at the stock exchange. Now look at me... I'm a mess. I have no house, no car, no job, no savings, and no idea what the hell I'm doing. I have holes in my hulls, a hole for a head, and a floating hole in the water to pour money into which I needed just about as much as a hole in my head. I may as well be bankrupt for all it's worth. After all, look at the reality," Rob thought analyzing his life, and taking stock of what was left. "The only real asset I have left to my name is a rather large liability, with holes in it, named after a tropical disease."

Rob pessimistically started to realize how little he had left, instead of appreciating what he'd gained. He didn't realize that sometimes when things start to go wrong, or at least differently than expected, it could be just the start of a great new adventure. But then again perception is everything – it could also be the start of a Kafkaesque nightmare as Rob had already perceived it to be. So, Rob sat down with Alex to budget the Island Fever's repairs and salaries. When it was over, he had a grand total of five thousand dollars left to his name. It was becoming rapidly apparent to Rob that Paradise was getting more and more expensive by the minute and that the cost of a rental car on the island of Sint Maarten, which he greatly needed in order to get to the airport for freight or to the docks to have something welded, was not going to fit into his budget for any extended term. So, both Alex and Raymond suggested that Rob invest in an 'island car,' as they were known in that part of the world.

An 'island car' could be best described as a mechanically sound vehicle whose engine will surely long outlive its sadly rusted–out body, and should only cost somewhere in the neighborhood of one to two thousand dollars. There are many brands of cars that fall into the 'island car' category, but the locals know only too well, never to be deceived by the modern day South American strain of the Volkswagen beetle, whose life expectancy rarely exceeds a day past twenty-four months without experiencing its first apparent symptom of island rot –

losing a fender or two along the roadside. But Rob was still naive to all the nuances of island life.

Volkswagen had sold the molds and machinery to the Brazilians several decades ago when they ceased making those classic, little cars, and in doing so relinquished all rights to any semblance of quality control. Rumor in the islands is, that's where they take all the recycled tin cans from that part of the world. But if the truth be known, it's more likely than not the product of what has become of the top half of all those fifty-five-gallon drums that are cut up to make what is known in 'de islans' as 'de steel drum' – a very romantic sounding instrument fashioned from the bottom half of that steel container which has been pounded into a concave configuration and tuned to hit a plethora of pleasing notes, depending on what part of the drum is tapped with a xylophone-like mallet. However, crude this may seem, it is in fact the sound that defined the birth of true island calypso music – that liquid, sensual, lazy, rhythmic beat that so well describes the island lifestyle.

Unfortunately, against all good advice from Grandpa and Raymond, Rob decided that if there was one thing he could handle alone without Alex or anyone else's help, it was buying a car. Even if his budget only totaled two thousand dollars. And of course, Rob had not allowed them to coach him on the number one rule of island car shopping – avoid used Brazilian VW's at all costs. So, when Rob pulled up at the boat that day in a bright yellow VW square-back wagon, Alex just shook her head and bit her tongue. Of course, Rob was quite proud of the great deal he had made for nineteen hundred dollars, especially since the car ran like a champ and was just two years old. To top it off, it even had a brand-new paint job, a fact which Rob never bothered to question about such a new car. However, he was quick to find out in the months to come that the paint job was in fact a temporary cover-up of a very progressed case of island rot – already halfway through the fenders, which were now held together by that fresh coat of paint. It was only a matter of weeks before the cancer began to spread faster than chickenpox on a six-year-old, revealing an incurable case of car–see–no–more fenders as Rob's bargain started shedding them one by one – only to be left by the side of the road as they dropped off like over ripened tamarinds* from a tree.

Eventually, the hole in the passenger floor board grew so large that whoever was riding in the passenger seat had to lift their feet in order to avoid the sand-blasting inflicted by the sandy, salty dirt from the unpaved roads, which of course was the reason the holes were there in the first place. But then,

TAMARIND – A tree which bears an unattractive brown fruit of the same name – used to make tasty juice, candy, and preserves – but is quite nasty and sour if eaten raw.

Lambchop usually managed to get the front passenger seat in the Yellow Submarine whenever they drove into town, forcing Rob to take the back seat if Alex was along.

One day during the island's normally dry season, it started to rain so hard and fast one day that it left eighteen inches of standing water in the street. Like Grandpa had warned – the weather in the islands had a penchant to change with little or no warning and Rob and Alex found themselves nearly drowning in the car from the water gushing up through the VW's holey floorboards like Old Faithful. It was then that they had christened their little underwater vehicle, the 'Yellow Submarine,' which it was known as for the rest of its short life span. Eventually, the front passenger floor board totally rotted out taking the passenger seat with it – to be replaced by a sheet of plywood and a little boat resin, patched back together somewhat like the Island Fever.

Oh, what a sad turn of events in Paradise. Poor Rob had been reduced from driving a German BMW to a Brazilian tin can in just a matter of weeks. Suddenly, Rob was beginning to realize how the other half lived.

"In a matter of just two months I've taken the back seat to a goat," thought Rob, "Gone from waking up to the sound of talk radio to waking up to chickens, digressed from living in a penthouse to living in a henhouse, and started taking showers out of an oversized douche-bag instead of the men's locker room at my two thousand dollar a year health club. Boy, have I taken things for granted," Rob suddenly realized. "I grew up believing that if I worked hard, life would always be what I wanted it to be. Maybe you just have to earn good fortune and a life in Paradise by doing more than simply working hard," thought Rob worriedly. "Maybe there are more dues to pay and lessons to learn before the Universe allows me to be happy."

What Rob did not yet realize was that there were indeed pipers to pay, and the bill collector it seemed, was already knocking at his door, even if he didn't own one at the moment.

"Stop feeling sorry for yourself," said Grandpa to Rob one day as he stared out to sea with a rum and Coke in his hand. "Things got to be looking up for you sometime soon. You've just got to stop wishing for bad luck and knocking on wood," sympathized Grandpa. "Luck be one of those things that come with change, overnight. Everything in life be just a roll of the dice and there be no denying that you've been on one mighty unlucky streak. You just got to start seeing yourself winning before you roll the dice."

On this count Grandpa was both right and wrong – his luck was about to change overnight, however, it was definitely not for the better, if that was possible. Unfortunately, Rob had not yet gotten the hang of visualizing himself the winner before he rolled his dice and he was unfortunately still letting life roll his dice for him.

CHAPTER EIGHTEEN

Dirty Laundry

"It doesn't always come out in the wash."

Grandma

Since Rob had deemed himself the official Captain of the 'Yellow Submarine,' one of Rob's newly assigned duties was to drop the ship's dirty laundry off at the only cleaners on the island. Of course, laundry hadn't been a conscious effort or even a consideration to Rob since his first year of college, before he had learned the ropes and figured out how to make his frat mates do his clothes for him. Prior to his years of academia, his mother had seen to it that if Rob threw something on the floor at night, it was clean and hanging back in his closet by the next morning. Rob's mother had spoiled him, not to mention the fact that Rob was somewhat lazy when it came to such domestic, menial things. The minute he was out of college Rob had been certain to hire a maid to come in three days a week, leaving nothing that resembled a household chore on his daily agenda.

So, when Alex had first suggested that he take on the duties of weekly laundry, Rob looked at her as if she'd eaten one too many green coconuts. However, once she further explained that the cleaner's widow had an affinity for young American men and always gave a fifty percent discount to any who entered her establishment, Rob agreed that it was indeed a wise move on his part to handle this simple chore himself. In light of his current financial situation, any means of saving money was a must for Rob.

As he entered the 'The Queen of Laundry's' establishment that first morning to drop off his dirty linens and underwear, Rob was greeted by Lucenda – a full figured, attractive native woman who could have given Jane Russell and her 'Cross Your Heart Bra,' a run for their money. Lucenda was dressed in a see–through lace tunic and tights, revealing enough fat to make even Rich Simmons wince, leaving little to Rob's imagination. The only accessories she wore was a rather oversized bow in her hair and an enormous smile when Rob walked through her door.

"Well, well, well... what do we have here. A new American maun cum to visit our beautiful islan'," replied Lucenda with her thick Papiamento* accent as she studied Rob from head to toe. "You know we have a special today on han' wash."

"I... I was just coming to drop off my laundry," stuttered Rob, quite aware that it was he and not his laundry that Lucenda was actually hoping to wash by hand.

Taking the duffel from Rob, Lucenda gave him a wink and her usual line – in her sexiest voice, "So, when you like to cum for dese? I mean, I wouldn't want ta miss you so I caun be sure ta geve you a discount on my services."

Rob, who was looking around for the closest exit to bolt from, just smiled and answered politely, "Wednesday, Wednesday would be just fine."

"Wednesday?" questioned Lucenda puzzled, "But it be only Tursdi, I wouldn't want you ta weit tat lon' a you clothes. I could tek care of dem mysef an halve dem for you later tonigh' if you like."

But Rob, who at this point was quickly backing towards the door, blurted out before making a dash for his car, "No, no that's all right. I wouldn't want you to rush or anything. Wednesday's fine, just fine."

"But don' you even want you tecket," cried a disappointed Lucenda as she followed him to the door with his claim check in hand, tip-toeing in her two sizes too small mules. But by the time she reached the doorway, Rob's VW was already tearing out of the driveway leaving poor Lucenda standing in a cloud of dust.

Rob had quickly decided that a discount on laundry was not going to make much of a difference in the grand scheme of things, so he opted to defer his new chore to Raymond who surely would be able to charm Lucenda as well as he. After all Raymond was an American male, which seemed to be the only qualification necessary for 'The Queen of Laundry's' discount.

Rob was aghast to find that when Raymond returned with their clean, folded laundry on Wednesday afternoon, all of his Calvins were MIA. Was it worth a visit back into the 'Queen's' lair for his briefs, or was he better off

*PAPIAMENTO — A language created by the native inhabitants of the Dutch Antilles. As with their general diplomatic policy regarding legislature, holidays, and customs, they have adopted a slang mixture of just about every other tongue that has ever graced their soil.

simply replacing several hundred dollars-worth of underwear with what the island had to offer. His present quandary was aside from the fact that, as Alex was quick to point out, Ludenda's was the only laundry on the island. So, unless Rob planned to do the Island Fever's wash by-hand he had better sort the situation out. Of course, Alex and Grandpa couldn't help but chuckle at the thought of Ludcenda chasing Rob around the Laundromat while he begged for his skivvies back. Missing briefs was not exactly Grandpa's expertise, so when Rob approached him for advice it was the first time that Grandpa seemed a little lost for words. However, he did point out that if Rob was unable to deal with a small matter of missing britches, he was likely in denial of the other more important issues in his life.

And indeed, there was a bigger life lesson that Rob was about to learn here – that you may be able to pass along those undesired chores to some sucker who is willing and able to do them for you, but inevitably at some point in life, one must tend to their own dirty laundry themselves – at least in the 'Karmic' scheme of things.

Of course, not everyone believes in Karma – all of those debts that have been rung up in this life or a previous one, not to mention all the interest that has also been accrued. It is in fact, that cosmic list of transgressions which all of us must at some point cleanup by paying off the accumulated debt. And unfortunately, cash is not the accepted currency – not even MasterCard will do. This is also one accounting system that one cannot simply file bankruptcy for, since this type of creditor actually follows you from lifetime to lifetime finding every opportunity they can to collect.

Most souls participating in this human experience called life, decided before they came into this world the course of events most likely to enable them to pay off their debts quickly and cleanly so that they could move on to bigger and better things. However, as I mentioned before, you do still have the final say in life to make your own decisions, and there are many people who insist on living their life strictly by the 'freedom of choice plan.' There is truly no right or wrong way, only the short way or the long way. But choosing the latter school of thought can indeed delay one's forward momentum substantially and keep one in cosmic hock for an eternity. This is the type of person who keeps on trying to work off of one of those deferred payment plans, somewhat like the one your local furniture store offers on the Fourth of July – charge now, pay later. And unfortunately, this was the plan that Rob had subscribed to this time around. But, with the recent turn of events in his life, he was slowly beginning to realize that maybe there was some validity to this Karmic theory since it seemed that those cosmic bill collectors were hot on his trail and indeed starting to catch up with him.

As far as this life went, Rob had been a pretty decent guy. A little shallow at times maybe, but certainly never one to intentionally hurt anyone. But G.O.D. only knew what indiscretions had gone before. A gypsy palm reader once told him that he was the reincarnation* of Casanova himself. If this were the case, then his present luck with women could definitely be attributed to his past life's indiscretions, and chances were – Lucenda had been one of his prior conquests who was seeking her vindication this time around.

"What could this woman possibly be doing with my underwear?" wondered Rob. *"No, that's not a picture I really want to conjure up. I'm sure it was just an accident that only my Calvin Klein briefs were selectively excluded from the rest of our laundry. I mean all of Raymond's boxer shorts were there,"* reasoned Rob. *"Maybe she just has a boyfriend that she decided should start wearing designer labels."*

Rob was smart enough to realize that this was all hopeful speculation on his part which made the task of retrieving his briefs no easier. However, Rob knew that reclaiming his property from the 'Queen of Laundry' would afford him the opportunity to stand his ground and clean up any future or past misunderstandings that he may have had with this woman. Besides, Rob had never been afraid of a woman, at least not since Sister Agnes from first grade. Which had been his parents' first and only attempt at a conventional education for Rob.

Upon Lilly's urging, Rob's mother had enrolled him in Catholic school his first year – against Thomas' wishes, of course. In fact, Lilly had provided her meager savings to pay his tuition she felt so strongly about the continuance of her family tradition, since she had not had the money to send Helen when she was a child. Of course, the nearest Catholic school in the city was some thirty miles away from where they lived outside of Iowa City, in Cedar Rapids, and it was up to Helen to drive poor Rob there in the morning and then return to pick him up in the afternoons. Thanks to Sister Agnus, who frightened the wits out of Rob with her stern righteous countenance and her steel yardstick, Rob had decided if this was school, then he'd just as soon forego an education all together. She had ruthlessly wielded that yardstick on those poor innocent six-year-olds hoping to scare the be-Jesus and the fear of God into them – both literally and figuratively. After the third week of Rob locking himself in the closet every morning before school, his parents had finally given in and transferred him to the neighborhood public school.

Dreading the task ahead of him, Rob climbed in the Yellow Submarine and headed off to the Laundry. Somehow, Lucenda's sixth sense had told her

---

*REINCARNATION — *The cycle of rebirth on the earth plane where you continue to be born again and again until you get it right. The heavenly edict for right and wrong, however, seems to always be in revision.*

that he was coming and she was waiting in ambush for him when he walked through the front door.

"There you are you sweet young thing," cried Lucenda as she grabbed him round the neck the moment he stepped into her establishment, laying a big juicy one on him before he could get a word out.

Feeling as if he'd just lip–locked with a Hoover, Rob tried as hard as he could to pry himself away from those lips that were as overly endowed as the rest of Lucenda's ample body. Finally, with an effort of super–human strength Rob managed to pry himself off her, sending himself reeling backwards knocking himself out cold on the laundry room floor. Seizing her opportunity, sweet Lucenda, 'Queen of Laundry,' sprung from her station behind the door onto a helpless Rob who never knew what hit him. Rob awoke an hour later to find himself nearly naked in Lucenda's den of red and purple draped walls and an alter holding numerous lit red and black candles, strange dried animal parts, and Rob's Calvins. Lucenda, by this point was dressed in some sort of a see–through ceremonial robe, revealing the last of what little had been previously left to his imagination. It seemed that once again Rob was marked as the evenings sacrificial lamb and this time, he was definitely going to put up a fight. What was worse – the smile on the 'Queen's' face said more to Rob than he needed to know in order for him to start looking for the quickest way out of there.

"This has to be a bad dream," thought Rob. "All I have to do is pinch myself and I'll wake up, this isn't really happening. 'OOUUUCH!'" screamed, Rob out loud as he pinched his left cheek hard enough to leave a bruise. "Oh, yes it is, this is real! This is real... real fucking scary! I've got to get out of here! And I was worried about Sydney putting some sort of curse on me."

Frantically, Rob scanned the room to find that there was no apparent exit, via a door at least. Spying an open window, Rob didn't bother to take the time to see what floor he was on and made a running leap out of the second story window above Lucenda's prized cactus garden. Rob wasn't sure what hurt worse – his shoulder from the fall itself or his behind from the prickly pear* that broke his fall. Needless to say, Rob had forgone the recovery of his briefs, even though it meant that she still had his personal belongings upon which to perform her voodoo. As far as his pressing need for underwear went, it was going to be a while before he'd be able to wear them anyway, due to the hundreds of cactus-needles he now had to extract from his left buttocks.

Luckily, Alex was off-island for the day taking care of personal business in St. Kitts, since Grandma spent the rest of the afternoon and the better part of the evening plucking prickly pear from Rob's posterior. Rob made her swear that she would never utter a word about his recent liaison with the

---

PRICKLY PEAR — *A very spiny cactus with paddle shaped pads and a prickly edible purple fruit.*

the 'Queen of Laundry' and the true reason he would be unable to sit normally for the next several weeks. It took some doing to hide the fact that it was impossible for him to actually sit down, especially when he needed to drive into town, but Grandma had made up a story about him being stung while swimming by a Portuguese Man-O-War, which Alex pretended to buy even though she knew that it was definitely not jellyfish season.

158

CHAPTER NINETEEN

Wisdom

"A river begins as a brook but grows ever larger until it flows into the great ocean... as is with enlightenment."

Siddhartha Gautama - Buddha

Rob had no way of knowing that first day that the Island Fever landed on Grandma and Grandpa's beach, how much importance they would play in the rest of his life. Looking at this kind, friendly, but uneducated couple, he never could have imagined how much wisdom was waiting to be bestowed upon some confused but deserving pilgrim that might stumble across their beach in search of Paradise.

Grandma, a loving, wonderful soul who had given birth to a 'baker's dozen' and raised her surviving twelve on little more than love, sunshine, and a prayer, was in fact, a rather profound poet; and Grandpa who had spent most of his life drinking, dancing, and carousing – in the name of work, was somewhat of a prophet in his own right, as Rob was soon to discover. Living alone on that beach, their blue–eyed, brown–skinned children all grown and gone to seek their fortunes, Grandma and Grandpa could possibly have been described as two of the most content sojourners of Paradise imaginable. By this point in their eighty-some odd years, they had indeed discovered its true locale and the bearings by which to reach it. The wisdom that Rob was to gain during the time he was shipwrecked on that tiny beach, would prove to serve him well in the years to come. Both Rob and I had asked the Universe to send him a teacher, and it had complied – with not one, but with two wise souls.

Grandpa's brother had also been a sailor Grandpa pointed out to Rob late one afternoon over a game of dominos and a rum & Coke. In fact, he had spent his life traveling the world by sea and died doing what he loved most, when his island trader, "Dark-Eyed Woman," was blown onto a reef one night in a tropical storm after he'd lost his engine. He had gone down with her trying to save her, his surviving crew had reported. She had been the love of his life – named after a woman he'd met and fallen hopelessly in love with in a port, stateside. In fact, it had been because of her that he was returning to the States during hurricane season and was caught in the storm. Grandpa had always known that one day he would get word that his big brother had gone to that big ocean in the sky, and he was not surprised when a telegram came reporting the sinking of his brother's ship. A part of Grandpa had died that day, but he held comfort in the knowledge that his brother had truly lived his life to the fullest. He had always reveled in his journeys, and Grandpa knew that for his brother, the destination had never been the reason for the trip, except maybe his last.

Grandpa was quick to point out, that his brother, the oldest of five *(only one year older than Grandpa),* known as Itchy by his friends and family, had taken on the job of raising Grandpa – then known as Stanley. Their mother had been a beautiful, exotic, wide-eyed West Indian girl who'd fallen in love with a rogue sailor named Xavier whom she had met while selling fruit on the dock in St. George's Harbor, Grenada,* her home town.

Xavier, like his son, had been a seaman most of his life in the French West Indies. Hailing originally from Mauritius, he had lived the better part of his life on a French Navy vessel in the Caribbean sailing from port to port. He had married Stanley and Itchy's mother, a fervently religious woman, on a long furlough only three days after meeting her. For five years after their union, Xavier had sailed into port for one weekend every two months which allowed Rose a precious two days with her husband – her whole reason for living. For five years, Rose sold produce on the docks and gave birth every eleven months to another strong son sown from Xavier's seed. Back then the Coconut Telegraph traveled a bit slower than it does today and Rose had fortunately, or unfortunately, been spared the details of Xavier's reputation. Throughout the navy and many harbor taverns, Xavier was known respectively as 'Eleven

*GRENADA — An island in the lower Windwards at the bottom of the grouping of islands known as The Grenadines. Grenada was originally named Concepcion Island by Columbus, then renamed Granada by the Spanish after their beautiful city – later called Grenada by the British who have had the greatest influence on the sizable Caribbean Island. In a more recent past, it made the evening news when the U.S. decided to invade and undo Castro's take-over under the guise of freeing a handful of American medical students from their communist regime. In 2024 the Grenadines were devastated by a rare Category 4 hurricane early in the season..

Quarters.' Since you see, drunken sailors often bored while in port, competed to see whose manhood measured up. Their measure of choice being one always at hand – the American quarter – just shy of an inch, it managed to give the less endowed some measure of advantage. Xavier or 'Eleven Quarters,' by which he was renowned, had believed it his God given gift and his born duty to spread his seed as often and as far as opportunity offered.

When he died in a knife fight in a barroom brawl in San Juan, and the Navy discovered addresses for seven wives scattered throughout the islands in his seabag, not to mention seven different wedding rings, they were understandably bewildered as to how to divvy up the remains and send a small part of him to each wife.

Rose had received the smallest but most endowed appendage from the undertaker and a note from the Navy providing her with names of the six other women, each bearing the name of "Mrs." Xavier Bellier – residing on different islands throughout the West Indies. They had even managed to forward her the wrong wedding ring. Rose's fantasy of a loving husband was shattered to say the least, along with her will to go on. She sent 'Eleven Quarters' to the local taxidermist, who was in the business of mounting trophies of quite a different kind. Nonetheless, he had presented it to her in a mahogany box, which was buried with her two years later when she inevitably died of a broken heart. She had however died content, knowing that if she couldn't have all of him, she at least had possession of the most important one seventh he had to offer. Alas, Rose had been buried a poor woman with only 'Eleven Quarters' to her name – just twenty-five cents short of three bucks. And her five dear sons, including Stanley and Itchy, had been left in the care of an aging grandmother, who had pretty much left them to fend for themselves the rest of their childhood.

"So, what is it you running from Rob?" asked Grandpa as he set up a new game of Dominos and refilled their rum & Cokes.

"Running?" said Rob looking at Grandpa truly puzzled.

"I'm not running from anything," Rob answered almost defensively.

"Then you must be searching."

Rob hesitated a moment thinking long and hard about what Grandpa had just said.

"I guess I am down here looking for something," thought Rob.

"Maybe Paradise?" queried Grandpa in his infinite wisdom.

Rob just stared at Grandpa for a moment surprised that this simple island man had so astutely summed up his quest and his life in a coconut shell. "

"Is it that obvious?"

"Like I sai, most sailors that land on this beach either be running or searching. And if it be searching, it's usually not for lost treasure, at least not the kind you can be spendin' anyway," said Grandpa.

"I'm still not certain what I'm looking for really exists," confessed Rob.

"Some can't believe in a thing they can't see with their eyes or feel with their hands," Grandpa responded sympathetically. "But a few still have the faith they can find it, even if few ever do."

Rob looked at Grandpa hoping that he would give him a clue on how to find this missing treasure in his life. "So... you know anyone who has truly found it?"

Grandpa sat looking at Rob, remembering Itchy and laughed his happy laugh. Itchy, Grandpa's brother had gotten his name one night when he'd passed out on the beach under the palm trees after a rum drinking competition, and had awoken the next morning at dawn with nine-tenths of his body covered in mosquito and sand flea bites. It had taken weeks for the bites and the itching to disappear, and in the meantime, the name had stuck, since he had nearly gone mad scratching himself.

When they were boys, Itchy had imagined he and his younger sibling sailing together to foreign ports-of-call and eventually buying a small island trader of their own. That was until he realized that Stanley was not cut out to be a sailor. To Itchy's disappointment, Stanley had not taken to the sea. In fact, he had taken to water like a cat, and had chosen at last to cross the ocean of life in a cottage rather than in a boat. He had found his happiness in his own way, which Itchy never understood.

Stanley remained Itchy's closest friend and family, taking him whenever possible on trips to the Americas and the larger ports-of-call – at least before Stanley had found himself with so many mouths to feed. If anyone understood Itchy, Grandpa did. He knew that men who wandered their whole life like Itchy were usually running from something – if not life itself, then usually a wife, the tax man, or the law. But in Itchy's case, Grandpa knew that he had truly found himself on the water, and had died a happy man. The sea had been his path, and in the end his ship his bride, since he stayed with her until death, they did part. This was not to say that he hadn't romanced a girl or two in the many ports that he had frequented. But unlike his father, he had never made commitments he couldn't keep – at least not until death had kept him from his pregnant wife to be who anxiously awaited his return.

Grandpa smiled reminiscently and tapped his finger to the side of his head, "First of all, you have to look here for Paradise. You got to look inside and listen. I suspect you be the type of man who listens when it comes to business but when it comes to life you just don't hear the answers."

"How could this man know so much about me?" thought Rob. "He's right, I've always paid close attention to that voice on the floor. It's never been wrong about buying or a selling, but I guess I never thought of using it for anything else."

ISLAND FEVER

Having taken an instant liking to Rob, as if he were one of his own sons, Grandpa was determined to set Rob on the right course. But he realized at the same time, that it was necessary to discover the true coordinates to the elusive whereabouts of Paradise for oneself and that it was not something to be simply given or acquired overnight. But then, Grandpa figured he had plenty of time to infuse Rob with his wisdom since the Island Fever was going nowhere fast. After all, nothing happened quickly or easily in the Caribbean, especially when one expected it to, like most Americans. Grandpa decided at that moment that the first thing he would teach Rob was to enjoy life in Paradise, since Grandpa knew that the only thing that separated a wise man from a fool was the wise man's ability to enjoy life, and this was one area of life in which Grandpa was very wise. "You know Rob," said Grandpa looking him square in the eye, "Real wisdom lies in knowing what to be concernin' yourself with and what not to. That be the first step to findin' Paradise."

Rob listened to every word Grandpa had to say and listened well, even though he was a slow learner. However, when he did finally get the 'big picture,' he got it. And that was the way his discovery of Paradise was to unfold, slowly at first, as Grandpa tried to paint a pretty picture for him. Eventually, Rob would get with the program when the Universe resorted to erecting a billboard for him.

"You be happy Rob?" Grandpa asked in his casual West Indian dialect, as he studied his next move on the domino board.

"Right now, I'd be happy to find a way to beat you at dominos," responded Rob.

Grandpa chuckled, "Hopefully, what you be looking for is not as hopeless as that," he said laughing triumphantly as he laid his last piece on the board and proceeded to set it up for another game. Grandpa grew silent for a bit as he always did when he was pondering life. "You see," he said finally, "Like life my boy, you got the hand you were dealt, and you got your startin' point," referring to the double ace he had just placed on the board as the center tile. "The secret is in learnin' to play the game with what you got, and realizin' you just never know for sure where it's going to lead. You also got to remember that everyone is dealt a different hand and they all be playing a different strategy. It's not so much what you don't have, but what you do with what you be holdin'."

Rob stared silently at the hand he'd just pulled thinking about his life and how he had neglected to use it to its full potential, while Grandpa poured him another drink and waited, giving him time to reflect on what he'd said.

"Sometimes all you got to do is just slow your headway a little. Give yourself time to chart the direction you be heading. Only a reckless sailor sets sail without at least plotting a 'dead reckoning'* course, even if he not be havin' all the coordinates."

"Doesn't that require knowing where you are... before you can figure out where you're going?" joked Rob, even though he was perfectly serious. As they sat pondering the wisdom of the Universe and more importantly dominos, Alex walked over and sat at the table with Grandpa and Rob. She carried her own glass with her – offering it to Grandpa. "I think I need a drink," said Alex quite seriously as Grandpa proceeded to pour the Mount Gay over a single cube of ice. Of course, it was quite rare for Alex to join them for rum & Cokes, so Grandpa and Rob suspected that something out of the ordinary had graced them with her company.

"Would you like the bad news now or after you've had several more drinks?" asked Alex.

"That depends," answered Rob. "If it's going to cost me money, can I opt for not hearing it at all?"

Alex just smiled sarcastically and proceeded to inform him that she had just discovered that the plywood in the underside of the Island Fever's bridge-deck was defective and had delaminated like layers of tissue paper, meaning an additional two weeks of work cutting out the old deck and rebuilding it, not to mention the extra expense. Needless to say, this news was definitely not music to Rob's ears as he hopelessly shook his head watching Grandpa make his move on the domino board.

Rather than stick around to listen to Rob's moaning, Alex took her drink and excused herself to join Grandma for their ritual of afternoon tea.

"Like I sai' before," said Grandpa seeing that Rob was about to burst a seacock.** "You have to learn to take everything as it comes. That's the only way you'll ever be happy."

"So, I should be happy about losing two more weeks of charters?" queried Rob.

"When there's a problem you know you can't be changing, you just gotta learn to go with the current or it be driven you crazy. You know, go with the prevailing wind flow."

Distracted from the game as he watched Alex on Grandma's verandah, Rob absentmindedly matched a 2/1 to Grandpa's opening play. Taking notice, Grandpa was quick to point out the other profound analogies that dominos offered, such as the similarities between dominos and relationships.

"You see, it takes two of a kind to be making a match," said Grandpa.

*DEAD RECKONING — A procedure by which a vessel's approximate location is deduced by its movement since the last accurate determination of position. In other words, a general guesstimate of where you think you are now, in relation to where you thought you were the last time you looked, and somehow never quite ending up where you'd hoped you'd be – which often involves missing entire islands. Assuming of course you didn't just miss the boat all together in the first place.
**SEACOCK — A valve that can close off a through-hull fitting, in the case of an emergency or rough seas – to keep the vessel from filling with water and sinking.

ISLAND FEVER

"If what you've got in your hand is no match with what you need to play the game, you just got to keep on drawing from the boneyard* until you find one that does. Take that big city girlfriend of yours up in the States. There just weren't no a match there. Just 'cause you think you love someone doesn't always mean you be making it work together."

Rob, sat there staring off at the ocean not thinking about Sydney, who he now knew he had never really loved – not in the true sense of the word. Instead, he was thinking about Julie Anne and the ways in which he had loved her.

"Why was it so easy to fall in love back then?" Rob wished that somehow, he could go back ten years and do it all over again – differently. *"Young love is blind love,"* he realized. *"It's in fact nothing but blind faith in another human being. It's believing that they feel the same for you as you do for them... knowing that this person in your life is never going to leave you. You never see the object of your love's faults because in your eyes they have none,"* thought Rob. *"It's as if love's a filter that strains them all out of the picture making everything about the other person seem perfect. How easy it was then to throw yourself into love with everything you possessed. Into the abyss of what you believed was everlasting, true love. Is there such a thing as true love or was it just blind desire to lose yourself in someone else? After all, if you have another person to rely on, you don't always have to depend on yourself for all the answers. But once you've lost that first love your heart is never the same, it never recovers from the wound, and sometimes it never comes home again. Like a rebellious child who's gone off in search of something better, or like the ancient Incas who would sacrifice a man by cutting his heart out. Some women have the talent of the executioner when it comes to slicing it quickly and cleanly from your chest... like Sydney,"* Rob realized, agreeing with Grandpa who had just wisely surmised that Sydney was not now, nor ever had been a match for Rob.

"The one thing that dominos are, that life is not, is that they be just plain black and white," continued Grandpa, jerking Rob out of his self-distraction. "With dominos, you can see what you got in front of you just as plain as day. Unfortunately, life not always be so easy to read. Sometimes we like to fool ourselves into believing we got a double-six in front of us when one be in truth a five. The most important thing you need to figure out is what it is you really be looking for, whether it be what you consider a 6/6 or a girl like Alex. Once you get that part right, all you got to do is learn to focus your attention on what you want an' just ask for it. Then you'll be seein' just how fast you get what you need to win the game."

• *BONEYARD — The main bank of dominos that players draw from when they can't make a play from their hand.*

Puzzled, Rob looked from the dominos to Grandpa about as lost as a weekend sailor without a compass. "Ask who?" questioned Rob uncertainly.

"The Universe, of course," replied Grandpa looking up to the heavens as if he were amazed that Rob would even question the source of all infinite gifts and wisdom. "It may not come in the exact form you want, but you be getting what you need if you just let go and keep the faith. It takes a lot more energy to make the world work the way you think it should than be accepting what it is. You got to stop your intellect from planning everything and lettin' it be the captain of the ship. Sometimes you have to let that 'great one source' guide you," Grandpa said pointing skyward, "It be always puttin' you in the right place if you just trust that it will provide."

Finally, someone was getting through to Rob as he followed Grandpa's gaze skyward.

"Why do I feel like I've just stumbled onto the world's first barefoot, domino playing, rum drinking guru?" thought Rob. "I always thought I could find all the answers on my own... at least until recently. Here I find this simple, uneducated soul who's lived under a palm tree most of his life, who makes me feel like I'm still in kindergarten in the big scheme of things. Four years of college doesn't have a thing on one game of dominos with Grandpa. I guess teachers can come in all types of disguises," pondered Rob.

"Yes, they can," I said agreeing with Rob's observation. With that Rob looked up as if he had actually heard. Finally, Rob was looking in my direction. Now if I could only get him to start listening, we'd be well on our way to that ultimate state of enlightenment or Nirvana, as Buddha would have it, or as Rob hoped – Paradise. I really shouldn't complain so much however about Rob's lack of awareness, since in truth he was far more advanced than many of those on Earth that my associates up here have been assigned. But Rob still had a long way to go and I was more than happy to finally have a little back-up help Earth side.

CHAPTER TWENTY

Fear

"There is no love without risk, and there is no love without loss. But... there is also no life without love."

Grandma

All the while that Rob had been shooting the breeze with Grandpa and doing that male bonding ritual that men do, Alex was in her own way becoming pretty close with Grandma. Everyday Alex would take her morning coffee and afternoon tea on Grandma's front porch to discuss life. To Alex, it felt as if Grandma was becoming the mother, grandmother, and sister she'd never had. And for Grandma, Alex was fast becoming the daughter who had finally come home. Alex would not realize until it was too late, how blessed she was to have found Grandma and her years of hard-earned wisdom, since not even her own daughters had ever been a recipient of the candidness that Grandma expressed with Alex.

Oddly, Alex found herself confiding some of her deepest secrets to Grandma, feeling as if she had found someone that she could trust for the first time in her life. Grandma had the ability to do that – make people feel that they could trust her with their life. She had all the qualities of a three hundred dollar an hour big city therapist – sans the insincerity. Grandma listened patiently as Alex babbled on and on about her painful relationship with Michael and how he had broken her heart. It was almost a relief to purge her pain to another human being for the first time in her life. Especially, to someone who always had the right answers, as if she had lived all the same sorrows as Alex, which indeed she had.

Not unlike Rob's grandmother, Lilly, Grandma's first child you see, was in fact not conceived from her husband's sperm. Grandma's first child as it were at the tender age of sixteen, had been the product of a childhood flame by the name of Warren Sparks. It seemed that Warren had professed his true love to Grandma, or Winifred *(Wini)*, as she was known at that age, and had even confirmed his intentions to her with a plastic Cracker Jack ring. She had given him in exchange the only possessions she owned – her undying love and her virginity. Two months later when she told Warren the reality of her most feared suspicions – that she was indeed pregnant with his child, he did what any gentleman would do faced with the given situation and gave his consent to plan the wedding. When the day rolled around for Warren to meet Wini at the church, to her horror, Warren was nowhere to be found. It seemed that he had jumped a freighter leaving for the Dominican Republic somewhere in the wee hours of the morning.

Seeing her heartbroken and rejected in that pretty white dress, Stanley, Warren's best man, had decided that very moment that he was going to make this young girl forget all about Warren and claim her for his own. It took nearly a year for Wini to get over Warren but in time Stanley had worn her down; and before the anniversary of that shameful day, she found herself back at the same alter once again wearing the same white dress, but this time her groom was in attendance, as was her beautiful four-month-old daughter. And, Stanley had remained so for some sixty years – loving Warren's daughter as if she were his own. Oh, Grandma knew that Grandpa hadn't been faithful for every minute of those years together, but nonetheless she knew that he was with her, for better or worse, until the day that she died.

"You know child," Grandma said to Alex in that charming, refined West Indian dialect which seemed to be so uniquely her own. She had stopped to correct herself, realizing that Alex was hardly a child, but a grown woman with many of the same concerns and insecurities that she had felt that day in the church. "My Dear," she continued, "You just have to let the pain of past heartbreaks go and move on with your life, otherwise you keep yourself from ever finding love again. You can't fill a glass that's already overflowing with heartbreak, you've just got to empty it to make room for something new. If you let it go, it will be refilled with all the right things, especially that sweet nectar of love."

"But love is too painful to just allow it to come and go like a revolving door," said Alex bitterly.

"What you truly need to understand is that someone can only cause you pain if you already have it inside you. Maybe you just need to look back a little farther than Michael to find where it all really started."

Alex looked at her strangely as if she had just uncovered something that she had known deep down inside for most of her life, but had been afraid to think about let alone discuss with someone else. Especially, someone who just a few short weeks ago was a perfect stranger.

Grandma, realized that she had hit a deeply hidden well for she had plumbed the depths of that same well herself since her pain had also gone far deeper than Warren. Grandma's mother had come from England, a country far away which Winifred had never managed to visit. Her father, Timon, was a doctor of some note throughout the Caribbean – a surgeon in fact who had gone to University in Europe, and in addition to his degree had brought back a beautiful redheaded bride named Victoria.

Wini had been born a year later to the happy, prosperous couple in her father's homeland of Grenada. Happy until that fateful day when Wini was five and Timon cut himself with a scalpel while performing a goiter surgery on a local woman. His patient recovered fully, however Timon succumbed to blood poisoning, which eventually claimed his life, leaving his grieving widow and daughter behind. Within a year, poor Victoria had developed consumption *(Tuberculosis)*, a common occurrence at that time, and had found it necessary to be committed to a sanitarium back in London, from which she never recovered.

Wini was left in the care of her Grandparents, her father's mother and father, who had raised her as their own giving her all the love she could have ever wanted. However, Wini had never quite recovered from her loss. Fate had taken her dear father from her, a man she had laughed and played with, and on whom she had relied for her security. And G.O,D., had returned her beautiful mother to rest in her homeland, robbing her of a mother's love and leaving her orphaned and all alone, or so it felt to Wini.

So, Grandma knew the face of loneliness and pain and recognized it in Alex when Alex dropped her guard enough to show her true feelings about the loss of her own parents. "Sometimes we experience bad things and people in our lives to take a better look at ourselves and make us appreciate the right person when you finally do come across them," Grandma said, "Just so we don't take the real thing for granted."

"But I'm afraid of falling in love again. I'm afraid I'll lose them or they'll betray me," replied Alex before she'd even realized what she'd said.

What Alex didn't understand yet was that it was fear itself and only fear that would create uncertainty and pain in her life. And, if she only had faith and trust in herself, and in her higher guidance, she would have found love by now. Fear is the one emotion that can control and overwhelm all other emotions and logic, and fear is truly the only thing in life that there is to be afraid of, since fear is the one thing that can destroy everything else.

* *FEAR* — (Synonymous with) *Doubt, qualms, hesitation, terror, and trepidation.*

"All fear* is dear, is just a part of you that hasn't discovered love yet. If you believe someone will hurt you, they will. You can't be afraid to feel deeply just because you fear you may lose someone. Fear is only your belief that something will be painful. The mind's a powerful thing, you've just got to stop creating your disappointment in your mind," answered Grandma sweetly as she took Alex's hand in her own and squeezed it. Grandma stopped a minute and looked at Alex, "You take life too seriously. You need to laugh more... it'll open your heart and soothe your soul. Give it time dear, love will find its way back into your heart. In fact, I think I can already hear it knocking at the door," Grandma said with a smile as she glanced over at Rob who was watching Alex intently.

Doubt, qualms, hesitation, terror, and trepidation were all the things running through Alex's mind at that moment as she watched Grandma watching Rob, watching her. What was Grandma seeing in Rob's eyes for her that she hadn't seen?

Grandma was a very perceptive woman who typified that age old paradigm of 'woman's intuition,' and had an innate understanding of human nature. Having raised eight boys, Grandma had learned by now to read the signs of lovesickness which imbued a young man's eyes at the height of its infection, and had recognized it early on in Rob's dreamy gazes at Alex. She knew however, that there were inappropriate times to meddle and inopportune times to not – this seemed to her to be one of those times where it was best to simply point out the obvious to the hesitant participant of the imminent amour, and let nature take its course. Of course, Grandma also realized that she was dealing with a woman who was nearly as strong willed and stubborn as she had been at that age and allowed herself a little indulgence in an attempt at out–and–out matchmaking. After all, it was obvious that these two needed more than a little coaxing to get over their fear of admitting their feelings for one another, and Grandma was more than happy to oblige with her services.

"You know dear," Grandma said to Alex, "I think you should answer that door, you never know what treasures might await you on the other side."

Alex caught herself with a doubtful laugh, "You can't really mean Rob? He's still so in love with that Italian princess that he can't even see that I exist. Besides, Rob and I always seem to find our way into an argument."

"Sometimes it's a sign that someone really likes you, when they care enough to be bothered by what you disagree about. Besides that, you have to understand that he's scared too, just as scared as you are about the two of you get-ting together," said Grandma with a strong measure of confidence.

"Now why on earth would he be scared of me? He's the kind of man who's always gotten everything he wanted."

*FEAR — (Synonymous with) Doubt, qualms, hesitation, terror, and trepidation.

"Maybe everything he thought he wanted. It seems that he's starting to reevaluate what's really important in life and realizing that maybe there's more to a good woman than pretty clothes and fine manners."

Alex thought about this for a moment in silence.

"Don't you realize that you intimidate him?"

Alex just looked at Grandma curiously.

"This princess you're referring to, only bossed him around but he still felt like the man in the relationship. Men want women to be women my dear. They just simply don't know how to respond to women any other way. You see, the problem you have is that you're more capable than him in the things that are an important part of his life right now, and it scares him. You're a strong and independent woman who's totally capable of taking care of herself. Don't you see that it makes him feel as if you don't need a man in your life?"

"But what can I do to make him feel more... manly, I mean, I'm just doing the job he hired me to do? It would be different if he knew how to sail and build a boat. Look at him, he's got so much to learn but he doesn't want me to be his teacher. I mean every time I try to show him how to do a job, he refuses to listen to me, and then he goes about nearly killing himself or a paying passenger."

"Well, it's a wise woman who knows how to recognize what a man needs and give it to him without him actually realizing you're doing it. You can be his teacher if you really want to without him ever even knowing it."

Alex considered this for a beat.

"Trust me girl, I've raised enough boys to be somewhat of an expert on what makes them tick. Nine all tolled including Grandpa there. Give him a chance to learn without him realizing you're his tutor. None of us ever stops learning lessons. Why even the master learns from his pupil."

Of Grandma's thirteen, only four had been girls – two older – two younger – placing the burden on the older two to help Grandma with the cooking and rearing of their younger siblings. Sara, the oldest, had run off with a young man from Barbados at seventeen and Myra had joined the Peace Corps the day she'd turned eighteen. As much as Grandma had adored her daughters it was her sons that had taught her the most about life, and about herself. They had inspired her, intrigued her, and exhausted her all at the same time. Girls were easy to raise, but boys were work – especially with a household of them underfoot. Grandma had gone gray early on and had longed for a husband at home to discipline them since Stanley was always on the road. Of course, she couldn't find it in her heart to impose punishment of any kind on them. In fact, they had pretty much run wild. But, as wild as they were, she had done her best to teach them values with love, even if her own meager education had limited her in worldly tutelage. All of her sons had grown to make her proud – all but two, her first and her last. And all had left the island to seek their own life, love, and fortune from North America to Argentina.

"You see dear, we were put here to learn and grow and the only way you can do that is through relationships with another. Now of course there's no denying that some relationships bring you pain and others pleasure, and some make you feel as if you've gone to heaven while some make you feel like you've woken up in hell, but it's all important, it's all part of growing. In fact, it's the only thing we're truly here to learn. Love is what feeds us dear. Why it's the fruit of life. It's what sustains us and makes us feel alive."

"Then I guess I haven't learned much this time around," sighed Alex.

"You know, if you're afraid to climb the tree to pick the fruit you starve yourself of the sweetness of life," responded Grandma. "Even if there are parts that are bitter there's always a sweetness underneath. It's like eating paw-paw.* You put lime on it before you eat it since the bitterness makes the fruit that much sweeter."

Grandma was indeed, as she had suggested, an expert on child rearing. But, raising her children had not always been an easy road, even if a happy smile had always somehow managed to grace that wise, serene face of hers since she had lost two of her sons, her first and her last along the way. You see, her thirteenth child, Dougie, born to her at the age of forty-four, had come into the world with Down's syndrome, and had lived only to the age of seventeen. But Grandma, who had always loved every little creature with everything she possibly had to give, felt in some way that this, although imperfect little guy, was the most perfect gift she had ever been given. Having pretty much raised her rambunctious brood by that point, she found Dougie to truly be her little heaven-sent angel. The day he died in her arms, she'd picked up a pen and had begun to write her first poem. A poem about her precious little boy who had loved everything and everyone equally, with no trace of judgment or preference. Since that day, Grandma had spent her time writing or reading, feeling the need to fill up her days turning her hard-earned wisdom into verse and rhyme.

*PAW-PAW – A slang word in the islands for the fleshy, edible, orange/yellow fruit – Papaya. Not to be mistaken with the North American tree, bearing fleshy, yellow fruit.

HINDSIGHT!

Had anyone told me when I was a girl,
Happily lost in a carefree whirl,
Not still believing in Elves and Fairies
But dizzy on Romance
And True Life Stories –
Had anyone warned me that I would give birth
To a Baker's Dozen!!!!!!!!!!!!!
I'd have hooted with mirth
Perhaps, or quietly fainted away
To sleep like Van Winkle
Until today!

Lorna Steele

CHAPTER TWENTY-ONE

AC–DC

*"How do you know if you're in love?
You don't have to ask."*

Grandma

As I said before, Rob was pretty ripe for Alex's affection, but she was not showing any signs of interest, and he was getting closer and closer to braving climbing that tree to pick the fruit himself. His misjudgment of Alex and her self–prescribed aloofness towards him only served to frustrate him and make him more and more uncertain on how to approach her. There were days that Rob felt he was making headway with Alex, and other days that left him feeling as if he were paddling upstream in a rowboat with a tennis racket. The fact that Rob's ego was still not totally intact, and the fact that he was a compulsive over-thinker, led him to such unreasonable conclusions as to even question Alex's preference of gender. Offering Rob, a far less painful solution to his lack of progress with her romantically than of course the most logical thought that she just wasn't interested. It never even crossed his mind that she might be as hesitant as he to take the plunge into deep water by making the first move. Little did he know that Alex was all the while wishing that he would just sweep her off her feet and woo her until the cows came home as opposed to Lambchop, Rob's new hooved companion who never left his side for a moment, especially when Alex was around. Lambchop, it seemed, had made himself right at home in their little boatyard.

In lieu of romance, work was progressing on the Island Fever at about the speed of the mail in the West Indies, and as per Grandma's advice, Alex had begun finding more and more small jobs which she felt Rob could handle without injuring himself or some passerby. Sanding appeared to be a safe enough task for Rob, given that aside from relatively minor skin abrasions, there was little damage to be inflicted by a sheet of sixty grit sandpaper. Of course, an electric sander was another story altogether, and Alex chose to play it safe and leave the power tools to herself and "Home Improvement," which they occasionally caught a glimpse of on local TV after someone had recorded it on their home VCR stateside, and sold it to their friends at 'de islan' TV station. Of course, it was several months out of date, but then, the same could be said for the daily news, since it was also pre-recorded on video tape then shipped air freight to the island. Thus, being broadcast at least two to three days later than it had originally happened. Of course, the great advantage in not getting the news until several days later was that the world could end and you'd have at least two extra days before you found out about it. And as far as the *New York Times*, the *Washington Post*, the *Miami Herald,* or the *Wall Street Journal* went, about the best that one could hope for was a pre-read copy which some tourist had brought with them on the plane. But then who cares about current events when you're living at least three steps behind in Paradise. Their theory was, anything that's of any great importance can and will eventually be heard via the island's most reliable source of information – the 'Coconut Telegraph.'

Regarding power tools, Rob still felt somewhat emasculated by the fact that Alex didn't trust him with any voltage higher than a D-cell battery, but then to be perfectly frank, Rob didn't really trust himself with any modern conveniences that could slice, dice, or chop vegetables, or digits effortlessly. But still, that didn't change the way Rob felt about Alex's assessment of his inadequacies in the power tool department. After all, weren't all men supposed to be capable of screwing things fast and efficiently? Meaning, any man who was still reliant on a handheld driver, was likely not getting a satisfactory job done. So, what in the end resulted from Rob's limping ego, were his unceasing attempts to impress her in other ways – like climbing a palm tree to pick her green coconuts and conquer his fear of heights, only to find himself hugging a nest of centipedes. It wasn't until he had regained consciousness from the fall that the sensations from the double spotted sting marks all over his chest began to feel something akin to being poked with a 110-volt cattle prod, not to mention the fact that Rob's rapidly swelling body was now beginning to resemble the Michelin Man, ala rouge. Needless to say, a trip to the local hospital was critically in order and had it not been for the visiting Miami dermatologist, there to borrow a needle and thread to stitch up his son's split forehead, Rob might have easily died of anaphylactic shock. Since, after all, it was Sunday and all of the local doctors were off on Sundays and nowhere to be found. Their theory was, since it was a day of rest – no one should get hurt, right? Grandma, Grandpa, Raymond, Alex, and Lambchop waited impatiently in the waiting room as Rob was given a shot of epinephrine and put on oxygen. It was touch and go there for an almost unbearable hour while Rob's breathing gradually returned to normal and the swelling subsided to resemble somewhat more of a Frosty the Snowman appearance, since his body was now in shock and he was whiter than the stained, yellow sheets covering the hospital bed. Unfortunately, no one had warned him that in the case of any life-threatening ailment, the vet or a jet were usually a safer bet than the town hospital.

Even though Rob's acrobatics had nearly killed him, his gallant intent had not gone unnoticed by Alex. In fact, she was well aware that the gesture was entirely intended to please her, since Rob knew that Alex's favorite treat was green, jelly coconut meat. She recognized the fact that he had finally found the courage to climb the tree of life to offer her a taste of his fruit, even if he had failed miserably in the attempt. Alex felt somewhat guilty knowing that Rob was lying in that archaic hospital bed in critical condition due to an attempt to impress her and win her favor. She had definitely been too hard on him, and now it might even be too late to make it up to him. Not to mention the fact that Alex was starting to realize that she might actually even be in love with him.

"In love with him?" thought Alex. *"Did I hear myself correctly?" repeated Alex to herself. "Is it love or just concern for his life, or even guilt that I'm responsible for what happened?"*

"Oh Grandma, what am I going to do if he doesn't wake up?" cried Alex sometime around sundown.

"Well child, love heals just about everything," assured Grandma. If you just talk to him and tell him how you feel you might just find that you can get him to row his boat ashore. After all, without love in our lives we're all adrift without purpose. If you give him a reason to live, I think he'll come around."

Alex looked at Grandma and squeezed her hand, thankful that she had found such an understanding soul. Alex never left Rob's bedside throughout the night, even when he started to talk about Sydney in his delirium – she sat, slept, and ate next to his bed – holding his hand and telling him how she felt and that everything was going to be all right if he would only wake up.

Of course, Rob was in Never-Neverland and it wasn't visions of sugar–plum fairies that were dancing through his head at that moment. In fact, had he been born about fifteen years earlier, his vivid dreams would have likely qualified as a microdot flashback. But since he was not a contemporary of the Leary and Kesey era, nor a participant in Tom Wolf's, "The Electric Kool-Aid Acid Test," one would have to attribute his hallucinations of being chased by giant centipedes and huge rolling coconuts, to the concussion he had suffered from falling fifteen feet from Grandpa's palm tree onto his head – laced of course with copious amounts of centipede venom. Life it seemed was indeed offering up Rob's share of pain and brick walls this time around. In fact, it seemed to be trying to tell him something. After all, painful was short for pay-in-full, to be credited of course against that overextended laundry tab that I mentioned earlier.

This wasn't the first time Rob had fallen backwards on his head, which could attribute to his current hard-headedness. I remember when Rob was eight and he and his cousin Marie had decided that since there were no mountains to climb in Iowa – they would get a better perspective of their little world from high above the town via the local water tower. Rob had gone first, and before he had gotten to the third-landing he had made the mistake of looking down. Frozen, hanging there from that ladder on the Iowa City water tower, Rob had realized how big the world outside his little one, truly was. It had taken two hours and the local fire department to get him to come down, since he was stubbornly determined to do it on his own. It was the first time he and his parents realized the severity of his fear of heights. One step at a time, Rob had eased himself down rung by rung. It wasn't until he reached the fifth step from the ground that he had unfortunately looked down and painfully took those last few steps back to earth in one-fowl-swoop, landing on the unforgiving concrete on his head, requiring as many stitches as his father's switches that were used later to teach him the lesson he'd already managed to learn on his own.

Luckily, this time Rob had landed on a stretch of somewhat soft sand, which prevented him from suffering any serious brain damage, or the need for stitches to any body parts other than his ego, which was still in tatters from his original balls-up with the Island Fever. However, it had taken a great deal of courage for Rob to climb that tree for Alex, since it was the first climb he'd attempted since his Iowa City water tower excursion to see the world.

Rob was in the midst of a dream about grinding large gaping holes into the Island Fever's topsides with an electric rotary sander, when he heard the faint calling of Alex's voice begging him to wake up. It wasn't until he dreamed that he heard her saying that she was in love with him that he put down the sander long enough to listen to what she had to say. Suddenly, the sun had come out in his dream and he was at the helm of the Island Fever, sailing through crystal blue water and sipping a tall rum & Coke. Alex was busy on the foredeck coiling lines and asking him if there was anything more that she could do for her Captain.

"Captain," thought Rob now in a state of semi consciousness. "She actually called me Captain!"

For the first time in months Rob felt in control. He was about to take the helm of his life, and his love life, or specifically, his insecure relationship with Alex. He knew then that she loved him and that they would be together, forever, sailing off into the sunset and – –

– – "CRASH!" went a metal bedpan as it hit the floor, ejecting Rob's amazing dream abruptly from his memory bank and catapulting him back to reality and a somewhat foggy state of consciousness. Since his body was still swollen to least twice it's normal size, he found it difficult to open his eyes to anything more than tiny slits, which were sufficient enough to find Alex leaning over him, with eyes closed, ready to kiss him tenderly on his swollen lips. Being of sound enough mind to recognize a fortuitous opportunity when he saw it, Rob lay there continuing to feign his state of unconsciousness until the moment that their lips met. Well trained in his line of work to be prudent in never making a move pre-maturely, and to always wait until one was assured that a commodity was ripe for the picking, Rob saw his opening and grabbed it, and laid one on her.

Alex was shocked and embarrassed to be caught in the act of openly demonstrative affection to a member of the opposite sex, which had been totally unsolicited, since it was entirely outside of Alex's modus operandi – totally against all her years of training in aloofness where men were concerned. Alex jumped back with a scream, utterly caught off guard by Rob's unexpected recovery – knocking over the antiquated IV stand which fell to the floor with another crash yanking the IV-drip right from Rob's arm. Rob screamed as he bolted upright in bed right into the tray table which was stationed over his chest knocking the wind out of him. Aside from the fact that he was fighting desperately to catch his breath and the fact that blood was streaming down his arm from the disconnected needles which still hung from his puffy, bruised flesh, Rob was a happy man. It was at that moment that all hell broke loose as Grandma, Grandpa, Raymond, three nurses, two doctors, and Lambchop burst into the room to see what all of the ruckus was about – finding to their surprise, Rob and Alex in a lip-locked embrace.

CHAPTER TWENTY-TWO

Black-Out

*"You can make the world go round,
or you can watch it turn."*

Grandpa

One thing the Caribbean has always lacked in the way of First World efficiency is an adequate infrastructure – thanks to the carefree attitude of the West Indian culture. Not to mention the rapid growth of tourism which has inspired the never-ending building of more and more hotels and those cursed timeshare resorts sought after by American tourists desperately seeking a brief taste of that very state of indifference so well honed by the West Indian. Like the phone system or lack thereof, which is always beyond maximum capacity due to a lack of needed phone lines on the island, the other utilities such as power and water, equal communications when it comes to being inadequate. On the island of Sint Maarten/Saint Martin, Dutch residents living at the end of the water main nearest the French side, have gotten used to going without water for weeks on

Cistern — A tank for storing rain water in the islands that is usually in the foundation of any given structure, and serves as their back-up water supply – allowing one to avoid relying on the island water plant. Since the system works off the principle – the roof catches the rain and everything else which happens to fall on it or in its gutters and thus runs into the storage tank under the house, one has to get used to the fact that the bottom foot or so of the cis-tern contains a sludge comprised of island dust, insecticide, palm fronds, decaying insects, and geckos who were unlucky enough to be caught unaware sunning themselves on the roof just prior to an island downpour.

end just prior to the start of tourist season when all of the major hotels between their house and the water plant decide to fill their cisterns* at the same time. Likewise, one never quite knows when the electrical plant is going to be shut down, due to either West Indians to run it, or a shortage of fuel. So, when Alex returned to the boatyard from the hospital once Rob had been released, she was not surprised to learn that the power on that side of the island was indefinitely off due to a strike by the barge crew that brought the power plant's fuel to the island every week from the storage containers in St. Eustatius. Thus, keeping Alex and her crew from operating any of the helpful power tools as aforementioned in order to quickly and conveniently expedite their progress on the Island Fever's repairs.

What was one more delay in Paradise? Progress on the boat may have slowed, and the island may have been in the dark, but Rob had finally seen the light, at least where Alex and love were concerned. Up until now Rob had been in the dark about love in general. He had grown to believe that he would never find true love again, at least not love like he had felt for Julie Anne. What he had never realized was that he hadn't really been looking, he had simply settled for other less important things in a relationship. What he hadn't been able to understand due to that gaping black cavern in his chest, was that once one finally starts to seek true love, it begins to seek them.

Thanks to the lack of power on the island prohibiting the use of power tools, Rob was on equal terms with the workers in the tool department. Rob's self-esteem was soaring as he happily sanded away at the inside port hull, feeling as if he were finally being useful to Alex. After all, Rob had to do something that made him feel worthy in his new found love's eyes. Having sworn off tree climbing, not to mention putting himself anywhere near the proximity of any creature with more than four legs, and the lack of electronic devices, Rob was relatively safe at this point – at least from himself.

Grandma and Grandpa were pleased to see the electricity sparking between Rob and Alex in the love department, even if Rob still had a torch waiting to be ignited in the area of self-love, self-esteem, and ultimately true happiness. Rob didn't yet understand that one couldn't fully love another unless he had learned to love himself. Grandpa was aware that he still had his work cut out for him in the task of mentoring Rob, but in the meantime, he knew that new love would keep Rob content for a while and quite possibly even deceive him into thinking he'd actually discovered Paradise. But Grandpa knew all too well, that until Rob learned to love himself and be happy within and not just without, or more accurately, with another, he would never be able to discover true happiness. In the meantime, it gave Grandpa and I a short respite while Rob happily went about being in love.

Rob was indeed feeling pretty happy at that moment in time, Paradise or not, having gone to the brink of death and back again only to find love waiting for him at the other end. He was now beginning to truly appreciate what he had, and the fact that he had been given a second chance to enjoy it. He finally understood what Grandpa meant by learning to work with the hand that you're dealt in life instead of always looking to draw another card. Of course, it helped that Rob had finally drawn a Royal Flush instead of his usual pair of deuces.

    Now that he had finally slowed down to enjoy life instead of letting it pass him by, Rob was feeling like a million bucks even if he was down to his last thousand. Finally, Rob had stopped sacrificing the present for the future and was learning how to live in the moment. He was beginning to realize that Grandma and Grandpa were right. Giving and receiving love and learning to enjoy life were the only things in life that truly counted. And to my relief, he was stopping on his walks with Lambchop to the marine store to chat with the Universe and to smell the hibiscus, as Grandpa had suggested, even if they didn't emote any fragrance. Maybe now he'd start to listen to what I had to say to him.

    "Well Universe, or whoever's in charge up there. Isn't life beautiful? I mean what a lucky man I am. Grandpa was right, it seems my luck has started to change," said Rob to nothing and everything at the same time. "So, I don't have a lot of money in the bank. I've got all the wealth that counts in the world. I've got people who love me. But more importantly, people I love in my life. Boy, did Sydney ever do me a favor when she left. She made me wake up and realize that I'd been pursuing her dream instead of my own. This is the first time in my life I've ever felt I'm worth more than my portfolio."

    "YES!" I exclaimed thrilled that he was finally starting to understand, "Now you just have to start investing in yourself instead of in the market."

    Rob looked around puzzled as if someone was there on that beach with him. Slowly, he looked up as if it were finally sinking in about the source of his intuition in business. It had, or rather, I had always been there for him, even if it hadn't ever been acknowledged.

    By the time Rob arrived back at the boat yard, a smile of contentment graced his face, as if the weight of the world had been lifted from his shoulders.

    "You see, it not be necessary to be dead to see the light, contrary to popular belief," said Grandpa noticing Rob's peaceful expression as he poured their first rum and Coke together since Rob's accident, "Even if it sometimes takes being faced with death."

    "You know, at one point there in the hospital I felt as though I were in a tunnel drifting towards that really bright light everyone talks about," Rob answered distantly as if he were caught up in reliving the experience. "But I wasn't scared. It was almost as if I was an observer. I knew it was my choice...

you know, whether to go or to stay, but I knew it wasn't time. And besides, how could I leave Alex. I mean she was sitting there begging me to come back. Actually, I think I stayed longer than necessary because I was enjoying listening to her talk. You know it was weird but it was as if I was able to really take a look at my life for the first time. Like that vantage point outside of my body, made it all clear."

Nodding his head as if he understood, Grandpa grew quiet for a moment remembering a time long past "You know, I be just about your age the first time I came close to dyin'. Until then I never understood what livin' really be about. I took life for what worked at the time... I was always waitin' for something better to come along instead of appreciatin' what I had. When you get too close to something like life, it be hard to make out the picture real clear. You know, it be like one of those impressionist paintings, where you need to take a step back for the picture to make sense."

Rob looked at Grandpa with a knowing look as if there was suddenly a deeper bond between these two men who couldn't be more different on the surface, but had just connected on some inner more meaningful level.

"We all pass up opportunity because we think we have plenty of time to go back and do all those things we always wanted to do," continued Grandpa. "But then one day we wake up and realize that we be either too sick, too tired, or just dead and we never had the chance. You have to take life as it comes... like what you're doing here. You saw a chance to live the life you wanted and you took it. Good and bad, you're living it, right here, right now."

"How does he do it? Why is it that this man always seems to know what I'm thinking and feeling?" thought Rob staring at Grandpa.

Rob froze, suddenly realizing that he was actually feeling something. And, like an appendage that had been asleep too long he felt a tingling sensation run up his spine as if his soul had just reawakened after a long winter's nap.

"He's right," realized Rob, "I have always taken life for granted... knowing that everything would just be the way I expected it to be. I guess that just doesn't work in this part of the world. I assume this was a wake-up call for me to realize that I have a lot to be thankful for and that I'm a pretty lucky guy when it comes down to it," reasoned Rob to himself. "I mean, look at what I've got. I'm alive and healthy, all of my appendages still work, even if I am a little bruised. I have a beautiful woman who's in love with me and half of a million-dollar boat. Even if it does have a few holes in the hull. That's where I went wrong with Julie Anne. I took her for granted – I believed that she would just be there for me, and then one day, she wasn't. I guess since then I just didn't believe I deserved someone who truly loved me, since I hadn't taken what was given me seriously the first time around," finally admitting it to himself.

ISLAND FEVER

Satisfied with Rob's progress in the learning to enjoy life department, Grandpa decided to allow himself a brief sabbatical from Rob's tutoring to give himself a chance to catch up on a little of the latest island gossip, and a lot of lucky hands of poker.

Grandpa rigged kerosene torches under the palms in order to provide him and his drinking and card playing buddies enough light to pour their rum and Cokes by, and determine which of them held the winning hand for the nickel-kitty and the shots of rum for which they played.

Sans the fully operational power plant, Rob and Alex were creating a fair amount of wattage by themselves. In fact, there was enough current in the air to make one think that they were sitting on a boat in the midst of a storm with Saint Elmo's Fire* crackling away in the rigging.

And Grandma, well she was basking in the knowledge that once again her instincts about love had been on target, and relieved to know that her matchmaking skills had not grown rusty from a lack of suitable candidates. In her eyes, Rob's unfortunate accident couldn't have been more fortunate. As Grandma well knew, a little dose of crisis in one's life is all it takes to recognize one's true feelings that have been tucked away in some compartment for safe keeping, in order to avoid the possibility of any self-inflicted disappointment, pain, or suffering.

Due to the fact that romance was in the air, the last thing on Rob's mind at that moment was making sure the boat got launched before hurricane season. Rob was in love for the first time since Julie Anne, who was quickly fading into his subconscious memory like a pleasant dream which is not written down the moment one awakens – where the feeling remains but all the detail is missing. In fact, it was almost as though Rob was fully awake for the first time in his life instead of living in his dream world. All of his senses were working overtime, and as far as the island blackout went, Rob wasn't in the least bit worried about the lack of light. He didn't need light to see where he was going since the glow of love radiated like a beacon all around Rob and Alex.

The only unfortunate thing was that there wasn't a great deal of privacy to be found from prying eyes and curious ears in their little boatyard. Not to mention the fact that there was so much sexual tension brewing between Rob and Alex, that Alex was somewhat concerned they might actually knock the boat right off the rollers used to haul her out. So, they decided it best to pack up their dinghy with numerous blankets and a bottle of French wine, and head up the coast one evening to the deserted beach by the power plant in Cole Bay. Normally, with the island's power plant fully operational, one could barely hear oneself think on

---

**SAINT ELMO'S FIRE* — *An impressive glowing electrical discharge seen at the tips of pointed objects such as... a ship's mast which is stimulated by the negative charge of the storm's intercourse with the positive charge of the pointed object, and unjustly named after St. Erasmus, the patron saint of sailors.*

this stretch of beach so poorly chosen as the location of the power station. But, with the recent black-out, the beach was as quiet as a downwind sail, and as deserted as the local church on Saturday night – the only sound being that of the gentle waves of the leeward side lapping on the shore.

Upon their arrival at their clandestine tryst in the deserted bay, Rob and Alex pulled the dinghy ashore, making certain it was clear of the high tide mark. Then Alex proceeded to spread the blankets on the sand while Rob opened their bottle of wine. The time they had spent in jail together, unable to act upon their attraction to one another, not to mention the last month or so of their impassioned gender war, had created a combustible situation, and it was more than obvious to both of them that it wasn't going to take getting struck by lightning to ignite the explosion. In fact, before Alex had even finished straightening the blankets, Rob gave into his rising testosterone and swept her right off her feet. Within seconds, they were lying in the sand totally ignoring the fact that they had even brought the blankets in the first place. This time Rob didn't give Alex a chance to initiate the kiss. For the first time since Alex could remember, she melted into his arms like ice cream on a warm summer's day, realizing how good it felt to let someone past her wall of steel. However, as much as she desired him, she was still nervous as hell. After all, it had been years since she'd made love to someone she cared about – not since she placed her misguided faith in Michael.

As Rob undressed her, Alex started to giggle like a school girl, and remembering her father's good advice with regard to rail travel – decided that it was wisest to add a little more coal to the fire and make the train a little harder to catch, to ensure that Rob would appreciate the ride that much more. Without warning, Alex jumped up and ran into the ocean – daring Rob to come and get her. Within seconds, Rob had stripped down to his bare essentials and was splashing into the water after her.

"Now this is what life in Paradise is supposed to be like," said Rob taking her in his arms and kissing her in a passionate embrace that even Alex could not resist.

To Alex it felt more like Heaven than Paradise as they finally allowed themselves to be lost in the pleasures of the moment. Together they fell onto the shore, and there, with the warm waves lapping over them, they made slow passionate love. Either she'd forgotten what it felt like or Alex had never been with a man as sensitive and caring as Rob. She didn't know that it could feel so safe, yet at the same time, so exciting. Rob kissed her gently, and then deeply as he made love to her. His body felt amazing against hers, and the feel of him deep inside her drove her to climax over and over again – something she'd always found to be a challenge with other men. Like most women, she'd often pretended just to avoid hurting her partner's manhood.

Unbeknownst to them, two Frenchmen sat watching all the while from the tree-line – smoking cigarettes and enjoying the show. Rob and Alex were deep into their lovemaking when they heard the sound of a dinghy engine being started a few yards down the beach. Caught by surprise that they were obviously not alone, the unsuspecting couple turned to find the two men absconding with their only means of transportation.

"HEY! WAIT!" shouted Rob, as the dinghy sped by them at a safe distance. "Nagez bien," *("Have a nice swim.")* chortled the Frenchman in the bow, waving as he passed.

"Reviens iu, abruti!" *("Come back here you shit-heads!")*, screamed Alex in her worst French, angrily cursing herself and hitting the sand in frustration for being so stupid as to not pay closer attention during 'dinghy season.* "Damn Frogs!** I should know better," shouted Alex as she watched the two thieves round the point with the Island Fever's rubber Zodiac, headed South to the lagoon and on to the French-side – only to be deflated and stowed away in some French boat heading northeast for the Med.

It wasn't until they looked around that they suddenly realized – not only had the lowlifes stolen their dinghy and engine, but they had also pilfered their clothes and blankets as a sick joke. So much for the consummation of their blessed union in Paradise, since poor Rob had yet to even reach climax. "DAMN!" shouted Rob. "Couldn't they at least have had the decency to let me come?! I hope you had a good show, you assholes!" He vented in the direction they had gone. Alex looked apologetically at Rob and gave him a hug, "Rob I'm so sorry... I should have known better."

Suddenly, like Adam and Eve, they both became excruciatingly aware of the bare facts of their situation. How would they get back to the boat with nothing to wear. It was only a few minutes to the main road from which they could walk home, but without attire they were rapidly realizing that this was not an option that was high up on their list of options. In fact, Alex was starting to realize that it was going to be a rather long swim home since several large ledges of jagged lava rock separated Cole Bay from Simpson Bay making it impossible to traverse the water's edge – especially if one was barefoot.

For Alex it was a far more logical choice to brave the dark ocean than taking to the main road butt naked. Luckily, they had the current tides with them but Alex was far more receptive to the thought of swimming the distance of several bays in the pitch dark than Rob, who had always heard the theory that fish feed at night, especially those large enough to make a meal of an unsuspecting swimmer. But there was no way that Rob was going to allow Alex

*DINGHY SEASON — *That time of the year in the Caribbean, between May and July, when the boats headed to the Mediterranean – especially the French, find it game to commandeer another boat's dinghy, since there is little chance of being caught once one's vessel is well on its way to another continent.*
**FROGS —*The French are referred to in this part of the world as 'frogs' by all that are not of continental French origin.*

to go alone, nor let her see what a chicken he really was. So, he decided if he couldn't appear as her savior, he could at least show her he was as brave as she was.

Unfortunately, the moon was just setting and due to the gathering clouds, there were relatively few stars shining, not to mention the total absence of manmade light of any kind. In fact, it was hard to see the coastline due to the blackness of the water and the rocks. Much like the night of the Island Fever's demise, it was as black as tar out there, leaving Rob with that ill sense in the pit pit of his stomach of impending doom. All he could hear above his pounding heart was the "Jaws" theme reverberating in his skull.

Forty minutes after they swam around the power plant point, Rob, totally breathless and exhausted, crawled up on Simpson Bay Beach like some amphibious creature from the Black Lagoon. Alex who had reached the shore ahead of him was already wrapped in a towel from the Island Fever and was compassionately offering Rob one, since his fear of trolling had shriveled his manhood to the size of a stunted green fig.*

What luck, now Rob was out an additional five grand for a new dinghy since no marine insurance ever covered those magical rubber rafts that had the disappearing act down better than even David Copperfield. Alex felt so guilty about her carelessness in leaving the Zodiac unattended that she offered to forgo several month's wages in consideration of Rob's loss. Of course, Rob wouldn't hear of it even though he was starting to panic once again about finances, since he was just about clean out of money. Boy had the euphoria been short lived. Not even the glow of new found love was helping to dim this newest dilemma of where he was going to find the money for a new tender. The only consolation was that since the boat was not in the water at present, a dinghy was not an immediate necessity – at least not until they got the Island Fever floating again.

---

*FIG — Figs in the islands are those wonderfully sweet, but miniature, finger bananas that at best reach three inches long when fully ripe.

CHAPTER TWENTY-THREE

Dinghy Fever

"First you have to row a little boat."

Richard Bode

As Rob's luck would have it, it seemed that it was dinghy season in more ways than one. Not only was there an island wide epidemic of missing dinghies, but it was also fast approaching that time of the year known as 'Dengue Season.' Hurricane season it seemed had started early and the intermittent rain showers had left more than a little fresh water standing on the island in such receptacles as old tires, abandoned plumbing fixtures, and the leftover tops of those 55-gallon drums. Leaving of course, numerous havens in which mosquito larva could breed – especially the strain of mosquito known to carry Dengue Fever.*

Dengue epidemics, although not a yearly occurrence, had hit the island enough years in the past to make most of the local population immune to the most common strain – a three on the scale of four. Luckily, Alex fell into this statistic having already suffered the excruciating symptoms her first year in St. Kitts.

However, Rob was new blood on the island and unfortunately every mosquito in town had gotten wind of the news. Rob awoke the morning after

---

*DENGUE FEVER — A non-parasitic virus carried by the Aedes mosquito which displays malaria-like symptoms that will eventually disappear forever, unlike malaria, in exactly eleven days – not without first putting the stricken through eleven days of living hell. Actually, there are four known strains of Dengue varying from mild at one – to the deadly hemorrhagic type at four; and the latest research suggests that the virus is likely mutating into a plethora of strains of the virus.

his swim, to a body that felt as if he'd been stoned, *(with rocks – not weed)*, since his symptoms included chills, body aches, and a rapidly spiking fever. His bones, his muscles, an even his skin hurt. In fact, every square inch of his body was in excruciating pain. Rob realized that he wasn't in the best physical condition but he couldn't even imagine how his swim could have made him feel so incredibly wretched.

Alex was beginning to worry that he had suffered from hypothermia due to his extended stay in the water the prior evening, even if it was a relative eighty degrees. It wasn't until Rob described the unbearable post-orbital pain behind his eyes that Alex diagnosed the source of his misery. She barely had the heart to tell him that he faced ten more days of sheer agony. And, unlike malaria, for which one could take Quinine to quell the raging symptoms and receive at – least moderate relief, there was no prescribed drug aside from the painkillers Tylenol or codeine, that could assist in relieving the pain or curtailing the term of ones suffering for even a day.

Upon learning of Rob's latest malady, Grandma took pity on him and sacrificed her bed in lieu of the sofa to save Rob the added agony of lying in his sweltering bunk on the Island Fever during the midday sun. Although grateful if ever a man was to receive such loving care from two women at once, Rob, whose fever rose daily like clockwork to 104 degrees by the time the sun was high over the yardarm, was in such a delirious state that the last thing he wanted were two doting women hovering over him every minute.

Realizing this, and knowing what difficult patients' men could be, Grandma hoped to save Rob and Alex's newly budding relationship from the test of Rob's illness. So, she suggested that Alex drive into town to buy the largest bottle of Tylenol she could find. Alex left with hopes of also returning with something resembling ice in order to help cool Rob's raging fever. But, due to the continuing power outage, she was referred to the French side for the frozen substance which had suddenly become the most valuable commodity on the island. Some three hours later, after trying every marche and bistro in French St. Martin, Alex had given up the quest. It seemed that due to the shortage on the Dutch side there had been a run on the ice plant on the French side. That precious frozen gold had become as scarce and as valuable as a snowball in hell. As a last resort, Alex collected various roots, leaves, and fruits for Grandma, to enable her to work her magic, since she had nursed thirteen children through their childhood years with hardly any help from modern conventional medicine.

In fact, Grandma took to caring for Rob as if he were one of her own. This was what she did best, since her only job in life had been taking care of others. It had been a while since any patients had been in need of her services, so Grandma took to her duties as Rob's nurse as if it were her life's calling.

Once Alex had returned and was secure in the fact that Rob was in good hands, she felt she should at least make an attempt to search for the Island

ISLAND FEVER

Fever's missing tender which had been so appropriately named, 'Dinghy Fever.' To alleviate her own guilt, Alex borrowed a fifteen-foot Boston Whaler from her friend's marine store, Island Waterworld, and set off with Raymond across Simpson Bay Lagoon to the French side, out through the channel to Bale de Marigot in search of suspicious French boats. Of course, Alex truly believed that by now the thieves were well on their way across the Atlantic Ocean headed for safe territory, but she felt it her duty to at least try. Even if it were still somewhere on the island, she figured that all traces of the name and registration had been removed, which would make it tough to prove ownership. Several turns around Marigot Bay and the town dock proved fruitless, so Alex decided to make an attempt at the next several bays to the northeast. As the little Whaler rounded the point at Friar's Bay and headed into Grand Case, Alex couldn't believe her eyes. There was the Dinghy Fever, tied under the bridge deck of a French proa.*

Slowly, Alex circled around dead ahead of the proa, cut her engine, and allowed the Whaler to drift down on the proa's anchor-line. Quietly, Alex and Raymond managed to maneuver the Whaler between the hulls of the Proa allowing Alex to reach up and cut the painter *(bow line)* to the Zodiac. As she had suspected, the name and registration number had already been scraped off of the rubber hull and wood transom, but there was no mistaking the makeshift hand-pull on the engine that Alex had fashioned from a piece of driftwood while she waited for a new handle to arrive from the states. Carefully, Alex and Raymond maneuvered the two boats between the hulls and out the back, or front of the boat, depending of course on which way you looked at it. They had almost made a clean getaway when a sudden gust of wind hit the proa on its beam and spun it around on its mooring, bashing the main hull into the Whaler with a loud thump. Realizing her dilemma, Alex quickly lashed the Zodiac onto the back of the Whaler as Raymond started the getaway car – too late, they were caught in the act of stealing back their own dinghy as two irate and indignant Frenchmen burst out of the main hull of the Proa. One of the Frogs – packing a flare gun, proceeded to unload a white phosphorous flare just inches above Alex's head.

*PROA — A strange vessel designed by the French from the principle of the outrigger canoe, which is definitely suffering from an identity crisis as to whether it is a trimaran or a catamaran, since it has one main hull and only one outrigger. What this means is that there is truly no bow and no stern, or no front and back. Every time one finds it necessary to change to the opposite tack one must completely turn the vessel around and point into the wind with the opposite end of the boat, in order to always keep your one outrigger to leeward so that the wind doesn't just simply dump the boat on its side due to the absence of any type of keel, such as on a monohull.

Within seconds, the two Frenchmen had radioed another boat for help and before Alex realized what was happening there were several French guys from the monohull next to the proa piling into their rubber Zodiac in hot pursuit as Alex and Raymond fled the scene as fast as their seventy-five horsepower Yamaha would carry them, towing the little Dinghy Fever.

It seemed as though Alex might actually make a clean getaway to the Dutch side. That was, until she turned into the cut for the French bridge to the lagoon to find, the French militia – two French police boats filled with Gendarmes, blocking the entrance. Alex spun the Whaler into a hard U-turn but the Zodiac and the Frenchies were on top of her, blocking the exit back to the bay. Alex was trapped in the channel unable to make an escape out either end so she opted to stake her luck on the French police, even though she spoke a minuscule amount of broken French. She coasted up next to the police boat and cut her engine, rafting the Whaler up alongside the boat. Suddenly, Alex and Raymond realized they were looking down the wrong end of an AK 47, as the Gendarme politely took the bow line of the Whaler and motioned with the rifle for them to climb aboard. Within minutes it was a shouting free-for-all in French as the proa owners arrived to claim the Zodiac as theirs, since they had just purchased it from another French monohull. Unfortunately, with the name and registration scraped off, Alex didn't really have a leg to stand on, not to mention her inability to hold her own in their dialect.

Alex pleaded her case to the officer in charge but to no avail. Finally, they decided that the only diplomatic way to resolve the situation was to hold the dinghy, Alex, and Raymond in custody, until either Alex or her accusers could produce adequate proof of ownership of the dinghy or the engine. Of course, if she didn't come up with proof within seventy-two hours, the dinghy would then be returned to the Frenchmen so that they could be on their way to Europe. There was only one small problem with this plan, since Alex and Raymond were thrown into the Gendamerie, and the Gendarmes were not about to let them out until they had proven that the dinghy was indeed theirs – a small Catch-22. Once again, as on the Dutch side, one phone call was not amongst a prisoner's first rights. Ironically, dinghy theft in the French West Indies seemed to carry almost as much weight as horse thievery had in the old West – that was of course if you were not French. Had the same accusation been made on the Dutch side, the Dutch police would have simply laughed it off and let the yachties fight it out amongst themselves. The Frogs definitely held the upper hand in this situation due to the fact that Alex was an insulting American who slaughtered their language with her poor attempt to explain the situation in their native tongue.

Once again faced with the problem of communication to the outside world from inside a jail cell, Alex was trying to figure out how to get a message to Rob who was nowhere within range of a phone and not likely monitoring the ship's radio in his present state.

Even though Alex begged and pleaded, they were not accommodating in any way regarding getting a message to the marina where she had borrowed the Whaler. Surely, they would be wondering by now where she was. They were her best chance at getting a message to Rob to bring the ships papers to the French jail, in order to get them released and to reclaim the Dinghy Fever.

As she gazed out of her cell window between the bars, Alex's attention was drawn to a young island boy catching land crabs outside the Bastille walls.

"Spshh... hey... kid," whispered Alex in the lowest tone possible and still be heard.

Looking up, the little boy was so surprised to see a pretty American woman behind bars, he couldn't resist his curiosity.

"How cum you be in dere missus?" questioned the boy totally puzzled by the sight. "They not be puttin' gurls'n jail... mostly locals who seen de bottom of one too many bottles of rum.

"Well, you see, it's all a big misunderstanding," reasoned Alex, as she extended a twenty-dollar bill through the bars toward him. "Do you think you could do me a favor?"

"Sure missus, for two of dose I do just about anythin' cept clenin' or kookin'."

Quickly writing a note on a scrap of bread paper with a broken pencil stub and handing it through the bars to the boy, Alex looked the boy square in the eye. "I need you to go to the marine store in the lagoon and give this note to the manager. Tell him where I am and that I need his help. He'll give you the other twenty."

Although she had piqued his interest, the boy looked apprehensively at the twenty-dollar bill.

"How do I know dere be anoder twenti when I get dere?" "Please, I promise he'll pay you the other twenty," assured Alex as the boy approached a little closer for a better look at the bill. "Do you know how to drive a boat?"

"Of course, I knowed how ta drive a boat," replied the boy indignantly.

"Then go to the lagoon dock and get the Island Waterworld Whaler, it'll be quicker. If anyone gives you any trouble tell them you were sent by Jeff, the manager, to pick up his boat, okay?"

"You mean I get two of dese, an, I get to drive de boat too?"

Tentatively, Alex handed him the note, the Whaler key, and the twenty, "Don't forget to tell him I'm here and to give him the note and the key to the boat."

"Tanks missus," answered the boy gratefully with a big smile that showcased two rows of perfect, enormous, white teeth.

"My name's Alex," she responded with a warm smile.

Snatching the note and the bill from Alex, the boy took off at a trot towards the docks, leaving his bag of crabs behind him. Alex was hopeful wanting to believe that he would follow through with her instructions. Yet there was a doubtful knowing that he would likely not even get the boat off the dock, and he would happily settle for the easy twenty he had just made by doing nothing other than being in the right place at the right time.

The young boy, Christian, as he had been named by his mother before she died when he was six, was fast approaching thirteen and had lived more of the last seven years of his life on the streets than at home – hustling his living to make up for his drunken father who although present in body, was mostly absent in sobriety. In and out of school since the age of ten, Christian, although a smart kid, had far more aptitude for boats, engines, and tools than he did for books. He had an amazing gift of gab, and had managed to develop his skills at scamming tourists into giving him money for any number of services from serving as tour guide, to renting grocery carts, not to mention, showing them where to find an obscure reef that was still somewhat populated with brightly colored fish.

When he was a month old, his mother had been brought to Sint Maarten from the neighboring island of Anguilla by his father who was originally from Aruba. This interesting combination made Christian a handsome mixture of Latin and West Indian blood. It was that Latin blood that made his father hot tempered. That, and his Dutch affinity for alcohol made for a volatile combination that unfortunately erupted in drunken tirades which were usually directed at poor Christian. He had gotten used to having to sneak into his own house to see the condition of his father's mood before letting his presence be known at home. It was rare he went there for anything other than sleep, but some nights he found it better to just sleep in one of the boats on the dock – the owners being none the wiser.

Of course, Christian, although creative in different means of making a living, was inherently honest – a virtue instilled firmly within his morals by his saintly Christian mother in the few short years that she was with him. He indeed had every intention of delivering the boat and the note to the marine store, however, how could it hurt to keep the boat for twenty-four hours or so to show it off to his friends, and take a spin around the lagoon, and out to the reef to dive for a lobster or two. Not to mention using it as a comfortable place to sleep for the night. After all the lady had not specified when he had to have the boat there.

By now the sun was setting, and back at the boatyard Grandma and Grandpa were beginning to worry about Alex and Raymond's whereabouts. Trying to cover to avoid worrying Rob, they kept telling him that Alex had from decided to wait for the ice to freeze so that she could bring Rob some relief his fever. Lost in his delirium, this explanation seemed quite plausible. Of course, by closing time the marine store had begun to worry as well, not only about their Whaler, but Jeff who'd been a friend of Alex's long enough to know that she was pretty reliable, was beginning to suspect engine failure or the like and sent a boat to look for them.

All the while, Christian was comfortably camped out on a small island of mangrove trees in the middle of the lagoon cooking his lobster and conch over the fire he'd built, and preparing himself for a comfortable night under the stars in the bottom of the little Whaler.

CHAPTER TWENTY-FOUR

Lost at Sea

"The real voyage of discovery consists not in seeking new landscapes but in having new eyes."

Marcel Proust

Having tried every other possibility, Jeff, the manager of the marine store made a visit to the Island Fever in hopes of finding that Alex had been delayed there, and thinking the store already closed, had decided to return the boat the next morning. When he arrived at the boatyard to find that they had no more information than he on her whereabouts, the whole boating community was alerted to their suspicions that Alex and Raymond had broken down in the Whaler and could possibly have drifted out to sea. Within thirty minutes, a search party had been organized amongst the charter fishing fleet and half a dozen boats had set out of the lagoon to first search the bays and coastline of St. Martin, and then the shores of Anguilla, where a disabled boat might drift across the channel without ample anchor line. They decided it best to first exhaust all of these possibilities before venturing into the worst case scenario that she could have actually drifted out to sea and across the Anegada Passage.*

The thought of Alex lost at sea was something that Rob could not totally comprehend, especially in light of her advanced seamanship skills. But, the thought of her being in any kind of danger rocked him to his core. In a

*ANEGADA PASSAGE — Also known as the "Oh My Godda Passage.' Better known as one hellacious body of water, stretching between the eastern most Leeward Islands and The Virgins.**

matter of just a few short weeks Rob had developed a deeper love for Alex than he had ever even imagined for Sydney. One that was quickly rivaling his adolescent adoration for Julie Anne, and he couldn't even fathom the possibility of losing her. Alex had been a hard-won challenge for Rob, making him appreciate her all the more. It seemed the Universe had realized that it was human nature to not always appreciate those things that came too easy and Rob had been forced to work for this one. Rob was pretty sure that he could feel something stirring once again where his heart should be, especially when Alex kissed him. Maybe like the tin man, the wizard had granted him his wish and he'd indeed grown another heart. He didn't dare raise his hopes too high – maybe they simply wouldn't be compatible, or even worse, maybe he wouldn't be able to keep Alex happy. After all she had lived a pretty exciting life and must have experienced many extraordinary lovers. All of Rob's short comings passed before him at that moment like a dying man, even though it was Alex's life that might actually be in danger, since his present disease wasn't terminal. Even so, he felt like he wanted to die at that moment due to his fever and chills and the fact that his body was feeling like it had been run through a meat grinder and poured in a Jell-O-mold – into a poor replica of himself. He knew he looked like death warmed over but his own condition was the last thing on his mind as he crawled out of bed and drug himself into the boat with Jeff to aid in the search.

The news of Alex missing struck Grandma and Grandpa hard as well, since they had already grown to love Alex as one of their own in the short-time they'd known her. This news in fact struck a frightful chord with them since it took them back to a sad day when they had received word of their oldest son, Matthew, who was it seemed, unofficially missing in action. Matthew had always dreamed of becoming a pilot as a child and had realized that his only hope of flight school would be to immigrate to America and join the Air Force. So at eighteen, he moved to Puerto Rico and signed up. He survived a stint flying reconnaissance in Vietnam and had returned to the Caribbean with only two choices – spend his life flying bush planes ferrying passengers from island to island, or join Air America, the unofficial air force which was funded by the CIA and make a shit-load of money flying 'rice-kickers' *** over Nicaragua. He had chosen the latter. Or… lets just say that it had chosen him since

**VIRGINS — (a place) Not to be mistaken with female nymphets – who knows what Columbus had in mind when he named them. The Virgins are instead, the western most grouping of islands in the Lesser Antilles which lay west of St. Maarten and east of Puerto Rico – the western islands – St. Thomas, St. Croix, and St. John, are now owned by the U.S., who bought them from the Danes. They are divided from the eastern islands – Virgin Gorda, Tortola, and Anegada, by a channel called 'The Narrows'. The eastern islands are owned by the Brits.
***RICE-KICKER — The term for food drops made by Air America, where a robust man would literally kick bails of rice to rebels from the open hatch of a DC3.

adventure was in his blood. Knowing the U.S. would disavow any knowledge of his very existence should anything happen to him, he joined none-the-less. And, they were true to their word, since Grandma and Grandpa had never been able to find out more information than what they had been able to read in the telegram they had received one afternoon from an anonymous source – "Mat's plane missing, whereabouts unknown." So, when they heard of Alex's misfortune, they felt they were suddenly reliving the past.

Poor Rob, whose temperature had finally subsided to a mild 102.5, felt it his duty to look for her, although the bouncing on that pounding Bertram fisherman had actually caused his aching body and mind to start hallucinating by around sunrise. He was certain he had not only spied the Whaler several times in the middle of the channel, but he could have sworn that it was being towed by a team of harnessed dolphins. Not to mention that he was certain that there was a fourth crewman aboard the boat when there were indeed only himself and two others. A man who resembled a handsome *(even if I say so myself)*, thirtyish year-old West Indian sailor. Indeed, for the first time in Rob's life, thanks to this altered state of mind, he had finally seen through the veil – he had seen me. Although this new sight of his was not to last long.

Frightened, Rob shook his head and rubbed his eyes hoping to ward off his hallucinations. Having been on the search party end of lost at sea, I can appreciate the fear of the unknown that was going through Rob's mind at that moment. For when I was a young boy in the West Indies at the age of thirteen, my younger brother had fallen asleep while fishing in our row boat and drug anchor – drifting out to sea. Of course, that was before we had any fancy instruments or radios to assist us in the search. So, several of the local island traders set sail to search the waters of the Caribbean in hopes of finding my brother and bring him home safely. We searched for days with no sign of even an oar of the little boat which was likely drifting faster than we could sail. I was afraid to think the most likely – that it had already filled with water and capsized. I seldom went to church in those days, but for two days and nights I prayed that my little brother would be brought back to me. It seemed the Universe heard, since on the third day, the wind and sea changed direction and blew that little row boat right back the way it had come – right into the harbor where we lived. From that moment on I knew there was such a thing as miracles and that there was indeed someone to watch over us if we just simply asked for help.

I even tried my best to assure Rob of Alex's safety, however his brief moment of sight was gone. And, thanks to the fever and his fear, his mind was working in overdrive to distort his reason.

By morning, the local boats had given up hope and had resorted to radioing the U.S. Coast Guard in St. Thomas, since they thought the boat was likely drifting fast in that direction. An all-out search was called with two USCG cutters sweeping the Anegada Passage for hours without success – even the choppers had given the area a good search only to find a disabled French monohull loaded down with stolen dinghies.

Rob was really starting to worry, sitting in Jeff's office back at the marina as he attempted to swallow a handful of Tylenol and down a cup of coffee in order to keep his throbbing eyes open. By this point he had resorted to turning his head rather than moving his eyes from side to side to avoid the severe pain from this simple bodily function. By now, Rob was beginning to feel like he was in dinghy/dengue hell from which there was no reprieve, and he was rapidly gaining a whole new appreciation for what he had once again, and what he stood to lose if Alex wasn't found.

It wasn't until ten o'clock that morning that Christian finally pulled up anchor and slowly motored the Whaler across the lagoon towards the marina dock. By the time he arrived and tied the boat up in one of the slips, everyone was in such a tizzy that they never even noticed him or the Whaler arrive. Christian wandered around the store in amazement looking at all of the wonderful tools and gadgets available to the consummate sailor. There was so much commotion at the front of the store he hadn't found an opportune moment to ask someone who the manager might be, so he had simply gotten lost in a Disneyland of fishing gear, bang sticks, and boat paraphernalia. Finally, Christian noticed an American man headed his way towards a storeroom at the back of the store. As he passed, Christian saw his opportunity to ask if he by chance knew the manager of the establishment.

"Yeah, that's me, I'm the manager," answered Jeff annoyed by the distraction. "What do you need?"

"Well, you see, dis American lady tole me you'd give me twenty-dollar if I brung you dis note."

"What note!?" snapped Jeff as he snatched the scrap of paper from Christian's hand.

"She said to tell you she was in de French Bastille and to bring your boat back," continued Christian trying hard to remember everything he was supposed to say in order to be assured of his other twenty – wrapping it up with one of his enormous smiles as he held up the Whaler key.

The place was suddenly in an uproar of relief at the news that Alex and Raymond were indeed on dry land, however, inconvenienced they may have been at that moment. Alex's note briefly explained her dilemma requesting that Rob come to the Gendarmerie, as soon as he could with the ship's papers, the dinghy receipt, and its serial numbers.

ISLAND FEVER

Of course, all that was easier said than done since Rob had no idea where Joey kept such things. It took Rob an hour to search the Island Fever for her papers. Joey obviously had a reason for building the secret compartment Rob finally discovered under the master berth's floorboards where he found the ships warranties, thirty thousand dollars cash, all of the needed serial numbers, and a colorful collection of passports bearing different names and dates of birth all containing Joey's smiling face. Hidden amongst the cache were numerous charts of Colombian waters and land maps of the interior of the country known for its agricultural products which plied the drug trade throughout the Caribbean and the U.S.

Suddenly, everything was crystal clear to Rob – Joey was a drug smuggler and the Island Fever was likely known throughout the islands as a drug boat. It was no wonder Joey had no apparent source of income yet could afford this luxurious vessel – no wonder the police were so quick to incarcerate her crew.

"Oh my God," thought Rob, "Now I've got to go to the French police. Forget getting Alex and Raymond out, they'll probably just throw me in there with them and throw away the key. Surely, they know. They think I'm his partner not only in the boat but in this line of work too. This time they won't make the mistake of letting us get away. This is it, I'm destined to spend the rest of my life behind bars," Rob reasoned with certainty – starting to sweat. "They're going to impound the boat and everything I have left in the world, and there I'll be, rotting away in an island jail while Joey is off scot-free spending my money."

Rob was panic stricken as he stuffed the ships papers in his pack and replaced all but a thousand dollars back under the floorboard. Frantically, he gathered up the illicit passports and Colombian charts and raced up to the galley* to light a fire to destroy all the evidence. His hands were shaking as he lit the gas burner on the stove and set fire to the passports one by one throwing them into the sink to burn insuring that nothing remained of Joey's illicit dossiers. By the time he had started to add the charts to the fire, Rob realized he'd created somewhat of a small barn fire. When the dish towels went up in flames, Rob decided a little water was in order. But when he went to pump the salt water foot pump, all he got was air, since of course the boat was on dry land and had no access to sea water. Nor did the freshwater pump offer any resemblance of H20 since her tanks had been drained to haul her out. What to do now that the entire galley was quickly being consumed by flames? "A bucket! I need a bucket," screamed Rob! "Water where's the closest water!? No! A fire extinguisher! That's what I need is a fire extinguisher!"

*GALLEY — The nautical term for a ship's kitchen not to be confused with a medieval ship propelled by sails and oars, although some ships' galleys (kitchens) border on medieval with regard to their sparse appointments, which are generally designed by men who don't cook.

Frantically, Rob looked around the deckhouse for anything resembling an extinguisher. There on the wall next to the doorway hung a dry chemical extinguisher which he ripped from the bracket then fumbled to figure out how to operate the thing, since of course he'd never had cause to use one before and never the forethought to read the instructions in case of such an emergency. By the time he had found the pin and pulled it releasing the entire contents of five pounds of dry chemical onto the now blazing fire, it had managed to singe everything in the forward half of the galley right down to melting the plastic dishes in the cubby-holes. Looking at the thick layer of white powder which could have easily been mistaken for a kilo that Woody Allen sneezed on, Rob had to wonder which had done more damage, the fire or the extinguisher. Covered from head to toe in white dust and black soot – sporting singed hair – sans eyebrows and eyelashes, Rob emerged from the deck-house in a stupor carrying his pack of documents and looking as if he had just survived an explosion in a talcum factory. Poor Christian, who sat waiting for him on the beach in the Whaler, thought he'd seen a ghost at the first sight of Rob who resembled a fresh baked Beignet,* straight from the oven.

"You all right mista?" questioned Christian as Rob stumbled to the shore and climbed into the boat without saying a word. Not daring to ask any more questions, since Rob was obviously not in the mood for talking, Christian pushed the boat off the beach, started the engine, and drove around the jetty then under the bridge to the lagoon.

By the time Rob walked into the Gendarmerie, the French police had been contacted by Jeff at the marina and told that Rob was on his way to clear up any confusion as to the ownership of the dinghy. In fact, he had even sold Joey the Zodiac and its Evinrude, and was certain that if Rob couldn't produce the serial numbers, that surely, he could find the required documents. Upon seeing Rob walk through the door, the on-duty Gendarmes took one look at his condition and a superficial glance at the documents and quickly released Alex, Raymond, and the dinghy without another question asked.

Of course, Alex couldn't believe her eyes when she walked into the Captain's office and find Rob in such a state of disarray. As she threw herself into his arms, Rob was so happy to see her that he barely even noticed the pain when she hugged him. "Oh my God, what happened to you?" gasped Alex.

Barely able to speak by this point, Rob somehow managed to mumble something about the fire being out and for her not to worry because he'd taken care of all the evidence. To himself, Rob was thanking God, the police, and the Universe for bringing her back to him safely. What a lucky man he truly was indeed, for not only had Alex and Raymond been returned to him, but the

*BEIGNET — A French puff pastry (in essence – a donut), which is generously dusted with powdered sugar.

Dinghy Fever had found its way home as well. Now, he just hoped his string of bad luck had run its course, and that maybe he'd finally erased some portion of that karmic debt he owed. Now he just had to hope that the other Dengue Fever would quickly run its course along with his bad luck.

Aside from his pain, Rob felt as if he'd hit the lottery. Little did he know however, that his outstanding debt was in fact only half paid by this point, and the lotto he'd won had only brought him five out of six winning numbers – the sixth was yet to be earned, over time. The real question was – what indeed was the grand prize – true happiness – Paradise? Or, would Rob instead be the lucky recipient of life's booby prize? But then, that's what the game of life is truly all about when it comes down to it – a gamble that one hopes will pay off in something other than coconuts and boobie birds. When they arrived back at the boat that afternoon with the Island Fever's dinghy, Alex was not surprised to find the winter wonderland that Rob had left for her in the galley, not to mention the medium-well-done cabinets underneath. At least the Island Fever was still there. After all she had survived four hurricanes, surely, she could survive one Rob. I can't leave him alone for a minute, she thought to herself lovingly as she dove into the task of cleaning up the disaster.

CHAPTER TWENTY-FIVE

Paradise Peak

> *"There are no guarantees what will happen when you jump off an emotional cliff. You might crash on the rocks or you might develop wings. But you will never really know which one it is until you jump."*
>
> Marianne Williamson

It was eleven days to the day before Rob was finally feeling himself again, even though he was temporarily fooled into believing that he actually felt better on day eight. If nothing else, dengue fever was predictably reliable, and by day twelve Rob was back at work beside Alex doing his best to make up for his prolonged absence in the boatyard.

The strike was over and the power plant had resumed operation, providing the Dutch side once again with electricity. It was the Fourth of July, which oddly enough, was a holiday more enthusiastically celebrated in the upper Dutch Antilles than in the 'States' itself, providing one more reason for festivities and one more official holiday on the island's calendar.

That afternoon, Alex sent Rob over the hill to the commercial docks in Philipsburg to get a bracket welded on the new engine sled she had built. It had been weeks since Rob had followed anything resembling the news, since it had been far too painful for his eyes to watch TV due to the dengue fever. The last thing that Rob was up on was the state of current world events or even local island gossip for that matter. So, when the Yellow Submarine crested the hill affording him a clear view of Philipsburg harbor, Rob slammed on the brakes in a panic. "Oh my God, we're at war," stammered Rob when he saw what seemed like half the American Navy sitting anchored just outside the harbor. Six U.S. destroyers and two nuclear subs made for an imposing sight to an American expatriate living in a foreign land. Terror seized Rob at the thought of being stranded on foreign soil with unrest brewing. Luckily for him, these were his own native land's troops surrounding the harbor.

At the next turn-off, Rob jerked the car off the road making an abrupt U-turn, and headed back as fast as the little sub would carry him to the boatyard to warn Alex and the others about the apparent invasion.

"What could they possibly want with St. Maarten?" thought Rob. "Other than some bad rum and a lot of discount electronic stores, their temporary home didn't offer much in the way of prime strategic advantage, especially since it was so close to the American Virgin Islands."

Alex, winked at Grandma and Grandpa and almost managed to keep a straight face as Rob carried on and on about this newly developed crisis that had descended upon their quiet little island. Wasn't it strange that the local radio hadn't mentioned a thing about America's military presence. Finally, Alex, unable to contain herself any longer, burst into laughter, along with Grandma and Grandpa. "It's the Fourth of July," cried Alex, as if that should explain everything.

"So?" puzzled Rob totally baffled as to why the American holiday would have any significance whatsoever with what was happening on the other side of the hill.

"Well, they come here every year to celebrate and salute the island of St. Eustatius.* Without them, America would have never won the Revolutionary War. It's just a minor detail that was left out of America's history books."

"Oh, come on, what could that little rock have possibly done to help us win the war?" questioned Rob skeptically.

So, Alex proceeded to tell Rob the story of how 'The Golden Rock' came to unknowingly orchestrate their own demise for the cause of the great country now known as the United States of America.

---

*ST. EUSTATIUS — (Statia) An island in the Caribbean originally named by the Caribs as 'Alo' (cashew tree) and then renamed St. Anastasia' by Columbus. It was later settled by the French in 1629 and changed hands more than twenty-two times between the Dutch, the French, and the British – making it eventually, not only the largest duty-free trading port established by the Dutch in 1636 – but the most traded port in the West Indies. Infuriated by their support of the Americas, Admiral Rodney settled the score by launching a naval attack against the tiny island – ransacking warehouses and auctioning off their goods. The Dutch managed to regain possession a few years later, leaving it in its currently impoverished state of being known as the Deserted Rock, or, 'Statia' by the locals instead of 'The Golden Rock, which it was known as in its wealthy years. Today it remains part of the Dutch, Netherlands Antilles under the governance of Holland via Curacao.**

ISLAND FEVER

You see, St. Eustatius is a small island with a large history and was actually known at one time as the trade capital of the West Indies. But since they were a trading port owned by the diplomatic Dutch, who have always put commerce ahead of political loyalties, they were neutral – feeling it their right to trade with any nation who sailed into their port. So, they had every intention of selling arms, gun powder, and provisions to Americans from New England, even if the Brits, who had made their island rich from their business, considered it as rebellion. Although, any trace of the deed has been omitted from American history books, Statia was the first to acknowledge a passing American war brig, the Andrew Doria with a merchant salute – two guns less than a warship. They paid for it dearly when ole Admiral Rodney got wind of their betrayal. He swooped in and cleaned out the place leaving what was the richest island in the Caribbean to the goats and the land crabs. He even took most of the inhabitants to St. Kitts or to England and was later sued in Parliament by the island's English inhabitants who lost their property. Pretty much the only thing it's used for today is fuel storage for this part of the Caribbean, since with its deep-water harbor, even super tankers can unload their cargo.

Rob was greatly relieved to learn that he was not on the verge of finding himself in the midst of some island military coup. Like when the Americans chose to be the heroes of the day and storm into Grenada to save a handful of American medical students from their communist intruders for a little international PR. Or, worse yet, when the American CIA did a half-ass job of trying to help Cuban ex-pats liberate Cuba from Castro during the Bay of Pigs.

Confident now that it was perfectly safe to complete his mission to Philipsburg, Rob headed off to his little yellow tin can which was already about to lose its two front fenders, in order to get to the machine shop before the docks closed.

Coaxed by Grandma, who had suggested that they take a small romantic excursion to the top of Paradise Peak, Alex ran after Rob, catching up with him just as he was backing out of the yard. "How would you like to go up to the top of Paradise Peak*** to watch the sunset and the fireworks tonight?" Suggested Alex shyly.

"Sounds like a great idea," said Rob hardly needing to answer since his smile broadcasted it all. "I'll pick up some things for a picnic in town."

**CURACAO — *A Dutch island off the coast of Venezuela which is part of the ABC Islands – Aruba, Bonaire, & Curacao – like all Dutch colonies still ruled by Holland. In 1986 Aruba succeed, leaving Curacao the main governing body which reports to Holland for all of their holdings in the Caribbean including Sint Maarten, Saba, & St. Eustatius, which not only report to Curacao, but send all of their taxable income to them to be doled out evenly between the five little islands. Once of course, Curacao has skimmed off their desired share.*

"Great," replied Alex happily as Rob pulled away, "I'll break out the picnic basket! OH! And you'd better pick up some new blankets!"

Regarding fireworks, Rob was hoping that he and Alex would set off a few of their own that night since he was finally feeling his old self again, and he had yet to experience the rocket's red glare and the bombs bursting in air with her in more than one sense of the meaning. Rob had much to celebrate, as did Alex, since they were both safe, out of jail, and relatively healthy at that point. Overall, it promised to be a rather celebrative evening, as opposed to a celibate one for a change. Not only was there likely to be a fireworks display in Philipsburg harbor, but an American owned hotel in Long Bay, on the French side, took a diplomatic stance and alternated between the 4th and Bastille Day**** every year – this being their year to acknowledge their homeland.

It was just before sunset when the Yellow Submarine chugged its way to the top of Paradise Peak with Rob and Alex onboard. Oddly, there was only one other human at the popular spot – a local man working on his land. So, Rob and Alex parked the car and packed their dinner and blankets up to the perfect plateau of rocks to claim the best seats in the house from which to view the setting sun and the upcoming evening's events.

Upon returning to the car to get the corkscrew, Rob noticed the sail bag in the back of the wagon moving with something crawling around inside. Cautiously, he crept around the back of the vehicle and quietly opened the back hatch fully expecting some sort of island creature to spring from inside the bag. Picking up the tire iron, which lay next to it, he prepared himself for the attack as he jerked the sail bag open. Instead of some furry creature, Christian popped out smiling his big, broad, endearing smile.

"What on earth are you doing here?!" cried Rob annoyed, but relieved to find his new buddy instead of some such fur-covered thing as a monkey or a mongoose.*****

"Well I jus' wanted to see de fireworks too," said Christian with so much sincerity that there was absolutely no way that Rob could be angry with him.

***PARADISE PEAK — *Offering grand vistas – it's true name being Pic du Paradis since it is located on the French side. It is the tallest peak on the island which catches most of the rain leaving it the closest thing to lush and tropical that the island has to offer.*

****BASTILLE DAY — *A French national holiday celebrated every year on July 14th, in much the same tradition as our own Independence Day. It was deemed a holiday in order to recognize the storming and capture of Bastille fortress in Paris by the French revolutionaries on July 14, 1789, which instigated the start of the French revolution and the beheading of Louis the XVI and Marie Antoinette.*

*****MONGOOSE — *A small mammal imported into the West Indies from India for the purpose of ridding the islands of rats, mice, and snakes. Unfortunately, the rat being a nocturnal animal and the mongoose not, the islands, although snakeless, still abound in rats and mice.*

ISLAND FEVER

"So much for the bombs bursting in air," mumbled Rob shaking his head.

"What bombs?" said Christian looking at Rob confused.

"The one I'm going to have to drop on Alex when I tell her we're not alone," said Rob as he helped Christian from the back of the car and headed back to their picnic site to surprise Alex with the news of their unexpected stowaway.

In the last couple of weeks Christian had grown on Alex, and he had quickly adopted the Island Fever's little boatyard as his new home – offering his services as Alex's new assistant in exchange for a bunk in the forward berth and a few dollars a day for food. However, as fond as she had grown of him, now was not a time for him to be included in the festivities. But what were they to do? Here they were – the three of them. So, together, they toasted the setting sun and shared the roast poulet, aged camembert, fresh fruit, crusty baguette and a bottle of the best French wine Rob had found on the island, while overlooking the island's most spectacular view.

From their perch atop the mountain, the rocket's red glare was breathtaking, and the bombs bursting in air – well... Rob just had to use his imagination. But by now, Rob and Alex were getting kind of desperate to pick up where they left off that night in Cole Bay, and they had decided it wise to get a room for the night. After all, Rob had found Joey's cash stash and he felt as if he and Alex really deserved this one small indulgence.

Alex had calculated that by the time they walked back to the car and drove Christian back to the boat yard, they could make it to the Horny Goat Guest House in Simpson Bay, which was owned by a friend of Alex's and more than appropriately named for the occasion, by eleven – leaving a few hours for them to romp and play before the sun came up the next morning.

By the time they arrived at the guest house Alex had to wake her friend, Maureen. But hearing the urgent need in Alex's voice and understanding the anxious look on their faces, Maureen gave Alex a wink and tossed her the key to her best cottage – the honeymoon suite, suggesting that they settle up with her the next morning when they checked out.

They had barely shut the door to the quaint cottage when they threw themselves into each other's arms never even bothering to turn on the lights, since they hardly needed to see in order to resume where they left off that dark evening in the surf in Cole Bay.

For Rob, exploring Alex's firm, golden skin was like basking in warm sand on a tropical summer's day, with the fragrance of gardenias wafting down from the hillside as the crystal blue waves crashed over them. Unable to hold out a moment longer, Rob entered Alex, whisking her away enveloped in a magical glow. That moment when they both reached a pinnacle where they felt as if they would surely fall from the summit, they suddenly found themselves soaring on a wave that took them high above the perilous cliffs of which they had both been so afraid – the treacherous terrain of love – that terrain of pain and rejection that they now intuitively knew they would never fear again. There they flew together hand-in-hand over that peak so often mistaken as Paradise itself. Rob felt an instant fleeting glimpse of bliss, and indeed a twinge of what Paradise must be like. Alas, their brief union had only offered him a temporary glance of what he was capable of achieving.

Suddenly, Rob was a believer that there was indeed such a thing as one soulmate* for a privileged union during his lifetime. Obviously, Rob had done something right along the way since he had earned the chance to find Alex. Rob was convinced at that moment that no other woman existed, not even Julie Anne who had momentarily vanished from his memory as if he'd suddenly entered an amnesiac trance.

Alex was simply lost in a state of bafflement, never really having believed that love would find her again. But as Grandma had predicted, she had overcome her fear and opened the door, and there it was – just waiting for her, on the other side. After all, the other side of fear is love, is it not?

---

*SOULMATE — *The theory that there is at least one perfectly compatible soul for every soul living both in and out of human form, from one reincarnation to another. Compatible of course being a relative term given that humans are never perfect. Timing is everything in finding your soul mate, since it is common to meet one's soul mate at inopportune times in your life, or when the other person is already unhappily married.*

CHAPTER TWENTY-SIX

Mistaken Identity

"If there were no illusion there would be no enlightenment."

Eckhart Tolle

Christian was panicked that something serious had happened to them when Rob and Alex didn't return to the boatyard for three days. However, Grandma and Grandpa knew that indeed something serious had transpired between Rob and Alex, and smiled as they patted themselves on the back for their insightful, successful matchmaking. Thank goodness they were better at these things than I.

Grandma's first great success at matchmaking had been for her best friend, Lorna, whom she had relied on throughout her lonely childhood as her lifeline to happiness. Wini had spent many an afternoon playing house with Lorna, fantasizing about their life to come, and the men they would wed and live with happily ever after. Of course, it was Lorna who had gotten Wini through Warren's desertion and her humiliation of being left standing at the alter sans a bridegroom, with her friend Lorna in attendance as her 'maid of honor.' Lorna had pointed out to Wini that she had been mistaken about the identity of her true love – she had simply chosen the wrong man, and encouraged her to look elsewhere with open eyes.

Just after Wini had married Stanley, who had hard-won her heart during that year following her annulled marriage, Wini had enlisted in a plan to wed her friend to Stanley's cousin, Albert. He had recently returned to the island with his degree in tourism – a career not yet needed on the island since the little island of

Grenada was yet to hit the tourist map. Being far wiser than her years, Wini knew that outright matchmaking on her part might shy Albert from her target. So, she set out on a campaign to make her friend Lorna appear to be the most popular and sought-after girl on the island. And of course, totally unattainable to Albert – leaving Albert none-the-wiser since he'd been off-island the past four years. Within a month, Grandma's magic had worked and Lorna and Wini set about planning the second wedding in their little town that year. A wedding for Lorna and Albert.

It was because of Albert that Wini and Stanley had eventually moved to St. Maarten to raise their family, since Albert had found a greater need of his services on the more traveled island than he had in his homeland. And Stanley, had found a better paying job at the island's rum factory as their regional salesman. Unfortunately, Albert's job had later taken him on to New York, where he would head up the tourism center for the island. This left Grandma lost without the woman she called sister to rely on during her tough years of childrearing – often spent alone since Grandpa was on the road, or in his case, off island entirely.

On the third night of Rob and Alex's tryst, they decided to emerge from their love nest to go out and celebrate their new found love, and begrudgingly share one another with the outside world. Since Rob was feeling fortuitous in his wealth of happiness, he decided to wine and dine Alex with the best the island had to offer. They were not quite ready to go back to the boatyard and dare fate to burst their pink bubble, so Rob took Alex to Marigot to buy her a new dress and himself a respectable outfit.

Once attired for a romantic evening, Rob called a taxi to drive them out to the Lowlands at the end of Simpson Bay Lagoon to the chic hotel, La Samanna. He didn't want to embarrass her by pulling up in the Yellow Submarine – their now fenderless, rusted excuse for an automobile.

La Samanna, had been built by a wealthy, eccentric American, who believed when he built it that to truly taste the lifestyle of the islands, one must sacrifice such state-side luxuries and expectations as screens, air-conditioning, and phones in the rooms. Eventually, the novelty of spartanism faded and the hotel added those luxuries that Americans have come to expect as a normal fact of life and find it impossible to live without. Offering the only more-or-less private beach in the Caribbean, where presidents, princesses, celebrities, and the mega riche' could find seclusion, the hotel had gained a reputation as the most desirable escape in the West Indies. Of course, it was off season so Alex knew they would pretty much have the restaurant all to themselves, providing them with a romantic evening that they could look back on as an evening to long remember. Even if it turned out to be for reasons other than they expected.

ISLAND FEVER

Hurricanes had come and gone on the island, along with the beaches, but somehow the sea was always forgiving. The sea always brought the beaches back, especially to this beautiful bay – Long Bay, or Baie Longe since it was across the line on the French side of the island. Sitting high on the terrace overlooking the breathtaking view of the stars glistening on the water and the moon setting to the West, Rob and Alex felt as if they were the two luckiest people alive. Rob had finally arrived, he thought in Paradise and he was ready to risk everything he had and invest heavily in life's futures. He was closing in on the decision to ask Alex to marry him – at least sometime in the future, since he was still uncertain as to Alex's feelings for him and he didn't want to risk rejection when things were going so well. What he didn't realize nor did she, was she was already smitten by that merciless condition called island love. Since, Alex was unfamiliar with love's symptoms, she had not yet diagnosed the cause of her lightheaded intoxication, uncharacteristic distractedness, and the butterflies in the pit of her stomach. It didn't matter to Rob that he had only known her such a short time – there was no question in his mind that she was 'the one' he'd been searching for his whole life. Even if he hadn't even known he was searching. After all, he'd been told that love was the only thing to happen expediently in the islands.

Being the more well informed and seasoned island inhabitant of the two, Alex simply accepted the evening and the last few days as a brief reprieve from the trials and tribulations of island life, which allowed her to enjoy it all the more since she knew that an end to their state of bliss was as imminent as the onset hurricane season.

Alex had lived in the islands long enough to know that status-quo was a term only applicable to the endless stream of chaotic events that took place daily, and certainly had nothing to do with describing the local lifestyle. As Grandpa had suggested to Rob, Alex had learned to go with the flow where change was concerned, and had pretty much mastered the art of island living, even if she was still adjusting to the thought of living in love.

Dinner was unforgettable, as were the few other patrons, who consisted of a well-known reggae star and some famous French designer whose dresses started somewhere in the neighborhood of the cost of a small villa on Anguilla. Exhausted from their three-day passionate marathon of lovemaking, Rob and Alex decided that it was finally safe to return that evening to the Island Fever for a good night's sleep – realizing that the most damage they could possibly do that night was to themselves. Several bottles of fine champagne later, they went for a stroll along the beach and ended the spectacular evening with a romantic kiss stolen here and there along the way.

Rob and Alex climbed into a taxi and headed back to the guesthouse to collect their little yellow submarine, with Alex contentedly resting her head upon Rob's shoulder. They arrived in the boatyard a little after midnight to find that the only one awake to greet them was Lampchop, who was thrilled to see them return home. It wasn't until they were on-board the Island Fever they realized, they were not as alone as they'd thought.

As Rob climbed the boat's makeshift ladder and stepped down into to the cockpit, reaching his hand inside the portlight to get the key to the back door, he suddenly sensed the presence of another human being sitting in the shadows on the far side of the boat. A faint smell of cheap aftershave tipped him off that it wasn't Christian, as well as a glint of light from Grandpa's porch light which reflected off something in his hand. As Alex climbed down behind him, Rob realized that the shiny thing aimed at his chest was a gun so he jumped in front of Alex.

"Well, well, if it isn't Joey Wilson. Finally decided to come back to the stash huh," said the gunman in a heavy Spanish accent.

Caught off guard for a brief moment by this obvious case of mistaken identity, Rob let out a nervous laugh realizing that this man was indeed looking for Joey and had assumed that just because he was on the boat, he logically had to be Joey. At that moment, all sorts of things were going through Rob's mind – the most prominent of which was the quite obvious fact that by the look of Guido here, the whole affair must have something to do with Joey's illicit profession and drugs, and that it was not a social call since Guido obviously meant business.

"No, you don't understand," answered Rob laughing nervously, finally able to collect his wits about him, "I'm not Joey, I'm his partner Rob... from Chicago," then suddenly realizing the implications of being Joey's partner, Rob blurted out – "His partner in the boat I mean... not in his other line of work... ahhh whatever that is."

As Rob floundered in water well over his head, Alex stood behind Rob squeezing his arm in order to assure him that she was there to back him up.

Laughing, the man just looked at Rob as if amused at his feeble attempt to squirm out of his present predicament. "Sure Joey, and I'm Jesus Christ. I've been told all about your many personalities. The way I understand it, you have as many names as the telephone directory," he said laughing for a brief moment before suddenly turning serious again and jamming the barrel of the forty-five into Rob's ribs. "You owe Miguel money and it's time to pay up. He wants his money and he sent me to collect. Figures you have it stashed somewhere here on this boat of yours."

Suddenly, realizing the gravity of the situation, Alex decided it was time to step in and lend her help to Rob who was shaking so badly by this point he could barely speak.

"I can vouch for him... I've known Joey for years... looks nothing like Rob here. Didn't Miguel tell you that Joey's short and blond?"

"Miguel told me nothing other than not to trust anything he says, and not to come back without his money or the boat. And seeing's how this boat ain't going nowhere, I guess it's going to have to be the money, or you, Guido said. Gesturing to the stand of palm trees along the edge of the yard, "You see Raul over there? He's here to make sure you pay."

Turning their heads slowly in the direction of the shadows under the trees, Rob and Alex searched apprehensively for a hulking, gold toothed, cannon toting, South America thug from a Bond film. They weren't far off from what their imaginations had so vividly portrayed when he finally stepped from the shadows, except the gun was bigger.

Suddenly, an idea dawned on Rob, "Wait, I can prove what Joey looks like.... the passports! I found his passports!

"Where are they!" asked Alex excitedly, "I'll go get them!"

"I ah... burned them all."

Alex just looked at Rob speechless realizing that that was in fact how Rob had nearly burned up the boat.

"Well, how was I supposed to know that they'd come in handy? I was just trying to keep the police from finding them."

"What police?!" demanded Guido concerned, pointing the gun threateningly in Rob's face.

Reaching for the sky, Rob backed off. "Oh, it was just a small misunderstanding we had with the authorities here, it's all cleared up now."

"So, where's the money!" demanded Guido again, obviously impatient as he nervously waved the gun around in front of them.

"I've tried to tell you, I don't have any money, I put everything I had into buying half of this Goddamn boat from Joey and now he's run off with your money and mine. And he's probably having the time of his life spending it while I'm here going to jail, rebuilding his boat, and getting held at gun point by a buffoon who can't tell the difference between five-foot-eight and six-foot-two," Rob blurted out breathless and agitated.

"Let's just make this easier on all of us here, Joey. You tell me where the money is and I'll leave you and your pretty little girl here alone," said Guido in a menacing tone even though he was smiling a wickedly, sinister smile at Alex. "Otherwise," continued Guido with a lecherous sneer as he grabbed Alex around the neck and held the gun to her head before Rob knew what was happening, "I'll just have to take your girlfriend since I can't take your boat."

Panicking, Rob had to think fast. It was one thing for his life to be threatened but another all together for Alex to be in danger.

"I've got it... buried!" Rob blurted out before he had time to think about what he was saying.

Alex's eyes grew wide in disbelief as she looked at Rob realizing his tack to try and lure them away from her. Thinking fast Alex looked Rob square in the eye, "Boy if I'd known this was going to happen, I would have stayed longer to see the rest of the fireworks," she said winking at him to make him understand, realizing that she would have better luck getting the support of the French Police than the Dutch. Since after all, they did owe her a pretty big favor at this point.

"Paradise Peak?" said Rob suddenly catching on to her coded message. "That's where I buried it, at the top of Paradise Peak!"

Looking at him somewhat suspiciously Guido tightened his grip around Alex's throat.

"I swear! I have this spot up there that no one knows about. I buried it in a cooler," Rob said having seen one too many movies. "I... I'll take you there if you let her go." Of course, the movie running through Rob's mind at that moment was the one where Guido cuts off Rob's left ear and sends it to Alex to get her to pay up. However, Rob was having a tough time picturing himself going through life resembling Van Gogh.

"She goes with us," demanded Guido, "You give us the money, I let her go."

Standing firm, more from being frozen with fear than from bravery, Rob took a chance, "No! She stays here... I go... alone! And your gorilla goes with us!"

Seeing the determination in Rob's face, Guido realized that Rob meant it.

Reluctantly releasing Alex, Guido gestured to Rob with the gun to climb down off the boat as he followed him – the gun pointed at the back of his head.

Ah, wasn't life on 'The Friendly Island' fun. You just never knew what was waiting to greet you just around the next corner. Rob was about to make his second trip to Paradise for the evening, however, this one could definitely prove to be even more challenging than deciding with whom he would be spending the rest of his life. This trip could be the deciding factor as to whether he would actually have the rest of his life to spend.

It was about now that Rob was finally starting to get the hang of communion with the big Kahuna, and he was desperately searching for that frequency which would tune him in to the help that he was so in need of to survive this new curveball the Universe had just pitched him. And I, was scrambling to round-up all the help I could find on this side. Sometimes even I, don't see these unexpected turns of events coming, since they are written into Rob's plan to serve as much of a test to me as it does to Rob.

CHAPTER TWENTY-SEVEN

Heart and Sole

*"Have a care what you ask for,
it might be given you."*

Ancient Proverb

Helpless, Alex watched as Guido led Rob away at gun point to their black sedan. Shaken to her core, she waited in the cockpit of the Island Fever until they had started the car and pulled out of the yard. As their tail lights receded into the darkness, Alex jumped from the boat, climbed into the Yellow Submarine, and drove to wake Louis St. Bernard at his shack in Cole Bay – one of her reliable workers who was the size of a Sumo wrestler, black as a crow, and as solid as a rock, both in character and physique. Since he was French from Les Saints,* Alex knew he would have much better luck explaining to the Gendarmes the nature of the Island Fever's latest need for police intervention.

    If it hadn't been for Louis' ability to explain to the police the gravity of the kidnapping in French, Alex knew she would have never solicited their aid. She was grateful that she had this big, lovable hulk to rely on at a time like this. Alex had known Louis for years – in fact, she had worked side-by-side with him building the Island Fever in the St. Kitts boatyard. The minute she had realized that they would be in repair mode for the summer, she had called him to offer

---

*LES SAINTS — Les Saintes are eight tiny French islands off the southern coast of Guadeloupe, only two of which are inhabited – Terre-de-Bas & Terre-de-Haut. Originally settled by seafaring Normans and Breton Colonists, it is now owned by the French and is the epitome of quaint.

him a job helping her put the Island Fever back together. He had accepted instantly, respecting Alex's abilities as a sailor and a shipwright,* but had informed her that he first had to head home for a few weeks, since his wife had taken ill and there was no one to look after his five young children. With such a large family, Louis had found it necessary to move away to find work capable of supporting his brood. The only means of making a living in Petite Anse on Terre-de-Bas was fishing, and Louis was unable to take to the sea due to an inner ear problem, which caused him to reel the minute he set foot on a boat on the water.

Of course, the Gendarmes remembered Alex all too well and were hesitant at first to get involved. Unbeknownst to Alex however, Louis had managed to entice them into a little swat team and sniper action. By the time he had convinced the Gendarmes of the urgency of the situation, Rob and Miguel's goons had gotten a pretty good head start on getting up to Pic du Paradis and Alex was getting worried. Riding with Louis in the back of the police van, Alex said a little prayer for the first time in as long as she could remember, that Rob was safe and that they would get there in time to save him before the thugs realized that Rob was only bluffing about the money. She also appealed to her dad, who she knew was looking over her to lend Rob a hand in dealing with his abductors.

Her heart was aching at the thought of losing him. Oh, how easy it had been to not care about anyone or anything. But now that she had found Rob, she realized that she loved him with all of her heart and soul, and that losing him might be the second most painful thing she would ever experience in life – the first being the loss of her father. Her only comfort was in knowing that the Universe couldn't possibly be so cruel as to take him away from her now that she had found true love.

Alex had always possessed an intuitive gift that sometimes allowed her to see the future. In her heart she searched for some assurance that Rob would be okay but found nothing there but fear. This was the most distressing part of it all – her intuition had deserted her and the only thing she was able to rely on was the faith that they were destined to be together. She was determined that their future would not be cut short by a couple of low-life, gun-toting, drug dealers.

When they arrived at the top of the road to Pic du Paradis the black sedan was the lone car parked at the end of the paved road. Before Alex could say a word, the French militia had swarmed out of the two vans and up the hill, wearing flak jackets and snapping ammunition clips into their automatic weapons. Panicked, Alex wondered what she had done. She'd unleashed the French Brigade – Rob now stood a greater risk of getting injured by the police than by his captors. If all hell broke loose, Rob might quite possibly get caught in the crossfire.

SHIPWRIGHT — A carpenter who builds or repairs wooden boats.

ISLAND FEVER

Alex leapt from the van trying in vain to catch up to the captain but it was too late – they were well on their way to the top of the crest where she had clued Rob to lead Guido and Raul. By the time she arrived breathless at the top of the lookout, the Gendarmes had already surrounded the perimeter and had the outlaws pinned down behind an outcropping of rock on the edge of a precipice. Alex felt helpless – unable to do anything about the volatile condition of the situation.

One of the good guys shouted instructions in Spanish through a bullhorn for the bad guys to lay down their weapons and reach for the sky, as if they were just going to give up that easy. Alex felt as if she had just been transported to Tombstone, Arizona for the "Shoot Out at OK Corral." In the meantime, Rob was at the mercy of Guido who held him hostage behind the rock with the barrel of a small cannon pinned to his ear. All Alex could see of Rob was one deck shoe sticking out from behind the rock, and she unfortunately understood enough Spanish to garner the terms of the banditos – the bad guys were refusing to come out with their hands up, and they were threatening to shoot Rob if the policia didn't back off.

By that point, Rob had nearly soiled himself from the cold, hard barrel of steel pressed against his temple. And, Rob had been afraid of spending the rest of his life in jail due to Joey's illicit calling. Right now, a life sentence was looking quite preferable to the option currently at hand. He was wondering what he could have possibly done karmically to deserve the recent turn of events in Paradise and realized that he was quickly slipping over that fine line back into Hell – surely, he had already reached purgatory. Instead of thinking about the gun lodged tightly above his left ear, he tried hard to focus on his future with Alex rather than the thought of going through life, if he was lucky, resembling Van Gogh.

The situation couldn't have gotten any more tense with an interminable wait, which felt like nearly an hour for Alex, and for Rob was starting the fourth re-run of the documentary of his life. Frightened to death, Alex was beginning to realize that someone or something had to give. She knew that her nerves had reached a point where she might not be able to make any clear judgments and worried that the bad guys might have reached the same breaking point.

What she and Louis didn't realize was that several sharp shooters had made their way around to another outcropping on the far side of the mountain where they could get a clear shot at the banditos. Alex's heart stopped when the Gendarmes suddenly opened up on the rock behind which Rob and the bad guys were hiding in order to distract them enough from their hostage for the snipers to get a clean shot at them, taking them both out with one shot each. It was all over but the crying in that one deafening moment. Not even Rob realized what had hit him until all was quiet and he suddenly felt a throbbing pain in his left foot. Alex was afraid to breathe as she waited to hear something from Rob, not knowing if he was dead or alive.

As I said before, it's our job here on 'The Otherside' to protect the lives of the charges we are assigned when they return to a human existence. And as of late, myself and everyone I could enlist here on this side have been working over-time to protect Rob from his recent string of mishaps. Although we try hard, it isn't always possible to prevent or even soften the inevitable events that have been written into one's life-plan. After all – that is what they are here for – to experience the pain and suffering of human existence that simply doesn't exist on 'The Otherside.'

It seemed that a bullet had ricocheted off the rock in the first volley of gunfire and gone clean through the sole of his deck shoe and out the other side of his foot. Once again, it was hard to believe, but Rob had actually written this newest setback into his recent package of calamity and mayhem that was rapidly speeding up his tutelage on the physical plane. In fact, Rob was about to graduate with his masters-degree and move on to obtain his Ph.D.

"Ah guys... I think I've been shot," announced Rob flatly once he had finally gotten his wits about him and realized that he was indeed still alive, however, there was a gaping hole in his left shoe. Of course, that was all that Alex needed to hear for her to spring to her feet and rush to Rob's side without regard at all for her own safety. After all she had no way of knowing for sure that the bad guys were well on their way back into utero of some poor unsuspecting mother who was about to give birth.

Louis could barely pry them apart when he went to pick up Rob and carry him down the mountain. All the way down, Alex kept a firm grip on Rob's hand until they reached the police van where they loaded Rob, Alex, Louis, and half the police, while the other half of the Gendarmes were busy carting the two stiffs down the trail to be taken off to the island morgue.

Of course, Rob and Alex left out all of the particular details regarding Joey as they told the story of Rob being taken hostage in their debriefing by the French police. In turn, they simply wrote Rob's involvement off to a case of mistaken identity.

This time, Alex didn't think twice about chancing the local medical care since the French hospital was twice as bad as the Dutch. Instead, Alex and Louis put Rob in the back seat of the Yellow Submarine and drove him up to the island vet where Doctor Don cleaned his foot, slowed the bleeding, gave him a hefty shot of antibiotics and Demerol, then patched him up enough to get him to Puerto Rico. Refusing to argue with Rob, who was not up to going anywhere, Alex had him on the first plane out the next morning to San Juan where she checked him into the Pavia Hospital. By noon, Rob was in surgery having the gaping hole in his foot sewn up and the shattered bone grafted back together from pieces of bone taken from his hip. It would be a miracle if Rob would ever walk normally again, but Alex knew that he stood a far better chance in an American hospital than at the mercy of some French or Dutch Antillean surgeon.

It was eight o'clock that night when they finally wheeled a semi-conscious Rob into his room where Alex waited impatiently for news. It seemed that the operation had been a success but it would be months before Rob would be healed enough to take the cast off, let alone knowing if he'd be walking like Hopalong Cassidy for the rest of his life. Nothing mattered to Alex other than the fact that he was safe, and in her arms once again – back where it had all started – in a hospital bed waiting for him to come to his senses, in more ways than one.

CHAPTER TWENTY-EIGHT

Tropical Depression

*"I have not failed. I have just found
10,000 ways that won't work."*

Thomas Edison

It was late July when Rob finally returned to Simpson Bay in St. Maarten with Alex, who had stayed with Rob confidently entrusting the repairs of the boat to Louis. She knew would be able to make progress without her. Especially, since they were down to the final stretch – sheathing the damaged hull and bridge deck to make it watertight, a job she knew Luis could handle in his sleep.

Raymond was there to meet them at the Princess Julianna Airport to assist Rob as he hobbled off the plane and through immigration on crutches – returning to the island like a casualty of war. Back at the boatyard, Grandma, Grandpa, and Christian awaited him with a welcome home party, as did Lambchop, who had grown to nearly double his size in the few weeks they'd been gone. He met Rob standing on his hind legs with his front hooves planted on Rob's chest in order to give him a famous Lambchop kiss right on the lips – nearly knocking him off his crutches in the process.

Being the later-half of July, tropical waves were rolling through one right after the other, like cruise ships in high season. But, since it was still early into hurricane season, the Atlantic had not yet spawned anything stronger than a number of tropical depressions,* which rolled across the island bringing endless rain showers, gloomy skies, and the muggy, stale air of summer. These showers did serve to slightly cool the ninety plus degree temperature and blow away the mosquitoes, which were multiplying at an alarming rate that the department of tourism wished it could generate tourists. But alas, it was off season in the West Indies and most of the expatriates were smart enough to travel elsewhere to spend the miserable summer and fall months and avoid hurricane season** altogether.

The island had been lucky the last decade or so, nothing stronger than a few 'category one'*** hurricanes had passed near the island, doing little or no damage. For that very reason, Alex was nervous this year. She understood the odds of keeping up this ten-year stroke of good luck, not to mention that the water temperature was already hotter than normal for that time of the year, which disturbed her since warmer waters were usually responsible for a greater than normal tropical storm activity in the Northern Atlantic.

Alex's daily afternoon swims were hardly a relief from the sweltering heat and the total stillness that followed a tropical depression. However, she had gotten used to this time of the year and in some ways welcomed it, since the island was a peaceful place without the throngs of tourists lining the beaches and driving rental cars around the island roads in a manner in which a novice might drive the Indy 500.

The good news was, they were well on their way to finishing the boat. Alex figured that by late August, they might actually have her back in the water before the peak of hurricane season. Alex was concerned that the Island Fever wouldn't stand much of a chance getting pummeled on shore by the swells like a beached whale should a storm decide to clock in from the west or northwest. This would be an unlikely turn of event, but then in the West Indies, anything is possible – not to mention Rob's bad luck.

Rob however, was in the midst of his own kind of tropical depression, since his uncomfortable cast and his throbbing itchy foot made life relatively

*TROPICAL DEPRESSION — The second stage in the development of a hurricane with winds up to thirty-three knots – the first being a tropical wave. Of course, the term 'tropical depression' also stands for the first stage in the development of the disease known as 'island fever.' But with regard to the weather, a tropical depression goes on to develop into a tropical storm before potentially becoming a hurricane once it reaches sixty-four knots (75mph) or above.
HURRICANE SEASON — That time of the year from June through November when hurricanes* can develop in the Atlantic Ocean and head for the Caribbean, Mexico, the Bahamas, Bermuda, or the southeastern United States. The true risk of hurricanes doesn't usually start until late summer, and at least by the book, should end by November 15th when the Tradewinds start to blow steadily from the southeast at an average 16 mph, thus cooling the ocean's water temperature.
***HURRICANES — A tropical system that develops off the coast of Africa due to winds from different directions converging over the summer's warm ocean waters (over 81 degrees). These perfect conditions added to the earth's rotation make thunderstorms circulate counterclockwise forming a churning mass known as a tropical cyclone. Once the winds from this cyclone reach 75mph it is classified as a hurricane.
****CATEGORY ONE HURRICANE — A hurricane's severity being categorized on a scale of one to five with category one starting with 75mph and a five being the equivalent of a 10.0 earthquake.

miserable in the sweltering tropical heat. All he was able to do for relief was to scratch his left foot inside his cast with a piece of palm frond as he sat on Grandma's porch watching the windsurfers come and go from the nearby watersports shack.

Rob was bored, since like all Americans he felt it necessary to be doing something every minute, no matter how meaningless. He still hadn't fully gotten the hang of three-quarter time and was getting antsier by the day, but at least some of his 'sturm and drang'* had subsided. Instead, he had simply found himself in the middle of the doldrums** it seemed both literally and figuratively.

Of course, Rob was able to catch up on a few games of dominos with Grandpa during his extended break. Once again being of little or no help to Alex, which was just as well since it prevented any unnecessary tension in their relationship and further potential injury to Rob's person. For now, Rob was simply playing voyeur to the workings of the boatyard and a student of life as far as Grandpa was concerned. Rob had even taken Alex's advice on resuming his mariner's course which would take some of the burden off of Alex to teach Rob all of the textbook nuances of sailing and piloting his vessel. As far as the practical application went, Alex figured that they had plenty of time ahead of them to work on that once the Island Fever was back in operation again.

"Let yourself be bored," said Grandpa one day over a challenging game of dominos, since Rob had at least learned how to give Grandpa a run for his money at his own game. "There be a lot to learn from just lettin' your mind be still. That be when the answers cum," continued Grandpa as he focused on his next play.

"You mean meditate?" asked Rob confused at Grandpa's new-age approach to life.

"Meditate, shmeditate, I not be carin' what those swamis want to call it, there's no need to be puttin' a label on it. That be the whole point. It be about nothin'... not somethin'. The minute you be puttin' a name on it becomes someting'."

Rob sat there thinking back on his life 'B.C.' – 'Before the Caribbean' – remembering how much he'd wished he could lose himself in that void of

---

*STURM AND DRANG — A German literary movement of the 1770's which embraced impulse, instincts, and emotion – all the things that got Rob into this mess in the first place. It implies personal crisis and disorder of the material world.
DOLDRUMS — The area of ocean which lays calm close to the equator and near 30 degrees latitude – known as the 'Horse Latitudes.* The doldrums can also describe that period between storms during hurricane season where the wind and one's mental state start to feel stagnant.
***HORSE LATITUDES — The area of ocean in the Atlantic near the Bermuda Triangle which was named for the Spanish galleons that made a habit of getting becalmed there. In order to get moving again they would dispose of any and all unnecessary weight, by throwing it into the ocean, in order to get moving again – including many of the horses that were bound for the Americas.

nothingness. But because he never seemed to be able to find a moment alone, he'd always been unable to find it. Here he was now with as much space and time on his hands as he could have ever dreamed possible and he was afraid of it – as if he might discover something about himself that he didn't want to know. As if ignorance was bliss and if he actually understood too much, he might have to take more responsibility for his life. After all, one does tend to learn the most at the lowest point in one's life.

"You know, the life you be living right now is exactly what you created," said Grandpa picking up on his thoughts.

"The trick to life is to be careful what you wish for, because it usually come to be. The problem is, we don't always think through all the details too well. I mean, you likely wished you had more free time on your hands, but you forgot to ask for it from some other means than getting shot in the foot." Grandpa paused studying Rob, who seemed quite puzzled by this recent revelation.

"You should be lookin' at the bigger picture of life. I mean you be havin' all those things that you thought you wanted. You be livin' in a beautiful tropical part of the world, you own a luxurious yacht, you have a beautiful girlfriend who loves you, and except for a small hole in the bottom of your foot and a hole or two in your boat, what more could you possibly be needin'?"

Rob thought about what Grandpa had said for a moment and then nodded his head realizing what a lucky man he truly was, holes or no holes. After all, it could have been worse. He could be dead right now instead of looking at that beautiful ocean.

"Problem is," said Grandpa, "When you dream'n bout the things you be wantin' outta life, you sometimes forget to fill in all the details in between. And those details don't always turn out the way you pictured," chuckled Grandpa. "In fact they be the things that make you appreciate the good parts and teach the hardest earned lesson."

"Well, then I must have learned an awful lot over the last few months. Funny, I don't feel a lot smarter," said Rob somewhat sarcastically since his sense of humor was fading rapidly along with his sanity.

What Rob didn't realize was that Alex had taken Grandpa aside, due to his waning state of mind, hoping that Grandpa would have the answers to snap Rob out of his current tropical depression, which was developing faster than any storm that had ever moved through this part of the Caribbean. Both Grandpa and Alex realized that Rob was at present, taking life a little too seriously.

"You got to ease up on yourself Rob," Grandpa continued hoping his ongoing tutelage would eventually get through. "Don't be so hard on yourself. Making money or not, it be time you learn to be good to yourself and allow yourself a time to rest. You need to take the time to be findin' your spiritual anchor. You be havin' plenty of time to get out there and make money again.

Just be grateful for the gifts the Universe has sent you... and learn to laugh more."

"Seems to me, the kind of gifts I've been receiving recently, I could live without. I mean in the last two months I've been given the gifts of ten days of incarceration, being robbed by my ex-girlfriend's father of my home, I have holes in my million-dollar boat, a miserable disease from a mosquito, I've been kidnapped, and then shot by the police... all for a boat I can't even sail. Besides that and the fact that I'm nearly broke again with no hope of work for the next three months, everything's just great," lamented Rob wallowing in self-pity. "Like the 'Twelve Days of Christmas,' I'm just waiting for the remaining half dozen gifts from the Universe."

"In fact," thought Rob to himself. "Miguel might just send another couple of his goons or even come back himself to collect from my hide, or even sail off with the boat once it's back in the water." But these were thoughts that Rob was keeping to himself. Since of course, Grandpa knew nothing of Joey's apparent illicit endeavors.

"I know it be hard to see, standin' in the middle of it, but look what you be gainin' in return," pointed out Grandpa. "You be that much wiser than you were before you began... and you found the love of your life."

Rob nodded, considering this fact and smiled at the thought of Alex. But underneath it all, he still looked miserable with himself. Grandpa could see the fear in Rob's eyes and he knew fear was the one thing that could ruin a man, or turn to ruin any great plan. He realized he somehow had to help Rob gain his confidence back – in himself and in the Universe.

Deep down Rob felt he'd failed the test of this new life of his. Compared to his previous ease of success in his old life, his new life was a shambles. He was scared – scared of what lay ahead and how he was going to survive his new life in Paradise.

"You know it be all about attitude," insisted Grandpa. "With the world changing all the time it really be the only thing we can control. You can be vexed by something that happens and feel like the world be out to get you, or you can choose to not let it bother you. You choose to be happy or to be unhappy, it be totally up to you – it be all about how we feel about something. In fact, the way we feel about things controls all that cum to us... good and bad. To truly find happiness you have to choose to be happy, not sit around and wait until it be happening to you and be vex at the world in the meantime."

"Well…it's kind of hard to be happy about getting shot. I mean I can't really say I'm happy I got shot in the foot," said Rob stoically.

Grandpa couldn't help but chuckle at Rob's literal interpretation of his philosophy on life. Although Grandpa understood the principal now, he hadn't always appreciated the things for which one should be grateful – like simply waking up every morning in a sound and working body. In fact, when Grandpa, or Stanley, was Rob's age, he had felt nearly as ungrateful as Rob did about the gifts in his life and the trivial trials he was faced with day after day. That was until he woke up one morning with viral encephalitis after one of his trips down-island to Trinidad. And, as the doctors had prognosticated, he thought he would surely die before the sun had set that day. Although he lived through that day and the next, his condition fluctuated for the days to come between seizures and unconsciousness. When he was conscious, he hardly knew his own family as he ranted and raved night after night. Even though the doctors had given her little hope to cling to, poor Winifred knelt by his bed day and night praying to his guardian angels for his recovery. It seemed her prayers were heard, for amazingly, on the fifth day of his torment, his dementia cleared and his senses returned to him – even if his body hadn't since he had been left paralyzed from the waist down. Life wasn't worth living, thought Stanley feeling sorry for himself, if he could no longer make love or dance – the two things he loved most in life. And what good was he anyway – he could no longer even support his family and was just one more mouth to feed.

In fact, at that point Stanley had been ready to give up living, forgetting all the wonderful gifts he possessed and the people who truly loved him. If ever the Universe had confronted him with a test to see how much he'd learned in his life this had been the one, since it took a full year for Stanley to recover from his paralysis. And, it wasn't until he realized that his life was truly in his own hands, that he stood up and walked again, to the doctor's amazement. Within a month, Stanley had totally recovered and he was so much his old self again that his extended illness was nearly forgotten. But deep inside Stanley knew that he would never truly be his old self again. He was a man changed by the lessons he'd learned about life and his newly earned credentials for living, which had so painfully been accredited him.

Grandpa knew that he could share his miracle with Rob, and tell him how he had not appreciated his life until it had been nearly taken from him or worse – left him unable to live it. But he also knew that this was a lesson that no teacher other than life itself could bestow upon another. So instead, Grandpa presented it to him as simply as he knew how – "Do you think the fish in the sea feel sorry for themselves when they get caught on your hook or eaten by a bigger fish? They just accept it as part of life. Like they say, shit happens, so get on with it."

Hearing Grandpa coin that famous phrase found on American bumper stickers, Rob couldn't help but let out a small chuckle. After all, life wasn't truly so bad. Although, he was still feeling like the one that didn't get away.

Time passed, and so did the tropical depression that had been hanging over their little boatyard. Once Rob finally began listening to Grandpa's advice

ISLAND FEVER

and acquiring a new appreciation for life, the days started to fly by. Before he knew it, Alex and Luis were wrapping up repairs and putting the finishing touches on the Island Fever's paint job – including applying a fresh coat of bottom paint* to her hulls.

It was fast approaching the end of August – the heart of hurricane season. Alex knew she had to get the boat into the safety of the lagoon, but first she had to get Rob to Puerto Rico to have the doctor find out how his foot was progressing. To the doctor's surprise, Rob's foot had healed completely and was ready for the cast to come off. There was something to be said for his recent change in attitude, Rob thought. Of course, it was still going to be a while before Rob was doing the Rumba or windsurfing, but at least he would be able to shed that awful plaster prison his leg had been in for the last six weeks.

The weather forecast was predicting no storms in the immediate future, so to celebrate, Rob decided to take Alex to 'The Baths,' a natural mineral spa and retreat on Virgin Gorda, in the British Virgin Islands. Rob knew Alex needed a few days of R&R – something she'd certainly earned. She had after all, put their world back together again and the Island Fever was about to be launched for the second time in her short existence.

Rob's life was on an upward swing once again and he was beginning to see all sorts of wonderful possibilities that awaited them. Maybe they should head off with the boat to some new part of the world where no one knew its history – once they had a little cash to fall back on. The South Pacific sounded attractive – uncharted territory just waiting to be discovered. To Rob, it seemed the possibilities were simply endless.

BOTTOM PAINT or ANTIFOULING PAINT — *A special paint for the bottom of a boat below the waterline – formulated to limit marine growth such as barnacles and green slime from attaching itself to your vessel. The paint is designed to sluff off in fine layers once the boat reaches a certain speed. Unfortunately, this does not entirely rid the hull of unwanted passengers and a good monthly scrubbing with a mask and snorkel is required to keep the boat clean and running at its optimum speed through the water. Although they are non-environmentally acceptable, many bottom paints contain high quantities of copper and arsenic to assist in discouraging those little organisms from climbing aboard in the first place.*

CHAPTER TWENTY-NINE

Changes in Latitude

"If we couldn't laugh, we would all go insane."

Jimmy Buffett

Upon returning to the island after their long-needed rest, Alex busied herself with preparations for getting the Island Fever back into the water where she belonged, leaving the island buzzing with excitement of the prospect of a launching party. You see, there is nothing quite like the launching of a boat and a lot of Carib beer to bring an island together. Of course, Alex could arrange to have one of the island salvage boats tie a rope to the Island Fever and drag her back down the beach into the water, but why pass up such a great excuse for a party?

    The technique was quite simple, especially since the steel pipes used to roll her out of the water were still in place. First: Purchase copious amounts of beer and rum and hire one steel drum band; Second: Gather several hundred islanders for one hell of a party; Third: Put the muscle-bound men on the back end to lift the sterns of the hulls as she starts to slide back into the water and just have the rest of the able-bodied beer drinkers push like hell. Eventually, the boat will find its way into enough water to get her floating again. At that point she could be towed around the sandbar to deep water where her rudders and dagger boards could be reinstalled. What was important to remember, was to be certain to commence with launching procedures before one unlocked the serious stash of libations in order to keep the incentive for hard work under de hot sun, higher than the receding tide.

Grateful that the boat was finally finished and that he no longer had any gaping holes in his sole or his topsides, had splurged and sprung for five cases of the locally bottled Guavaberry rum liqueur.* Even his friends at immigration partook in his hospitality and leant a hand with the launching. Of course, they had an ulterior motive in mind – to get the Island Fever off the island as quick as possible. As remuneration for their earlier faux pas they had even been kind enough to supply the steel drum band to liven up the afternoon's festivities.

Christian did the honor of re-christening the boat with a cheap bottle of champagne poured over her hibiscus lei-covered bows, as two hundred happy islanders carried her into the water. It was a magical day for all concerned and Rob was actually beginning to believe that maybe the scourge had lifted as he and Alex climbed aboard his, once again, floating vessel.

Even Alex took the rest of the day off to join in the celebration, once the Island Fever was safely on anchor in Simpson Bay. She danced the night away with Luis and the guys as Rob watched her smile, laugh, and enjoy herself. He didn't even mind that he was unable to dance with her to the steel drum band, since inside, he was already dancing to the beat of Alex's drum. And I, well I was never one to miss out on a good party. In fact, in my day I had been a rather good dancer, so I took the opportunity to join in the festivities. After all, we need a break here on 'The Otherside' too.

It had finally dawned on Rob that he had indeed gotten the hang of living in three-quarter time for the first time in his three decades of life on the planet. He had begun to realize that the only thing that truly counted was how one perceived life, and it was finally starting to sink in that the present was the only stuff to build his life on – everything else was just a cerebral exercise. After all, you can grow old and lose your memories of the past, and even give up on your dreams of the future, but it is truly impossible to lose the present and still survive, is it not?

It only took Alex and Luis a few days to put the final touches on preparing the ship for seaworthiness. The new engine sled was ready, but the engine had strangely been delayed in shipping and had not yet arrived. No matter, they were going nowhere immediately since they still had more than two months to weather out the rest of hurricane season, and there was no reason to leave since they were sitting just outside the safest hurricane hole in the Eastern Caribbean – Simpson Bay Lagoon.

Even though they were ecstatic to be afloat once again, Rob and Alex already missed Grandma and Grandpa, not to mention Henry and Lambchop.

*GUAVABERRY RUM — A legendary folk liqueur of St. Maarten/St. Martin which was made in native homes for centuries – an essential feature of the island's folklore. The fruit, the guavaberry, is found in the high tropical hills at the center of the island and is not related to the fruit, guava in any way. Today the Guavaberry liqueur is produced commercially along with many flavors of rum by a local distillery.

ISLAND FEVER

It was just as well that Rob was not yet able to take him windsurfing, since Lambchop was much too large now to fit on the board. Lambchop's horns were developing rapidly and created a bit of a hazard when he jumped up with his hooves on Rob's chest to nuzzle his chin. Lambchop's adolescent hormones were also rapidly blossoming and he was becoming a very horny goat in more ways than one.

Of course, being anchored in Simpson Bay, Rob and Alex were only minutes away from Grandma and Grandpa's beach and still made a habit of parking their other two vessels there – the Dinghy Fever and the Yellow Submarine, so they could stop for a quick visit whenever they came and went. Alex continued her morning ritual of coffee with Grandma and of course, afternoon tea, and Rob made certain to never miss an opportunity for elevenses or happy hour, and a quick game of dominos with Grandpa whenever time allowed. And time, it seemed, was the most plentiful asset Rob currently had on hand.

Alex had done more than a little exploring over the years in the waters around St. Maarten and she was dying to show Rob her favorite anchorage in the entire world aside from Barbuda – Tintamarre,* *(or Flat Island as it was called by the locals)*. Its beach was one of the most pristine, beautiful deserted beaches around, and Alex wanted to share sleeping on the beach all night under the stars with Rob – the water lapping along the shore. Sleeping on the beach in the islands was only possible to do on Flat Island since the overabundant hermit crab and lizard populations left nothing resembling an insect *(i.e. sandfleas and mosquitoes)* alive on the island to nibble on you during the night as Itchy had painfully experienced.

Since the repairs were finished, and the Island Fever was staying put in that part of the world until November, Raymond set off for a little surfing in the Dominican Republic, and Luis headed back to St. Kitts to start on the newest boat in the yard. This left Rob and Alex to themselves, with the exception of their new found foster son, Christian. Assured by Grandma that she would look after Christian for a week or so, Rob and Alex decided to venture out of Simpson Bay, sans engine, and take the Island Fever out for her first shakedown cruise since the accident. They'd be only an hour and a half from the safety of Simpson Bay Lagoon and close enough to get back in an emergency.

*TINTAMARRE OR FLAT ISLAND — A private, deserted, French owned island off the windward side of St. Martin, which is home to nothing more than a herd of goats, lizards, and hermit crabs. It did however, serve at one time as a Vichy French provisioning stop in the Eastern Caribbean for German subs. The ruins of the old sub dock and landing strip, along with the remains of many small buildings, still exist today not to mention parts of wrecked aircraft.

Unfortunately, the satellite which monitored the weather for that part of the Caribbean also decided to take a vacation and had taken off for some other galaxy, leaving the Caribbean on its own in predicting approaching hurricanes. But, since the weather looked promising for at least the next few days or so, Alex decided it was safe to sail the ten miles to the other side of the island and visit Tintamarre, which was just off the coast of Club Orient on Orient Beach – the nudist resort on the French side of St. Martin.

As usual, Alex sent Rob off to town for provisions while she readied the boat for sailing. Upon his return, Rob gave the boat a thorough once over to check for any stowaways named Christian, who may have decided to join them on their little expedition once they were sure they were alone. They left about midday on Monday hoping to miss the weekend warriors on the little island and find it deserted. It didn't matter that they were engineless, they wouldn't need it to sail around the island to the northeastern corner where Tintamarre lay – an easy sail to weather then a comfortable beam reach past Guana Bay and Oyster Pond. After all, what did sailors do prior to the invention of the internal-combustion engine? Like Alex, they had to rely solely on the wind for forward propulsion of their vessel to carry them to their intended destination.

Alex raised the main while they still sat at anchor, then helped Rob pull up their extra anchor – a much easier job with an engine. They dropped off their anchorage as Alex raised the main-staysail and set the mainsail hard to starboard, then turned the helm hard to port to back her around under sail alone. Once around, Alex fell off the wind and headed out around Pelican Cay at the entrance to Simpson Bay as Rob raised their light weather genoa. They headed southeast past Philipsburg on a tight hauled port tack – off in the direction of St. Barth.

Today, Alex would turn the helm over to Rob since there was no one on board to get hurt and they had no schedules to keep. Taking Grandma's advice, she had decided to teach him to sail without him even realizing it, and make him think that he was learning all by himself. Besides, from teaching kids to sail for years, Alex knew that the only way to truly learn was by feel. One had to sense the ocean through the helm – feel the movement of the boat and the direction of the wind and learn how the boat responded. Sailing was purely an instinctual thing once one understood the technical side. A seasoned sailor could smell a reef or land without ever seeing it, feel the approach of a low-pressure system without a barometer, time the tides by an inner clock, and sense a wind shift by watching the waters ahead. If only one could live their life with the same astute awareness of approaching storms and shifts in the prevailing winds. The well-honed, experienced sailor, learned to become one with their vessel as well as the elements – the way a professional athlete becomes one with their body.

With his confidence somewhat renewed Rob took the helm of the Island Fever as if he'd been doing it his whole life. He finally felt as if he were steering his own course once again instead of being adrift at sea. He had been a student of life for more than thirty years, but now he had to become a student of the sea, which like life, was far bigger and more unpredictable and uncontrollable than our wildest imaginations. The day had given them a small reprieve between tropical depressions with the wind blowing only about eight knots. The temperature was high in the nineties, and the water was about as calm as a duck pond. For the first time on board, Rob felt in control. What Rob didn't yet understand was that he might feel as if he were in control at the helm steering his course for a while, but total control of the sea, as well as one's life, is as impossible as changing the course of a waterspout.*

Once they had Tintamarre in their sights just aft of their beam, Alex asked Rob to jibe** the boat around and head right for the flat looking rock straight ahead. Alex had chosen not to tack the boat with the winds so light and the water so calm. She was afraid that they might end up 'in irons'*** as catamarans are known to do in such light wind. As they reached the little bay in the lee of the island, Alex had Rob turn straight into the wind dead at the beach as she unwrapped the halyard for the genoa, letting it slide down effortlessly to the net on the bow of the boat. As Rob did the same with the main-staysail halyard from the cockpit, the boat coasted to a stop only three meters from the shore. As she drifted backwards on the light breeze, Alex lowered the anchor and fed out enough rode to give them a secure hold, then tied off the line on the windlass,***** coming up short with a slight jolt like a yearling who's just reached the end of her tether on her first halter.

*WATERSPOUT — The dangerous marine cousin to the tornado which can play havoc with small boats, since they are erratically unpredictable and a rather common occurrence in the tropics.
**JIBE — The opposite of tacking with the boat turning downwind instead of into the wind. It is the stern, not the bow that swings across the wind in a jibe. An accidental jibe occurs while steering downwind and not paying attention to the accuracy of one's course or an unexpected change in wind direction. An accidental jibe is when the wind catches the back of the mainsail and throws it and the boom violently across the boat to the other side – risking damage to the rigging, or as mentioned earlier, damage to crew members' heads by booms unsecured by a boom vang or strop. All of which is somewhat analogous to life slapping you upside the head when you aren't paying attention to the prevailing forces of nature.
IN IRONS — A term used to describe a condition when sailing to weather where the vessel has tried to point* too close into the wind and has become stalled – 'in irons.' This condition can also occur during tacking, especially on some multihulls, since they are lighter and don't always have the weight to carry them through the tack to the point where the wind has filled the sail on the opposite side.
****POINTED OR TO 'POINT' — To 'point' into the wind is to turn the nose of the boat too close to the direction that the wind is corning from. As mentioned before in 'beating to weather;' pointing too close to the wind stalls the boat, preventing forward propulsion from its sails. This is also a quick way to stop the boat or curtail one's forward momentum rapidly if you are close-hauled, since unlike a car, a sailboat does not have brakes.
*****WINDLASS — A type of winch located on the foredeck of a vessel which holds the anchor rode – the end of the anchor line which is attached to the boat and not the anchor. As opposed to a gypsy which holds the anchor chain.

It seemed that Rob's luck was changing since the only boat visiting this popular picnic spot turned out to be a day charter boat that was in the midst of loading up their sunburnt, waterlogged passengers and gear, and was already busy pulling up anchor for the afternoon cruise back to Philipsburg. He was alone at last in Paradise – something Rob had only dreamed of back in Chicago. But this time, his definition of 'alone' included Alex.

Once the sails were down, bagged and put away under sail covers, and the Bimini top* was strung over the cockpit to offer some reprieve from the tropical sun, Alex stepped into the galley to make up a batch of her famous rum punch, so loved by both sailor and tourist alike, while Rob unlashed the dinghy from the deck and hauled out the engine from the rear lazarette.**

It's a deceiving illusion how life at latitudes in the teens can easily be perceived as Paradise, especially if one doesn't have any specific agenda to meet. There are few inhabitants in your Earthly form who don't need the perfect locale in order to manifest Paradise. Funny... I always seemed to find happiness where ever I went. For me, it was always hard to understand why discontentment seemed to be the prevailing disposition for the human species, and it wasn't until I had returned home back here on 'The Otherside' that I finally got it. Humans just don't know how to have trust in the greater power of the Universe. They don't realize that if they were to simply tap into that great 'One' energy that is the source of all life, including theirs – everything they could ever dream of could be theirs.

A tall rum punch later, Rob had finally started to settle into the 'changes in latitude,' as the song goes *(another Jimmy Buffetism)*, and Alex had prepared little cocktail lanterns*** to illuminate the evening as well as a fabulous dinner ready to go onto the grill once they had built a fire on the beach. They loaded up the blankets and cookout provisions, and motored to the shore to set up their bar-b-que at the northeastern end of the beach under the red sandstone cliffs. Alex placed the lit lanterns in the nooks and crannies to add a little ambiance just as the sun was setting, while Rob stacked the last of the driftwood they had collected with the charcoal and lit their cooking fire.

Alex had planned ahead and came prepared with a feast of scraps for the lizard population of the island to leave off in the bushes. This would keep them at bay and uninterested in Rob and Alex's dinner long enough for them to

---

*BIMINI TOP — A fixed, collapsible, or removable awning or top created in the Bahamian islands, used on a boat for shade.
**LAZARETTE — A storage area in a boat's hull, generally located in the aft or stern of the vessel.
***COCKTAIL LANTERNS — Make-shift lanterns made from empty Heineken bottles – stuffed with rags and filled with kerosene.

eat, since Alex had actually witnessed a starving Tintamarre lizard, deprived of mosquitoes and no-see-ums, actually jump onto a hot grill in order to get to the marinated chicken legs before the tourists. Of course, the land crabs did move a little slower, but eventually they would seek out any morsel that resembled food on their barren little isle as well.

Dessert had never tasted so good thought Rob as they made love after dinner on the beach – on an island which they, for the moment owned – in a world that they alone inhabited. Then they lay content and euphoric with the surf lapping at their feet as the evening breeze gradually cooled the heat of their passion. There under the heavens – with an endless blanket of stars caressing them, they fell asleep in each other's arms, breathing in the essence of one another's being. And, as the full moon rose over the ocean behind them, Rob was certain that he'd finally arrived – at least at a way station on the course to his destination.

CHAPTER THIRTY

Hurricane Hole

*"Life is not measured by the number of breaths we take,
but by the moments that take them away."*

Internet Wisdom

The next morning Alex woke just before dawn and disengaged herself from Rob's embrace, careful not to awaken him. Slipping on her shoes, she climbed to the top of the cliff overlooking the eastern end of Anguilla and Scrub Island and greeted the new day. It was a beautiful morning, thought Alex, breathing in the exhilarating sea air. Partaking in her morning meditation she found it hard to focus as she basked in a feeling of great wellbeing and the warmth of Rob's love.

When she returned to the beach, Rob was still sleeping so peacefully she decided to let him be, and swam to the boat to shower and change and prepare a grand breakfast. It had been years since Alex had felt a desire to be the least bit domestic but she found herself enjoying the thought of cooking for him. A housewife she wasn't, but it was fun to have someone in her life once again whom she wanted to pamper. Aside from Michael, the only other man lucky enough to witness Alex's domesticity had been her father, whom she had cooked for since she could reach the stove without a footstool.

Meanwhile, back on the beach, Rob was beginning to stir under the fast-rising sun as were the crustaceans and the reptiles. Totally unaware of the rapidly approaching army, Rob kept right on dreaming – basking in the warmth of the golden sun and sand. The crumbs from the previous night's dinner had lured them from their home in the bushes and into the open, since any other source of food on the island had been polished off the night before both the stash Alex had left for them and the final remains of the previous night's bar-b-que. For these crusty little island dwellers, breakfast was about as scarce as a banquet in Ethiopia, and to them, any available crumb constituted a feast.

Rob was busy dreaming about acupuncture when he suddenly realized that the needles were moving across his body. When he cracked one eye trying to ascertain exactly where he was, he found himself eye-to-eye with a miniature version of Godzilla who stood on his chest, licking the corners of Rob's lips. Rob, it seemed, was breakfast. Screaming, as if he'd been bitten by a rattlesnake, Rob sprang to his feet and tore into the water like a man with his pants on fire.

Hearing Rob's screams, Alex stuck her head through the companionway hatch just in time to see Rob hit the water with several crabs still attached to his clothing. Alex felt terrible for not realizing that the natives might be restless and stirring that early, but she still couldn't help the chuckle that slipped out at the sight of Rob, with crabs.

Rob and Alex spent the next four days swimming, spinnaker flying,* and making love on deck, morning, noon, and night. Of course, Rob barely needed a spinnaker to fly at that point since he was soaring pretty high on his own, thanks to Alex.

At night they lay on deck – Rob now the one pointing out the constellations above, since he was still studying celestial navigation in his seamanship course. It amazed him how clear the heavenly bodies were out there away from civilization, as on the night of his first passage to St. Barth from Antigua. Rob was finally closing in on tapping into 'the source,' even if he wasn't totally proficient at direct communication at this point with us celestial inhabitants.

On the fifth day, while checking in on the VHF radio** with Island Waterworld to get a recent weather report, Jeff informed Alex that he had received word that there was a tropical depression headed north, which had

---

*SPINNAKER FLYING — A sport which takes place off the bow of a boat with the spinnaker fully up, yet not sheeted in. In fact, the person flying the spinnaker sits in a sling strung between the two tacks of the sail and rides it up and down on the wind – often being dropped into the water when the wind dies.

**VHF RADIO — An FM radio band which is used on boats as a ship-to-ship and a ship-to-shore means of local communication. VHF transmissions are line-of-sight – consequently it is restricted to a limited geographical area – 10-15 miles for ship-to-ship communications and 25-30 miles for ship-to-shore. These distances do however depend on the height of the transmitting and receiving antennas and could reach up to 40 or 50 miles if being transmitted from the top of a tall island.

ISLAND FEVER

just been upgraded to a tropical storm (over 33 knots*). It was currently two hundred miles southwest of them and heading north at about twelve knots. It had entered the Caribbean down around Martinique and had, as most hurricanes do, hooked a hard right once it was well into the Caribbean. The weather had snuck up on them since they had had little warning due to the lack of a satellite for their area. Although it would likely pass the island causing nothing more than squalls and rain showers, Jeff suggested that they head back for the bridge opening at five that afternoon. That way they would have time to set up their mooring and secure the boat safely inside Simpson Bay Lagoon – the safest hurricane hole in the Caribbean. Just in case. After all, it was pushing August.**

    Alex knew that storms and hurricanes in this part of the world almost always tracked north to northwest, and since it was already well to the west of them, she felt confident there was no imminent danger of it becoming a threat. After all, it was still only a small tropical storm and posed little danger of becoming more than that before it passed well west of them.

    Alex often lived her life irreverently, however the two things she did respect were the weather and the sea. Most of her life was somewhat controllable, but the weather and the sea were beyond her control – beyond human intervention. Man had been unable to harness them – the weather – the wind – the sea. They ruled him – played him, and brought him to his knees to beg for mercy at times. A hurricane or waterspout were two of weather's most magnificent, yet terrifying displays of its indisputable power. Once formed there was no stopping it – diverting it – managing it. It was impossible to control – one could only avoid it, prepare for it, and pray.

    Disappointed that their little sojourn had come to an end, yet grateful that they had been allowed the time together, Alex and Rob packed up the dinghy and took off the sail covers preparing to head for home. By the time they had gotten underway, the winds had picked up to a brisk twenty-five knots from the south-east, and by the time they had traveled the downwind leg along the coast of St. Maarten to Simpson Bay, it was gusting up to thirty-five, raising the stakes ever so slightly. As far as Alex was concerned, this was a bad sign. It meant that the storm was probably closer to the east than predicted and was probably traveling faster and growing stronger than anyone had thought.

    Luckily, the seas had not had a chance to build, which made it easier for the growing line up of boats in Simpson Bay to make their way through the bridge to seek safety from the approaching storm.

*KNOTS — One nautical mile (knot) per hour is the equivalent to 1.15 miles per hour.
**AUGUST - OLD ISLAND HURRICANE SAYING — "June too soon; July stand by; August come you must; September you'll remember; end of October all over."
However, in recent years, October would have to be revised as "End of October wish it were over," since there have been many hurricanes as late as the end of November.

The Island Fever arrived at the bridge with a few hours to spare before its opening so Rob decided to take the dinghy and go ashore to pick up Christian. That way he could assist them in readying the boat should their approaching tropical storm *(33 – 64 knots of wind – or* 39 74 *mph),* decide to become a hurricane.

Everyone was quite relieved to see the Island Fever round the point, especially Grandma and Grandpa, since the 'Coconut Telegraph' lines had been sizzling with the news of the weather heading their way. Grandpa had been busy and had already gotten all of his hurricane shutters closed and had put away all the outdoor furniture and anything else that wasn't nailed down. The last thing anyone wanted in a hurricane was to have flying lawn chairs hurtling past at a hundred miles or more per hour. Grandma had already filled the sinks and every available jar, pot, and pan with water. She had brought out the candles and the flashlights since she knew that the first two things to go on the island would be electricity once again, and of course water that was safe to drink, since the flooding from the rain often washed sewage and unwanted debris into their cistern. And, depending on the severity of the storm, they were likely to be without such for at least a week, if not more, until the little island could regroup from such an emergency.

Although, Grandpa knew that Rob and Alex would likely as not stay with their boat, as most sailors do, he invited them to weather out the storm in their little cottage under the swaying palms. After all, it had survived sixty-years of hurricanes and was still as far as Grandpa was concerned, the safest spot to weather out a storm on the island, since it was on the leeward side and nestled under the palm trees.

Rob thanked him and said that he would be sitting out the storm on board with Alex but he would greatly appreciate it if Lambchop and Old Henry could weather it out in Grandma and Grandpa's shed. Even better than that, Grandma had already made them a comfy bed in which to pass the storm, in her shower. With his mind set at ease that his pals were well looked after, Rob headed over to the marina to pick up Christian. Grandpa informed him Christian was picking up some extra money helping to move their boats off the dock.

On his way into the lagoon, Rob swung by the Island Fever to give Alex an update and let her know that he'd be back in time to help her with the bridge opening.

"Swing by the storage locker and pick up a couple cases of canned food and fill the extra water jugs," called Alex, shouting to be heard over the fifteen-horsepower dinghy engine as Rob backed away from the boat. He gave her a thumbs up, then headed off at full speed under the bridge – through the cut, and around Snoopy Island* to the marina. There he found Christian just putting the last boat from the dock on its mooring. Within minutes they had hit the storage locker and picked up their stores and extra water jugs, which they had stashed away just for such emergencies. Then after filling them on the dock, Christian jumped in the dinghy and headed back to Simpson Bay with Rob.

Without an engine, getting the Island Fever in through the bridge would not be a cakewalk, but the wind was just forward of their beam, making it an easy shot to sail right through the cut with just her mains and a baby staysail. That is of course, if they didn't get a header** as they came through the channel. Christian would stay in the dinghy in order to lend assistance should it be needed, but Rob had every confidence that Alex had the situation well under control.

By the time Rob had returned through the bridge to meet Alex, the seas had already started to build and the swells were wrapping around the rock jetty and rolling into the bay like soldiers marching into shore. Alex lowered the engine box to the floating position for Christian to motor the dinghy close enough for Rob to climb aboard since the boat was still underway. Then she winched him up so he could climb over the back bridge-deck – the seas being too big to safely board on the transom.*** It was ten minutes to five by the time Rob was back on board with Alex, and she was tacking back and forth at the end of the line-up like an anxious race horse waiting for the starting gate to open. As planned, Christian stayed with the Dinghy Fever, motoring behind the boat, mirroring its every move.

Once on board, Rob learned that Alex had just received an update on the storm – the reports they had received earlier had been a bit delayed. It seemed that the storm had done the unlikely and had changed course and was now heading northeast, which would bring it substantially closer to the island than they had thought, even though it would likely stay on the other side of the Anegada Passage and wreak havoc with the Virgins. The effects of the storm, which at that point could possibly reach a category one proportion hurricane, were expected to hit Sint Maarten/St. Martin by just after dark. Not only was it closer, but it had officially been upgraded to a hurricane *(64 knots)*. Now, there was no time to lose and it would take every spare minute once they were inside to get their anchors out, the sails off, and the boat battened down for the slightly more than inclement weather which was about to hit.

---

*SNOOPY ISLAND — A small man-made island just inside Simpson Bay Lagoon next to the Dutch bridge in St. Maarten – illegally filled from the sand dredged from the channel under the bridge in the 70's. The island, unused for anything other than an anchorage for South African yachties for years, is now home to a marina and several businesses. It has unfortunately become a barrier which prevents the water from flowing freely in and out through the bridge – resulting in a very polluted body of water on the southwest end of the lagoon.
**HEADER — A quick wind change that brings the wind closer to the head of your boat, requiring that you fall off the wind and change course, or you will go into irons.
*** TRANSOM — The sterns of the hulls or the farthest aft point on a catamaran.

It was one minute to five – with the binoculars, Rob could see the lights flashing on the bridge and the gates starting to close to stop traffic. Within seconds the bridge tender had unlocked the bridge and was walking to the middle with the big lever which he inserted into the center hub. Once it was in, he walked the huge lever around in a circle to manually crank the swing bridge open. Gradually, the old bridge shuddered and creaked as it started to turn slowly clockwise. The bridge was rather antiquated and had long ago seen better days. In fact, it had been retired some twenty years earlier from the Intracoastal Waterway in North Carolina to be replaced by a more modern version, and had been brought to the island by Holland in lieu of their dutious support of their little wanted territory. This aging bridge served as the only access on the Dutch side of the island into the lagoon.

By that point the boats were all in a tight formation, lined up ready to rush through to safety the moment the channel was clear. Rob was nervous since it was his first time through the bridge, but he knew that within minutes they would be sitting on the hurricane mooring that Joey kept in front of the marina in the southwestern corner of the lagoon.

As the first boat in the line-up pulled into the cut, they heard a loud scraping sound of metal on metal as the bridge's opening came to a grinding halt, causing the boats already idling in line to throw their engines into reverse, as their passage to the other side had been abruptly terminated. Alex could see the bridge tender running to look over the side at the gears, and the minute she saw him climb down to inspect the problem she knew they were in trouble.

Within minutes, the radio was buzzing with sailors shouting for those in boats already anchored inside to come lend a hand, since there appeared to be some sort of serious problem with the gears which opened the bridge. In no time, dinghies were headed from all directions as sailors tied off on the bridge and climbed up the pilings in order to help old Mr. Brown, the bridge tender, get the bridge open. Christian motored over in the dinghy to get a first-hand report and returned with the bad news – no matter how hard they tried it appeared that the bridge was stuck. One of the teeth on the large cog had broken off and had wedged itself in between the gears. Not only could they not open it the rest of the way – they couldn't get it closed. They even tried having one of the tugs lash a line to it and force it open, but it seemed that everyone's prediction that the old bridge would surely give out one day soon had come true, and it had happened at the worst possible moment, at least for Rob and Alex and all the other boats in their current predicament. The situation was rapidly turning into an island emergency since at least twenty-six boats, which were now nearly on top of one another, were stuck outside their hurricane-safe harbor. They were all starting to panic since it looked as if they would not be riding out the storm in anything that resembled a safe hurricane hole.

Alex's heart sank since she knew that the boat was far too wide to make it through the French bridge safely, especially with the wind on her nose.

ISLAND FEVER

It seemed it was going to be a very long night since their only real option was to head south to try and sail away from the storm, since she calculated that she should be able to sail out of the storm's effects within a few hours. There was still a slim chance that she might make it into Oyster Pond or Le Galion's harbor on the eastern side of the island, but with the rapidly increasing size of the swell, even that possibility was likely closed out due to breaking waves. Had she just slipped in there when they were leaving Tintamarre, she thought berating herself. How could she have been so unprepared? But then again, how could she have known that this storm would do the unlikely.

Alex had read reports that one of the cats caught in a hurricane at sea during the Route du Rhum Race,* had actually just lowered their sails, lashed their rudders, pulled up their dagger boards, and simply drifted through it like a raft with the wind just ahead of their beam – the waves sliding under them. Given a choice in the matter this definitely would not be her first. But with the swells already rolling in, there was no other safe harbor she could reach in time. Simpson, Great Bay, and Marigot all got pretty nasty from the swells wrapping around the island and were not a safe option.

Alex looked at Rob guiltily, as if she felt the weight of the world on her shoulders – solely responsible for their predicament.

"I trust your judgment. Whatever you say captain, just give the order, I'm behind you all the way," said Rob to Alex attempting to bolster her confidence as he realized the gravity of the situation.

Alex smiled, relaxing a little – eased by Rob's faith in her.

"By the way, does this thing have a name yet?"

"Yeah, it's called Claire," answered Alex.

Rob's heart sank at the news, "Now I know we're in trouble," groaned Rob, turning several shades whiter. "That's Sydney's middle name." Indeed, hurricane Sydney Claire was finally on its way and there was, it seemed, no stopping it.

*ROUTE DU RHUM RACE —A French single-handed multihull race leaving from France, which crosses the Atlantic Ocean, and ends on the French island of Guadeloupe.** A race which the Island Fever had won in an earlier incarnation.
**GUADELOUPE — A large butterfly shaped island right in the center of the West Indian chain of islands, originally inhabited by the Carib Indians who resisted Columbus' invasion. A hundred years later, the French succeeded where the Spanish had failed and drove the Caribs off the island, planted sugarcane, and established a slavery-based plantation system. The British stepped in and took over for four years in the 18th century until they signed the Treaty of Paris — exchanging Canada for Guadeloupe – then came back later that century to take it over again. Finally, the French sent in Victor Hughes, a Black Nationalist, to arm Guadeloupe slaves and drive out the British. Once the British left – Hughes decided to kill most of the island's Royalists and attack U.S. ships – causing the U.S. to declare war on France. The prosperous island continued to be a pawn between the British and the French for centuries. Today it remains solidly in the possession of the French.

Alex smiled and kissed Rob, then went to work, knowing that she had a job to do. It was too rough to drop anchor so Alex turned the boat into the wind and waved for Christian, who was still motoring around, to tie the dinghy between the sterns and climb on board via the engine box to help them ready the boat.

It was about to be a very long night for the two of them and although Alex would have welcomed Christian's help, she did not want to put the boy in jeopardy. As much as he argued, Alex insisted that he stay with Grandma and Grandpa. But Christian was young and fearless, and he didn't want to miss out on any excitement. He was committed to seeing the storm through with whatever he could do to help. After all, this was the first time Christian had finally felt he was part of a family. Somehow, Rob managed to convince him that Grandma and Grandpa needed him more. He would take the dinghy ashore and put it into Grandpa's shed where it would be safe. The last thing they needed on deck was anything to create more windage.

Rob was beginning to feel a little like Gilligan as they went about their checklist of things to do before the Island Fever headed out to sea on their slightly more than, "Three-hour cruise" – readying the boat for the treacherous night that lay ahead of them. They had much to do and Alex set Rob to the task as a commanding officer might dispense orders on a battleship – for once, Rob gladly obeyed. The headsail had to be removed, the baby staysail reefed,* the main staysail double reefed, and the main triple reefed. The weight had to be balanced between the hulls, the RDF, radar, and all other navigational devices set in order – the Satnav being useless at this point due to their MIA satellite. Alex also decided to unlace and remove the aft trampoline** to cut down on windage and sea under the boat. Their survival gear was broken out and of course, safety harnesses, life lines, and PFD's*** were prepared, each with its own EPIRB**** attached in case, God forbid, one of them should go overboard.

Once all the gear was assembled in the cockpit and Alex and Rob had donned their survival suits, their safety harnesses, and their PFD's, Alex picked up one of the hand-held VHF radios to slip it into her waterproof pocket so that she could hear the radio outside the deckhouse once things got rough. But, to her

---

*REEFED — The past tense of reefing a boat's sails as a method of lessening or shortening sail due to higher winds, where one ties the sail up so that it's shorter – not to be misconstrued with reefing the boat, which might find one high and dry on a coral reef.

**TRAMPOLINE — A netting or webbing of straps that replace portions of the deck between the hulls of a multihull in order to cut down on windage under the boat, and the overall weight. Also, the open weave of a foredeck trampoline helps prevent capsize if the boat does a nose dive into a wave – it allows water to pass freely through the trampoline reducing the tripping effect.

amazement the case of the radio had expanded like a carton of milk that had sat in the sun a bit too long. She felt her stomach turn over as she realized that this could only mean one thing – the inside pressure of the radio was greater than the rapidly dropping barometer – signaling that the storm was even closer to them than had been predicted.

Alex radioed Jeff at the marina on the boat's VHF and requested that he notify the U.S. Coast Guard and the French Navy that the Island Fever and nearly a dozen other boats would be heading south towards Guadeloupe and likely as far south as Martinique if necessary. Several of the faster monohulls had headed around to the French bridge in Marigot in hopes of making it there before dark, and a few boats had foolishly been brave enough to take their chances and stay anchored in Simpson Bay to ride out the storm.

Ideally, Alex would have liked to have positioned herself in the southwestern or weakest quadrant of the storm, however this time luck was not on her side, and the best she could hope for was to get southeast of it as far and as fast as possible. Although it would be a beat until they out-sailed the grip of the storm, Alex knew that this would be the safest course to take. She was slightly uneasy about the untested newly rebuilt boat, but she had faith that her repairs were even more sound, than even the boats original construction.

She also realized that just because the storm was currently on a heading which would bring it just due west of Sint Maarten, it didn't mean that it might not change course and continue heading northwest towards Puerto Rico. What Alex didn't know however, was that this storm had a mind of its own and would perform the improbable if not the impossible before the next forty-eight hours were over.

Alex had been through many a hurricane, but the last thing that she wanted to tell Rob, was that this would be her first not sitting it out on a safe hurricane mooring. To Rob, Alex portrayed the epitome of cool, calm, and collected.

But he had to admit that he was feeling hesitation, terror, and trepidation at that point, which as far as he was concerned, qualified as out and out fear. Not only had Rob never sailed in a hurricane before, he had never even witnessed a hurricane. The fact that he was from the Midwest, and more than familiar with tornadoes, filled him with terror all the more. He had seen the destruction that tornadoes had caused in his hometown. If it was anything even remotely similar, then Rob was borderline scared out of his wits and he was starting to pray like he'd never prayed before. More even than he had prayed

---

***PFD'S — Personal Flotation Devices or life vests equipped with a strobe-type light, fluorescent tape, and a Class S or Mini EPIRB for rough weather.
****EPIRB — Emergency Position Indicating Radio Beacon – A modern day S.O.S. device which is invaluable for any vessel leaving radio range (20 miles), which transmits a signal on aircraft frequencies or to passing satellites, supposing of course that there is one or the other within range to receive the signal and report your high-tech MAYDAY call for help.

when the drug dealers held him at gunpoint, or at morning mass in Catholic school to get him transferred out of Sister Agnus' class. I attempted in vain to bolster his confidence but his mind had control of him, and he was too busy running scenarios of the worst that could happen to listen to me.

It was now almost 6:00 PM and there was still a little while before sunset, however the sky was so dark by that point that the light would likely be gone for all practical purposes by seven. The wind was now out of the south. Most of the other boats had motored in the same direction but they were much slower than the Island Fever and were still within sight by the time Alex sailed out of the bay on a port tack, carrying the smallest amount of canvas the rig could carry and still retain enough speed to get them out of immediate danger before the brunt of the storm hit. By the time they were out of the harbor and off shore enough to tack and head south on her course – a compass heading of 140 degrees, the clouds were so low they could no longer see Saba* or St. Barth. Alex headed out close-hauled against the south wind, relying solely on her instruments and a dead reckoning course she'd plotted on her chart.

On shore, Grandma and Grandpa were beside themselves. Christian had returned to tell them about the bridge not opening and that Alex and Rob had headed the Island Fever out to sea to ride out the storm. So, Grandma went to her room and lit a candle on her nightstand and started to pray for their safe return. Grandma and Grandpa had seen many a hurricane in their day and figured that they had seen the worst of them, but nothing had prepared them for what was to come. They had never seen a storm come from the west in more than half a century of living there on that little stretch of beach. They were about to witness the 'storm of the century'*** heap its wrath upon their little island.

*SABA — The smallest and the tallest of the Netherlands Antilles, known as "The Unspoiled Queen." Saba is nothing more than a tropical volcano jutting out of the sea claiming an airport more dangerous than St. Barth, which greatly resembles landing on the deck of an aircraft carrier 1000 feet in the air. Upon arriving in the tiny villages of the Bottom, St. John's, or Hell's Gate, one could easily believe that they had accidentally stumbled into Hobbitland. The top being the opposite of Hell – an incredibly lush rain forest. It's greatest value to the Leeward Islands has always been the tallest peak in that part of the ocean which offered the tallest antenna for the Saba Radio** station.
**SABA RADIO — A now defunct, land/sea radio/phone station based on the top of Saba – the tallest island around the vicinity which provided the closest thing to reliable phone service the islands had to offer.
***STORM OF THE CENTURY — The fictional storm, Claire, is based on two historical hurricanes to hit St. Martin and St. Barth in the last fifteen years — Luis and Lenny. Luis sunk over 1400 boats in Simpson Bay Lagoon and the SXM meteorological station stopped recording the storm when the wind meter blew off the building in 200 knots of wind. Lenny was the first storm of this century to travel west and then south and create massive swells, which came in from the shallow Caribbean onto the leeward side of the islands, causing millions in damage along the coast.

CHAPTER THIRTY-ONE

Weathering the Storm

"To be in hell is to drift, to be in heaven is to steer."

George Bernard Shaw

The reality of their circumstances had finally set in and Rob was destined it seemed, to weather out the storm both metaphorically and literally. He was on a runaway barge and no matter how hard he tried he couldn't find a way to get off the boat. He knew that he had to face this last hurdle that now loomed before them on the horizon, and he had decided that whatever the outcome, it was his fate and he was now finally man enough to own it. Rob was confident that Alex would be able to pull them through. But, as I mentioned earlier, Alex, although quite adept at her seamanship skills, had no first-hand experience in riding out a storm at sea. Only in theory had she prepared herself for such an event should the time ever come that she needed to perform such a service, and it seemed that the time had indeed come to prove her skill.

Knowing it would only get worse before it got better, Alex had decided that Rob should take the first watch since the seas were still only about twelve feet high and the wind was gusting no higher than fifty knots by the time darkness had fallen upon them. Alex unclipped her harness and hooked up Rob in the cockpit, then went below to try and get an updated weather report from Saba Radio. The news wasn't good. It seemed that the storm had actually slowed its forward momentum and intensified with winds now gusting to 120 knots, and it seemed to be building even stronger as it moved its way northeast towards them. Since it was moving at about eight miles per hour it meant that they would really be feeling the leading edge of it long before midnight, since they were only making way to the south at approximately ten to twelve knots. Alex checked the chart and plotted their course since they had left the harbor. She was on her course – a heading of 140 degrees, braving a straight shot southeast on a starboard tack with the wind out of the south. They would stay west of Antigua and east of St. Kitts and Nevis shooting the margin between the two, which would have never even been a concern on a normal night, but tonight required close attention.

The other concern that Alex had was that there were a dozen other boats, that she knew of, tacking around on approximately the same course, not to mention the fact that they would be heading into shipping lanes once they had cleared Montserrat and Antigua. Luckily, they were fast enough to at some point out-sail the other boats and pass them by, but until then, it would be touch and go. Just to be certain, Alex checked the radar to confirm that there was nothing that she had missed on the horizon in the immediate area. The last thing she could possibly think about was resting even though her whole body already ached with tension. Instead, she attempted to eat a bite of dried fish in order to keep up her strength, but her stomach was in knots. Giving up on the concept of food she gulped down a warm cup of coffee from a thermos that Christian had been thoughtful enough to make for them before he'd gone ashore.

An hour later, it was already a roller coaster ride with seas ahead of them the size of large hills. The bows were starting to punch through the waves rather than ride over them due to the speed they were making and it was becoming extremely difficult to maneuver below deck as Alex tried time and time again to raise someone, anyone, on the radio for an update on the storm's progress. It seemed no one heard, or they were too preoccupied coping with the storm themselves to answer. What Alex couldn't confirm, but suspected no matter how unlikely, was that the storm had turned and had actually started heading east. With the increasing size of the swells pushing in from the southwest, Alex knew that something big was close behind it, and indeed, she was right. The storm had done the improbable – it had turned east and was headed right for St. Maarten and St. Barth.

About every ten minutes or so Rob would find Alex's head poking out the companionway to make certain that he was okay, especially when a squall would blow past increasing the wind speed to sometimes almost half again in gusts. After another hour had passed, Alex had given up on rest of any kind and had sent Rob inside to monitor the radar as they passed the other boats. She clipped herself into her harness and took the helm from Rob, who although concerned to leave her in the cockpit alone, was quite relieved that his watch had ended. It was tiring, backbreaking work steering in that kind of sea, since one had to drive the boat up and over the swell fighting the tug and pull of the wind and the sea as it pitched and tossed the boat around.

"Wouldn't it be easier if we were sailing downwind instead of beating ourselves and the boat to death," shouted Rob looking white as a ghost as much from the chill as from the shear fear of the force of the storm – now that he had a voyeur's perspective.

"That would take us right back to where it's heading," Alex shouted. "We want to get as far south of this thing as we can. The problem is, it seems like it's turned and come east on us. That has to be what's causing these massive swells."

By that point, the seas had grown to well over twenty feet and every other wave would find its way into the cockpit, or pound the underside of the bridge-deck with such force it sounded as if the boat had been hit with a battering ram. As her bows punched through the waves, the Island Fever would shudder so badly from the impact, even Alex wondered how long the boat could take the pounding. Alex was thankful for the giant fish-pot they'd taken between the hulls, for without it, she may have never found the failing wood under the bridge-deck. Had they sailed out in this with the boat in its previous condition, she would never have survived this sea. Funny how something that appeared to be a catastrophe at the time, turned out to be a lifesaving occurrence designed by a higher power. Now, Alex was confident that the boat was likely to out survive them when pinch came to shove, and assured Rob that everything was under control.

Normally, the Island Fever could make good anywhere from nine to fifteen knots of headway on this point of sail in heavy winds, but with the winds now gusting well over seventy, the boat was pushing its limits of speed with the size of the sea and reefed sails. Alex left the harbor with the most prudent sail area the boat could carry in the conditions ahead, a reefed baby-staysail, a double reefed main-staysail, and a triple reefed main, so that they wouldn't bury her bows into the oncoming seas. She had planned ahead when she reefed the sails knowing that the easiest to lose in an emergency would be the main-staysail if the weather got really rough. What Alex hadn't counted on was the huge sea that was relentlessly slamming into the bridge deck, slowing the boat down between waves. The result was severe compression on the boat, and the last thing she wanted was to start breaking rudders, or boards, or even, God forbid, her rig. Alex was starting to consider dropping the main-staysail entirely since there was no race to win except the one to try and stay as much ahead of the storm as possible, and of course to stay alive. Although, she didn't relish the idea of having to go up on the deckhouse to tie down the sail.

By midnight, Alex and Rob were wading in greenwater* in the cockpit which was now washing over the deckhouse like a waterfall. In fact, Alex had

---

*GREENWATER — *That frothy wet stuff that manages to find its way into or onto a vessel at sea once it has been churned and agitated by the motion of the ocean into frothing white and green seawater.*

resorted to wearing her mask and snorkel just so she could see and breathe. The wind was gusting to well over seventy-five knots although the seas had lessened over the last hour due to the fact they were, for the moment, tucked behind St. Kitts and Nevis. But now that they were nearing the passage between Nevis and Montserrat, the seas would start rolling in through the gap, slamming the boat hard. The time had finally come, to Alex's dismay, to lose the main-staysail. She yelled over the howling wind for Rob to tighten the topping-lift,* while she ground the main-staysail sheet in as tight as it would go. She knew that if the boom wasn't tight when the sail came down, she would never be able to keep the thrashing sail under control, which could result in a torn sail or worse injury to herself or Rob.

Alex turned the deck lights on and waited until the squalls subsided. Then she instructed Rob to turn up into the wind. She steeled herself for the dangerous task ahead as she started the arduous crawl on the stomach out of the cockpit and onto the deck – then up onto the deckhouse with her lifeline attached to the jack-lines that she had rigged along the deck prior to leaving St. Maarten. Her mask allowed her to see in the pelting spray off the bows, not to mention the spume flying off the wave tops. Her rain gear was being pelted so hard it felt as if she were being hit by hailstones, and the wind was so strong she literally had to hold herself down on the deck for fear of being blown overboard. Once she reached the top of the deckhouse, Rob eased the halyard for the main-staysail from the cockpit. With his help, Alex managed to safely lash the sail to the boom with the tail of the jib halyard, without having it shredded into tatters by the wind or getting too badly beaten by it herself. Battened-sails** in that sort of wind had been known to put eyes out, break bones, and kill sailors just from the sheer force of the wind filling the sail as it was released. It was now two in the morning.

They had just made good at least seventy or more miles from St. Maarten, which meant the storm must be huge since they were now sitting at least sixty miles from the eye and they were still feeling winds the magnitude of a worse than average hurricane. Alex was getting worried. Not so much for their own safety since they were faring okay even if it was tiring work, but about

---

*TOPPING LIFT — A line of the boat's rigging that runs over a sheave at the top of the mast and is connected to the end of the boom to hold the boom up when the sail is dropped.
**BATTENED SAILS — A sail made with long tiny pockets which hold thin, flexible strips of wood or plastic, that give the sail shape when it's trimmed.
TRIMMED — The past-tense of the act of trimming or setting the sails to the perfect shape for sailing via the use of sheets, halyards, outhauls, and leech lines** — insuring the maximum performance from the sail for boat speed.
****OUTHAULS AND LEECH LINES — An outhaul is a line used to tighten the foot, or bottom of a sail on a boom; and a leech line is a line and small cleat built into the luff, or back edge of the sail which provides for making fine adjustments to the sail trim.

Grandma and Grandpa back on St. Maarten. Since they were out of range of Saba Radio, Alex finally managed to raise someone at the SXM* meteorological station on her SSB.** It seemed that the hurricane was now stalled just slightly west of St. Barth, with an eye twenty-five miles in diameter. This mean that St. Maarten was sitting in the northern quadrant or the worst side of the storm, and likely getting beaten and battered by the relentless winds which were reportedly gusting on the island to well over 150 knots. But worse than the winds were the southwest ten-meter*** swells that were pounding the leeward coast. In a nutshell, that little beach that Grandma and Grandpa's cottage sat on was getting hammered by thirty foot plus waves. Alex swallowed hard against the rising bile and the lump in her throat, panicked at the thought of Granma and Grandpa's safety – they should have gotten them to a safer location before they left. However, Rob, who was getting more and more nervous by the minute about their own predicament assured her that they would surely be okay. After all, they were seasoned hurricane experts. In fact, they had probably survived more hurricanes than most people on the planet. But what Rob didn't realize, nor did Alex, was that hurricane Claire would build into the biggest storm of the century and take up residence on top of that tiny little island for the better part of a night and a day.

Meanwhile, back on St. Maarten, due to the position of the storm and the counter-clockwise rotation of a hurricane, the winds were indeed clocking dead into Simpson Bay and pushing the sea straight into Grandma and Grandpa's beach. Grandma and Grandpa were starting to realize, like Alex, that they should have gotten out of there, but if was far too late to evacuate at that point. The sound of the wind and sea inside their tiny cottage had become a deafening roar, like and endless freight train crossing over their little roof. The waves had already reached their front door high up the beach under those frantically swaying palms, which now were menacingly bent over their vulnerable little abode, and Grandpa was beginning to realize that the cottage that he'd chosen this lifetime might soon become a raft after all. The radio report that Alex had received had greatly underestimated the wind velocity. In fact, the storm had been packing gusts of over 175 knots on the SXM airport anemometer just before it had blown off the roof – before the storm had even reached its peak. Not to mention that this was the first storm ever to turn out of the west and push the shallow Caribbean Sea full-force towards those vulnerable little isles from Anguilla all the way to Venezuela.

*SXM — The abbreviation for the Princess Julianna Airport in St. Maarten.
**SSB — SINGLE SIDEBAND – A radio which most ocean-going boats are fitted with that provides a wider range of transmission than the standard ship-to-shore VHF radio.
***METER — One meter is the equivalent to 39.37 inches – about three and one third feet.

The wind had died down again making Grandpa realize that the eye had passed over their island for the second time. He was busy packing rags around the front door to keep the water out from the waves which were crashing onto the beach with a deafening roar, and engulfing the foundation of their little cottage. Grandma was laying on her bed trying to rest, but had found herself doing more praying than sleeping, and Christian was in the bathroom trying to calm Lambchop and Old Henry who were pacing back and forth like expectant fathers. Suddenly without warning, a tremendous wave hit the little cottage with such force the front door was swept right off its hinges. Before they knew what hit them, the wave unleashed a torrent of water into their little home, turning furniture upside down, washing away their meager belongings, and sweeping Grandpa right off his feet. As the wave subsided, and Grandma's mattress floated along with it right into the living room, she saw to her relief that Grandpa, although quite shaken and wet, was luckily uninjured. Wasting no time in escaping the next deluge, Lambchop and Henry swam as fast as their little legs would propel them, right out of the cottage on the rapidly ebbing tide.

Concerned, seeing Lambchop and Henry fleeing into the treacherous storm, Christian ran out of the cottage after them as Grandpa struggled to pull himself back to his feet. Panicked about Christian's wellbeing, Grandpa ran after him without even a thought for his own safety. Struggling to get past the floating debris, Grandma managed to make her way to the doorway, where she stood frantically yelling in vain into the blackness and the blinding rain for the two of them to come back inside. To Grandma's utter dismay Grandpa and Christian were wandering around somewhere in the havoc of mother nature's wrath that raged just outside her door.

"What on earth is the old fool thinking, he'll be killed out there in this!" cried Grandma realizing that they must be in the 'eye of the storm'* since the wind had temporarily abated. She called their names into the blackness, but there was no answer. She couldn't see it but she heard the next wave coming as it broke across the harbor and that little stretch of coral reef just off of what was left of their beach. By the time she could see the water, it was half way up the beach and nearly on top of their cottage, leaving little for Grandma to do other than seek refuge in her concrete shower. She was panicked at what would become of Grandpa who had nothing whatsoever to protect him from the wall of water which was seconds from devouring them in its huge, monstrous, black mouth.

On the boat, the sun had been up for hours but they couldn't see it through the blackened sky which accompanied each squall-line – only a grey-

*EYE OF THE STORM — *The chimney-like column of calm air around which the wind and multiple thunderstorms spiral. Usually anywhere from 12 - 25 miles across.*

ISLAND FEVER

black haze which loomed above the pitch-black water, crested in white like a snowcapped dusting on a mountain top. In the squalls, the visibility was nil – when they passed, it was cut down to a mere five miles due to the humidity in the air. The wind was once again starting to build, blowing 110 knots in the squalls which whipped the white, frothy spume on the surface of the wave tops like a cappuccino steamer might steam cream. During the night as they cleared Antigua, the wind had veered more southwest, and Alex had been forced to ease off the wind to a course of 110 degrees in order to slip under the eastern side of Guadeloupe for protection. They were now traveling even faster than before due to their point of sail.

The squalls were coming more frequently now – one right after the other, giving them a reprieve of only a meager ten minutes or so in-between. The wind shrieked through the rigging like the cry of some unearthly creature – the din almost unbearable. The spray and spume in the 110 knot gusts now stung their bare skin so badly – like shot from a BB-gun, that Rob and Alex had to cover their faces and hands entirely. When the squalls came, the boat would pick up so much speed it would launch itself off the wave tops – nearly airborne. It was a wild ride with the bridge-deck slamming into the waves so hard Alex was considering taking down the main. However, there was no trampoline below the main boom, and she knew she couldn't get it secured safely without risking injury from the whipping sail once it was blown apart, as it would surely be by the intense wind. Instead, Alex opted to pinch up slightly into the wind to slow the boat down to a manageable speed. But, she also knew she couldn't come up too high or they'd be in danger of hitting the northeastern end of La Désirade.*

By that point, it was taking everything both Alex and Rob had to try and keep the boat on course since the pull of the boat's weather helm** was getting stronger and stronger. And, to complicate things even more, Rob had just informed Alex that the wind had increased to a steady 90 knots and that there were now two blips dead ahead on the radar screen. It seemed the storm was starting to move slightly south towards them, the St. Maarten weather station confirmed when Alex traded places with Rob and called once again on the SSB. Maybe they weren't going to be able to outrun this thing – maybe it was destined to catch them after all thought Alex, almost afraid to tell Rob the painful news. They had fared okay up until that point, however Alex realized that they wouldn't stand a chance if this thing got closer and the seas grew bigger. They had been at sea now for fifteen hours and were both exhausted,

*LA DESIRADE — A sparsely inhabited island, 11 miles long, projecting about 10 km off the southeastern tip of Grand Terre – the eastern half of Guadeloupe. Meaning, it juts out into the ocean nearly 25 miles east of Guadeloupe. On the chart its shape quite resembles an over turned boat.
**WEATHER HELM — Some sailing vessels tend to want to turn upwind on their own, requiring compensation in the steering of the vessel to keep it straight on course. This is sometimes built into the balance of the boat for safety reasons so that if a boat were unmanned, it would naturally turn up into the wind and stall instead of sailing away without its helmsman.

cold, and hungry. The tension in Alex's muscles had tightened into bands of steel and her head was spinning from the caffeine and lack of food. Maybe she would be smart to just turn around and head back to Falmouth Harbor* where she knew they could seek some sort of safety. After all, that was where her own little Dancer sat on a safe hurricane mooring in English Harbor, just around the corner. But to do that they first had to maneuver the boat around to run downwind which would mean they would have to get the boards up to prevent the waves from catching the leeward board and flipping them over off the wave. The next step would then be to try to get into the harbor through the breaking waves.

Of course, the testosterone which was now raging in Rob's body made him offer to be the one to go out on deck to handle the dagger boards, however Alex, knowing all too well that she had the more agile sea legs of the two insisted she take the deck while Rob manned the helm. They waited until the next squall had passed before they even attempted to set up for the maneuver. When the moment was right, Alex instructed Rob to turn into the wind as she readied herself to crawl out onto the deck to pull up the starboard dagger board. Although they were somewhat protected from the sea behind Guadeloupe and La Désirade, the waves were funneling through the channels between the islands like mechanical waves at a surf park, creating a strangely mixed-up sea unlike anything Alex had ever witnessed. The boat jumped and tossed like a can of paint on a paint mixer as Alex carefully snapped her lifeline onto the jackline on deck once again and unclipped the cockpit tether. She worked her way up to the starboard dagger board box on her belly. Thankfully, since they had nothing up at this point except a triple reefed main and a reefed baby-staysail, which was self-tacking,** it wasn't necessary for them to do anything to jibe the sails over to a port tack.

Alex reached the dagger board and pulled the pin. To her amazement, with the help of the passing wave, the board popped right up out of the box with ease, allowing her to replace the pin with the board in the up position. Slowly – cautiously, Alex clipped her lifeline to the foredeck jackline and worked her way over to the port side, half crawling, half climbing over gear on the deck until she reached the port jackline, where she now carefully reclipped her

---

*FALMOUTH HARBOR — Falmouth and English Harbors sit immediately next to one another only separated by a small spit of land. They were used as secure defensible harbors by the English in the early 1700's. English Harbor Dockyard was once Britain's main naval station in the Lesser Antilles. Falmouth Harbor's mouth is at least four times wider than English Harbor offering easier entrance in rough weather, even though English Harbor offers a much safer holding ground for hurricanes.
**SELF-TACKING — Meaning that a sail is sheeted into a metal or plastic fitting which travels on a track bolted to the deck. This allows the sail to swing to the opposite tack unaided. This is also known as a traveler.

lifeline. Quickly, she raised the port board as easily as she had raised the starboard.

"Okay!" Alex shouted to Rob from the deck over the howl of the wind and rain, "Ease the main slowly! Then the baby-staysail! The bows will start to blow off the wind... then take her down! Slowly!! Hold her with the wind at five o'clock. I'll help you jibe her through when I get back there."

Nervously, Rob turned the wheel down with some effort, but as he eased the baby-staysail it helped to blow the bows around off the wind. Slowly, the boat turned, starting into her passage downwind on a starboard tack. As the boat reached the point that the wind and sea were on their starboard rear quarter, Rob breathed a sigh of relief as suddenly the motion of the boat grew calmer. However, it was accelerating so fast he wasn't quite certain what to do next. It was as if some race car driver had suddenly taken over and stepped on the accelerator. He hung on until Alex could get back to the cockpit – feeling exhilaration and fear all at the same time. Rob smiled at Alex as she made her way back to the cockpit, crawling along the port side of the deckhouse. She smiled back – confident that they would pull through this together. He had proven after all to be a reliable crew in excruciating circumstances. Just as Alex reached the end of the deck line and unclipped her lifeline to climb back into the cockpit without first hooking into the cockpit jackline, they both felt their stomachs drop as the boat rose up in the air as if it had been swept up in a tractor beam. They heard it before they saw it – a rogue wave* as it loomed over them from out of nowhere. It was as if time suddenly stood still with the boat suspended in air. It hit the boat with the impact of a battering ram, tossing the Island Fever aside as if it were a toy sailboat in a bathtub as it washed clean over the deckhouse. Rob lunged to grab Alex, nearly going over himself, but it was too late! Alex was gone! Gone along with the sea that poured over the deck. Rob couldn't believe his eyes as he watched as Alex tumbled overboard into the dark agitated water which engulfed her instantly. This time, Alex was truly lost at sea.

*ROGUE WAVE — An unusually large or abnormal wave. As opposed to a rogue sailor which often falls into the category of abnormal.

CHAPTER THIRTY-TWO

Overboard

*"Even when the sky is heavily overcast,
the sun hasn't disappeared.
It's still there on the other side of the clouds."*

Eckhart Tolle

"ALEX!!" Was the only terrified sound that escaped from Rob's lips as he stood at the helm, momentarily frozen from the shock of seeing Alex being swallowed by the water and flying spume of the angry ocean. Then with no hesitation, as if he had been a seasoned sailor, Rob turned hard to port and hurled the man overboard rig* in the direction in which Alex had fallen. Blood was pounding in his temples, as the adrenaline surged him into action. Driven by an instinctual knowledge, he looked to the heavens and begged the Universe to give him the power to find her. All seemed hopeless, but Rob, in that brief moment – that split second of realization – knew that he wasn't about to give up the ship, let alone Alex. Rob was more present than he'd ever been in his life and he gave himself wholly to what he knew he had to do. Maybe it was instinct, or maybe it was knowledge from a past life – just maybe Rob had indeed been a sailor before, or maybe he was just channeling me. But Rob had no time to ponder such thoughts now, he had a job to do. The Island Fever was traveling dead downwind now and Rob had no time to sheet the mainsail to center for the jibe – he took his chances, slamming it hard to a port tack in that kind of wind might

*MAN-OVERBOARD RIG — A small buoyant, weighted pole with an orange flag and a water activated strobe light on top – about 8 feet high. Attached to it is a horseshoe life-ring, a whistle and a small drogue (a cone to slow its drift).

just take down the rig. As the wind passed to the other side of the sail, it sounded like cannon fire as the main slammed over and the impact on the rig jolted through the entire boat as if it had been hit by a freighter. But the rig stood, and Rob continued hardening up to tack to starboard in order to try and beat back upwind as close as he could get to the spot where Alex had gone over. He had no engine to help him maneuver and even if he did – in this sea an outboard engine would never get a bite into the waves to power the boat through it. Rob realized that the sea would be pushing Alex swiftly downwind and he knew that he had to quickly regain the distance that now separated them. Her life was in his hands and if she were to survive these treacherous seas, it was up to him to step up to the helm and don his sailor's cap, not to mention me donning mine, since it was time for me to do what-ever it would take to help Rob save Alex.

Rob would have to sail back a few thousand yards from whence he had come in order to recover the ground he had lost between them. However, what Rob didn't yet realize was that he would have to bring the boat fully around to weather again and tack several times to recover the ground he'd lost – a risky proposition in these seas. But Rob had no other choice, since the Island Fever was still engineless and totally reliant on her sails to make any kind of headway. As the boat came back around onto a close-hauled starboard tack, he slowly eased her back up the monster swells, grinding the mainsail back to center until the compass read a reciprocal heading of 110 degrees. He held his breath as the boat climbed up and over the first wave then crashed down into the trough with a shudder as it passed under the boat – the bows punching through the waves as it picked up speed with the forward half of the boat engulfed in water. Rob knew he wasn't far away from Alex. He was afraid that he might even hit her in the chaos which boiled and churned foam on the surface ahead of him, blowing spume off the wave tops in the howling wind. Four waves had crashed over the boat, each passing like another mountain as he tried to estimate how far southeast he had to travel before falling off again. He was uncertain – he had no points of reference – no land, no sun – nothing to judge by. He fell off the wind heading dead-downwind again for a few hundred yards, the point of sail they'd been on when Alex went over. She had to be close, Rob thought, but he was unsure – disoriented now that he'd made a full circle. He checked his compass to try to get his bearings. And then he saw it – the marker – dead ahead. He sailed as close to it as he dared, then turned the Island Fever into the wind to stall his forward momentum.

As the boat stalled into the wind, he felt her rise up the next wave – up and up as if the boat were a car on a roller coaster, creeping up the biggest dip. As it reached the crest, the Island Fever teetered a moment threatening to topple backwards as if his little car had run out of steam just short of reaching the summit. Rob held his breath. Then the wave rolled past and Rob let out an exhale as the boat slid down the back side as if it were sledding down a snowy hill. He prayed he hadn't overshot his mark since he felt blind in these huge seas that blocked his vision beyond a few feet. He now sat in irons, stopping the forward propulsion of the boat through the water. Rob was grateful for the reprieve from the pounding, however the sight of the seas from this angle was so menacing that he had to catch his breath. As the boat rose up and teetered on the next wave-crest he felt as if it would surely fall off into space over the other side or topple over backwards. But then the wave gently slipped under him as the massive wall of water rolled beneath the boat. Confident now that the boat wasn't going to tumble down the face of the next wave as it drifted at the mercy of the giant forty-foot swells, Rob searched the water desperately for Alex. She was not with the marker or the life-ring. There was no sign of her as he stared at the angry black surface behind him that was broken only by the white spray. He knew that the strobe-light on her life-vest was designed to activate the second it hit the water – this and some rudimentary man-overboard skills he'd learned in his seaman's class. But Rob was praying that it was indeed working – if not, the chances of finding her out here in this mess would be slim.

    Rob stood silent – feeling alone in that big ocean. He looked to the heavens once more and asked for assistance. Amazingly, the cloud cover started to clear as he talked to the powers that be like he'd never talked in his life. "I need your help now if I've ever needed it damn it! Don't let me lose her like this! Don't bring both of us this far and take her away from me! Take me if you have to, not her!" he screamed, as he stood there clinging to the aft-mast. Rob was angry – he knew giving in was not an option. He had finally found his true love and no one and no thing, not even a force five hurricane, was going to take her away from him. Then suddenly, the wind started to weaken and the seas grew calmer. The squalls subsided, and Rob looked around puzzled, as if someone had turned the storm from high to low. Rob had asked for assistance and he had received a brief reprieve. The only problem was that the swells were still so big, he could barely see a few meters ahead or behind, or to either side of him. At that moment, he knew what he had to do – he had to climb the mast in order to see over the wave tops – he had to get a higher perspective. He knew that it was the only chance he had of finding her. He had failed twice at climbing the tree of life and his water tower, but this time he couldn't fail – Alex's life depended on it. Life it seemed was throwing everything it had at Rob, and he had somehow managed to navigate through the mire thus far – he wasn't about to give up now.

    Bravely, Rob crawled to the foredeck and started the dangerous climb up the sixty-five-foot foremast, foregoing the safety of a bosun's chair* or

---

*BOSUN'S CHAIR — A swing-like chair which is pulled up the mast by a halyard. It was called this since it was designed for the Bosun or Boatswain – a subordinate officer on a ship in charge of the boat's equipment.

halyard, since there was no one to belay the line for him anyway. Luckily, Joey had rigged the foremast with steps, but Rob still rocked and swayed clinging to it with everything he had as each monster swell rolled under the boat. The higher he climbed, the more the mast seemed to whip. Frantically, Rob searched from wave top to wave top, climbing higher and higher in order to see further – all the while risking being knocked from the wildly swaying mast to the deck below by the pitching boat, the higher he got.

Let's remember now that Rob's experience with climbing had not exactly been successful by this point. To say the least, he was scared shitless, but somehow, he managed to slowly pull himself up another five feet. He knew he couldn't look down at the deck or he'd freeze – like he did that day on the water tower. As he clung to the rungs of the steps for his life he searched the waves – still unable to spot her. Surely, he should be able to see the emergency light on her life vest by now.

"How can she be so far from the marker," Rob thought. "I dropped it within feet of where she went over. What if she's drifting much faster than I calculated... at a different speed than the boat? What if I haven't gone back far enough, and what if she's slipped out of her life vest somehow? What if?" thought Rob. "What if?"

He knew he would have to climb higher now in order to see just a little farther. The higher he climbed the more violent the motion grew. But he refused to give up as he pushed on step by step, hand over hand.

The thoughts that were running rampant through Rob's mind now were starting to interfere with his reasoning and his regard for his own safety. But at that moment his own safety was not at the forefront of his concern. The boat rolled up a huge wave teetering on the crest then dropped down the face of it as if he'd been in an elevator which had suddenly free fallen ten floors, knocking Rob's feet from the steps – leaving him clinging to the mast with his hands twenty feet above the deck. Kicking wildly, he managed to get his leg back around the mast and his foot securely onto one of the steps. But then he made that same, near fatal, mistake of looking down that he'd done that day on the water tower. He froze – unable to move. He hung there clutching the mast – the only thing that stood between life and death.

Things were getting out of hand and I knew that this was my cue to make an appearance, hoping that the sight of me wouldn't just be enough to frighten Rob into falling from that mast the way he'd dropped from that coconut tree on Grandpa's beach from the shock of the centipedes.

"Rob." I called softly from above "Rob, look up," I said hoping that this new perspective would take his mind off the deck below.

Slowly, Rob leaned his head back and looked up to find me, sitting just above him on the lower spreaders,* 25 feet above the deck of the Island Fever in the middle of the sea – in the midst of a hurricane. Rob shook his head and squeezed his eyes tightly shut as if he were hallucinating, the way he had that night looking for Alex, who was prematurely presumed to be lost at sea.

"It's okay Rob, don't be afraid. I'm here to help you. I'm your Guardian Angel. You can do this. You can save her. You know everything you need to know. You just have to believe it."

Rob hung there from the mast – his mouth gaping open as if he were seeing a ghost – which couldn't be more inaccurate since I am not an earthbound entity stuck between this world and 'The Otherside.' I, on the other hand, or on 'The Otherside,' am an ascended soul who's chosen to come back to this plane of existence to be of assistance. But of course, Rob did not understand this metaphysical stuff just yet and he was certain he had lost it. Even if he felt more alive, and sane than he'd ever felt in his life.

"Climb higher Rob. Come up here and sit next to me. From here you can see what you need to see," I said to him in a calm, encouraging tone as if I were talking a man down from a rooftop who was dead set on jumping. "I'm your Spirit Guide... my name is Ian."

Rob was speechless – unable to voice the questions that were bubbling up through his throat – unable to escape into intelligible sound. His arms had feeling in them again as he pulled himself up towards me – one rung at a time he slowly climbed the last five feet that would bring him to rest on the spreader next to me. As he climbed that last rung and eased himself onto the spreader, he just looked at me and smiled – he had remembered. Remembered the pact that we had made before he was born this time around. I had vowed I'd be there to help him, and as promised, I'd come to his aide when he called. I was there simply to give him guidance, not to do it for him. Just to make certain that he would pull through this okay. He could end it all now if he chose – it was an available exit point for him. But it was not his time – he had a lot more of this life to live – with Alex. There was no need for words – he knew what he was there to do as he searched 360 degrees around the boat. He scanned the water's surface in all directions knowing he'd find her. He knew that he didn't have much time since the calm break the Universe had granted him between squalls would only give him a short window to locate Alex and maneuver the boat close enough to retrieve her from the water. Contrary to earlier when Rob thought

---

*SPREADERS — The horizontal cross bars that are attached to the mast at one end and to the shrouds** at the other. The first spreader is usually about midway up the mast providing more triangulation for the shrouds from the top of the mast to the chainplates*** on deck. Often there is a second set of spreaders further up the mast.
SHROUDS — Wires, known as rigging that run from the top of the mast down to the midship** of a sailboat – as opposed to stays, which run from the top of the mast to the front of the boat or bow (forestay), or the back of the boat (backstay(s) – two on a catamaran).
CHAINPLATES — The metal plates fastened to the decks, which the rigging attaches to via a turnbuckle.**
****MIDSHIP — The middle of a ship – side to side or fore and aft.
*****TURNBUCKLE — An adjustable screw-like fitting which goes on the ends of rigging wire and attaches to the mast or chainplates.

Alex was lost at sea, this time Rob had taken control of his rampant mind – he had connected with his higher source, with me, and with the Universe.

Carefully, Rob managed to stand next to where I sat on the spreader to see more clearly. As the Island Fever rode up on the crest of the next wave Rob's vantage point gave him an extended view of the sea around him. As he peered over the wave tops several swells away, he caught sight of a glimmer of light and something orange floating in the water. It was nowhere near the marker, but he was certain that it had to be Alex's survival suit and light – about a hundred meters to weather. However, it was quickly apparent to him that the boat was drifting at a much quicker speed than Alex and it was rapidly broadening the gap between them. Of course, he was moving faster than her – the windage of the boat and sails created a far greater object to be blown backwards by the wind and current than Alex did on the surface of the water, especially with his boards up. Rob realized that his only hope to get to her at this point was to sail above her and drift down on her to pick her up. But of course, that meant that Rob would have to tack away from her on a starboard tack, then tack to port to get above her so he could drift down to her current position.

Rob looked down to speak to me but he was the only one who now stood there on that mast. He smiled, knowing that although he couldn't see me – I was there. Instead of afraid, Rob felt exhilarated. His tutelage with Grandpa on how to live in the present had prepared him for this, and Rob was now fully present. As present as he would ever be in his life.

Carefully, he descended the mast before the winds picked up again and blinded him with spray, obscuring Alex's location all together. Rob would have to work fast, but he was confident that he would beat the storm at its own game this time. Rob hadn't let fear takeover, he had given himself fully to the moment.

First, Rob lowered his port dagger board to provide as much resistance against lateral drift as possible, then he made certain the main was sheeted-in hard to center, knowing the baby-staysail would take care of itself. He turned the Island Fever off the wind onto a starboard tack, hoping she would pull herself out of irons and allow the sails to fill. But, with such a small amount of sail area up, it wouldn't be easy. He was still drifting backwards so he decided to take advantage of any momentum the boat had and backed her around the way Alex had backed her off her mooring in Simpson Bay. He cocked the mainsail to weather and turned the rudders hard the other way, allowing the sea to do the work for him as it brought the boat around – the sea now slightly off his starboard bows. Once he was far enough around, Rob sheeted the main back to midships, and turned the wheel hard to port to guide the boat back onto a starboard tack. Slowly, it responded as the Island Fever's baby-staysail filled and she eased forward up and over the next wave. Rob sailed a few thousand yards as tight off the wind as she would point, then came about onto a port tack.

Rob now headed off once again on a close-hauled port tack trying to make his way up above Alex, who he could no longer see. It was all guesswork now. Strangely however, Rob was calm – certain that he would succeed even if his logical mind tried to tell him otherwise. He sailed again as far as he instinctively dared and turned the boat up into irons. He searched aft of the boat, but still the seas were so big that he could see nothing of Alex in the water. Once again, Rob crawled forward on deck to the foremast and climbed easily up ten feet to have a good look around. As the first wave passed and the boat rode up on the swell, Rob saw her – dead downwind.

With the seemingly hardest part done, Rob suddenly realized that in his struggle to find her, he hadn't even thought about how difficult it was going to be to pull Alex aboard in these huge seas without going in the water himself. He still had to find a way to get her up onto the boat quickly or it could pound her to death should she be caught underneath the hull. Then he remembered how they had used the engine box for him to climb aboard while the boat was tacking back and forth in Simpson Bay awaiting the bridge opening. It was hard to believe that had only been yesterday – it felt as if it were a lifetime ago. Gradually, Rob unwrapped the line from the winch and lowered the engine box to the floating position, hoping that the huge waves wouldn't rip it from its hinges. Hove-to, the boat drifted backwards easily on the huge swell with Rob using the rudders and the mainsail to steer to where Alex floated in the water. He was close enough now to see that Alex was awake, although moving lethargically as she painfully raised her hand to ensure that he had seen her. Then he saw her injury – blood covered one side of her head.

When she saw the Island Fever backing down on her she thought she was hallucinating. Surely in this mess, having been unable to get to the marker, it would have been like looking for a needle in a haystack for Rob to actually spot her, let alone maneuver to pick her up. She felt as though she'd been hit by the blast of a nuclear bomb, from the impact of the wall of water that had collapsed on her head before it raked her over the lifelines. But she was alive, and, about to be rescued. When she had first come up for air, she had found it nearly impossible to breathe and had almost drowned in the foot of flying spume and spray above the water's surface. She had turned her back to the wind and sea as the waves came up behind her like a freight train with the impact of a 250 lb. linebacker. From that perspective, the waves were unbelievable, Alex thought – like a four-story building as they approached and swept her up on the crest – then broke over her, pushing her under in the violent turbulence as they passed. She had thankfully discovered that she was able to take a few breaths of air trapped in the pocket in front of her life-vest – it had actually saved her from drowning in the spray. At first, she'd started to panic, realizing she wouldn't survive long in those conditions when suddenly the wind subsided, quelling the froth and blowing spray. She had at some point relaxed – resigned to her fate.

Rob, she thought, would never find her in this and the next closest landfall in the direction she was being blown would he Newfoundland via the Gulf Stream, if she wasn't eaten by something first due to her loss of blood. Actually, there had been so much blood – she wasn't certain she wouldn't just bleed to death. But she hadn't entirely given up hope. Somehow, Rob's determination had gotten through to her. In fact, Alex's guide, Peter, and I had been busy helping Rob find her and keeping the weather at bay until he could get her back on board.

"ALEX! I'm coming, I'll throw you a ring and pull you in. Just try to hang on," shouted Rob excited to have finally made contact with her again, as he tied the end of a line to an orange life ring.

Certain that he had positioned the boat to drift over her, Rob secured his own lifeline in the cockpit, and taking the additional line with him, climbed down into the engine box which jumped and jerked violently with the swell, threatening to toss him out. By this time, Alex was so weak from the time spent in the water and her loss of blood, that swimming was impossible, especially in her water-soaked survival gear, let alone being able to pull herself into the boat. She felt truly helpless and was depending totally on Rob at this point to help her out of this grave situation.

Rob stood in the engine box and threw the life-ring towards her, just missing on the first try. He reeled it in as he struggled to hold himself in the box and threw again. This time it landed right at Alex's fingertips. Weakly, she hooked her arm through the ring as Rob started to pull her towards the boat – being careful to time the waves so that she wasn't too close to the boat as it reached the top of a swell, knowing that the wave might actually throw the boat on top of her as it dropped over the back side. Rob pulled with everything he had, lifting Alex out of the water by her lifeline and harness – somehow managing to pull her into the engine box and into his arms.

"Oh my God, I thought I'd lost you," Rob gasped with excruciating relief to finally hold her next to him as he wept tears of gratitude. Alex clung to him desperately, unable to speak. Instead, she too wept sobs of relief and exhaustion into his shoulder as the box bounced and jostled them. "Let me get you out of here," said Rob as he looked at the deep gash on her temple that oozed fresh blood which trickled down her face, looking much worse than it was. Quickly, Rob secured her life line to the box to keep her from being thrown out and climbed back up the bridge deck into the cockpit, then winched the box back up closer to the boat where he could reach her better. He knew it would take Herculean strength to pull Alex over the back of the bridge deck without hurting her, so he dropped the mainsail, which even though it was resting in the lazy-jacks,* it was whipped and shredded by the wind since Rob did not have

have time to secure it. With the more important task at hand, he clipped the main halyard to Alex's life-line harness, untying the line that held her in the engine box. Then he proceeded to winch her up to bridge-deck level where he was able to swing her safely into the cockpit and lower her onto the settee. Rob unclipped the halyard from Alex's harness and reclipped it onto the frenzied mainsail, grinding it up again with great difficulty since the wind was starting to blow as a squall approached them from the south. He had found her just in time. The wind blew, and it blew hard, as if whatever source that had held it back while he was looking for her had suddenly just let it go.

Rob quickly unstrapped Alex from the life vest and harness and tore the soaked survival-gear and clothing off of her. In the meantime, the wind was gaining force, but Rob's attention was on Alex, not the storm. He carried her limp, shivering body inside the deckhouse and laid her on the carpet, wrapping her in blankets and binding the bleeding wound on her head with a T-shirt which he tore into pieces. Alex was conscious but she found that she hadn't an ounce of strength to advise Rob of what to do next, let alone assist him with sailing the boat.

"I thought I'd never find you," said Rob smiling.

"You can't get rid of me that easy," Alex whispered attempting to pull herself up – realizing that her head felt as if it had been caught in the spin cycle as she reached for the bandage around her temple. "How on earth did you find me in this?" asked Alex impressed and grateful all at the same time. "If it had been you that had gone over, I'm not certain that I could have done it."

"Guess we were lucky it was you then, not that I would credit falling overboard in this to anyone as lucky. Actually, I can't take all the credit," admitted Rob not certain she would believe him if he told her about me.

Alex looked at him strangely. "I know Christian didn't sneak aboard this time," whispered Alex uncertainly, wondering if he'd successfully perpetrated some amazing disappearing and reappearing act.

"It seems I do have a Guardian Angel after all," said Rob smiling. Alex looked at him strangely, pleasantly surprised to find that he was indeed more spiritually attuned than she realized. He had tapped into his higher source.

"Well," said Rob as he looked out the companionway as a light ray was breaking through the clouds, "Let's just say I just relied on a little celestial navigation."

Alex thought to herself that Rob had learned well from his many teachers. He had saved her life and saved the boat, and he'd proven himself a true sailor in, not only her eyes, but his own. Rob was her hero. He was her

---

*LAZY-JACKS — Ropes or wires which run from midway down the mast to either side of the boom to cradle and restrain the sail on the boom when it's dropped.

white knight that only existed in fairy tales. But here he was, real flesh and blood, leaning over her to kiss her. In that time of crisis, Rob had surrendered to something bigger than himself – than his mind – his ego. Rob had found inner peace – strength – he had tapped into this higher source. Rob had finally learned to ask for guidance and divine intervention and his prayers had been heard and answered. He had learned the most crucial thing of all – to have faith that whatever he asked for and truly needed would be provided, or that he already had it within. Rob hadn't realized how much his father's condemnation over the years had taken its toll on his self-confidence and self-esteem. Because of his father's criticism Rob had always covered up for his self-doubt by being a man – never capable of admitting he felt unsure – never asking for help. He had let his ego run the show – that false-self that's trained to always take control in uncertain times. But this time Rob had been able to discard it – shed it. And because of that he had found himself to be a part of that 'Great One Destiny.' Even this horrible storm had served its purpose. Rob had finally found his real self-worth right out there in that angry ocean, and he was certain that he would never lose it again.

CHAPTER THIRTY-THREE

Eye of the Storm

*"Don't be afraid that your life will end,
be afraid it will never begin."*

Internet Wisdom

As foggy as Alex was from the concussion she had received as she was drug over the lifelines and stanchions* by the wave, she finalized the decision with Rob to run back to Antigua and slip into Falmouth Harbor. Pointe-a-Pitre, the main harbor on Guadeloupe was closer, however it was a narrow entrance and Alex didn't know it well enough to risk entering it in these conditions. Plus, the sea that was coming through the cut between Guadeloupe and Les Saintes seemed worse than in the open ocean. It was like a washing machine. To Alex, it appeared the storm was weakening or moving away since the wind had died down below 100 knots in the gusts, leaving Alex questioning whether it had indeed turned to the south. The sky was even starting to clear and the squalls were further apart. However, on the chance that it was headed their way, Alex knew that they had to seek the refuge of a protected harbor. They were far too spent to continue to outrun this thing. Unable to focus on the chart due to her blurred vision, Alex left the task to Rob to estimate a dead-reckoning fix. After

---

*LIFELINES AND STANCHIONS – Lifelines are lines that run around the outside deck of a boat through stanchions – upright metal posts, designed to keep people from falling overboard. Those lines are either wire or wire rope – usually covered in plastic.

some studying of their course and the use of the radio direction finder, which was able to locate three radio signals in the area in order to give him a fairly accurate triangulation* on their location, Rob determined that they were at approximately 60.75 degrees west – 16.5 degrees north – abeam of Guadeloupe, just north of La Désirade. He set a course of 293 degrees to take them just inside the point at Shirley Heights** – a port tack back to the southeastern corner of Antigua.

Rob made certain Alex was comfortable on the nav-station settee, before he backed the boat around and fell off the wind on a port reach just slightly aft of their beam – which clocked further aft due to their speed. Alex refused to simply lay down and do nothing even though her throbbing head made it difficult to sit up. She suggested that he sheet the sails in flat even though they were traveling downwind, although standard sail trim for that point of sail called for the sails to be out almost as far as they can go – to fill with the wind from behind. In this case, just the windage of the boat and bare poles alone would propel them faster than they wanted to travel down the face the waves.

Within minutes the Island Fever was racing down the monster waves at 20-25 knots – surfing as if it were a long board at Waikiki. The boat would ride a wave, picking up so much speed it would actually out sail it and start the climb out of the trough to catch the next one. At that speed, Rob calculated that they were less than two hours out from Antigua. Alex tried time and time again to raise someone from St. Maarten on the SSB, however there was no answer. Obviously, their antennas were history. Compared to the gut-wrenching sail to weather they had been on for the last twenty-four hours, the downwind sail to Antigua felt pretty painless, even if the huge seas rolling up their stern were disconcerting to say the least, when Rob looked over his shoulder to find a wave higher than the masts, feathering at the crests behind them – just before it swept the boat up and carried it a few hundred yards. Thanks to the somewhat clearing sky, the cliffs at Shirley Heights were visible from a good distance out – about 15-miles, as they approached the southern coast of Antigua. Alex, although groggy, dragged herself into the cockpit after donning a dry set of foul-weather gear and a life vest, and drew her hood tight around her bandaged head. Attempting to get a visual reading on the coastline, she searched for the opening to Falmouth in the endless line of white that stretched across the shoreline – the surf pounding the normally lee-shore of the island. English Harbor would

*TRIANGULATION — When navigating, one needs three accurate points of reference in order to get a true and accurate position.
**SHIRLEY HEIGHTS — Named after Governor General Shirley, it is the highest point on the southern side of the island for navigation around the shoals off Shirley Heights when entering into Falmouth and English Harbors. The ruins of the old fortress at Shirley Heights are also the popular spot to drink rum punch and watch the sunset.

have been more protection however the entrance was even smaller and trickier to get into in this kind of sea. Alex knew it was not going to be easy getting into either harbor in these conditions, but she believed Falmouth was their best choice.

They covered the 10 miles in less than twenty minutes – leaving them now about 5 miles off the coast of where Alex knew Falmouth Harbor should be, but she still found it impossible to differentiate the coastline from the opening of the harbor. Luckily, Alex had spent enough time there to know the landscape well and she spotted a house on Blackpoint overlooking Pigeon Beach on the eastern side of the entrance that she recognized. She knew the mouth of the harbor had to be there, but huge waves were breaking over the entrance. They were now only a mile off the entrance, cooking at 25 knots on a broad reach as Alex started setting them up to enter the harbor. She took a sighting with her hand bearing compass and set a new course to steer of 28 degrees – dead for the center of what should be the opening between Blackpoint and Proctors Point. The wind had veered even a little further to the west and was now coming from about 250 degrees.

She took the helm from Rob and took the boat through the jibe onto their new course and started their entrance through the channel on a starboard broad reach, which would allow her to harden up to the northeast corner of the lagoon. Within seconds, Alex realized the channel was totally closed out by breaking waves and quickly made the decision to abort their mission – that is until she looked over her shoulder and saw the 30-foot wave peaking behind her. In a split second she had to commit – continue on and risk getting pitch-poled in the breaking surf or take a chance on turning into the trough of the oncoming wave which was teetering on breaking on top of them. Just like certain decisions one makes in life, this was one that Alex didn't have time to ponder or regret – she had to react and realized that their only chance of not flipping was to surf the Island Fever in between two breaking waves. Alex, who had surfed a fair amount in her years and had as many years of experience driving these oversized cats around whose hulls surfed almost as well as a hand-shaped Big Wave Gun,* let the following wave catch up with them enough to lift the sterns. This allowed her to turn the helm down just enough to catch the wave. With the speed they were traveling, which was a little faster than the speed of the waves themselves, the Island Fever caught the wave and shot forward – sterns up, riding the wave that Alex prayed would be their savior as opposed to their

---

BIG WAVE GUN — A hand-shaped, hand-laminated foam and fiberglass surfboard – thicker, longer, and narrower than typical surfboards. This board is not designed for radical maneuvering on the wave face, but rather for speed to catch the wave and then to ride it out.

nemesis. Like a Pau Malu Set,* the Island Fever was off, surfing down the face of the wave like a pro at the Eddie Aikau Big Wave Championships.** Now there was no turning back – they were committed – Alex was about to ride the biggest wave of her life, like it or not. She feathered the steering carefully, to avoid picking up too much speed. She didn't want to get ahead of the wave and bury her bows which could send them careening ass-over-tea-kettle so to speak, the way most multihulls that have met their demise. It would surely be the end of the Island Fever in these conditions.

Rob made the mistake of looking behind them as he had often done in his life, and what he saw scared him more than anything he'd witnessed yet – the curl of the wave was looming above them, cresting – threatening to break over the boat. In fact, they were nearly inside the curl. Rob swallowed hard and quickly turned to look ahead.

"Okay Ian!" Rob yelled, looking up the mast at nothing other than the empty spreaders. "Don't desert us now! We need you!"

Alex thought Rob's ranting strange, but her attention was fully on the wave at that point. It stayed with them as if it were carrying some precious cargo to safety in its liquid arms. The Island Fever raced with it past the entrance to the harbor. It carried them all the way to the far northeast corner of the harbor, right past the Antigua Yacht Club where it slipped under them as Alex fell off the wind slightly to let the wave pass under them, the same way as a surfer would kick-out when they'd finished their ride. Alex then hardened up to sail back up to the more protected southeast corner by the Yacht Club.

Suddenly, they found themselves in the lee of the wind as it dropped to a mere 45-50 knots over the tops of the hills. Alex turned the boat hard into the wind as Rob hurried to ready their main anchor, a 75 lb. CQR.*** Alex hardened up and as the boat drifted to a stop Rob lowered the anchor. She knew that she would need several more anchors in this wind, but with no engine or

---

*PAU MALU SET — Meaning "to end secretly" originating from an old Hawaiian Pau-end, and Malu-from behind or to sneak upon you. It is the ancient name for the surf-break at Sunset Beach, Hawaii and it refers to the sneaky west swell sets that come across the channel catching surfers inside. If they can't hold their breath, they are Pau Malu.

**EDDIE AIKAU BIG WAVE CHAMPIONSHIPS — The surfing championship, held each year at Big Sunset or Waimai Bay – home of the biggest ridable waves in the world. This event was named after waterman Eddie Aikau who was lost at sea while trying to paddle on his Big Wave Gun to the Island to bring help for his comrades on their sinking Hawaiian sailing canoe.

***CQR & DANFORTH — Both are types of anchors. The CQR or plow, is designed to keep the anchor from breaking lose when the direction of the pull on the line changes as the boat swings. The CQR is a great anchor for grassy bottoms. The Danforth, named after its inventor Richard Danforth, is a lightweight anchor engineered with extremely high holding power for sand or mud bottoms, but does not work well in grass or weeds.

dinghy, properly setting a second or a third would be a tricky proposition. And if the storm got worse, they'd likely need as many as five. Since she had not yet hooked up their bridle,* the boat would naturally swing around more than normal with the gusts, allowing her to cover more ground in order to drop the second anchor at least 30 feet away from the first. Alex waited patiently until the boat stretched back tight with a gust and then sprang forward when the puff subsided. She steered the boat forward to the right of the anchor she'd already set. By then, Rob had prepared their 35 lb. Danforth and had it set to go from their starboard bow. When the boat settled to a stop, Alex gave Rob the go ahead to drop it and ease out the scope as the boat settled back on the next gust. Of course, without an engine, there was no way to insure it was set into the mud bottom aside from simply waiting until the boat pulled the 150' rode taut in that direction to see if they were dragging. She moved the 75 lb. anchor rode to the windless and then did the same with a third anchor off the port bow when they swung as far to the left of the others as the boat would go. Once it was down, she added the bridle to the center anchor.

Finally, they were safe, and both Rob and Alex breathed a sigh of relief. But their work wasn't yet over – they still had to get the sails down and clean up the mess. The deckhouse of the boat was floating in seawater which had washed in through the back companionway from the greenwater in the cockpit, and water that had blasted through the closed dorade vents.** Alex had capped all the vents, but a huge wave during the night had blown one of the caps off and had blasted water into the deck house like a fire hydrant. They had tried to plug it up with towels and rags, but every other huge wave had discharged them like shot, leaving the cabin a wet soggy mess.

The bandage on Alex's head needed changing since it had bled through the cotton shirt, so Rob unwrapped it and cleaned the wound just above her temple with hydrogen peroxide. She needed stitches, but it would have to wait until the storm had passed and they were able to get to a doctor. As a temporary measure, Rob used butterfly Band-Aids to close up the wound as best he could – then left it unbandaged for the air to dry. Seawater can be an amazing antiseptic and the two-inch cut appeared to be pretty clean. Alex's head still pounded, but she was so grateful to just be alive and safe once again with Rob, in a reasonably protected harbor, that her adrenaline high had masked the pain. Instead, the feeling of elation had overcome her whole being. Alex was ready to celebrate by

---

* BRIDLE — A V-shaped line which runs from the anchor line in the center, to each bow of a catamaran. Due to the wide beam, a cat tends to swing and prance all over its mooring without the use of a bridle.

**DORADE VENTS — Ventilation boxes on the foredeck, designed to allow air in and keep water out, however in huge seas, nothing is guaranteed to keep water out entirely.

opening a bottle of champagne although she knew what it would do to her throbbing head, but it was worth it. They had made it through alive, and they had saved the Island Fever from certain destruction.

"Look... the sky's clearing and the wind's died. We're okay now," she sighed with relief as she hugged him as if she would squeeze the life out of him. It was then that she looked up and saw the 150' motor yacht, which had been anchored off the Yacht Club, weigh anchor and head out of the harbor. She felt her stomach turn over realizing that they must be leaving for a reason. This was a ship that would surely have a Weatherfax* aboard. The storm must indeed still be headed their way. Why else would they be leaving the comfort of Falmouth Harbor to brave the seas outside? She radioed them on the VHF and it was confirmed – the storm was once again on its way in their direction.

That left only the Island Fever and three other boats in the harbor. Even though this was a safe haven to them in these conditions, it was definitely not the place to be in a full-blown hurricane – it was not like English Harbor which had several dogleg turns to protect boats once they were inside. The harbor was open to the sea and the type of wave that had saved them sailing in, surely could turn out to be their demise in the end. But now they were trapped – sailing in through those breakers had been one thing, but sailing out would be impossible.

Alex tuned the VHF radio into Radio Net to hear the Weather Report from Bubbly Joe – the "Voice of Doom & Gloom." He confirmed her worst fears – the storm was indeed on its way. Now, Alex had more work to do. She had to get more ground tackle** out before dark. They would never stand a chance on only three anchors But, it would be risky since she had no way to set the additional anchors properly. She would just have to drop them and pray that they would hold when she needed them to.

"Boy, does this kind of bad luck follow you everywhere?" Alex asked Rob half-jokingly – half-serious, "You're like a magnet."

"Seems that way, doesn't it?" answered Rob ironically. "Kind of like those people who get struck by lightning over and over again."

Alex looked at the sky and then at him sternly, "Please... don't tempt fate."

"You sure you want to stick around?" asked Rob uncertainly.

"Oh... I guess I can handle a hurricane or two I'm just waiting to see

---

*WEATHERFAX — A piece of electronic equipment which uses an SSB radio receiver to obtain an ongoing print-out of weather information on a chart.
GROUND TACKLE — All of the equipment it takes to anchor a boat – the line, the chain, all the shackles* used to attach it all together; and of course, the anchor.
***SHACKLES — U-shaped fittings which have a screw-pin to close them. This fitting Is used to attach chain to anchors or lines to other gear like masts or elsewhere on the boat. The snap shackle has a spring pin instead of a screw-pin for quicker release and is usually used to attach halyards to sails.

what's next... a volcanic eruption... a tidal wave?" said Alex jokingly, trying to be lighthearted about their unfortunate circumstance.

Their daylight was waning fast, so Rob and Alex set two more anchors, as best they could – a 34 lb. Danforth and another 28 lb. CQR off each stern about thirty feet apart. Alex reserved a 58 lb. CQR on deck in case they should break loose when the storm got bad and they needed emergency back-up. She set up all the anchors with chafe gear,* and checked the scope to make sure it was enough and that the anchor rodes were even. At least now, the boat wouldn't be able to spin freely, which could wind the anchor lines together – shortening their scope and decreasing their holding power.

The sun had gone down even though they couldn't see it set through the heavy cloud cover. Alex got on the SSB once more and finally raised a big power yacht in Simpson Bay. The reports of the destruction were almost impossible to believe. Nearly every boat in that huge lagoon had sunk – crushed upon one another along the shore, or they were sitting on the airport runway at the far end of the lagoon, leaving only a few dozen still floating. It seemed that their denial of entrance into the lagoon by the broken bridge had ironically been lucky after all. It had likely saved the boat. They informed her that the storm had left the island about five hours before on a heading of southeast, tracking at approximately seven miles per hour – straight for Antigua. Alex asked about the Simpson Bay coast, and the answer she received made her heart sink. Pretty much everything along the beach was gone. In fact, the breakers had been rolling all the way across the spit of land into the lagoon in some places. Alex thanked him and asked if he would be kind enough to check on Grandma and Grandpa's cottage and see if they were okay. Surely if it had gotten that bad, Grandma and Grandpa would have had the sense to get out.

They were sick with worry now but there was nothing they could do to help Grandma and Grandpa – first they had to help themselves. Rob and Alex wrung things out and closed up the boat, and waited – trying to rest as much as their racing minds would let them as they thought about Grandma, Grandpa, and Christian. Rob asked over and over again that I help them but that was something that was out of my hands. They had their own guides that were responsible for their fate and knew their destiny. Although, I did make certain to pass the message along to the parties in charge. As it was, Peter and I had our hands full just keeping up with Rob and Alex's crisis.

*CHAFE GEAR — Approximately five-feet of flexible plastic tubing used over anchor line where it runs through the chocks** to prevent abrasion.
**CHOCKS — A smooth metal fitting – normally placed at the edge of the deck where lines come aboard, which holds the anchor line in place and prevents chaff.

They prepared as best they could and waited for the worst. As exhausted as they were it was a sleepless night for both Rob and Alex. The leading edge of the storm arrived several hours before sunrise and the wind shifted to the northwest, leaving the Island Fever hanging from her two smaller stern anchors. They were now sitting only 150 ft from the docks of the Yacht Club – in the midst of breaking waves. If Alex had realized what was to come, she would have anchored further out, but she hadn't been thinking straight in her foggy state and she had wanted to tuck up into the corner as far as she could. But luckily, the storm had weakened by the time it reached them, bringing with it winds of only 40 - 50 knots sustained in the harbor – gusting to 75.

The wind was manageable – now what they had to worry about was the sea which was breaking entirely over the boat. Every time a wave approached and the boat rode up taught on her anchor lines, Alex prayed that the anchors would hold as the sea crashed over them and rolled past like an avalanche rumbling out of control down a mountain. As each wave approached, Alex held her breath and waited for it to pass. In some ways it was worse than being out at sea. Now, the only thing that stood between them and getting broken into matchsticks on the docks or on shore were those two little anchors and a few hundred feet of rope.

The sun rose that morning over the hillside bringing with it an incredible mauve and lemon sky. Alex was relieved, it was a good sign – it wasn't red* – a sure warning against approaching bad weather. The wind suddenly started to weaken, the clouds parted, and the sky became clear above them as a beautiful cloudless dawn awakened. Then the wind just stopped – they were in the eye of the storm. It was as if someone had simply turned off the storm's power.

Alex had been through enough hurricanes to recognize instantly that this was the eye – but Rob was confused. He looked around in amazement – stunned, "Where did it go?" he asked baffled by the sudden calm.

"It hasn't gone anywhere we're right in the heart of the storm – we've only seen the first half of it. This is just intermission." After all any great show would offer its viewers intermission to catch their breath, grab a drink, or make a bowl of popcorn, so why shouldn't Claire offer her viewers this same courtesy. After all, this was the 'Greatest Show On Earth' – presented by mother nature herself. At least it was the 'Greatest Show of the Century' in this part of the world, since no hurricane recorded in the last 100 years in the Caribbean had packed the wallop Claire had. Nor had one accomplished the impossible feat of traveling east and south – in the direction from whence it came.

*RED SKY — Like the old maritime saying goes – "Red sky at morning, sailors take warning. Red sky at night, sailor's delight."

Rob was awed by the beauty of the calm eye that existed within such a violent exterior. He grew quiet, no longer feeling disconnected from the source – no longer a meaningless bit of matter in this big, big Universe. He had connected with the storm in such a way as to almost understand it – like Rob, its outer existence was uncontrolled and chaotic and at its center, its inner core, it was somehow at peace.

"The worst should be yet to come," said Alex, concerned that they may still be in for more than they deserved, "Although the sky tells me different." After all they'd already been through this storm once in the last 24 hours, were they really due seconds?

HURRICANE!

Wherefore the use of the hurricane,
Gathering, whirling winds and rain?
Multiplying its forceful power,
To hurl at men, and snarl and glower?
Where lies the Beneficial Being Behind
such a monstrous, wicked thing Starting
from nothing, to grow and move Faster
and faster! To batter and shove. To toss
and level the crops and trees, And pick
great quarrels with the seas? Cutting an
enormous swath Of death and havoc in
its path.
Is it, that mankind must pay
In some great measure – for the day,
The sun, the moon, the stars, the night;
The privilege of having light,
The life we live, the hope we scan
Of being part of some Great
Plan?

Lorna Steele

CHAPTER THIRTY-FOUR

Dead Reckoning

*"Life is eternal and love is immortal, and death is only a horizon;
life is eternal as we move into the light,
and a horizon is nothing save the limit of our sight."*

Carly Simon/Teesa Gohl

Alex waited for the worst on the backside of the eye, but when the wind filled in again, it was weak – the storm had split and gone either side of the island. It took another three hours for it to totally blow itself out – gradually calming to a mild 20 knots from the north. At first Alex had been suspicious that the storm had simply stalled on them, but when she saw the sky all around the island clearing, she knew it was over.

Most importantly, they needed sleep, but Rob knew that it was best to get Alex's head stitched first. He called Alex's friend Roberto, the dockmaster at the Yacht Club, and asked if he could be of assistance in getting a doctor for her. Also, they needed a way off the boat – they didn't have a dingy and even if they did, the seas were too rough to land it ashore. Luckily, Roberto had his 25-foot rescue boat anchored just off the dock and he instructed his deckhand to swim out and bring the boat into shore close enough to the dock for the doctor to jump aboard – he would bring the doctor to them.

Once Alex's wound was tended – fifteen stitches later – the doctor gave her the okay to take some painkillers and more importantly, to take a nap, since she was oriented, able to converse, and her motor responses were good. Sleep sounded too good to be true at that point, thought Alex. They had been up now for more than forty-eight hours and her whole body ached almost as much as her aching head. Alex and Rob were anxious however, to get back to St. Maarten to check on Grandma and Grandpa. But they reasoned that the earliest they could safely make it out of the harbor would be the next morning. They made the decision to leave by dawn – if there was any wind, since a passing hurricane often took away every available breath of air. They could try to fly into St. Maarten, but rumor had it that SXM was closed due to the fact that the runway was littered with boats and debris.

Roberto offered to have his guys help pick up their extra anchors later that afternoon, since it would be too tough a job to do without an engine or dinghy. To set Alex's mind at ease, Roberto informed her that he had personally checked on her boat, Dancer, in English Harbor and it was safe and sound – there had been little or no sea to cause a threat like the waves had in Falmouth.

Night fell. Rob went out on deck to look at the stars which felt more important now. In fact, he had been certain just hours ago that he may never lay eyes on them again. He stared at the vast expanse of sky above him – at the millions of stars that he could see. He was awed at the thought of how vast the Universe must truly be for he knew there were just as many unseen galaxies – like little islands floating in space comprised of stars. How still it felt – how magnificent – full of promise. Finally, Rob fully understood that he was part of that vastness – a oneness. When Alex had fallen overboard, Rob had been present for the first time in his life, and he had felt the depth and oneness of the Universe within him – the all-knowing and the nothingness at the same time. He finally understood what Grandpa meant when he had said to live in the present – for if Rob had been anywhere but in-the-moment when he was up that mast looking for Alex, neither of them would be there now. For the first time in his life, he felt open to the source of all being, and for the first time ever he felt real love – not love connected to the body, but love that rose out of something more vast – more important – something more real than the body he inhabited. Finally, Rob understood the lesson he'd come here to learn, and I breathed a great sigh of relief since I knew I had finally gotten through to him. He had finally learned to tune in and now he could rely more on his own navigational skills.

Rob joined Alex in the master berth, and by nine o'clock, they finally fell asleep in each other's arms, comforted by the knowledge that they had lived through such a frightening, life-threatening experience together. Alex knew for the first time, that she had found a man that she could trust with her life the way she had trusted her father. Finally, she was able to trust – to love – unconditionally – to surrender.

With the wind from the north at 10-12 knots, they sailed straight out of the harbor on a starboard broad reach at the crack of dawn the next morning.

The seas were still big from the southwest, but with the storm to the east of them, there was nothing to push the sea any longer from the west. Almost as quick as it had come, it had gone. They hugged what was now the leeside of Nevis and St. Kitts all the same, to garner a modicum of protection from the sea, making the ride a little smoother and faster since it allowed them to crack off of the wind a bit. Progress was slow since once again they found themselves beating dead to weather on a starboard tack, due to the fact that the wind had clocked around and was coming out of the north – a result of the receding storm. Luckily, it would take only one tack to get all the way to abeam of Simpson Bay – some twelve hours later.

Alex set the autopilot and made herself comfortable in the deckhouse on the only part of the settee that had somehow managed to remain dry, as Rob took the first watch. Today's sail would be a pleasure cruise compared to their last. The going was slow, however, with a fair amount of canvas up they were making good at least eight to ten knots. Alex and Rob's primary concern still lay with Grandma and Grandpa's welfare, and the faster they could make it back to the island, the better. The little island of St. Maarten had taken the brunt of the storm and Alex wasn't certain what they would find standing along the coast. The report she had received yesterday, from the yacht in St. Maarten, sounded pretty grim.

As they got within 40 miles off the island, Alex was unsuccessful in locating anyone from the marina in Simpson Bay via Saba Radio, likely because everyone was preoccupied with rescue work – assisting the crews of the hundreds of submerged vessels which had not been as lucky as they thought when they cruised through the bridge a few days before in search of safety.

Although they had slept, Rob and Alex still felt as battered as the Island Fever looked. The boat had amazingly sustained little serious damage. Although her starboard dagger board had broken off at the waterline while Rob was maneuvering to save Alex, making the boat a bear to steer to weather in the confused seas. An hour into the trip Alex had realized that the autopilot was overtaxed, and Rob had taken over the helm, steering her as best he could in a straight line. Luckily, the only other damage to the boat had been ripped and tattered sails from the force of the wind. It would however, take them a week to get all the seawater out of the carpets and cushions and get them dry, but it had all been a minuscule price to pay for their own and the boat's safe return.

Alex owed her life to Rob, who had pulled her from the jaws of certain death with little concern for his own safety. Watching Rob at the helm, Alex realized that she was indeed looking at a different man – one who had found himself somewhere out there in the middle of this vast ocean. Ironic how only a few months prior she had given him up as hopelessly unseaworthy. She had been so wrong. She knew that their fates were now sealed and that it would take far more than a hurricane to ever separate them. A bond had been created between them that could carry them through the good times and the bad.

Almost too weak to stand, Alex struggled into the cockpit against Rob's wishes, and wrapped her arms around him – partially in an attempt to steady her-self, but mainly to feel her heart beating next to his. "Did I tell you how much I love you?" she whispered into Rob's ear as he leaned down to kiss her. "I owe my life to you. You were amazing out there."

Rob smiled at her, "I couldn't have gone on living if I hadn't found you. What would have been the point?" Alex smiled and buried her head into Rob's chest so she could hear his heart beat – Rob pulled her close, knowing that she would indeed find it there. Alex stared off in the distance – her attention caught by something large floating in the stream of flotsam that had been washed from the coastal areas and boats of the neighboring islands. She pointed it out to Rob and asked him to sail a little higher for them to get a better look. They had been seeing the trail of debris for hours, stretching nearly a mile wide from about the time they were first out of Falmouth. As they got closer to the floating object that Alex feared might be a person in the water, a cold chill crawled up her spine. There in the water with all but one chamber submerged floated the Dinghy Fever – their little rubber raft had finally met its demise after all. Alex had managed to save the Dinghy Fever from the clutches of the French, but it seemed that as fate would have it, Claire had gotten the best of her on that count. But, it wasn't the destroyed dinghy that concerned Alex and Rob who hove-to long enough to haul what was left of it aboard using the extra jib halyard – it was the fact that it had been locked away in Grandma and Grandpa's shed which sat behind their little cottage. If the sea had been high enough to wash the dinghy out of the shed, what was the condition of their home?

It was still a few hours before sunset. It had taken them all day to make it back to their mooring, which was no longer located in Simpson Bay. In fact, they would later find that their two-hundred-pound kedge anchor* and chain from an old tug boat lay instead on Simpson Bay beach – still tied to a monohull which lay on its side wedged between two palm trees. Alex couldn't believe what she saw when they rounded what was left of the rocky point at Pelican Cay into Simpson Bay. They had definitely fared better than the scourged little island which now hardly resembled the Paradise they left not more than a few days ago. Winds of over 200 mph had ravaged the island so badly the palm trees resembled bent telephone poles – stripped of their fronds, and the rest of the foliage on the island was history.

*KEDGE ANCHOR — *An older traditional style anchor which looks quite like Popeye's tattoo. Several of these type anchors are known as a Herreshoff, Fisherman, and Yachtsman. This type of anchor is no longer widely used since the development of modern lighter anchors, however, it is a good anchor in a grassy or weedy bottom, or especially in coral.*

But the wind had only done half the damage – what the wind hadn't destroyed, the sea had polished off, including all the beaches along the southern and western sides of the island. The few monohulls that had chosen to remain in the outer bay for the storm, now littered the coast like beached whales. But the worst of it was the massive toll collected amongst the boat population inside the lagoon that were crammed under the bridge – one on top of the other – like clams at a clambake. They were yet to see the devastation that awaited them inside the bridge along the southwestern shore of the lagoon at the end of the airport runway. The destruction of those who had been so unlucky as to have made it into the bridge on time, was almost complete, since only about four dozen or so boats remained floating in the entire lagoon including the French side – the remains of a fleet of 1400 plus. What they could see however were the masts along the shore inside entwined like tangled pick-up-sticks.

It had taken a while, but Rob and Alex finally got the anchor to hold quite far offshore in the churning bay. The swell in the harbor had diminished dramatically, but it was still so huge that even with binoculars, Alex was having difficulty surveying the damage on shore in the waning daylight. But, when she finally got a clear line of sight on Grandma and Grandpa's beach, once the boat rose up on a wave to give her a clearer shot, she gasped and dropped the binoculars. There in the spot where Grandma and Grandpa's cottage had sat for the last sixty some years, lay the Morgan 41 that had turned back to ride out the storm in the harbor.

"Oh my God!" cried Alex, turning whiter than she'd been the day before from the loss of all that blood. Her hand shook as she covered her mouth in shock.

Rob snatched up the binoculars and climbed up on the deck house to get a better view. "Oh... dear God," he cried as he surveyed what little remained of that stretch of beach that was once Paradise to two people they loved. Throwing down the glasses, Rob ripped his clothes off as if preparing to dive in after a drowning man. Alex, still in shock from what she'd seen attempted to remove her jacket, but the dizziness from her bump on the head nearly sent her reeling.

"You're staying here," insisted Rob as he removed his shoes and stripped down to his bathing trunks. "I'm going to swim ashore to see if they're all right. I'll get a boat from the marina to come back and get you as soon as I can."

Feeling helpless to do anything to help those who had become her dearest friends over the last few months, Alex's tears welled uncontrollably for the first time since her father died. Rob's heart sunk as he held her tiny body – shaking with fear over what Rob might find once he reached shore. Alex had never been so scared in her life, even the time she spent in the water trying to save her own life paled in comparison to the dread she was feeling about Grandma, Grandpa, and Christian.

Rob hugged her and promised he'd be back, then he dove off the bow of the boat and swam with everything he had towards shore. For the last few months, Rob had been flirting with life and death and each time death had seemingly caught up with him, he had cheated it by slipping from its grasp. Death had always seemed like such a distant horizon for Rob since he had never given much thought to his own mortality. He had only lost one grandparent so far – his grandmother, who had been old and quite ill for years terribly. At the time it had almost seemed a blessing, even though he missed her. As he swam, Rob cursed the sea that seemed so determined to steal from him all he cared about. Rob was starting to realize what might be just on the other side of that unseen horizon as he neared the shore, struggling to pull himself out of the crashing waves before they pounded down onto him or tossed him aside like some sort of jettisoned debris. Suddenly, it seemed that death was like the edge of the earth – out there somewhere on that elusive horizon just waiting for those unsuspecting souls to sail off the edge with little or no warning.

What he found on the beach that afternoon was almost beyond Rob's comprehension when he finally climbed and stumbled up the beach, which was now eroded away to the palm trees with an eight-foot drop to the water. The ketch sat with its keel in what had once been Grandma's living room. Rob raced towards what was left of the cottage, screaming and tearing through the wreckage like a rescue worker searching for earthquake victims, waking Christian who slept in the Yellow Submarine just behind the cottage. Christian jumped out of the car and ran to pull Rob away from the rubble. He had been sitting in the front seat of the Yellow Submarine for a day and a half, waiting – hoping Rob and Alex would come back – uncertain if they were dead or alive. He hadn't seen them sail in since he'd dozed off, having gone a total of three days without sleep.

"You've got to help me," Rob shrieked as he tore at the rubble, until his hands bled – frantic to find them.

"Dere's noting you kin do maun! Dey not dere Mista Rob... dey not dere!"

Suddenly, Rob realized it was Christian who was pulling him away from the rubble and he turned and grabbed him in his arms, relieved to see he was still alive. "Oh thank God!" he cried.

"Not to woury yousef none 'bout me... I be fine," said Christian unable to look Rob in the eye. "It be Granma and Granpa who need de woury."

"Where are they," demanded Rob, "Are they okay!"

Christian only shook his head. "Granpa, he be in de hospital. He not be hurd, bu' he don't seem to know'd whur he be. He not all dere," he said pointing to his head.

"And Grandma?" questioned Rob frantically, "What about Grandma?"

Christian shook his head again and lowered his eyes, "Sorry Mista Rob, she not maek it," he said as he burst into tears crying into Rob's chest. "I na do my job Mista Rob."

"Rob stood frozen – unable to process any of it – unable to move or think as he hugged Christian tightly to his chest. This time the Universe had brought out the big guns. It had pulled out all the stops and it seemed that he was being taught how to live, by being taught how to die, a little bit at a time. A part of him had indeed died on the beach that day – that part of the old Rob who had taken life for granted.

    Christian explained how he had run out into the storm during the eye after Lambchop and Old Henry, and Grandpa had followed – just in time to escape the huge wave that had brought in the ketch which had decimated the cottage. It had been the Yellow Submarine that had saved he and Grandpa. Lambchop had instinctively run for the car which he knew well, and was waiting next to it when Christian and Grandpa caught up with him. Christian opened the door and they all climbed in just as the wave hit. The missing floor boards it seemed, had saved them from being washed out on the receding tide since the car filled with water from underneath instead of floating back out to sea with the wave. The car had however, rolled over a few times, and ended up wedged between two palms trees, where it had stayed the rest of the storm. Miraculously, they had remained unhurt inside the little vehicle where they'd spent the rest of the night as the eye passed and the storm raged on – never realizing what had happened to the cottage.

    Then Christian told Rob about waking up the next morning to see the boat sitting on top of the little house. That's when Grandpa had snapped. He had lost his lifelong mate, and he wasn't able to accept the reality of life without her. Christian explained how some guys from a big yacht in the lagoon had helped him to dig out Grandma's body and get her to the morgue. Grandpa had been taken to the hospital on the French side since the Dutch hospital, for the most part, had been washed away. He was still there resting – under observation.

    Rob looked toward the Yellow Submarine which was buried in sand and debris, and there next to it stood Lambchop and Old Henry – guardians of the little vehicle that had saved their lives.

    Although he thought he'd planned an accurate dead reckoning course, Rob hadn't even come close to the mark he had estimated he'd be at by this point in his life. He certainly never imagined he'd end up here. Fate had plotted against him – swept him off his course onto a new one. One that had definitely not led him to Paradise. Instead, it seemed he had found himself in hell. This time death had snuck up on him and snatched away someone he loved, leaving him totally helpless. Grandma hadn't stood a chance to get away from the ton of steel and fiberglass, not to mention the wall of water that had come crashing down on her. "Whur be Mzz Alic," asked Christian, concerned for her safety.

    "She's safe, on the boat. A little beaten up, but she's okay thank God. We had a rough time, but not as bad as you," answered Rob gratefully, realizing now just how lucky they'd been. The gravity of their own experience had not really hit him until he had learned of Grandma's fate. "Alex needs rest," said

Rob, "She took a pretty hard knock on the head. I need to get back out there and tell her." "It be impossible to git de Whaler tru de brege, but I get a dinkee from de mareena an I row yew ouut," said Christian anxiously, relieved to hear that she was okay. "Sari bout de dinkee," said Christian apologetically, "I'd pud it in de shid lyk you say... bu' de wave, it tuk it."

"I know," said Rob shaking his head, "We found it floating south of here. That's when we knew something terrible had happened."

Together Rob and Christian sorrowfully walked to the marina to borrow a dinghy and some oars to enable them to get back out to the boat. The devastation in the little village of Cole Bay was frightening. Houses were missing roofs, buildings were flattened, palm trees lay across overturned vehicles, windows were blown from cottages, and water stood in the streets knee deep in some places. It looked like the aftermath of a war – the war that Claire had waged with the island. Unfortunately, the island had lost. When they reached the marina, Rob could see that most of the roof was missing from the showroom. The workers were busy cleaning up water, destroyed merchandise, glass, twisted metal siding, neighbors' patio furniture, and palm fronds. There was even another roof from a house across the way wrapped around what was left of their front entrance. Jeff was relieved to see Rob walk into the store and to learn that Alex was also okay. He was more than happy to loan him a rubber inflatable that had somehow been saved from the storm. Jeff looked as tired and harried as Rob, since they had been up for days saving boats and lives, and attempting to save the store. They'd given it their best effort, but once the roof had blown off, they'd given up the fight and crawled into the cistern beneath the building to save their own lives. It seemed that everyone had lived through their own hell the last few days. Rob and Alex's harrowing experience now seemed small in light of all the devastation sustained by their friends.

It was getting dark as Rob and Christian rowed across to Snoopy Island and carried the dinghy over the road to launch it in the rough surf of Simpson Bay. It was hard work rowing out to the Island Fever, but Christian was young and strong, and he was used to rowing around the lagoon on any type of floating craft he could get his hands on. Alex was so relieved to see Christian in the dinghy that her heart leapt with joy, hoping that quite possibly they had all gotten to safety. When they arrived at the boat and climbed aboard, Alex stood on the transom – awaiting news. She grabbed Christian and hugged him tight enough to squeeze the wind out of him, giving him a big kiss on each cheek. Although he was a little embarrassed by the physical display of affection, he secretly loved it and he hugged her back. Christian was equally as happy to see her alive and well, as she was of him. Alex and Rob were now his family – the only family he truly had.

"Are they alright?" Alex asked, her voice quivering as much from the excitement at seeing Christian as it was from fear of what their answer might be.

Rob hugged her, and she knew. "Grandpa's in the hospital... he's not hurt... but... Alex... Grandma's gone. She didn't have a chance... the boat."

Alex gasped and her legs gave way underneath her. Rob caught her and pulled her to his chest. He held her tight realizing how close he'd come to losing her too. "I didn't even get to say goodbye to her," she choked, "Like my father... he died when I was out sailing. I didn't get to tell them I loved them," Alex sobbed into Rob's shoulder. At that moment Rob knew without a doubt that his heart had come home to live since Alex's pain felt as if someone had stabbed him in the chest. He was heartbroken – not just for his own loss – but for Alex's, knowing how much that wise woman had meant to her.

CHAPTER THIRTY-FIVE

Life & Death

"Death only ends life, not love."

Ian

Alex lay on the settee, sedated from the tranquilizers Rob had insisted she take, since she was in such a state over Grandma she could hardly stand. Finally, the gravity of what they had been through had hit her and she had broken-down – blaming herself for not seeing Grandma and Grandpa to safety, and for not being there for her father who had died alone. Maybe she could have saved him, if she'd only been there. For the first time since his death, she wept – torrents – enough to fill an ocean it seemed to Rob who sat with her head on his lap, stroking her hair.

Alex should have seen it coming, it was inevitable that the boats in the harbor would end up on the beach, she reasoned. But how could she have known that the storm would come from the west. It didn't matter. She had still left Grandma and Grandpa's fate in the hands of a couple of inexperienced sailors foolish enough to believe that they could ride out the storm outside on their moorings.

All Alex could see was Grandma's smiling face as she sat on the verandah with a tea cup in her hand and the wisdom of a seer in her eyes. Once again Alex had lost someone she loved as if just the act of her loving someone somehow doomed them to such a fate. First it had been her mother who had given her life simply to give Alex hers, and then it had been the father who had raised her single-handedly – as brave, she thought as a sailor willing to circumnavigate the globe alone. Braver than her, since she had even been afraid to fall in love, let alone raise a child by herself. Her father had loved her mother so much that it broke her heart to think that he had waited patiently eighteen years to be with his wife again, on the Otherside. He knew Alex needed him as she grew into an independent young woman. He had been her life teacher, and he had taught her well. He had armed her with just about everything she would ever need in this lifetime before leaving to rejoin his soulmate – at least everything but this. She knew the day he died of a heart attack, that he had only stayed to see her grown and strong enough to take care of herself. Alex had never let herself grieve for him and the pain was almost more than she could bare as she wept for Grandma, her mother, and her father. She missed her father terribly, and now she would miss Grandma. A woman she had trusted – a woman she had confided in. She had been the only woman Alex had ever really known in her life, and Grandma had shown her how to open her heart. She had given her the true gift of life – she had helped her to love again. Alex hadn't known her mother, nor either of her own grandmothers who had passed away before she was born. Alex hadn't even had many girlfriends as a girl growing up since she was such a tomboy. All her friends had always been boys.

It had been easy when Alex was alone. She had simply shut the pain out – closed her heart, like she did on the day she sailed away from Annapolis. Like Buddha, she had taken to the road of life alone making the decision that one cannot truly be hurt if one does not get attached – to anything. But, now that she had opened her heart to Rob, and to Grandma, it all came rushing in – like the storm had ravaged the island – it had also ravaged her heart. As Alex fell into a semi-conscious state somewhere between sleep and waking, she felt herself drifting outside her body. She was floating above looking down at her physical body with such indifference that she felt she could easily just drift away and break the silver-cord that seemed to connect her. She knew she could just let go and the pain would be gone – forever.

Alex found herself walking in the most beautiful rainforest she could have ever imagined. So real, she knew she couldn't be dreaming. There by the waterfall, stood a young woman throwing gardenias into the pool – an attractive woman with golden skin. As Alex approached – the woman turned. It was Grandma – but young – beautiful – no more than thirty. Alex recognized the light in her green eyes immediately and the warmth of her touch as she reached out her hand to her. Then Alex felt an overwhelming sense of love. They spoke but without the need of words. "Don't blame yourself," Alex distinctly heard Grandma say to her, "You knew it was my time to go home. You did what you had to. You followed your path and I followed mine. Sorry I had to go out so dramatically, but the Universe works in strange ways, and there's not much we can do to change the big strokes once we've written our course."

Alex smiled at her uncertainly. "Am I dead?" Alex asked.

"No dear, you're very much alive for the first time in your life. You've just come to visit... it's not your time. You have much more love to live in this lifetime and you've only just found the soul whom you've waited your whole life for. Don't be afraid to love with all your heart my dear, it is the purpose for which you exist. If you don't, you'll die inside."

"My parents, are they here?" asked Alex hesitantly, uncertain where here was. She assumed it was the Otherside but Alex never was one to make assumptions without the cold hard facts.

"Remember... it's only love that truly matters. And that I'll be there whenever you need me." And then, Grandma was gone. Alex turned and on the hill above was her father – young, radiant, looking only slightly older than he had in his wedding photo. Beside him stood a tall beautiful woman with long golden blonde hair, dressed in pale sky-blue to match her vivid blue eyes, not unlike her own – the color her mother had worn the day she had married her father. They smiled at her, and she felt all the love they had for her pour forth like the warmth of a summer's day. It enveloped her and made her feel safe – the way her father had made her feel when she fell asleep in his arms as a little girl. For the first time she understood the bond between her mother and father – the immense love they held for one another. She understood what Grandma had meant about love. She knew now why they had left her, and she also knew now that they would never leave her.

Alex felt the lightness slowly disappear – the feeling of the heavy weight of her body returned. Her head ached, but strangely she welcomed the pain, rejoiced in it since she knew that she was alive. Struggling with consciousness, Alex opened her eyes to the man she knew she would spend the rest of her life with.

"Are you okay?" asked Rob surprised to see her smiling.

"I couldn't be better," answered Alex as she took his hand in hers. "I want to spend the rest of my life with you."

Rob smiled, confused but elated knowing finally that she had indeed fallen in love with him. "Will you be my wife," asked Rob knowing before she spoke what the answer would be.

"Yes," she said matter-of-factly. "Yes, I would love to be your wife."

Rob smiled and held her – his heart leaping for joy at the thought of Alex's love for him.

Alex smiled. "I spoke with Grandma," Alex said to Rob. "She's just fine... so is my father," Alex said beaming, "He's with my mother." Alex waited for Rob's response not knowing what he would think – had she gone balmy from her bump on the head or would he accept that she had truly seen them – spoken to them as if they'd been standing right there with her. But Rob didn't question the fact that she'd seen them for a second. Afterall, he had met me at

*OUT OF BODY EXPERIENCE — Better known as astral travel. When one's spirit body leaves the physical body for a little gallivant about the Universe staying connected to the body by a silver-cord.

the top of a swaying mast during a hurricane. Why then couldn't they still see their loved ones who had passed over? Alex, had simply had an 'out-of-body experience.'* She had been lucky enough to cross over to the Otherside** to see for herself that she hadn't been responsible for their demise. They had followed their own dead reckoning course home.

Rob thought again about meeting me. He still did not know who I really was or from where I'd come – from the Otherside he'd assumed. But, where-ever I resided, he knew I'd be there for him to see him through to the end – until he'd accomplished what he'd come here to do. For months Rob had questioned the Universe as to why? Why had so many bad things happened to him – what had he done to deserve them? But now Rob suddenly realized that all his experiences – good and bad, had happened to him for a reason. They had all led him to wisdom and all that was needed to fulfill his life plan. Rob was here for a reason as was every soul on the planet – he had a divine purpose in the greater plan.

Alex and Rob could not believe their eyes the next morning when they saw the devastation along the southwestern shore of the lagoon where the boats were pilled like discarded wrecks from a war – not unlike the shores of Normandy. The toll exacted on sailors' lives had not been quite as high as that fated day five decades before, but there were already seven known dead and dozens still missing. On shore, the death toll was uncertain due to the fact that there was quite a large, invisible, Haitian worker population that lived in the hills – with relatively little or no safe shelter from such a storm.

There were twenty or more boats scattered across the airport runway which had washed up and over the road at the east end of the airport on the western side of the lagoon, and several on the main road itself. The one island crane was busy working overtime attempting to clear the road and the runway by moving the boats to a makeshift boatyard across from the airport. It would take a lot more to clear the channel through the bridge, and then it would take even longer to replace the existing bridge with a new one. Most of the boats along the shore had been crushed by other boats – six or seven deep in some places. The ones on the bottom, which had sunk, actually were the lucky ones, it seemed. Once they were able to raise them, they had fared much less damage than the ones crushed on shore, since the bottom of the lagoon seemed to have been the quietest place to have ridden out the storm. Somewhat like inner peace – the depths of the lagoon had remained calm and undisturbed.

Alex and Rob borrowed a car from Jeff and drove to the French side to check on Grandpa at the hospital, and to make certain that someone had seen to

---

*OUT OF BODY EXPERIENCE — Better known as astral travel. When one's spirit body leaves the physical body for a little gallivant about the Universe staying connected to the body by a silver-cord.
**THE OTHERSIDE — Where a soul lives once it's left the physical body – the other side of 'the light.'

Grandma's arrangements. But, when they arrived, they found eight of his twelve children by his beside. The family had flown in from all over when they found out about Grandma. Luckily, the French airport was still open for business, and of all their children living in the islands, and a few from Canada, had been able to get there. At the door they were met by Veronica, the youngest, who informed them that Grandma had already been cremated that morning and the service was to be held that afternoon. They thanked her and hugged her, and quietly walked to Grandpa's beside. Their hearts ached when they saw Grandpa laying in that bed staring up at the ceiling at nothing at all. It was as if a part of him had died with Grandma, like someone had extinguished the light inside. Grandpa didn't even know them – he was in his own world – one that seemed to include Grandma since he talked to her as if she were there in the room with them. It was as if he were ready to give up – ready to go home.

    Rob and Alex introduced themselves to Grandma and Grandpa's children. They already knew Veronica, who lived nearby on the island. But her siblings had already heard all about Rob and Alex from Grandma and Grandpa who spoke about them constantly in letters and on the phone. Their oldest son and daughter planned to take Grandpa back with them to Toronto, since Veronica had also lost most of her home in the storm. They were planning to leave the next day, and Rob knew that this might be the last time he would ever see Grandpa again. In his gut he knew that Grandpa would not survive long without Grandma. They had been together nearly three-quarters of a century and their souls would be lost in the Universe without each other. Rob mourned as much for his own loss as he did for Grandpa's since he knew that Grandpa would soon join his true love on the Otherside. It seemed that Rob's life teacher had come into his life overnight, and had departed as quickly.

    Rob and Alex attended the service on the beach at sunset where the cottage had stood – where Grandma had lovingly raised her children who had returned to their island to put her to rest. Four of their children had immigrated back to Grenada to live, and knowing that Grandma's favorite spot in the world had been the rainforest there, they made the decision to spread her ashes in the pool beneath the falls. It had been her place to go to when she was a child growing up alone – her solace and her comfort. A place where Wini knew she could commune with her mother and father as Alex had done with hers.

    As she heard each child speak, Alex realized that even her own children didn't know how deeply enlightened a soul Grandma had been, since they spoke as if Grandma were the very ashes that were held within that urn. When they were finished, Alex stepped forward and laid a flower on the sand next to the urn and then turned to Grandma's children. "I'd like to say something… if that would be all right?" Alex asked hesitantly. "I know I'm not family but I did get to know her well in the short time I was privileged to have share with her."

    "Please," said Veronica who knew how close Alex and her mother had grown. "She would like that," she said as she smiled at Alex.

Alex hesitated a moment fighting back the tears and the lump in her throat that threatened to steal her voice. She closed her eyes for a moment trying to picture Grandma's smiling face clearly, but strangely, she could only pull up a vague image of the woman who had only a few days before told her that life goes on no matter what.

"Grandma taught me a wealth of lessons about living and dying," Alex said. "And she taught me that only a happy person can create happiness in others. She taught me that one can only be loved if they are willing to love themselves. She taught me many things in the short time I knew her, but the most important thing she taught me, was that the only truly important thing in life is love, and that you do take it with you when you go." Alex cried openly now ready to feel the pain of her immediate loss and the loss of her past.

A tear ran down Rob's cheek as he watched Alex – remembering what Grandma had once said to him.

"Life can end at any moment, and if we haven't loved... truly loved, we've missed the purpose of why we came here in the first place." Rob now understood what the true purpose of his life was. He knew that he had come here to learn to love – himself, his life, and everything and everyone on the planet, but most important of all – Alex. Rob had finally begun to understand life, but more importantly, for the first time, he understood death. Life and death no longer seemed like two totally juxtaposed concepts – life was about letting go and even being willing to allow some part of yourself to die for someone more evolved to be reborn. And death, was about living everyday as if it were your last. That day, Rob and Alex said their farewells to Grandma, comforted by the knowledge that she had happily returned home.

CHAPTER THIRTY-SIX

The Payoff

"True wealth is not the pot of gold at the end of the rainbow.
It is the rainbow."

Ian

The island was once again dark due to the absence of utilities, thanks to Claire having washed out the power plant – not to mention the fact that the water plant was not in operation due to the lack of electricity. The island's cisterns were quite full from the torrential downpour the island had received, however so were the island's many septic tanks which now overflowed into the flooded streets and into the cisterns – contaminating the drinking water. Historically, the average storm would rob the island of services for approximately a two-week period, however, Claire was not your average storm, and the island was predicting months before it would be fully operational again; and years before it could even begin to recover from the disaster, if ever. It had taken a major toll on some of the island's major resorts which had pretty much blown away in the storm. The island desperately needed the assistance of the Red Cross, however word was that the government was afraid to call them in, since they were in fear of the negative publicity that might hurt the island next tourist season.

Alex looked at herself in the mirror – she would definitely end up with a scar. But then, that was what made you appreciate life all the more – those reminiscent battle scars to both flesh and spirit that made one remember the pain and thus fully appreciate the pleasures of life. But aside from the scar, Alex was fine. It seemed that, as Rob knew all too well, Alex was a hard headed woman and had managed to absorb the glancing blow without too much residual damage. Alex was a survivor, as was Rob – determined to find her true purpose in this life and live it to its fullest.

Rob and Alex now had to take stock of where they were and what was next. Hurricane season wasn't quite over so the first order of business was to get the Island Fever inside the lagoon through the French bridge. Now that there were so few boats in the lagoon, the risk of damage from another boat dragging into them was slim.

Rob was at the point where he needed a vacation from his extended vacation – desperately. This time however, he needed a break from Paradise, and a little dose of civilization sounded quite appealing to him. Strangely, even a visit home sounded good to Rob. Maybe he'd take Alex to meet his family – maybe it was time for Rob to make peace with his father now that he realized how unpredictable life was, and how fragile.

Rob and Alex sailed the boat around to Marigot the next morning and had Jeff, from the marina, tow them in through the bridge. He dropped them in the southwest corner of the lagoon on Joey's mooring that had somehow survived the storm. Christian lent a hand putting the boat back together while Rob and Alex went to help the other sailors who were struggling to salvage what was left of their boats. Several large catamarans had ended up on shore in various stages of disrepair and the owners were vying for time from the island crane so that they could right their boats and begin to assess the damage. Lines of the 'Coconut Telegraph' were buzzing around the island with stories of the storm – of how a fifty-foot catamaran had been seen sailing through the air like a kite and had landed upside down on top of a small monohull, only to be blow away again onto shore in the next 200 knot plus gust. And of sailors who had abandoned ship to spend nearly 24 hours in the lagoon hanging onto mangroves* to keep from being blown away themselves. Rob and Alex worked most of the day lending a hand as best they could, but the devastation was overwhelming.

They had not attempted to go over the hill into town, but word was that the entire town of Philipsburg was under water from the flooded Saltpond – all the way up to the food market at the new traffic circle. In fact, most residents and shop owners had resorted to driving the streets in dinghies since there was no other way to reach their buildings to assess the damage. Due to the fact that the Saltpond had been turned into the island dump, no one in their right mind was dumb enough to wade through the waist deep water to get from place to place. Once again, another year had passed without the island officials allocating enough money in the budget to purchase a large enough pump to handle all the water that always accumulated in the Saltpond basin from the runoff of the surrounding hills. After all, that new Mercedes sedan for the

•MANGROVES — *A tropical or sub-tropical tree or shrub which grows along coastal areas, estuaries, and swamps. Usually found rooting above the water, the trees boasts numerous tangled aerial roots which embed in the muddy bottom along the water's edge. Whole islands have been formed from thickets of these trees and the accumulation of mud, sand, and debris over time.*

Senator was a far more important expenditure than a new pump that may not even be needed that season.

Dinner that night was an appetizing menu of post hurricane cuisine – consisting of canned Spam, green peas, and sardines, with Campbell's tomato soup for a starter. No restaurants were open since there was no refrigeration and all the food in their freezers had already spoiled and been delegated to fish food. The seas were still too rough for the local fishermen to go out, but even if they could, most of their boats had been turned to matchsticks on the French docks. The meager produce the island produced in Columbier such as mango and banana now lay on the ground rotting where the wind had stripped the trees of foliage, and blown fruit around as if it had been shot from a cannon. Even the main food wholesaler on the island had lost their entire warehouse from a tornado spawned by the storm – all that remained were a few cases of beer and sodas amongst the twisted steel bar that framed where the building had once stood, the rest of which had already been raided by the locals. All in all, the island was left with little or no sustenance and was totally reliant on the meager hurricane provisions that the islanders had hurriedly stored before the storm.

Rob and Alex fell into their bunk that night still in their grimy work clothes – exhausted from the last few days of relentless work and agonizing grief. The next morning Rob and Alex rose to a beautiful clear day with the sun reflecting blindingly off the surface of the lagoon, which now extended inland through-out parts of Cole Bay due to the standing water from the storm. They bathed sparingly, in about a gallon of water each. They only had a limited supply of clean water aboard since they hadn't had the opportunity to fill all their tanks before the storm. Alex was exhausted, both physically and emotionally – unable to offer a hand to other boat owners that day. The carnage amongst the yachts she'd witnessed the day before had sickened her and made her feel completely and utterly empty inside. Although, it had left her grateful that the Island Fever had survived and had safely seen them through the storm, she felt a sickening loss at the pit if her stomach to think how close they'd come to total annihilation. That morning she decided to stay aboard and work on putting their life back in order. Even with Christian's help the boat was still a mess, but the clean-up of their physical possessions would be easy. It was her state of mind that would be the toughest to unscramble.

Saba radio patched through a call on 16 that morning around eleven from Raymond in Antigua. He had just arrived back to find that the Island Fever had returned to St. Maarten – should he meet them there, or should he wait for them in Antigua? Alex, who knew no more of their future plans than Rob did, asked Raymond to stay with Dancer until they had had time to sort things out. All she knew for sure was that they needed a break, and would likely not be back in Antigua for the rest of the month of October – certainly not until hurricane season was well over.

Rob decided to check out the flight possibilities off the island on the French side since the Dutch airport runway had still not totally been cleared. He drove carefully through the flooded streets with downed trees and debris, to the airport in Grand Case. He wanted to see what the chances were of getting a flight off the island to Puerto Rico or some other nearby American territory, as soon as possible. Surprisingly enough, he was able to book seats for two days hence to Puerto Rico, which was not quite as surprising as the fact that he had actually gotten the Yellow Submarine running that morning after digging it out from under a mound of sand and palm fronds, not to mention having to clear the engine of seaweed and saltwater. The waterlogged seats still steamed up the windows but at least it was transportation, since all of the rental car agencies were closed due to the lack of tourists on the island. All those that could, had flown out on the last few flights before the storm.

Rob returned to the boat that afternoon with a few fresh lobsters he'd managed to buy from a fisherman in Grand Case for ten times their worth, and the exciting news that he and Alex were going to the States on holiday. Although apprehensive about meeting his folks, Alex was quite relieved at the thought of a respite on land for a while with hot water, real showers, and most of all, a dry bed. Dinner that night tasted like a feast. Alex cooked the lobster with rice and some canned escargot she had on board and Rob opened a bottle of red wine. It had taken three tries however, before he found a bottle that hadn't turned to vinegar from the shaking it had taken during the storm. Alex, Rob, and Christian sat around the table in the deckhouse that evening and gave thanks for the meal that lay before them. Only a few days prior they had assumed to be their last, and here they were – together – enjoying their meager offerings from the sea that felt so satiating. Rob thought he'd never tasted food as good as what lay before him.

Christian was already in his bunk, exhausted from the last week's excitement and Rob and Alex were busy cleaning up the galley from the evening's meal when they heard a power boat approaching. They felt the wake of it hit the boat as the engine idled down to a stop, and a bump against the starboard hull – then hushed voices. Assuming it was another sailor coming to check on them, or a boatless one in need of something that the Island Fever might have, Rob stepped out of the deckhouse into the cockpit. To Rob's surprise – there stood Joey on the starboard hull accompanied by several official, clean-cut men who were obviously Americans and looked quite out of their realm in their matching Hawaiian shirts.

"Joey?" questioned Rob thinking he was imagining things.

"Guess you thought I was never coming back ole buddy. Sorry 'bout that," he said as he slapped Rob on the back.

"Well... yeah... as a matter of fact..." answered Rob uncertain what to expect from Joey now that he had magically reappeared. Would Joey stop Rob from chartering the boat? Would he take it back? Would he ruin all that Rob had worked so hard for? Rob wasn't certain if he was relieved to finally see Joey again, or angry enough to take him out for leaving him in this position in the first place.

"The boat looks good, considering," said Joey looking around.

"Thanks," answered Rob a little defensively.

"I hear you've been through a lot since I saw you last... a hurricane, a renegade water buoy, a brief visit to the island jail--"

"--not to mention Miguel's goons and a bullet in my foot," added Rob more than a little sarcastically.

"Oh yeah, sorry about that. Actually, that's why I'm here," said Joey clearing his throat.

"Who're your friends?" questioned Rob referring to Joey's entourage.

"We just need to have a little chat with you Rob... you alone?"

"Alex's here...," he gestured inside." We're together you know, engaged."

"Really! I knew you two had shacked up together but I didn't realize it was that serious. I guess you guys haven't been doing your homework," Joey said casting a look at his white-collar thugs.

"What's going on Joey? Who are these guys?" Rob asked a little unnerved – assuming this was the other side of the drug ring – the American team.

Just then Alex stepped out of the deckhouse with a bottle of champagne and a stack of paper cups in her hand.

"We never opened that champagne Rob... I think it's time to finally celebrate the fact that we're even alive--" Alex said coming up short as she looked up to find Joey standing there smiling at her.

"Alex!" cried Joey enthusiastically as he stepped down into the cockpit to give her a kiss on either cheek and a warm, sincere hug – leaving his thugs standing at attention on deck. "I was relieved to hear Rob had hired you to take care of my baby, he's a smart man... not much of a sailor though I hear," Joey said laughing.

"Actually, it was Rob that saved your boat in the hurricane as well as my life," said Alex proudly as she looked up at Rob and smiled, uncertain of their fate now that Joey had returned.

"What's going on Joey... where've you been?" demanded Rob. "You deserted me to fend for myself down here."

"Looks like you managed okay. I mean you are one of the few boats in the lagoon still floating, and you've got this pretty little lady at your helm. Not bad if you ask me," said Joey chuckling. "So, you finally got smart and dumped that rich bitch from Chicago? The smartest thing you ever did aside from buying half the Island Fever."

"The former I might agree with, but the jury's still out on the purchase... as much as I love the boat."

"Well, that's kind of what we're here to talk to you about... your investment. You see we're here to buy you out."

Rob just looked at Joey uncertain what to say – then at Alex who looked as if she'd just received her pink-slip.

"Well... I'm not certain I want to sell," said Rob, unsure what game Joey was playing with him at this point. Maybe this indeed was Joey's game – sell the boat to some sucker – disappear and wait out the incubation period until a serious, incurable case of island fever had set in. Then, buy the boat back for half what he'd sold it for in the first place. But what Joey didn't realize thought Rob, was that he had become somewhat immune to that deadly disease in the time he'd spent on the Island Fever and in the West Indies, and he was not as desperate as Joey probably thought to be bailed out at fifty cents on the dollar.

"Well, you see... I'm about to make you an offer you can't refuse."

"Funny you don't look like Marlon Brando, Rob quipped."

Joey laughed and took the bottle from Alex unwinding the wire from the top, but before he had popped the cork, the bottle exploded all over the cockpit.

"Uh... I forgot to warn you... it sailed through the storm too," said Alex trying not to laugh at Joey who was dripping with champagne.

"Feels like I've just won a race," said Joey, looking around, "Where're the girls," he said snickering – always the jokester. Then he proceeded to pour champagne into three cups and offered them to Alex and Rob, totally ignoring his men.

"A toast! To Rob and Alex!" said Joey smiling as he raised his champagne to them – then downed half of it.

"How could you let me walk right into Miguel's trap, and how do you know what's been going on here?" demanded Rob, getting a little angry.

"I have to apologize for that Rob, that wasn't part of the plan. How could I have known that he'd send two monkeys who didn't know what I looked like?" Offered Joey as he lifted his cup in another toast. "I'm just glad to know that you two are okay. I realize I have some explaining to do, but there're some things you're better off not knowing."

"Why didn't you tell me you were a drug dealer before you took my money and made me your... partner? Do I have sucker written across my forehead?"

"Well... you see it's like this Rob. Miguel and I are actually on opposing teams. The drug dealer part is just a cover... you know, to get inside. In fact, you buying half the boat from me got my ass out of a lot of hot water. That money couldn't have come at a better time."

"Inside what?" asked Rob.

"The Cartel... the Medellin Cartel," answered Joey. "You see... we took them down since they paid you a visit and they need to think I'm dead, or I soon will be along with the two of you if you stay on this boat."

Alex looked at Rob concerned as he put his arm around her and protectively pulled her close.

"These nice gentlemen here are willing to take the boat off both our hands," Joey said gesturing for them to hand him the sail-bag the second guy was toting.

Joey sat the bag on the deck and unzipped it, exposing stacks of hundred-dollar bills.

"The purchase price is only a million cash for your share. Sorry Rob, that was the best I could do," Joey said winking at Rob.

"But I paid--" Rob started to say as Joey cut him off putting his arm around him and whispering into his ear, "That's double your money in less than six months. I'd say this has turned out to be a decent investment for you, wouldn't you?"

"But we don't really want to sell," said Alex, "There must be another way."

"Let's just say ma'am, that this is the only way," one of the big guys said in no uncertain terms. "Do yourself a favor, just take the money and walk away... no questions asked. If anyone wants to know why you sold out... Joey here came back and bought you out for a price you couldn't refuse."

Rob and Alex stared at the stranger who stood there unflinching – waiting for them to accept the money and simply leave their boat. Walk away as if they never had any attachment to it what-so-ever.

"Sorry guys, it's the only way," said Joey. "I couldn't live with myself if I knew something happened to you because I put you in the middle of this situation."

"Can we have the night to think about it?" asked Rob.

"Sorry... I need you to move off tonight as a matter of fact," answered Joey.

Rob looked at Alex hoping to read her thoughts but it was plainly written all over her face – the sadness of losing yet one more part of her life in such a few short days. Alex said nothing, understanding that there was nothing left to be said that might change their fate. She had lived in the islands long enough to understand the unspoken drug laws in that part of the world. Many seemingly retired, gentlemen marijuana dealers had lived in the area over the years she had resided in that part of the Caribbean – all harmless as I said before. None of them had been the gun toting criminals of the new cocaine cartels which had started infiltrating the area of recent, such as Miguel's goons. Alex was grateful to learn that her friend Joey had been brave enough to risk his life to put an end to what could have potentially become a plague in that part of the Caribbean due to weak corrupt governments that could be easily swayed by large sums of money – like what had been happening over the last few years in St. Kitts.

Joey gave Alex a big hug and thanked her for everything she'd done for him, and then gave a fond hug to Rob. "Thanks man... hope I changed your life a little for the better. Looks so," he said as he smiled looking at the two of them, together.

"Yeah... I'd say for the better or for worse," Rob said as he took Alex's hand. "Sorry I misjudged you man," Rob said to Joey apologetically. "You're a brave man."

Joey smiled at Rob knowing that he had indeed changed his life, forever. This would be the last time Joey would ever speak with his friends, since after tonight, he would need to disappear from this part of the world – at least as Joey Mitchell. He motioned to his men that it was time for them to leave, and they boarded the 17-foot black rubber Zodiac and sped away.

Sadly, Rob and Alex shared the last of the champagne with Joey and then packed up their meager belongings. As Alex brought bags and gear up onto the deck, Rob rowed them ashore to the marina to pack them into their locker and the back of the Yellow Submarine. It only took two trips since all Rob had, were the two bags he'd arrived with six months earlier, and Alex had even less since most of her belongings lived aboard Dancer. Joey sat smoking on the aft bridge-deck giving them time to say their goodbyes to the boat they had learned to love as home. Then they woke Christian telling him they had decided to go to the French side and get a hotel room. He was to come with them since they'd sold the boat back to Rob's friend Joey and they were moving ashore. Groggy and confused, they led the boy to the marina's tender tied between the hulls. Rob stepped back into the cockpit and extended his hand to Joey, who looked even sadder than they – this was the end of a grand era in the islands, never to come again for any of them.

"Thanks for the chance to do this," said Rob gratefully to Joey, "This was an opportunity of a lifetime. A scary one... but one that I'll never forget. You take care of yourself," said Rob as he slapped Joey on the shoulder and picked up the bag of money.

Joey just smiled, afraid that if he spoke, he might just lose it, which would be totally out of character. Rob climbed in the dinghy and ferried Christian and Alex ashore. They watched over their shoulders as the Island Fever disappeared into the liquid blackness – all except for her cabin light which appeared to levitate over the darkened lagoon like a small spaceship. Alex's heart was breaking once more – she had grown to love the Island Fever as if it were her child. She was a beautiful, swanlike creature which had risen from a dirty old boat yard into an elegant, almost sentient being. Only sailors can understand the personality a boat takes on as if it were a living breathing being, and not just a stack of plywood, glue, and metal. They grow to understand how a boat responds to the wind, the sea, and most importantly, to one's touch.

Rob had also grown to love the boat, and to hate her as well. Yet Rob knew that she had become his accomplishment, and leaving her was harder than if he'd laid up every plank of her with his own hands. The Island Fever was the reason he had met Alex – had come to know her – and to fall in love with her. But most important – it was the reason he had come to know and love himself.

They tied the tender on the marina dock, and Rob carried a sleepy Christian to the Yellow Submarine and sat him in the back seat with Alex. He locked the last locked the last of their unneeded belongings in their locker for locker for safe keeping and padlocked it twice. Carrying a million dollars cash around the island didn't seem to him to be the smartest move he'd ever made, so Rob left it in the locker for now. He needed to sleep on it, clear his head and try to regain his reason so that he could figure out what to do with that much cash. He could bury it as he had pretended with Miguel's goons, but that was hardly a safe option, and there weren't too many places in the world that one could just walk in and make a cash deposit of that size without being scrutinized or arrested. Rob started their faithful little car that had been one of the few things to survive the hurricane and backed out of the lot, then drove slowly through the standing water which washed up through the floorboards to their knees. He dodged debris and vehicles which blocked the dirt roadway until he made his way out onto the hard surfaced road to Marigot.

The island was pitch black, including the lagoon, which was now void of boats. Rob pulled out onto the deserted road and started up the hill to the French side. As he crested the hill overlooking the lagoon, the concussion of the blast hit the little vehicle – lighting the sky like a premature dawn. Rob jerked the car off the road and jumped out looking back at the ball of flame that hovered over the lagoon. There, where the Island Fever had laid on anchor, blazed an inferno on the water – engulfing what little remained of her hull.

Joey's cover was now complete. As far as the world knew, Joey, or at least his identity had died that night aboard the Island Fever. Investigators would later find a body – so badly burned, it was beyond recognition. And, since the island police were so incompetent in forensic science – Joey's dental records were never even requested for positive identification. Whose body the police found in the lagoon that night, Rob and Alex would never know. Some drug dealer they assumed – they hoped.

In a state of shock, Rob and Alex returned to the marina and were questioned by the Dutch police who arrived on the scene, surprisingly fast. They arrived just as the last of the flames had extinguished themselves in their watery grave. Both Rob and Alex had testified to the fact that Joey had indeed been aboard when they left only twenty minutes before. Initially, when they arrived at the makeshift police station in Simpson Bay, since the Philipsburg one was flooded out, their old friends in charge had been unduly suspicious about Rob and Alex's role in the explosion – questioning if they had been angry at Joey for wanting the boat back.

Thank goodness Rob had stashed the cash in the locker before they had driven away, since that kind of cash would have raised their suspicions that much more. But, when Joey's DEA and Interpol* friends in the Hawaiian shirts, turned up in the outer office and spoke to the official in charge, it was only

*INTERPOL — The International Criminal Police Organization – founded in 1923 to serve as a clearing house for police information world-wide – specializing in counterfeiting, smuggling, and drug trafficking.

minutes before he and Alex had been ushered out of the station. It was well before dawn when they got back to the marina, where Christian still slept in the back seat of the car. The police had obviously been enlightened as to the nature of the whole affair and were told in no uncertain terms that this was simply not their jurisdiction and to lay off. Rob breathed a sigh of relief that amazingly, this had not gone the way of their last police escort and that they were free to go – no questions asked. The certificate confirming Joey's death was signed by the island's coroner and the case had been closed – forever. That night on the boat, Joey had officially ceased to exist, as had the Island Fever.

Alex knew another piece of her had died that night as she watched the Island Fever burn to the waterline. She had given so much of herself to her, and she'd learned so much from the building of her. She was thankful that Rob had at least afforded her the opportunity to captain her, even if it had only been for a brief time.

Rob looked at the sail bag the next morning when they returned to the locker from the French guesthouse where they had left Christian. Rob had lost everything – the toll had been high to reach enlightenment. It was true that he'd been repaid two-fold, but he would've gladly given that bag full of money to simply bring Grandma and Grandpa back and return the island and life to the way it had been only a few days prior. But he wouldn't have traded the experience of sailing through that storm for ten times the amount of money in that bag. Through it, Rob had learned the value of life and what was truly important. And the commodity for which he had struggled and toiled for the last ten years, he realized was like the rain from a storm – it came and went being only one of the necessities to sustain life. It was never meant to last. Like everything else in life except love, it eventually evaporated, just as the sun consumed the moisture and turned it back to rain. His toil had been like the sun and the clouds – to extract a living from his environment – only to pour it back into it. Money was simply a liquid ever-flowing substance. It was not the tree that grew into life, only one of its many fuels for growth – what it needed to sustain it and allow it to achieve its purpose here on the planet. Rob had learned that money was not the goal in life. Sure, it couldn't bring him a certain kind of happiness, but it hadn't brought him love. Surely it had not been the means of discovery of Paradise or happiness for Rob, since those things he'd found on his own – at a time in his life when he'd been the poorest – at least where money was concerned.

By the time they had arrived back at the marina, the 'Coconut Telegraph' was already sizzling with the news of the Island Fever's demise, and rumors that Rob and Alex had been aboard. Everyone was greatly relieved to see them drive up in the Yellow Submarine, yet disheartened to learn that although they were safe, Joey had been aboard. A faulty propane line on one of their refrigerators had been blamed for the 'accident' Jeff had told them – making the propane tanks a bomb that had blown the boat right out of the water. Rob and

Alex found no need to act as if they were shocked or surprised by the tragedy – they truly were. Joey's plan had been so quickly enacted, the reality of it had not had time to sink in. They had expected that Joey would go missing and the boat would have been seized as a drug confiscation or at the very least, put up for sale – not blown to pieces. Couldn't they have spared her? After all, she was the one innocent victim in the entire mess. But, what better way to publicly announce Joey's demise than with a spectacular show for all the island to see. With all certainty – news of his death would reach South America within days via the 'Coconut Telegraph', and reach Miguel's followers who still believed Joey to have millions of dollars of Miguel's money buried somewhere. Not to mention being the one responsible for his 350-year internment in Leavenworth.

Rob and Alex took the ferry to Anguilla that morning from Marigot, with the cash in hand. Somehow the ferry had survived Claire in the lagoon, tucked up into the mangroves. Their reason for visiting the tiny little storm ravaged island was to open a new bank account and make a rather substantial deposit. Like I said before, Rob knew there were few places in the world where he could walk into a bank with a bag of cash and not raise some eyebrows, other than Switzerland and the Cayman Islands – no questions asked. But Alex had informed Rob that Anguilla was part of that elite private banking enclave where one could hide whole fortunes from the rest of the world, as St. Maarten had been until the world found out that it was where the Marcos' had stashed much of the national treasury of the Philippines, not to mention where Mrs. Marcos had purchased most of her shoes.

Rob had indeed made much larger transfers and transactions in the past for his clients, but this was the first time that he had held a receipt in his hand with his own name on it showing his net worth to be one million dollars cash. Nervously, Rob walked out of the bank, expecting to be stopped and questioned. When he climbed into the taxi scot-free, he started to relax and turned to Alex and smiled. "Do you think there might be a restaurant open on the island where I could buy my beautiful lady lunch?" he asked the taxi driver.

"Ah... de resorts, dey hab dere own genarta, dey awl be'd in bidness sur," he answered, happy to even have a paying patron on the island as he drove them to lunch at a five-star resort/spa, on the north side of the island that had managed to escape serious damage from the storm.

With the money taken care of, Rob and Alex needed to focus on what was next. Where was their life to lead them now that they had every possible option open to them that they could imagine, and little or no obligations except to Christian, Lambchop, and Old Henry? In the last 24 hours their lives had taken a 180-degree course correction. Their options were plentiful – they could choose to go anywhere – do just about anything. But as they discussed their future plans, they both realized that they wanted the same thing – to go back to the life they'd worked so hard to create. Maybe they would build another boat – maybe they would just cruise the world for a while. Rob had imagined it as a distant dream, but how quickly the gap had closed and he had suddenly found his dream was in reach – there for the taking. After all, they still had Alex's Dancer, which would afford them a great little cruising cat, even if she wasn't big enough for charter. In fact, they could cruise a long time with a million dollars in the bank. Wasn't that what he'd truly wanted, Rob thought? Cruise around the islands – around the world – his dream had indeed been dropped right there in his lap. But now that it was real, Rob was uncertain. Could he just drop out – be an unproductive member of no real community? Rob was unsure that he could totally shed his domesticated upbringing and need to fit into the working society – another cog in the wheel of the big machine. But he would work on it. Somehow, he was sure he'd find a way to overcome the guilt. But first there were more important considerations. What of his and Alex's relationship?

"While we're in the States I think we should get married," said Rob out of the blue. "Just a simple wedding. Life is too short and too precious... I don't want to waste another minute. You just never know what's in store for you over that next wave, do you?" asked Rob, taking Alex's hand in his.

"Well I... guess I don't really need to walk down the aisle wearing white. After all, who would give me away?"

"No one in their right mind," answered Rob as he tenderly brushed her hair from her face and kissed the back of her hand.

"With everything that's happened over the last few days it almost doesn't feel right being so happy," said Alex.

"I want to adopt Christian," Rob said surprising himself as much as Alex. "Adopt him? But he has a father."

"One that probably hasn't even wondered if he's still alive. He's a good kid. He needs a chance to make something of himself."

"The question is, what would Christian want?"

"He just wants to be part of a family.... our family," said Rob smiling at how that sounded.

Alex snuggled next to him as he wrapped his arm around her and they stared out at the beautiful turquoise ocean – sparkling – like diamonds on the surface of the calm water which had finally given up the struggle and now rolled gently in, lapping its wet tongue onto the shore. They walked the beach with the water racing up around their bare feet. It soaked into the white sand like a sponge, and then trickled back to sea leaving only bubbles where tiny crabs burrowed holes to hide from the sandpipers who zigzagged up the beach chased by the water. The ocean had made peace once again with the world, and like the ocean, Rob had finally learned to give up the struggle. He felt different – lighter – centered – at peace, like the ocean. Rob had finally found his true self even though he'd been stripped of his worldly possessions – his work – his social status – even many of his beliefs. He had shed his ego and his ever-calculating mind which had raged like a boulder filled river, and now laid calm like the placid channel which flowed offshore. He had let it all go – everything that had at one time comprised his self-worth. And it had come back to him ten-fold. Rob had found prosperity, but it was not in that bag of money. Rob's real payoff was that he had learned to finally allow the Universe to participate in the creation of his life instead of struggling to manage it all himself. He had found his true place in the Universe. He was a key part of the giant breathing organism that needed him to make it work. Rob realized that he had finally stopped waiting for life to happen, and had started living it. He soaked in the silence – and in that silence I heard him say, "I haven't had an opportunity to thank you for what you did out there Ian... and all the other times I'm sure you've been there. I hope someday I'll get an opportunity to know more about you."

"In time you will," I answered, "In time you will."

Rob smiled knowing that indeed he would. All the answers would come as he needed them – of that he now was certain. Rob was no longer waiting for them – for the future – he was happy now. Along with his heart – Rob's happiness had decided to come home.

CHAPTER THIRTY-SEVEN

Paradise Found

"Paradise is where I am."

Voltaire

Rob and Alex returned to St. Maarten that afternoon to make arrangements for Christian to stay in Jeff's back room at his house, helping him to put the marina back together again while they were away. Jeff didn't hesitate to accept since he had grown to love Christian almost as much as Rob and Alex had. They told Christian of their plan to try and adopt him when they returned. Christian was thrilled – he started counting the days until Rob and Alex would come back to the island – unbeknownst to him, as husband and wife. School was an issue that they'd definitely have to address when they returned. But for now, Christian was content just to be needed by Jeff, and to have the opportunity to play with all the great stuff at the store as they took inventory of what was left. Lambchop and Old Henry became the marina mascots, and even though Lambchop was too large for Christian to take on the windsurfer, he pulled him behind the marina's Whaler every day on the hydroslide-board.*

      Rob and Alex flew out the next morning, as planned, on the 9:00 AM flight to San Juan from Grand Case. The plane circled the little island and headed northwest towards the Virgins. They watched out the window as the seemingly untouched little atoll faded away into the azure blue of the Caribbean.

---

*HYDROSLIDE-BOARD — An abbreviated surfboard of sorts, or what is known as a wave board or buggy board – designed with a bridle to be pulled behind a boat like a type of ski.

Once again – all appeared perfect from the right perspective when one didn't focus on all of life's daily problems and its minutia.

Thirty minutes later they were touching down on American soil – something that had never before seemed important to Alex, but today, made her feel as if she'd finally returned home. Rob checked them into an exclusive resort on the western coast of the island, after they had stopped to purchase two wedding rings and something respectable to wear to a wedding – theirs.

They stayed on in Puerto Rico for another week, basking in the glow of their happiness. Rob called home and told his mother he was coming for a visit, and that he would be bringing a surprise with him – to set another place for dinner. Rob's mother had been crushed when Rob had called to tell her his engagement was off, even if she'd never been close to Sydney. She had already started buying baby clothes in hopes of a little granddaughter or grandson to fulfill her life. Rob had been her only child and was destined to be their only source of grandchildren.

When they arrived three days later and she opened the door – Helen knew in an instant that the woman standing on the other side of that threshold was to be her new daughter-in-law. Rob just smiled as the smell of fresh baked pies wafted through the house to greet them. "Mom... this is Alex, my fiancée," he said beaming with pride as he introduced her. "Alex, this is my mother, Helen."

Nothing needed to be said, as Helen wrapped her arms around Alex and pulled her close in a warm, motherly embrace. Alex knew she'd finally found her family. Grandma it seemed, was not to be the last woman in her life as Helen instantly melted all her fears and apprehensions away about meeting her new in-laws to be. Rob's dad would be easy – she always knew how to be one of the guys, but she had never felt totally at ease when making new friends with women.

"Thomas! Come say hi to your son and his beautiful fiancée," Helen shouted with excitement to her husband who sat in his recliner with his feet up, watching Sunday afternoon football. Not much else could have torn him away from his game. Even Helen was amazed at how fast he had made it to the door.

As Alex stretched out her hand to Rob's father, Thomas grabbed them both instead and hugged them as if some wish of his had miraculously been granted. His son, it seemed, had finally brought a woman home who wasn't, in his words, "Store bought."

They had an endless string of questions as they sat over Helen's home-cooked Sunday dinner that took Rob back to his childhood – when he and his mother worked for hours putting up preserves and baking fresh homemade bread and pies and perfecting her recipes. Thomas sat quietly listening to Alex tell the tale of Rob's miraculous rescue at sea – when she floated adrift helpless in the water at the mercy of the storm. She told them how he'd climbed the mast of thrashing boat at sea to find her and how he had maneuvered the boat around to save her from certain death. For the first time in Rob's life, he could see the awe in his father's eyes – the look of respect that he now held for his son. For the first time in Rob's life, his father was openly proud of him – proud of his son who he'd never quite seen before as a man. And, for the first time, Rob truly felt like a man in the presence of his father.

Helen got up to clear the dishes and Alex got up to join her even though Helen resisted her help. Alex had never had a mother to help in the kitchen – she had been the woman of the house when she was growing up with just her father at home. It felt good to wash dishes next to the woman who had given birth to the man she loved, and the woman who had raised him to be the loving man she planned to spend the rest of her life with.

Rob sat at the table talking to his father – man to man – for the first time in his life. And, he realized that he really liked him – the man inside that hard outer shell that he'd always hid behind. Rob had found a confidence that day in that big ocean that even his father could never diminish. He no longer based his self-worth on other's measures of success for him. He had found success in his failure and in hindsight – saw his failure to truly live in his success. He had found peace – he was finally free. Free from the fear of lack, of need, of want. Rob was living life now no longer struggling to make a living. He was living every moment as it came – good or bad. His life was his to do with it what he chose, and he chose to make it the best it could be, instead of discarding the moment for something better in the future. Up until now, Rob had been living in the future while identifying with his past. Rob had been obsessed with his need to arrive in Paradise, and the present had only become his ride to get there. Finally, he had awakened to the fact that he was not his ego. He was not that old Rob who had gone to the islands in search of an unfulfilled dream, craving fulfillment and prosperity from the future. He had found his present – his joy – his Paradise. He had given up his pursuit to be happy and it had found him. He had finally realized that Paradise was not a destination resort – it simply was. Rob now realized where the coordinates to Paradise lay. It lay to the north of him and it lay to the south of him – it lay to the east of him and it lay to the west of him – it lay above him and below him – it was always there – where he was, as long as he was fully there, in the moment. Rob had ended his quest for the Holy Grail – he had finally found it within. It had been there all along.

When the dishes were done, Helen made coffee and asked Rob if he wouldn't mind going down into the storm cellar to bring up a jar of peach preserves for the warm pastries that she had in the oven. It had been years since Rob had been to the cellar, but he had spent so much time playing there with his cousin Marie when he was a child, that he knew it like the back of his hand. He knew how many steps there were in the dark as he descended the stairs and exactly where the string hung for the overhead light. As he opened the door and started down the steps into the cellar, all the memories of his childhood flooded back to him like the sea returning with the tide. He found the cord and pulled on the light. Then he saw it – there in the corner where it had been stored after Lilly's house had been torn down – Lilly's sea-chest. The chest that had so inspired Rob's imagination as a child. He stared at it, more intrigued by it now than he had been as a wide-eyed boy – still wondering in awe what lay inside.

Rob thought about his Grandmother Lilly, and how she had been the one to broaden his concept of the world and interest him in something outside of Iowa City. He thought about her stories of her homeland and wondered if she was happy now, wherever she was. He remembered her stories of arriving in New York with only that chest to her name, and how she'd bravely left her homeland alone as a young girl. He remembered the look in Lilly's eye as she had told them stories about an amazing man she had met, who had sailed out of her life never to return. Rob thought about that chest and wondered after all these years, what was inside. Did it really contain the magic that Rob had always imagined?

Rob looked around the cellar and easily found the shelf where his mother stored her preserves. Not much had changed over the years. It was amazing how organized and industrious she was since the cellar was always filled with shelves and shelves of canned vegetables and fruits that she spent all summer and fall preparing. The last jar of peach preserves was buried behind several rows of plum and it took some rearranging for Rob to get to the jar. As he reached to the back of the shelf, his arm just barely brushed his grandmother's old piggy bank – a ceramic sailing ship which leapt from the shelf as if someone had intentionally sent it crashing to the floor, scattering pennies throughout the cellar. Rob looked down, upset with himself about the mess. But there, nearly hidden by the coins lay an old ornamented skeleton key – like one that fit a piece of furniture, or an old chest – Lilly's chest – the key to her hidden treasure. Rob stared at it for a moment. For years he had ached to know its contents. And now, entry lay right before him and he wondered what Lilly would think if he breached her secret – the mystery she'd kept locked away all those years. But he had to try it – at least to see if it was indeed the right key. Rob knelt down and picked it up. It was quite possibly the key to the one possession that had meant anything to Lilly. He walked to the chest and knelt before it, nervously. Inserting the key – he looked over his shoulder as if he felt Lilly watching him. It slipped easily into the slot and he effortlessly turned the tumbler in the lock. At long last Lilly's secret was unlocked – there for him to assuage his curiosity, but still he hesitated. At my prompting, Rob slowly lifted the lid – it was his destiny to be the one to finally learn of the secrets of Lilly's chest. Somehow, he knew that she would have wanted it that way.

There inside lay scraps of lace, buttons, and photos – mementos of a lifelong past. And there, in a tray at the top of the chest, lay a bundle of letters tied-up with faded yellow ribbon. Instinctively, Rob lifted the brittle parchment envelopes from the tray and turned them over. There on the bottom of the letters was a photo. Rob untied the bundle and lifted the photo into the light so that he might see it more clearly. It was a picture of two men and a woman standing arm-in-arm in front of the Statue of Liberty. The young woman was his grandmother, Lilly, looking close to the age of her wedding photo with Canton that had always sat on their bureau. Oddly, the two men in the photo looked Mulatto. In fact – Rob looked closer – the one on Lilly's right looked like a younger Grandpa. Rob shook his head knowing that the odds of his grandmother knowing Grandpa Stanley were almost impossible, but there it was in black and white right there in front of him. And, the man on her left looked like a slightly older version of Grandpa, yet taller. Could this be Itchy Rob thought – puzzled that his present and his grandmother's past could have been one and the same. Had she known the man he'd come to know and love as Grandpa – his prophet and his teacher? Could Lilly have been Itchy's 'Dark-Eyed Woman?'

Rob opened the last postmarked letter and started to read the words written more than six decades before. He read the words of a man called Itchy whose love would traverse an ocean to be with his true love once again, and his child that she carried. He would return to New York on the full moon and take her to his homeland of Grenada, where their child could grow and thrive in the sun and learn to be a sailor like his father and his father before him. But, as Rob well knew, Itchy never made it back to New York – instead he'd died there in the ocean that had been his first love. Lilly was never to learn of his fate – why he'd never returned for her, and Itchy was never to know in that life, that the son that she carried was indeed a little girl – Rob's mother, Helen. After waiting at the docks every afternoon for two full moons, Lilly had gone that day to the Empire State Building to find herself a husband. The rest was history – the history of Rob's family with much left unwritten, since Lilly was never to tell her husband that Helen was not his real daughter. Not even when she'd arrived two months early. Lilly had died before her husband taking her secret with her to the grave, and now Canton was living out his life in the next county with his mother's younger brother, none the wiser.

Rob read the letter twice again then looked at the photo of the three who had never known of the other's fate, since Lilly left New York before Grandpa's letter had arrived. Grandpa it seemed was Rob's real Grandfather's brother. Rob looked in the mirror in the lid of the chest – now he could see the resemblance. He looked more closely at the photo of the man he'd just discovered to be his real Grandfather and turned it over. There, on the back inscribed in Lilly's hand – "Stanley, Lilly, and Ian (*Itchy*) – May 1st, 1939.

That is why you see I have come to guide my Grandson, Rob, on his journey across his ocean of life. In this life of his, I never knew him. But when Lilly crossed over, we took on our preordained appointments to guide Rob to Paradise. Rob smiled – he now knew his true heritage. He knew why Grandpa had meant so much to him – why he'd always been so intrigued with stories of travel and adventure. It was in his blood – it was in his genetic makeup – it was his destiny. He had had many teachers throughout his life, Rob thought. Lilly had been his first, and I was destined to be his last. But then Rob realized that pain, suffering, failure, and loss had truly been his greatest teacher in the end. It had taught him that when all else is gone – the mind, the body, the ego, and one's possessions – the only thing that survives is love. At the time Rob had seen his pain and suffering as bad, but once he'd been able to climb that mast to get a better perspective, he had been able to see the bigger picture. It was all about perspective after all – wasn't it? If one learns to just be, one doesn't perceive the 'bad' things as bad – just simply a lesson to be learned towards one's higher purpose.

Standing side-by-side amongst a sea of corn – their friends and family in attendance, Rob and Alex said their "I do's." Rob had finally realized that only his ego had been in love before he'd met Alex – his love for Sydney had not been love from his heart. It was simply love from his ego – fulfilled by Sydney's physical attributes and standing in society. Looking at Alex dressed in pale blue to match her eyes, Rob knew that his love for her came from a much deeper place – it came from a source within him which brought him peace and joy he'd never known before.

As they said their vows to one another, Rob suddenly understood what was meant by joining in a union of Oneness, but at the same time remaining free to each be who they were for the rest of their lives. "I do take this woman to love and to cherish, to honor and respect until death us do part," said Rob, meaning it from the very depth of his soul. Of course, he took her for better or for worse – for richer or poorer – after all they'd already covered all that ground. Alex was glowing as he slipped the ring on her finger and kissed her, feeling the warmth of her inner light, which he welcomed into his own being. He was ready – ready to step out of the darkness and into the light – forever. Alex knew that her mother and father were watching, as was Grandma, whose smile she could see beaming clearly all the way from the Otherside when Rob slipped that ring on her finger.

Rob had made it nearly halfway across that ocean called life. He had learned to let his past go but he was still working on the future. Working on not letting it run his life. But, most importantly, he was learning to live in the present, leaving my job yet unfinished – at least until Rob reaches the other shore and comes home – many, many happy years from now. Until then, I'll keep working on him – keeping him aware and focused on his course. But more importantly – keeping him always living in the moment, and ever learning from the University of Life.

THE END

To Be Continued

Somewhere

WEST OF THE EQUATOR

AUTHOR'S EPILOGUE

Upon the first publication of Rob Mariner's journey in his quest for happiness, DuBois' most often asked question has been, "Are you Alex, and is the book based on fact."

"As I stated in the previous disclaimer, 'The names and details have been changed in order to protect the 'survivors of Paradise,' since many of us have only scraped through by the skin of our teeth, a colloquialism which has never made sense to me. Do we have skin on our teeth? Or, does it just refer to that fine line of getting worn down to the very core of our potential self-destruction – that state that we are all susceptible to – that line that some manage to avoid crossing, but others trip over into the abyss.

In fact, many of us ex-pats simply self-combust in the loosely woven structure of humanity we find ourselves suddenly immersed in when we run away to hide in a third world country or the laid-back islands of the Caribbean – where there is truly no social structure to keep one from just slipping over the edge into rum soaked, or drug induced oblivion. I've watched as many a friend slipped into that bottomless barrel of distilled sugarcane at one of the local watering holes – designed to tempt bored sailors and pirates alike to this fate far worse than death – a fate somewhat akin to purgatory, a place from which most never escape – a place called 'escape from ourselves' – somewhere between the 'real world' and the Otherside of reality.

As Grandpa knew well – most are running from something – if not the law, the IRS, or an ex-wife, then some demon that will inevitably follow them to those tropical waters – since until we make peace with our demons, even 'Paradise' cannot offer us any semblance of peace. But somehow that spirit-induced oblivion can keep those demons at bay – for a while. I was one of the lucky ones. For aside from my addiction to sailing and writing, alcohol and drugs had never had a lure for me. In fact, I had never found the need to escape by any means other than getting on a boat and sailing to some location where no one in the world knew where to find me, or locking my door and simply dropping out for a while.
What, you ask was I running from? A live-in boyfriend about to go to jail for trying to save his hard-earned boat factory from bankruptcy by selling a few bails of pot supplied by some neighborhood Cuban exiles. I was of

course, hoping to avoid being called to testify against him when he did go down, as I watched DEA agents hide behind my palm trees and learned that my phone bills had recently been confiscated from the phone company by the DEA, who pretended to be our friends, so they could get inside his 'operation.' I ran from fate – I ran from a country whose policies I questioned, but most importantly – I ran away from me – and, I ran in search of myself.

But, to get back to my answer to that often-asked question of whether I wrote from fact or simply fiction – "Of course it's based on reality. Isn't all fiction really just a part of some writer's own version of reality that they have experienced in some manner – if only in their minds, then put down on paper? For a writer to write the lives of their characters – their faults, their strengths, and their weaknesses, it's necessary to live the very essence of each of those characters – to experience their pain and their suffering – their pleasure and their joy – their confusion and their uncertainly, so that they might offer the reader a compelling, heartfelt story that can truly move you to tears, make you laugh, or inspire you to enlightenment. Each word put down by a writer of any worth, is but a piece of a world in which they have lived – then shared for all to read and to relive – in turn, the reader will experience their own version of the story, which has been provided by those characters who have been brought to life by the author.

I had been a witness as many of my friends drowned in the enchanting chaos of that unrestrained island lifestyle. I watched as a friend in deep despair hung himself the day after I fired him for drinking on the job and hurting a passenger, the day after his girlfriend had dumped him. I watched as a friend I loved dearly, with the IQ equal to that of a genius, self-destructed from his inner demons that had followed him back from the terror he'd witnessed on the Mekong Delta. I watched as a young friend, a girl I loved and protected like a daughter, nearly died of a heart attack from over-indulging in cocaine. I watched, knowing that no matter how much I cared, no matter how much my heart broke for them, I could not battle their demons for them. And, as I started to write about the islands, many of the catastrophes that awaited my character, Rob, could not avoid mirroring my own outrageous experiences. The saying that truth is stranger than fiction is a fact, for if I had written my story of real experiences, no one would have believed it as truth. So, under the guise of fiction, I told my story of a man and a woman who most definitely sprung from my own life. Of course, I am Alex, but then I'm also Rob – a soul who innocently journeyed off, like I, in search of Paradise.

The first year I was in the islands I suffered every possible tropical illness known to man, shy of malaria – including typhoid, meningitis, and dengue fever; I watched as friends were air-lifted off the island after being shot in the stomach and in the foot, during a shoot-out between bank robbers and Gendarmes; I spent months in a dirty, sweaty boatyard repairing my beloved, Ikhaya, after my partner ran over the cruise ship buoy and ripped the underside of the bridge-deck of our little Spronk catamaran to shreds; I spent many an afternoon under the coconut palms in that little boatyard on Grandma's veranda, sipping tea and learning of life and heartache from a woman who always had a smile on her face for everyone, and had raised her baker's dozen on nothing more than that love she shared with all; I sat waiting for two weeks for word of friends who had been thrown in jail, with no reason given for their arrest, only to learn that they had been innocent bystanders in an international drug bust and never offered 'one call,' 'counsel,' or an explanation of their arrest, until they were unceremoniously deported from the island, and I had missed being one of them by no more than thirty minutes of sheer luck; I found myself being held a gunpoint by a drug dealer who wanted my friend to return money that had been lost in a deal gone bad; I found my best friend and I being held for kidnapping, after our boyfriends took matters into their own hands to stop two local yacht thieves who had robbed the American yachties blind and had received no relief from the police; I found that I had fallen in love, only to learn three and a half years later, that the love of my life was, quite literally, not the person I thought he was; I found myself living in the wild, wild, West Indies, then I took a sabbatical back to Miami, while a piece of me died inside – only to become engaged once again to another man, who I learned, had decided to resort to running drugs in order to save his home from the IRS. Then I ran… I ran back to the islands once again to look for what, I wasn't sure. I had waited five years for work papers and a telephone in order to open my design firm, only to watch helplessly as my young friend and right-arm in business, died from a ridiculous hospital error; then… I ran again… I ran from Paradise… I ran as fast and as far as I could go. I ran back to the security of the States… I ran back to the safety of being an American. I ran back to the deluded security of competent healthcare, and back to that secure little box I had lived my life in before I had left to go in search of Paradise. Ironically, I ran back to find myself, finally realizing that the locale of ones' enlightenment is not truly a factor in the equation after all. I ran until I found myself, and what I had gone to the islands for in the first place.

And although, unlike Rob and Alex, I am still in search of that one true love, I am, as Grandma insisted, still willing to climb that tree of life in order to taste the sweet, sweet nectar of the fruit that life offers. I have found my reason for being here if only to offer tiny snippets of illumination for other seekers of truth and enlightenment. I have found my Paradise in writing, even if I falter sometimes in living in the realization that we are all creators of our own lives. We are all authors of our own stories, and we must accept responsibility for our lives and learn that if we want things to be different than the reality we perceive, we must re-write our lives to fulfill that destiny. We all came here with a plan however we just don't always remember what that plan entailed. Sometimes, like a writer, we must write and rewrite our lives until we get it right, or at least feel as if we have reached that elusive destination we yearn for, which we define as Paradise."

"If a diver is to secure pearls he must descend to the bottom of the sea, braving all dangers of jagged coral and vicious sharks, so man must face the perils of worldly passion if he is to secure the precious pearl of Enlightenment."

Siddhartha Gautama - Buddha

FINAL SCENE

*"Age looks down from her balcony, and sees
Youth, an army of Quixotes
Tilting at shadows with fine new lances
While the audience laughs
And the Devil dances."*

Lorna Steel